'The power of this finely crafted novel lies in its raw, high-energy, coruscating language which is the world of young Jimmy Flick, who sees everything . . . *The Eye of the Sheep* is an extraordinary novel about love and anger, and how sometimes there is little between them.'
—Miles Franklin Award 2015, judges' report

'Sofie Laguna faultlessly maintains the storytelling voice of Jimmy, who is oblivious  and hauntingly knowing and observant in other. The places in which such a story could tip over into sentiment and melodrama, but Laguna's authorial control and intelligence keep the story on track and the reader engaged and empathetic both the humour and the darkness of th  ity and control.'
—Stella Prize 2015, judges' report

'The greatest achievement here is making this family's world not just compelling but utterly entertaining. Laguna does this by showing the way her characters all the parts that make them . . . It is quite a feat to write characters with such nuance. In harnessing her storytelling facility to expose the flaws in the system with what is becoming trademark empathy, Laguna is an author proving the novel is a crucial document of the times.'
—*The Australian*

'This book should be impossibly bleak, but Laguna has managed to imbue it with luminosity. This is a story about how to find your place in the world and how to accept what you have been given. *The Eye of the Sheep* will break your heart – a small price to pay to hear Jimmy's story.'
—*Readings*

'By getting inside Jimmy's mind and showing what an amazing place it is, this book goes a long way towards explaining what a library of textbooks could not.'
—*Sydney Morning Herald*

'Jimmy is a tour de force of a character, brilliantly maintained . . . Laguna's great skill is in conveying contradictory human depths.'
—*Adelaide Advertiser*

'. . . an extraordinary, haunting tale about love, anger and family. Adopting the sweet but manic voice of six-year-old boy, Jimmy Flick, Laguna cleverly navigates the tensions of a struggling working-class family in this surprising, heartbreaking and funny story.'
—*Canberra Weekly*

'. . . tender and delicate novel, rich with sympathy and understanding.'
—*Compulsive Reader*

'Sofie Laguna has perfected the voice of a child, *The Eye of the Sheep* is a dark tale told with perfection.'   —*Culture Street*

'If you liked *Room*, *The Lovely Bones* or *The Rosie Project*, you'll like this too. The main character is a young boy, Jimmy Flick, who has a unique (and unspecified) way of looking at things. It's such a joy to be presented with a character who thinks so differently and feels so authentic. Jimmy lives in a poor family where violence is never far from the surface and life is chaotic. This is compelling and arresting.'   —*Geelong Advertiser*

'A beautifully written novel, refreshingly raw, though the eyes of a child. I couldn't put it down.'   —*Launceston Examiner*

'. . . truthful and beautiful.'   —*Newcastle Herald*

'Laguna has a way of beautifully illustrating the deepest of emotions, with Jimmy providing an alternative look at the world of domestic violence, love and family relations. Full of both happiness and heartbreak, this novel deals with elements of human nature in a deeply touching way.'   —*Weekend West*

PRAISE FOR *ONE FOOT WRONG*

'An extraordinary achievement . . . original and compelling . . .
compels us to see our familiar world as new and intriguing – no
small feat.'   —Jo Case, *Big Issue*

'. . . a book that intrigues and affects every essence of your humanity
. . . a dark and terrible tale told in lyrical, poetic language and
stark imagery.'   —*Australian Bookseller and Publisher*

'. . . intense, disturbing and hallucinatory.'
                    —Kerryn Goldsworthy, *Sydney Morning Herald*

'The language is pitch-perfect – it is the light in this dark tale
. . . a haunting story of horror, but also of friendship and love
. . . Despite the darkness of the subject matter, it is surprisingly
uplifting, cathartic and affecting.'   —Louise Swinn, *The Age*

'. . . harrowing, beautifully written, insightful and absorbing . . .
unique, forceful and absolutely hypnotic . . . Fresh honest writing
. . . makes this dark journey well worth taking.'
                    —Emily Maguire, *Canberra Times*

'Laguna creates a world and a character and a language that we
become immersed within . . . This is humane, passionate, true.'
                    —Christos Tsiolkas

Sofie Laguna's many books for children have been named Honour Books and Notable Books in the Children's Book Council of Australia Book of the Year Awards, and in the Queensland Premier's Literary Awards. She has been published in the United States, the United Kingdom and in translation in Europe and Asia.

In 2008 Sofie published her first novel for adults, *One Foot Wrong*, also published by Allen & Unwin. It was shortlisted for the Prime Minister's Literary Awards, and longlisted for the Miles Franklin Literary Award. *One Foot Wrong* was published throughout Europe, the United States and the United Kingdom, and screen rights have been optioned. First published in 2014, *The Eye of the Sheep* was shortlisted for the Stella Prize and won the Miles Franklin Literary Award in 2015.

Sofie lives in Melbourne with her husband and their young son.

The
Eye
of the
Sheep

SOFIE LAGUNA

ALLEN&UNWIN

First published in Great Britain in 2016 by Allen & Unwin

First published in Australia in 2014 by Allen & Unwin

**ARTS
VICTORIA**

This project is supported by
the Victorian Government
through Arts Victoria.

Allen & Unwin
c/o Atlantic Books
Ormond House
26-27 Boswell Street
London WC1N 3JZ
Phone: 020 7269 1610
Email: UK@allenandunwin.com
Web: www.allenandunwin.com

A CIP catalogue record for this book is available from the British Library

Paperback ISBN 978 1 76029 248 5
E-Book ISBN 978 1 74343 705 6

Set in Mrs Eaves by Bookhouse, Sydney
Printed and bound in Great Britain by Clays Ltd, St Ives plc

10 9 8 7 6 5 4 3 2 1

For TL, in memory

Part One

It was Saturday morning and I was doing the gardening with Mum. My dad was still asleep.

'When will he wake up, Mum? Mum? When will Dad wake up?' I asked as she watered the fern, its tentacles bouncing under the pressure. If I stood close enough I could hear the same tentacles inside my mum, waving at the dust in her air ducts. 'Has he had enough yet, Mum? Does he still need more rest?'

My dad worked at the Mobil refinery in Altona, getting rid of the rust. Rust came back every time it rained, but even if it left my dad raw, his skin corroded so you could see the fibres that joined him, he didn't stop scraping. He learned at the Western Car Yard in Laverton. Mum said all the Flick brothers knew how to work.

'You help me in the garden, love, and let Dad have a bit of quiet. He'll be tired after the night shift. Here, take the hose.' Mum passed me the hose and I felt the water pushing its way through the rubber tube. The hose gave it a direction. I aimed at the leaves and then I aimed at the path, blasting leaves against the edges.

'Keep it on the plants, Jimmy, that's the boy,' said Mum.

I watched as the leaves drank, absorbing fluid and light, and growing greener as water dripped down the stems and back into the ground. When Mum was getting her gloves and her kneeling pad from the laundry, I let go of the hose. It whipped and wriggled like a snake under attack and water flooded the paving. I grabbed the hose-snake by the neck and felt the water rushing through my fist. I looked at the soil refining to mud. I heard the plants drinking, their stems gulping back the drips. The darker the soil the more it had to drink. It processed the water the same way the refinery processed oil.

I got to see it up close one day. Dad left his thermos behind, and Mum took Robby and me, and drove it in to work for him as a surprise. Mum parked the Holden in Mobil Car Park A and through the high wire fence I saw the inside of a body with intestines made of steel and no skin around its precious metals. It smoked grey clouds and a flame blasted from the end of a huge pole like a giant pilot light. It was the same network that was in the rabbit that my Uncle Rodney shot and pulled open. The same network that was in my mum, the same network that was in me, in plants and leaves and machinery and all shops and underground in the earth's core. It was the whole inside of all living things, but on the outside, and that's where my dad worked. There! In that refinery! My mouth watered. I couldn't look away.

Robby and me were eating Weet-Bix at the table when Dad walked into the kitchen. 'Morning, boys,' he said, his voice croaky with sleep.

'Morning, Dad! Morning,' I said.

Robby barely looked up – he was reading the instructions on the milk bottle; it was just Robby and the bottle. 'Morning,' he mumbled.

Dad leaned against the island and rubbed his eyes. The skin of his face was still red from the rust. 'Might take my coffee down to the shed, love,' he said to Mum. 'Take a look at that chair.'

'Good idea, Gav,' she said, passing him his cup. 'A chair with three legs isn't much use, hey?' She smiled.

'Good idea, Gav,' I said.

Dad looked at me and frowned, then he took his coffee and went through the back door.

A horn beeped outside. Robby took his bowl to the sink and pulled up his football socks. 'Mrs Davids is here,' he said, looking through the window.

'Good luck for the game,' said Mum, grabbing him and squeezing. 'And thank Mrs Davids for the lift.' Robby was twelve – six years older than me – and Mum's first miracle. Her ovarian was crusted with cysts like barnacles on a boat. I saw a picture on Dr Eric's wall. The boat was deep in the water and there was hardly any space. Only one tiny hole that took me six years to find – her second miracle.

Robby headed for the front door.

'Bye, Robby, bye. Good luck in the game,' I said, but he was already gone.

Dad's shed was a garage with a roller door that didn't roll. Dad used the thin door in the side instead. The shed was the one place Mum didn't tidy. 'You leave Dad alone when he's in there, Jimmy,' she said.

I hung around the doorway and looked in at Dad and rode my three-wheeler up and down the concrete path and onto the grass then back onto the path then onto the grass. Dad was drawing something on the wall. I dropped my three-wheeler and went closer to the open door. He was drawing lines around his tools with a texta.

'What are you doing that for, Dad?' I asked him. 'Dad?'

'So I don't lose my tools, son,' he answered. 'Look.' He took the hammer off the wall. Left behind was the outline of the hammer. 'Now I know where the hammer should go. I'll know when it's missing. I should have done this years ago.' He shook his head, then put the hammer back into the drawing of itself.

In the corner of the shed was a small fridge where Dad kept beers. There were stickers on the fridge door: pictures of highways that led to the beach. One said *Golden Valley Highway*, another said *Southern Lands Highway*, and one said *Great Coastal Road*. Some of the stickers had a wave curling over. Others had a fish or a fishing rod.

The shed was where Dad went to fix things like a chair. I stayed at the open door and watched him where he stood, gripping the chair between his legs, his mouth tight with a nail sticking out, his lips bitten back as he hammered at the place where the leg had snapped. The refinery's magnetic powers streamed through him and drew me. I couldn't leave him alone.

Soon he came out of the shed, pushing past me with the chair. 'Paula!' he called.

Mum came into the yard. 'Oh, love, that didn't take you long!' She looked closer at the leg he had fixed. 'Think it's strong enough to hold your other half?' She smiled at him.

''Course it is,' he said, before turning away. Her need was

4

like a blanket you throw on a fire to extinguish the flames. Dad couldn't breathe under there.

Dad pulled the lawnmower out of the shed. I wished I could mow. I liked the way the grass got sucked under then sliced off. While Dad took out the jerry can I ran my fingers down the long handle of the mower until I reached the round orange body. I wished I could turn the mower upside down and put a stick in the blades and see it get cut in half. I wanted to see how fast those blades could go.

'Careful, Jimmy!' Dad called out to me. He unscrewed the lid of the jerry can and poured the petrol into the mouth of the mower. I squatted beside it and watched the air shimmer and cloud. It didn't matter how far the fuel travelled or how long it was stored, it never lost energy. If you lit a match and held it near, the air would catch fire.

When he'd finished pouring, Dad screwed the lid back onto the jerry can and put it beside the shed wall. I watched him cross the yard, his body small and quick. He stood over the engine, legs apart, and pulled the cord. The ladies on his arm shot up into the air, nearly knocked off his muscle. The sun behind him shone bright in my eyes.

'It didn't work, Dad. It didn't work,' I said. Dad pulled at the cord again, harder. The motor still didn't start. Underneath the metal body of the mower the blades waited. 'Are you going to pull it again, Dad? Are you going to pull it again?' I asked him.

The answer was yes yes yes! He pulled the cord again, his arm a fast red streak up into the sky, sending the ladies on his muscle through the air, squealing and shrieking. This time the motor started. 'Rrrrrrrrrrrrmmmmmm!' Engines send my cells into a spin as they try to keep up. I ran towards the mower then away from it, then towards it, then away from it, then around it in a circle, then another circle, then another circle then another circle.

'Paula! Paula!' Dad shouted over the rumble. 'Come out here and get Jimmy!'

'Get Jimmy, will you! Get Jimmy!' I shouted. 'Get the kid, get the kid!'

'Paula! Paula!' Dad called. The engine kept chugging, and I kept running. I jumped over the top of the mower, first from the back and then from the front. 'Paula! Paula!' Dad grabbed at me as I leapt but I was too fast for him.

'Whooooeeeeeee!' I called as I jumped. 'Paaaauuuullllllaaaaaa!' The blades or me, who was the fastest? Nobody knew! Nobody even *knew*! I jumped again then I ran to the fence, touched it and ran back. Dad swiped at me. Mum came running, rocking like a rowboat on the sea, down the back step and across the gravel path, towards me and the mower and my shouting dad. 'Wheeeeeeeeeee!' I screamed as I jumped, falling against the handle of the mower, tipping it on its side so its whirring silver blades glinted in the sun. I jumped again, Dad reached for me, but he went too close, too close!

'Aaaahhhh!' he called out, falling back from the mower.

Mum screamed, *'Jimmy!'* and hauled me up.

Dad held his arm against himself, his face white and blue and green and grey, blood bursting across his shirt. Mum dragged me to the back door and pushed me through. She locked it from the outside and ran back down to Dad. I pressed my face to the glass, and watched their mouths moving around and up and down and around. I looked at their eyes and I saw that they were filled with tiny sharp rocks. I shouted to them, 'Your eyes! Your eyes!' but they couldn't hear me. Mum tried to check Dad's arm, but he pulled away. He shook his head, then looked back up at me. All of his face was closed, hard as the blade slowing to a stop beneath the dying engine.

I ran into the bathroom where the tiles were white and cool and I leaned my cheek against the wall. I looked at the crisscrossing lines. I traced my finger up and down the grooves where the mould collected, growing thick and black with spores that shot out from strings attached to the main body. Each spore was poison but you would need to lick every crack in the bathroom wall and the guttering at the base of the shower and the circles around the taps before you showed the symptoms.

The cold of the tile against my cheek slowed my cells to a cycle per second. One . . . turn . . . two . . . turn . . . three . . . turn . . . I closed my eyes and made a picture of my dad's hands.

Mum told me Dad was the first one to hold me. He hadn't been at the hospital for Robby's borning, but times had changed – *it was 1980, after all*, said Mum – so he was there for mine. Mum told me I was pre-nup. She was too tired to lift her head; it stayed on the pillow, and Dad held his out hands instead. The nurse said, *No, no, not yet, Mr Flick*, but Dad said, *Pass him to me*. So the nurse, who was young, passed me, the baby, to him and because my skin was so raw and untamed I could feel the imprint of his hands on every part of myself. The nurse said, *Please, Mr Flick*, but my dad took no notice. He raised me to his face and because I was still so new, not yet obstructed by pollution, I had vision, and with it I could see through his eyes, past his thoughts, to his core. It was shining and there was a Jimmy-sized place for me inside it. My dad kissed my forehead and his lips imprinted on my intelligence. The nurse said, *Mr Flick, please*, and slowly, without wanting to, he passed me back.

I heard the back door open and Dad come inside. I heard him go into the sitting room.

I went out to where Mum was pushing the mower into the toolshed behind Dad's garage. She couldn't close the door; the fat black bottom of the mower was in the way. She pushed and pushed, then she leaned against it so the door had no choice and dragged the lock across. 'Bloody hell,' she said. She turned around. Her face was damp with sweat from her effort. It evaporated from the hotplates under her pores.

'Come inside, Jimmy. Come on,' she said, holding out her hand. It was shaking. Dad's blood was on her fingers.

'What about Dad, Mum? What about your other half? Mum? What about Dad?'

'I know you didn't mean it, Jimmy,' she said. 'So does your dad.'

I followed her into the kitchen where she got out eggs and a saucepan. She dropped the saucepan onto the floor as she reached for the tap. 'For God's sake,' she said. Mum picked up the pot and filled it with water, then she put it on the stove. The tentacles in her air ducts began to wave as they tried to catch the dust. She reached into her apron pocket, took out her puffer, shook it and sucked. I stood next to the stove and listened to the eggs knocking softly against each other when the water started to boil. Steam rose up into the kitchen air. I tried to watch for when the molecules collided so I could catch them before they escaped, but it was too late. The droplets hovered over the bubbling water.

'Don't stand so close, Jimmy. How many times have I told you?' Mum pushed me back. 'Go watch the telly for a while, Jim. Just while I do this for Dad.' She got his tray out, her hands still shaking, and made a pile of sandwiches, one on top of the other, their edges lining up like bricks in a wall, egg with salt and no sauces.

She went down the hall and into the sitting room. I heard her say, 'Let me drive you to the hospital, Gav.'

'I'm fine.'

'But your arm, love . . .'

'I've seen worse done at work.'

'It must be painful.'

'It's fine.'

Merle Haggard began to sing 'Kern River' as Mum came out. She looked at me, pulling her bottom lip in with her teeth then biting softly on it. I slid down the kitchen wall then up it then down it then up it then down it again.

'Give it a rest, Jimmy, love — just give it a rest. I'll bring you your manuals in a minute,' Mum said as I followed her into the kitchen. I kept the instructions for new equipment; my latest was for Mum's clock radio. The manual showed you how to set the timer and tune the stations. A counter told the numbers when to change. Mum reached up above the stove to the high cupboard with the vitamin C and the aspirin. She pulled down a full bottle of Cutty Sark Blended Scotch. Next she took the ice tray from the freezer and one of Dad's heavy glasses from the bottom shelf.

She bent back the ends of the ice tray so that ices went flying across the island and onto the floor. I got down on my hands and knees to find one to eat while Mum dropped the rest into Dad's glass. Then she poured the Cutty Sark over the ices so that the ices were drowning it in. 'Help! Help!' I shouted.

Mum swung around, her face pale. 'What is it, Jimmy?' she asked in a hurry, tentacles waving faster.

'I'm an ice,' I told her.

She frowned and sighed. 'For God's sake, Jimmy, give it a rest.'

I followed her skirt to the sitting room and stood outside the door, hidden by the wall. When Merle thought about Kern River he thought of his friend who went under. Merle couldn't stop the river rushing and swirling and pushing at its banks, breaking rocks and making a waterfall and drowning a dog that had jumped in for the ball. 'Bloody kid!' I heard Dad say.

'We've just got to keep him inside when you get that thing started.'

'It's not bloody normal, Paula. Who has to keep their kid inside when the lawnmower starts?'

'We don't know what goes on behind closed doors, Gav. Could be anything. Could be things that make our Jimmy look like a saint.'

'Bloody idiot kid. You keep him like that. It's the bloody Paula and Jimmy show.'

There was a gap then, without words or moves. The bloody Paula and Jimmy show was a show without a part for my dad. He was in the audience, watching.

'Can I get you anything else, love?' said Mum, finally closing the gap. In her question I heard the top world and the invisible world simultaneously. There was more in the invisible world. When Merle finished his song I heard the ices trembling in

Dad's glass. I wondered if Dad had drunk enough Cutty Sark to lower the level and save their lives.

'Some bloody peace,' he answered.

Dad thought I'd taken over the part of Paula's other half in the show. But he was wrong. Why couldn't Paula tell him? Without each other's halves their vitals fell out. Didn't she know?

Dad stayed in the sitting room all day. He only came out to get the Cutty Sark, which he took back with him. I sat outside his door and listened to him sing along with Merle to 'I Had a Beautiful Time'. I closed my eyes to see him dance as he sang, swinging in circles, his quick feet stepping, his thin tight legs moving with the music. He wore a black suit with a white tie in a bow, and he held a microphone, and when my mum stepped onto the stage wearing a long red dress that kicked out, he looked across at her as if he had never seen a woman so lovely, so big, so much all at once. He went to her, circling her, then he swung her and sang and danced and Mum threw back her head and laughed and it was a beautiful time.

'What are you doing out here, Jimmy?' Mum frowned, looking down at me. 'Please leave your father alone. Come and help me outside.' Mum pulled at my arm and we went out into the garden together.

'Come and dig with me,' Mum said, giving me the spade. She set down her kneeling pad and pulled at grasses that grew beside the trees and in between the flat purple flowers. I dug beside her. *Crunch, crunch, crunch*, the dirt tipped into my spade. I tipped it out again, digging deep holes, seeing worms and tiny flies and rocks. *'Won't you tell me that you love me?'* sang Mum. *'Won't you tell me that you do?'*

SOFIE LAGUNA

'If I could ever come back again it would be as Doris Day,' she said. 'Doris is perfection.'

Birds in the trees swooped down low and lined the branches to listen to Mum. *'So won't you tell me that you love me? Won't you tell me that you do?'* they sang together.

Digging slowed me down, my cells like bicycle wheels coming to a stop. I could hear the movement of my own air, each *in* an equal to each *out*. The same sun that shone behind Dad's arm when he pulled the cord now shone over us. The dirt we were digging used to be big things like rocks and cliffs and cars, but the worms sucked it with their lips through the tube of their bodies until it was in smaller and smaller pieces and then it was dirt. It packed the space behind my fingernails tight.

'What about Dad, Mum?' I asked.

'What about him?'

'Will his arm fall off?'

'No, love, it won't fall off,' she said, stopping her work and turning to me. 'It will be alright. You just do your gardening and don't worry about it.'

I saw a red smear underneath her eye, like a finger pointing.

After a while she went in for snacks. Soon she came back out with lamingtons and chocolate fingers and glasses of Passiona. She was chewing on her lip, trying to hold back messages she'd received on her trip to the kitchen: *Dad is drinking Scotch, Dad is in the sitting room, Dad has a bad cut.*

Robby came through the back door, his football socks loose around his ankles, mud on his knees. He looked around and saw the lawn not mowed and he heard Merle singing 'I'm a Lonesome Fugitive'. 'Where's Dad?' he asked.

'Your father had an accident,' Mum answered, passing him a glass of Passiona. 'Best just to leave him alone for a while.'

Robby frowned. 'What happened?' He looked at me.

'I did it,' I said.

'No you didn't, Jimmy. Your dad'll be okay. Have your drink,' said Mum.

Robby looked up at the sky and then he walked to the fence, stood on his tiptoes and tried to see over it, as though he was searching for something in the distance beyond the houses and the streets, something far away like a speck of light.

'Are you seeing Justin this afternoon?' Mum asked.

'Yeah.' Robby drank his drink and looked up to the house then back at me. All his thoughts and words and wishes were growing thick inside him. There was a world beyond the fence. There was the sea. When Robby won the Best Player trophy for 1984 two years ago he forgot to bring it home from the awards night in the school hall. He didn't care if it was on the mantelpiece or if I dug a hole for it in the sandpit. A part of him had left already. I tried to get it back sometimes but it was no use. It was out there in front of him, waiting.

It was almost the end of the day and Mum stood at the fryer. I sat at the kitchen table with my manuals opened around me like a fort – heater, stovetop, hairdryer, toaster, clock radio. When I looked over the fort wall I saw Mum, her apron strings, her legs, her bottom moving as she turned the sausages. I read about how to connect the hairdryer nose to the body, and then I checked that she was still there, still frying. I kept looking up and checking, then reading, then checking. Was she there, was she staying? What came after? What was next? What would it be? What would it feel like? When would it happen? When? When? Now? Now? Next? Next? What next? After the frying, then what?

Dad never left the sitting room; he didn't even go to the TAB or the newsagency to pick up the paper. I knew because when Mum couldn't see I went and checked. I saw the back of his head over the top of his recliner that was tipped back and rocking to Merle singing 'Someday When Things Are Good'. Dad was smoking a cigarette and the hand with the glass was making small dance moves to Merle, the cigarette a conductor's stick telling the music which way to go. All the ice was gone from his glass. I looked at the Cutty Sark bottle and the level was past the sails, almost touching the sea. Dad said some things I didn't understand, noises but no language.

Robby came home from Justin's and I followed him to our room. 'What makes the aeroplane stay in the air, Robby?' I asked him.

He lay on his bed and picked up a comic. There was hardly any light. I looked over the top of his comic; all the superheroes were in shadow. He pulled it back.

'What, Robby? What makes it?' I asked him again. He rolled away from me. I pushed his shoulder. 'Is it the fuel? Is it the propellers? Is it the wings?' He didn't answer. He was inside the square frames with the superheroes, scaling buildings and putting out fires. 'Is it the engine, Robby?'

He rolled onto his back. 'Mum!' he called out. 'Can you get Jimmy?'

I gave the back of his comic a flick and left the room. I went back down the hall. I saw the sitting room door open and heard Merle sing 'If Anyone Ought to Know'. I walked up the hall. One of my hands was on the wall and I drew wings and a propeller and I hummed to the music coming from the sitting room. But I did it with an aeroplane engine. *Anyone anyone anyone anyone Rrrrrmmmmmmmrrrrrmmmmmm, louder and louder.*

Suddenly the chair swung round and Dad shouted, 'Get out of here, you little shit!' His words ran into each other like liquid.

Robby ran into the hall. 'Jimmy!' he hissed.

'Get out of here, you little shit!' I hissed back. Robby tried to pull me away from the doorway. 'No!' I shouted.

'Leave Dad alone,' he said.

'Why?' I asked.

'He's drunk.'

'Let go of my arm. Let go.'

'No,' he said, still trying to drag me.

'Mum!' I called. 'Mum!'

Mum came out with a cleaning cloth over her shoulder. There was sweat on her face and the hotplates under her cheeks were up so high I could see the coils. 'Come away, Jimmy!' she said in a whisper.

'Why are you whispering?' I asked.

'I'm not,' she said. 'Come away.'

'You are!' I shouted. *'You are! You are! You are! You are!'* Sing that, Merle Haggard! Sing that!

Robby and Mum were both trying to drag me away when out came Dad, swaying as if there was a small breeze in the room. His face was flushed and he held his arm in a tea towel, patches of blood over the roosters, his conductor stick burning close to his fingers. 'Can't you bloody kids give me some fucken peace?' He spat little white balls with the words. The blood on his shirt had spread to his eyes; there was no white left.

'Sorry, love, I'll take them out the back,' Mum said, her voice smooth as milk.

'I can still bloody hear them from out there!' He spat more.

I saw a ball land on the carpet. It balanced on a carpet fur, like the ball on a seal's nose at the zoo. I pulled away from Robby and lay down beside it. 'Spit!' I shouted. *Spit! Spit! Spit! Spit!*

'Don't, Jimmy,' Robby warned.

'Bloody little idiot!' Dad pushed Mum.

'Robby, take him out the back,' she said quickly, shoving me into Robby's arms.

'Spit! Spit! Spit! Spit!' I shouted, all of me fast, my cylinders and cells revolving, my tubes turning, molecules colliding. 'Spit! Spit! Spit!' Robby tried as hard as he could to pull me away — my brother Robby who'd just turned twelve, his shoes leaving dots of mud from the field when he had run for the ball, the best on the team, the best and the fastest and the fairest, my brother! I couldn't feel myself. I was as fast as the helicopter when you pull the string and off it flies, rotors spinning fast enough to cut off a head. I was too fast for my skin to hold. If something spins that fast, speed turns it invisible and all the invisible silent languages come at you in a rush and blow you apart, like a bomb.

Dad pushed Mum into the wall. 'Hah!' Her breath bounced from her as she fell back.

'Not in front of the kids, Gavin!' she said, fast and low. He couldn't hear the things she wanted. He was going on, forward.

'Look at what he did, Paula! See this?' He pulled back the tea towel from his arm and showed her the long split with the blood turning darker, cutting the ladies in half, blood crusting around their bosoms and thighs. 'How am I going to go back to work on Monday with this? Bloody little retard!'

I fought in Robby's arms. 'Bloody little retard! Bloody little retard!' I shouted, each word heading for my dad like a rocket.

'Gav, don't . . . please don't . . .' Mum begged him.

A fire engine raced along my pathways, its siren screaming *Emergency! Emergency!*, its lights flashing on off on off. 'Eeeeooooooooeeeeeooooooooooo, bloody little retard, Paula! See what he did, Paula, bloody little retard!'

Dad looked at me with a backwards light in his eyes.

'Shush, Jimmy, shush. Robby, can't you get him out of here?' Mum was trying to hold my arms still, but they swung out like blades.

'I'm trying,' said Robby.

Mum turned to help him but I mowed her down with my arms of metal.

'Can't I even cut the bloody grass? Can't I even do that?'

'Stop it, Gav. Please . . .' Mum's words were broken and breathy as she tried to contain me.

'It's always you and the bloody kid.'

'Let's just leave the kids out of it. Let's just keep it between us.'

'Between us? Ha! That's a bloody joke, that is.'

'Eeeeeeeeeeeeooooooooooeeeeeeeooooooooo!' My siren rang out, its light beaming from my holes, lighting up the room in red. 'Keep it between us, keep it between us! What a bloody joke!'

'For Christ's sake, shut up! Shut up!' Dad stepped towards Mum and slapped her on the side of her head as if it was her who'd been shouting, her who was the retard, her with blades of steel.

'Get him out of here, Robby!' she shouted. 'Go!' Then she was quiet. No more begging or pleading, as if she knew what happened next and it was too late to stop it. There was only the sounds of our bodies – skin rubbing skin, our breaths – trying to get away as if the centre was our dad and we were spinning around him but the gravity was him and it dragged us towards him. Another slap, the same place, the same ear, and down Mum went. She never tried to stop him, she didn't shield herself. She just let him – there was so much of her for him to choose from. Mum got up slowly, having to balance her weight.

Dad was shaking, as if the pressure was too much and he might explode. That's why Mum offered herself. She didn't want him in pieces all over the walls – there'd be too much to clean.

'Fuck this.' Dad growled. He smacked her again and then Robby got me out of the room and through the back door. He dragged me down the concrete path between the two squares of grass, under the washing line hung with sheets, past Dad's shed. One of the boards of the back fence leaned to the side and one next to it was loose. He pushed me down and through the gap and he followed on his hands and knees.

The wetlands were made of mud and water and stiff silver grass, floating plastic and seaweed. Robby pulled me to the edge of the stream and then we sat and he put his arm around my shoulder. I breathed in one out one, and looked at the grass and the clouds and the sun half hidden and the birds on the water and I felt myself joining with the swamp. On the other side of the grass and the stream, way in the distance, the flame leapt from the refinery pipe – like the light in the sheep's eye, it never died.

We sat there for a long time, Robby's arm around me drawing speed and fear from my cells. The arm wasn't too tight or too loose. Its temperature set mine to itself, cooling me from hot to warm.

The stream that ran through the middle of the swamp rose when it rained, and fell in the summer. Spoonbills and black swans, sandpipers and pelicans nested on the banks and on the tiny islands away from the snakes. Ducks had their babies on the sides, leading them into the deep when foxes came.

'Okay, Jimmy?' Robby said.

'Okay,' I said. 'Okay, Robby.'

Robby moved his arm, and stood. 'Come on,' he said.

I followed him to the trench – half there already and half made by us. We dug it deeper to catch the water. I breathed in then out, keeping both breaths the same length. The wetlands air had a potion that came from the refinery flame and slowed me down. That's why Mum let me go; when I got home I was quieter.

We cleaned out the dirt from the fridge that lay upside down at the end of the trench, and wiped the sides. We dug and scraped and across the fields the flame blasted from the pipe without ceasing. Smoke rose and turned to cloud until there was no difference.

We built up walls to support the fridge, smoothing them so the enemy couldn't get a foot-hold. The grass prickled our knees. The end of the sun was warm in my nostrils.

'What are we making?' I asked Robby.

'A boat,' he answered.

'Like the *Lady Free*?'

'Yes.' When Robby was younger Dad took him on the *Lady Free* and they stayed away for two nights and caught fish as long as Robby. I counted the hours; I got as high as I could then began at one again. In the sitting room, beside Dad's recliner, there was a photo of him and Robby on the deck of the *Lady Free*. They stood together and the smiles on their faces were matching. I smoothed the mud up the fridge in a boat shape, sharp at the ends and round in the middle. I stuck a shell in the side for a cyst.

Robby fished off the fridge, dangling an invisible line into the mud. I looked up into the sky and counted twenty-six pelicans, their wings outstretched as they rode the currents, their beaks telling them which way to go, storing messages from the sun and the tides. On the other side of the swamp, I saw the tank farm and the tyre factory and the LKA chemical plant where they boiled vitamin pills, and the Quality Endorsed Industrial Park Established 1979 where the steel sheds stood as big as ovals. Trains ran back and forth along the tracks between the swamp and the factories, like moving guards.

I lay on my stomach and put my ear to the ground beside the *Lady Free* so I could listen to the core of planet Earth. The core held planet Earth's network and made the sound of *shush*-ing.

'Shhhhhhhh . . .' I whispered back, the core's echo.

'Boys! Dinner!' Mum called from over the fence.

Robby stood and wiped his muddy hands down the front of his trousers. 'Come on, Jimmy,' he said.

The loose board knocked against our shoes on the way through the fence. As soon as we walked into the house through the back door I felt my cells speed up. The potion from the flame couldn't pass through the plaster.

Later that night, when Robby and me were in bed and the lights were off, Mum came into our room.

I rolled over, eyes open. 'Mum?' The light shone in from the hallway. In her long white nightdress she looked like a candle.

She sighed. 'What are you doing still awake?' She got in beside me. I had to move over to the far edge, so that I was pressed against the wall, to make room for her. The wall was cool against my cheek and knees. Mum was as wide as my bed. She was so big there were parts of her I'd never seen. She held on to me and counted sheep. 'One sheep . . . two sheep . . . three sheep . . . four . . . You count too, Jimmy,' she said. Her arm was hooked over my body. I could feel her breathing, her warmth. She held me tightly to her as if I was a sponge that could absorb the extra.

'Five sheep . . . six sheep . . . seven . . .' we counted together. If you look deep into the eye of a sheep you can see a light. It burns right at the back of the head and it never goes out, no matter what happens to the sheep.

'Does anything happen to the sheep?' I asked her.

'Keep your voice down, you'll wake Robby.'

'Does it? Does anything happen to them?' I whispered.

'Nothing happens to them.'

'Are you sure?'

'Jimmy, do you want to keep counting or not?'

'Yes, keep counting,' I whispered.

Once we were in the Holden, caught in the traffic beside a truck full of sheep, so close I could hear their hooves clacking against the boards. I could see them shuffling, pushing against each other for room. They were jammed in, one layer over another, their noses pressing against the wooden sides of the truck, tails covered in mud. What happened to those sheep? What happened to the light?

'. . . Eight sheep . . . nine sheep . . . ten . . .'

I never liked to wake and find her gone. There was too much room, as if the bed had grown to make space for her and not shrunk back to its original. I lay awake and waited and listened. Robby breathed slow and even in his bed on the other side. I could smell Mum's Intensive Care left behind on the sheets.

I lined up shadows of bottle, Matchbox car, book, window, shell, bus painting and birthday card while I waited. I was at birthday card when I heard a *thump* coming from down the hall. *Thump.* Like someone falling without power or muscle or fibres, as if the power and muscle and fibres had been lost. There was nothing to hold up the body.

The particles under my skin scratched at the surface. Robby slept on, the smooth air going in then slowly out. *Thump!* again, louder this time as the powerless body tried to stand and couldn't and fell again.

I jumped from my bed and ran to Robby's. He moaned and moved over. I pressed as much of myself against him as I could, legs, stomach, knees. I breathed him in, he smelled of Johnson's Baby Shampoo after it had been heated and cooked with his sweat. I lay there, shaking and listening, my whole body tuned as an ear, but there were no more sounds.

'Jimmy,' Robby whispered. 'You wet the bed.'

'Sorry, Robby. Sorry. Sorry.' I felt the spread of wet, warm as the last of Mum's tea, beneath us. I got out and so did he, and he pulled off the sheet in the dark and threw it under the bed. Then he pulled down my wet pyjama pants and threw them under there too. We slept on the mattress, its buttons sticking into my skin as I held on.

When I went into the kitchen the next morning Mum wasn't there. Dad was sitting on the high stool at the island drinking his coffee, holding his arm in a bandage against his chest. He didn't look at me. The morning after my dad drank Cutty Sark he hung his head, as if it was too heavy for the rest of him. The weight of the Cutty Sark blocked the valves that led to Paula. Dad tried to clear the blockages with his hands and that's what left Paula with the bruises. But if he didn't drink the Cutty Sark, the valves inside pressed against his heart and other vitals, carrying the past through his bloodstream. The pressure built like the boiling water in the refinery pipes that led to steam and flame. It wasn't bearable.

When the phone on the wall rang Dad left the island to answer it. 'She's not up yet, Anne,' Dad said into the tiny holes of the receiver. 'Yes, I'll tell her.' His voice was gruff and sung out from too much time with Merle. He put his coffee cup in the sink and took his work vest off the hook.

I was on my way into Mum's room when Dad called me back. 'Stay here, Jimmy, she'll be out in a minute.' He looked at something high-up to the side of me that only he could see.

Robby came into the kitchen. He opened the cereal cupboard and took out the cornflakes. He only made contact with the cornflakes; they shared a world that nobody else could enter.

Dad put on his jacket. 'Righto, I'm off,' he said to the high-up thing. Robby and me kept quiet. *Click* went the front door, and he was gone.

Mum came slowly out of her room, walking as if her feet were sore. She wore a white dress with little pink baubles on her ears. I liked to press against her blue morning gown while she drank her tea. Where was the gown? Why was she wearing the baubles? There was a coating of pale mud on her face almost the same colour as her skin. It looked as if it had been painted on. It went down her cheeks and stopped at her neck. There was the mark of a wave that had rolled in then rolled out again, leaving a line of froth, dirty and uneven.

I ran to her, pressing myself against her. What had happened to her face? 'Mum!' I cried out.

Robby didn't speak. He didn't seem sure. He stood on the other side, watching, his spoon in his hand above the bowl.

'What is it, love?' she answered, stroking the top of my head. Then she bent down and came close. 'What is it, pet? Had your breakfast yet? Had your soldiers?' She tickled my side and rubbed her nose against mine.

I peered through the mud and saw the same face – the round pieces and the brown lights, the lines and the tiny wells. Tears trembled and clung in her eyes. Mum! I hugged her tight and her warmth transmitted on to me. Robby stayed where he was, on the other side of the island. He didn't like to cuddle long; he'd grown out of the need.

Dad kept away the whole morning. Mum stood at the sink and told the detergent and the hand cream and the cleaning cloths that the bastard was healing his wounds at the TAB. She wiped surfaces, her hands straining against the insides of her pink rubber gloves. She wiped around the stove and up the walls and down the sides of the island and under the fridge. Before the water dried I saw the swirls, and then she went over them again.

Robby said, 'Come on, Jimmy,' and we crawled through the hole in the fence.

There was a burnt-out car on the other side of the steel bridge. Seagulls sat along the rusted edges. I stopped halfway across and watched the water rushing under my feet through the steel. 'Jimmy! Come on!' said Robby. I gripped the rails and followed him across. With every step the bridge shook. Just on the other side was where I'd seen the snake. Robby kept heading for the car. It was the furthest I'd ever gone with him. He picked up a long stick and poked it into the grass to scare the tigers and the browns. 'Ssssss . . .' he said.

When Robby hit the sides of the car with his stick the seagulls flew up, screeching over our heads. There were empty bottles inside the rusted bones, and a pair of black underpants. Robby flicked the underpants out onto the grass. He climbed in and took the steering wheel, the car's only remaining organ, and changed gears with the invisible gearstick. He leaned forward, closer to the bonnet. I could see he was headed for the ocean. Out to the end of the pier, where he'd wait for an ocean liner to come and take him away.

Then he climbed out and walked slowly around the car. 'We got to dig the wheels out,' he said. He bent down and started scraping the dirt away from around one of the iron wheels.

'But, Robby,' I said, 'the car doesn't have an engine. It doesn't have tyres, Robby. It can't go.'

'The wheels are stuck,' he said again. 'Help me dig.'

'But, Robby,' I said.

'Dig.' His hands moved quickly in the hard dirt. There were small stones mixed in. He had to pull up grass. I got down beside him and started to dig. Neither of us spoke. Our hands made their own talk of scraping and clawing and digging, until our fingernails stung and bled. I kept up with Robby as we made trenches around the wheels. Deeper and deeper, as if we kept on digging we might free the car. What was under there, underneath the wheels? Where would we end up if we didn't stop digging? After the car was freed, if we kept going and going, where would we be if our hole never ended? Down passageways, under with the worms, to the core, then beyond, to the other side. And if we still didn't stop, then where?

Soon Robby's digging slowed down and the talk of his hands grew quiet. He stood up and kicked the car. Then he climbed inside its bones and put his hands on the steering wheel. I got in the passenger side. I tucked my feet up over the grass beneath and Robby drove. The wind blew back our hair and every traffic light was green and Robby put his foot to the floor and we sped through the wetlands laughing and listening to loud songs on the radio. *Gonna get you baby, gonna make you mi-i-ine!* Robby shook his head in time to the music and I shook my fist then Robby changed his gear and the car lifted higher. Robby said, 'Look, Jimmy! Look!' and we were in line with the twenty-six pelicans. We had freed the car.

When we got home I could hear hammering as we crossed the yard; Dad was working in the garage.

Mum lay on her blue kitchen couch reading an Agatha — her head against the *Home Sweet Home* pillow. The kitchen smelled of bleach, like a swimming pool. She sat up when we came in, *The Mystery of the Blue Train* falling to the floor. 'You boys were gone for hours,' she said.

Robby went straight through to the bedroom without stopping. If Robby stayed quiet, the distance between him and something he didn't like or want grew more quickly, but only if he didn't say a word about it. If he said a word, even one, the word made a space for the thing he didn't like or want to come crashing in and detonate him. It was the words that made the opening.

Early on Monday morning Dad went back to work. He wore long sleeves even though it was going to be a scorcher. It was to hide the cut from Bill Philby, his boss. Dad was scared that if Bill Philby saw it he would start asking questions Dad didn't want to answer.

Before he walked out the door to meet his lift, I said to him: 'You could roll one sleeve up, Dad, so the cool won't have so far to travel. It will go under your shirt, and come out the other side like a breeze through a short tunnel.'

Dad laughed. Sometimes it happened. Why? Where was the engine of laughter? There was no time to ask him; he was through the door and gone, a full day of rust ahead of him.

That day Mum took me to Dr Eric's. Dr Eric had been seeing me since I was born. He was the one to give me my first injection – I felt it enter my sub cuticle. He put a bandaid over the two holes when he was finished and told Mum to press. Dr Eric was as old as some of Mum's Westlakers. Mum cooked for the seniors at Westlake Nursing. *I may not be a women's libber, Jimmy, but I still like to have a bit of my own.* Dr Eric had white hair on his head and on his face that kept him insulated. There were always mints on his desk. It didn't matter what time of the day it was the bowl was full, as if there was a pipe that ran the length of the table underground to a mint tank and whenever a patient took a mint, the mint tank shot one up and replaced it.

I looked at the books in the children's box while Mum talked to Dr Eric.

'Couldn't you come round to the house?' Mum asked. 'Gavin's so stubborn he'll never come in by himself. You might just say you were popping round to check on me, the way you have before; my asthma's been playing up . . .'

'If Gavin makes an appointment I'll look at his arm, Paula. That one's up to him,' said Dr Eric. 'But it's not Gavin I'm worried about. Something might have happened to Jimmy. I think it's time you took the boy to see a specialist.'

Every time I came it was the same books in Dr Eric's children's box. *Little Black, a Pony, Hello, Mr Train* and *How Many Puppy Dogs?* There was a wooden crane in the box too, but I'd already lifted everything there was to lift.

Mum said, 'Why do I have to go and see a specialist? What do they bloody know? Nothing. I'm the specialist. I'm his mother.'

Dr Eric wrote a number down on a piece of paper. 'Just give it a try, Paula. You might be surprised.'

'I would be surprised,' she said. 'Very surprised.'

'There are some really good learning programs . . .'

Mum looked disgusted. 'I won't be drugging Jimmy.'

'Nobody said anything about drugs. Just go and talk to him; he's at the Royal,' said Dr Eric, passing the paper to Mum. 'It might make things easier.'

'Easier? Winning the lotto would make things easier. Not a bloody visit to a bloody specialist. I just wanted you to look at Gav's bloody arm.'

'Take it easy, Mrs F.' Dr Eric smiled. 'Have a mint.' He passed us the bowl and Mrs F took three. 'If Gavin makes an appointment I'll look at his arm. Tell me how it goes at the Royal.'

Mum stood, pushing past Dr Eric's desk, her legs squeezing against the edges. 'I'll be telling you how it goes, alright,' she said, the mints clacking against her teeth. 'But I'd be better off with that lottery ticket.'

'Next time you visit I'll have one ready,' said Dr Eric.

Mum shook her head, holding back a smile.

'Why is it called *The Royal*?' I asked Mum, as the bus rocked us towards the Westgate Bridge.

'It's the name of the hospital,' Mum answered, her hands gripping each other in her lap.

'But is it royal?'

'It's the *name* of the hospital, Jimmy.' She looked away from me and out the window.

'But is there a king in it, or a queen? Is there a castle?'

My words set Mum's laughing gear in motion. 'I reckon there might be a few people who are paid like bloody kings!' She pulled softly on the end of my ear. 'My Jimmy,' she said.

As we crossed the Westgate Bridge I saw the whole mechanics of the city spread before us; a thousand refineries at work, processing the oil and information, making the crude into usable. Cranes lifted the parts that were falling into the sea, raising them up and pushing sacks of sand underneath for support. Trucks weaved in and out, dodging pipes and tanks, carrying loads of dirt and jerry cans full of petrol to the empty vats. Lights flashed as the engines operated the levers, building walls and jetties and monuments and roofs and rooms and erecting poles and pipes and scaffolding. The sea surrounded it all. I saw sharks circling, looking for waste, biting at the borders, missing nothing. Mum never took me to the city. She said, 'Why leave Altona when we have everything we need right there? Bloody specialist.'

The specialist sat opposite Mum and said, 'You can't expect too much.'

I drove a train up over Mum's chair, crossing the hills of her thighs onto her lap. I said, 'If you're a king, where the hell is your crown?'

Mum gasped. 'Jimmy!' She turned back to the specialist, 'Gosh, he can be silly sometimes. Just having a joke.' She pushed me away but I didn't stop, choo-choo-ing choo-choo-ing, right up the slope of her side.

'Choo-choooooo.' I said, sending the sound deep into the specialist's ears.

'Some things will change and some things won't,' he said. 'You can't expect him to be at the same stage as other children his age . . .' I watched as the redness moved up over Mum, washing her chin and her cheeks pink. It was a mother's fury coming up from her core. She had tried to cover it with chocolate cake and tea from the hospital cafeteria, but it was linked to a vat of mother's fury that could power the world and she couldn't hold it down. She bit back her lips and held her own hands tight and swallowed.

The more the specialist talked the louder I choo-chooed. I tooted so loud I made the specialist put his hand to his ear.

'Can't expect too much,' Mum mumbled on the bus on the way home. 'I'll show you too much. Too bloody much. Too right it's too much. Too much bloody money. Too bloody much. Mind you, Jimmy, you did ham it up in there. What did you have to do that for?' She didn't wait for an answer. 'Still. Talk about an arm and a leg. An arm and a bloody leg.'

'Mum,' I said, 'you sound like mad Mr Henry from the bench at Myrtle Park.'

Mum laughed. 'Jimmy, you're sharp as a tack, you are. Ha! Mad Mr Henry, ha! The same stage as other children. Ha! Who'd settle for being the same, hey, Jimmy?'

For weeks Dad wore shirts with long sleeves and then one morning he said, *Bugger this*, and he wore a short-sleeved shirt. The dark lightning of the cut on his arm rose up between the ladies and severed their heads from their bosoms and one rode it like a surfboard.

Even though it was a weekday and all the other six-year-olds were in school, I was doing the morning shift at Westlake with Mum. Nurse Gallantinis, who was in charge of the maternals, said I'd be best kept back another year and what was the hurry. Mum agreed. She said, 'Oh, I love to have my little man at home, I'll miss him when he has to go to school.' Robby had to go to school. But Justin and his other friends were there. The oval was there. The other things he did and learned. He wanted to go.

'Come on, love, get a move on. Get your manuals together, we can't be late.' Mr Barker, the manager of Westlake, turned a blind eye when I was there. Mum said Mr Barker was always at the pokies spending his hard-earned, so who was he to say I couldn't come? She puffed as she moved her bulk around the kitchen; filling bags and moving dishes, picking up empty teacups and looking for keys. There was already a shine on her face even though it was only the very start of morning when it was still cool. 'Come on, Jimmy. If you want to come to work with me we have to leave now.' Underneath every word I heard the pull of her breath, as if it was unwilling.

'Okay, Mum, instruction manuals on the ready. Westlake Nursing, here we come.'

'That's my boy,' she said.

I followed Mum out to the Holden parked over the crack in the driveway. The wheel was an obstruction. Insects who used the crack for a river to drink from, or to store food, had to go around the tyre. I stopped to check the distance.

'Come on, Jimmy. Hop in the car – get a move on.'

When I was slow I should have been fast, and when I was fast I should have been slow.

At Westlake Mum sent me to Mr Barnes's in Number Six to read to him while she did breakfast. I didn't read the words on the page; I made up my own. I told Mr Barnes the story of my dad's job at the refinery, the way he could get in the corners, where rust grew the thickest. I turned the page and told Mr Barnes the story of the lump in my dad's throat that jumped up and down when he talked and told him what to say. It tells all men what to say, it's the control box and it gives the orders; it doesn't matter that it's small, the voice box holds the power! I told Mr Barnes the story of the earth's core. How the core is hot but it doesn't move. It is the voice box of planet Earth and it gives the orders! *Rain! Storm! Hail! Sun!* Soon I saw Mr Barnes was asleep.

I went into Number Seven, Mr Roger's room next door, but it was empty and the bed was stripped. The photos were down and the books were gone from the shelf and the vase with the rose made of plastic was missing. The window was open, letting in the factory air.

I found Mum in the kitchen. Her face was pink from the steam of boiling macaroni. Underneath her arms, on both sides of her dress, were big damp circles. There was wet in her hair. 'Where did Mr Rogers go?' I asked her.

'Mr Rogers?' She frowned, as if she had forgotten who he was.

'In Number Seven. His room is empty.'

'Oh, Jimmy, it's all part of working in a nursing home. We have to get used to it.'

'But, Mum, *where* did he go?'

'Don't you worry yourself about Mr Rogers. He's in a better place, that's all you need to know.'

'A better place? Mum, *what* place?'

'Oh, love,' she said, wiping her face with the end of her apron, 'can we leave it for now? I still have to finish the mince. You go and have a chat with Mr Olly in seventeen. Mr Olly likes to see you.'

'Okay, Mum, okay.' I'd seen a lot of seniors come and a lot of seniors feed the refinery flame.

We got home just before midday. Mum swept the garden path and I rode my three-wheeler through the dust and hair and dirt that rose up as she swept.

'Don't, love,' she said, smiling.

I did it a few more times then rode at the fence to make the posts shake.

Mum kept sweeping. She hummed Doris, *Won't you tell me hmmmmmm, won't you hmmmmmm,* then when I looked around again she took her puffer from her apron pocket and gave it a shake. She sucked back on it. 'Empty,' she said.

We went inside and she looked for other puffers and found one in the bathroom cupboard but it was empty, and I found one under my bed but it was empty too. Mum sat down and read *Murder on the Orient Express*. Agathas were Mum's specialty and she did the same ones over and over. I sat next to her and built a block and rod refinery. I didn't have enough rods to make all the pipes and smokestacks, but I built the base and assembled the ladders and got the tanks ready. Then I read my sink manual to check the positions. I matched the plug with the refinery exit.

Mum turned on the television in the sitting room and we watched *Days of Our Lives*. She lay on the couch with her head tilted on the arm holder. When she breathed in it sounded as if the air was made of metal shavings. Soon she sat up. 'I thought it would be better with a rest, but it's not. We'll just have to wait for your father to get home, Jimmy. We'll take it easy till then, won't we, love? Really easy . . .' She touched my cheek. When Mum touched me it lit her up. 'You light up my life, little man,' she said. I let her do it anytime.

I rested against her and hardly moved. The end of my finger tried to — up then sideways then down. I stopped it. My leg jiggled. I stopped it. My other leg jiggled and I stopped that too. I took it really easy just like Mum asked me to but it didn't help; all that afternoon her air wouldn't go in. Nothing moved the blockages. I wished I could turn the hose-snake on full and blast it down her throat.

'Get the telephone, love,' she said.

On *Days of Our Lives*, Bo and Hope Brady kissed and Bo said, *'Hope, Hope, you know I would never give up on you.'* Hope had a medical emergency and only Bo could help but he was so tall he couldn't fit through the doorway.

'I'm sorry, Hope . . .'

'Jimmy, Jimmy, you need to help me get to the telephone.'

'What for, Mum? What for?'

'No time for questions, Jimmy. You have to help me.'

I looked at Mum; she was turning the colour of a bruise. 'Yes, Mum, yes.'

She got herself to the edge of the couch, pushing her bottom to the rim. Water sat in droplets on her forehead. She put out her arms. 'Help me, Jim,' she whispered.

I took her hands so she could balance and I pulled as hard I could.

Mum tried to stand but she couldn't get the weight on the right side of the couch. It kept tipping back. 'Oh love,' she said.

I looked in her eyes and the blue of the bruise was spreading to her whites. 'Come on, Mum.'

She leaned forward and put her muscle in her legs. I gritted my teeth and I pulled so hard I thought my eyes would pop. Harder and harder, leaning back against her as if I was pulling oars in a boat on the water, pull, pull, and at last up she came.

She stood panting against me, one hand on my shoulder, the metal shavings in her air passage tearing at the sides with every breath. I was her little man walking stick as we made our slow way up the hall.

I led her to the kitchen couch.

'Get me the telephone, love,' she wheezed, sitting down heavily.

'Yes, Mum, telephone.'

I took the telephone from the bench and brought it down to

her, the cord stretching over the island so that the loops were pulled out.

'Good boy,' she said, putting her finger in the circle. She spoke to someone at the other end of the cord, her voice a mix of whisper and scratch. She said our address – 'Nineteen Emu, nineteen . . . yes . . . yes, I think so . . .' – then she hung up. She tried to lift her mouth into a smile but the rope and pulleys behind her cheeks only got it halfway.

Next Mum called Dad. She had to wait, the telephone pressed against her chest while they dragged him out of the pipes and cleaned him off. The rust was too toxic to expose to the oxygen. Mum never called Dad at work. Once I broke my finger in the sliding door and when the nurse said, 'Did you call your husband?' Mum answered, 'Oh no, not at work, love.'

At last they let Dad on the telephone and Mum said, 'Gav, the ambulance is coming . . . Jimmy's with me . . . I'm sorry, Gav, I just wasn't sure . . . Oh good, oh thanks, love . . .'

I found another puffer under the couch but there was no puff left in it.

'I thought I bought one,' Mum said, hanging up the telephone. 'Jimmy, I need you to . . .' She was pulling in, but there wasn't enough air to support her words and they came out dry. The tentacles were trying to wave but they were heavy with dust and dirt, metal shavings and throat-water.

'What, Mum, what? What do you need? Mum? Mum?'

'Open the door.'

'Yes, Mum, yes.' I ran to the front door and turned the lock one wrong way, then another wrong way, then another, then one right way. I pulled and the door opened. I heard the siren *'Eeeeooooeeeeooo!'*

'Eeeeooooooeeeeooooeeeooo!' I cried out with the

siren, both of us loud through the streets for my mother. 'Eeeoooeeeeeeeeeeoooo!'

I ran back to the kitchen where she lay on the couch. 'Mum, it's coming.' Her head was tilted back, eyes closed, mouth open. 'Mum! Mum!'

'Eeeeeeeooooooooeeeeeoooooooo!' the siren kept calling.

I leaned over and looked into the dark tunnel of Mum's open mouth and I saw a knot. I reached in with my fingers to undo it. She turned away from me. I was getting faster. I shook her shoulders. 'Mum!'

I heard voices. I ran up the hall. Three men wearing blue uniforms said, 'Where is she? Where is your mother?' Dad came through the door behind them. He wore his shining refinery vest and his boots, round at the ends, and his face looked as if a fist had screwed it tight into a ball.

'Through here,' he said, leading the men into the kitchen. They carried a thin white bed in their arms.

Dad went very close to Mum, closer than me or Robby had ever been, so close he was almost under the surface, and he whispered something to her. I couldn't hear what. Nobody could. They were words only for Mum. Her eyes opened as she looked at him, into his eyes, then closed again.

The men lifted Mum up onto the bed. One of them put a mask over her face.

'No! No!' I shouted. 'Open her! Open her!' But the men took no notice. I followed them as they carried Mum out to the ambulance. They moved like the robots in my Sourcebook, hooking her up to a blue plastic bag dangling from a pipe, sliding her into the back. 'Release! Release! Return!' I called out commands but they didn't stop.

'Shush, son, shush now,' my dad said. He stood behind me on the pavement and put his arms around me. They felt strong as trees as he pressed me to him. His voice vibrated in my cavities. 'Take it easy, son,' he said. We watched as the men took Mum away.

I didn't cry. I didn't know how. I didn't know where crying started. I never had, even when I was born and wanted to cry because I didn't yet know words to say what it was to be parted from my mum in that way. Every other baby knows how. When they cry the tears block out the memory, but I didn't know how, even in the first seconds outside the membrane. That's what alerted the authorities.

The street was very quiet without my mother and the siren. Dad was still holding on to me. I looked at the round ends of his boots and stood on one with my bare foot. 'What now?' I said.

'We wait for your mother to come back,' Dad answered. Our bodies were touching at the hands, at the shoulders and down the back. The strength of him was behind me, heating me. We went inside and he turned on the television in the sitting room. *Doctor Who* was on. He left his recliner alone and sat beside me on the black couch instead. For the first time Mum was gone and there was room.

'Dr Who? Dr Who? Knock, knock. Dr Who?' I said.

Dad said, 'Who's there?'

'Dr Who? Dad!'

We watched as the doctor led his friend down many passages, each one narrower than the last. They were running out of time. Three-eyed worms caught them by surprise, rearing up like cobras. 'Give us your secrets, Doctor,' they said. But the doctor never stopped. He crept along as the passages grew thinner. He kept going. He knew he could. The knowledge from the

TARDIS never left him, even though he was only given it once. That one time was enough. Dad stayed for the whole episode. He didn't get up to pour a drink or open a window or make a telephone call. He sat beside me and watched. The story of the doctor and the three-eyed worms came to us at the same time. When the doctor exterminated the worms with death foam, Dad said, 'Good job, Doctor.'

After *Doctor Who* finished we went into the kitchen to make a snack. We were spreading butter onto biscuits when Robby came home from school. 'Where's Mum?' he asked.

'Robots took her to the hospital,' I told him.

'What are you talking about?' Robby's eyes grew wider; rings around rings around rings around the black centre, where the vision entered.

Dad put his hands on the island. 'It's okay, son. Your mum's okay.'

'But is she in hospital?' he asked Dad.

'Yes, she is,' he answered. 'She had an asthma attack. She didn't have her medicine. But we just called the hospital and they said she's doing well; she just needs a bit of quiet time and she'll be home tomorrow.' Dad put the biscuits on a plate, spread with more butter than I'd even seen before.

Robby still hadn't moved. In the deep of his eyes, water wheels turned, processing the information.

'It will be okay, Rob. If she has to stay another night we'll go and visit her. Jimmy took care of things, didn't you, Jimmy?' Dad touched me on the shoulder with the same hand that sent Mum's head wobbling on its stalk. His touch was dry and light and sent messages like a battery charge. I didn't want it to stop; it rooted me to the ground, sending tendrils out from my feet, deep into the earth.

Robby was looping things together in his cognitive. Him and Dad used to go for whole days. Fishing. Kicking the ball. Driving. I wanted to go with them but Mum stopped letting me. I could have swallowed my tongue or broken glass or been run over.

'Paula, Jimmy'll be fine with me. I can manage,' Dad would say.

'Just you and Robby go, love,' Mum said, holding me back. 'It'll be a bit easier that way – more fun. And more whiting.' I saw the wink she gave him; she was trying to pretend she was holding me back for him, and not because she was worried about me.

Until I was three and a half my words were made up and Paula couldn't understand the language. Only Dad and Robby could. *Better than all the bullshit I have to listen to at the car yard*, said Dad. Dad linked my wooden trains one to the other and drove them slowly along the tracks. When he came to the tunnel, he took my hand and said, *It's only short, son. Any minute and we'll be on the other side*. Back then, Dad hardly ever reached for the high cupboard. I didn't even know what was in it.

But when I learned to speak I repeated. Every week that went by I grew faster; words quickened me. Paula stopped letting me out of her sight. She did all the Jimmy jobs. Cleaning and feeding and changing, teaching and holding and clamping and counting and taking my temperature on the nights when the pain in my canals reached the speed of light. She took over with her bulk and when he tried to get to me from around the sides she wedged him against the walls. He began to reach for the high cupboard more and more. 'He bloody drives me to it, Paula,' he said.

'You want to go outside?' Dad asked us.

Robby frowned. 'What for?'

'Because it's only half past three. I'm never home at half past three.'

'What about Mum?' Robby asked.

'She's going to be okay, Rob, mate. I promise.'

Robby looked away to the window.

'You want to throw the frisbee?' Dad asked.

'Not enough room,' said Robby.

'There is on the other side of the fence.' Dad grinned. Mum once showed me a picture of Dad when he was a boy. He wore shorts and he didn't have front teeth and he held two fingers up in a V at whoever took the photograph. *Up yours!* 'Come on,' Dad said, picking up the green frisbee from the step where it lay as a dish for bird water.

Dad, glowing with the powers from his refinery vest, put his hands on the top of the fence and pulled himself over. Robby and I crawled through, the way we always did. We were on the other side, in the wetlands. Birds sat on the shallow water like statues, watching us. Dad ran across the steel bridge, not checking for snakes, not looking through the grid at the water flowing underneath, not holding the bars as he ran, his quick legs like pistons through the silver grass.

The air was fresh in my face, and far away, on the other side of the wetlands, the bright flame leapt from the pipe. When he was far enough Dad stopped and called, 'Ready, boys?'

We called out, 'Ready!' and the green frisbee cut through the grey sky towards us. Back and forth it spun as we ran and threw and ran again. The three lines that joined us shortened and lengthened, the three points stretching and returning, stretching and returning.

Later, back inside the house, red-faced and puffed with sweat dampening our hair, Robby said, 'Drink, Dad?' and passed him water, pouring one for himself and me too. Robby's thin arms moved loosely, his fingers touching Dad's as the glass of water passed between them. We drank our water and Robby said, 'Knock, knock. Who's there?' I said, 'Jimmy!' And Dad said, 'I am, ya mug.' Robby said, 'No, Dad, say *Who's there?*' and Dad said, 'Me, mate, it's me!' and messed Robby's hair. Robby said, 'No, Dad, not *you!*' and Dad said, 'What's wrong with me, mate? You saying there's something wrong with me?' Robby laughed and I saw Dad's reflection in his face with Mum coming up from underneath and entering the cheeks.

It was as if a spell that we didn't know had been in the kitchen of Nineteen Emu was broken. We weren't waiting for anything; we were already there. There was nothing in the invisible world, as if there never had been; it was empty and quiet.

Dad made eggs and bacon. He wore Mum's pink apron with a frill up the sides and the ties went round him twice. Robby laughed and said, 'You look pretty, Dad.' Dad put his hands on his hips and flipped his hand and said, 'More bacon with your eggs, sir?' We moved around the island easily, each of us taking a different side, then joining sides, as if the island was a raft, and we were changing places at exactly the right time to keep it afloat.

When Dad rang Mum at the hospital he said, 'Us fellas have got it under control, love,' and he winked at Robby. 'You just take it easy, sweetheart. I'll make the boys tidy the house top to bottom.' He turned away from us. 'I love you, Paula,' he said, close to the holes, as if it was a secret.

That night, in bed without Mum in the house, I counted sheep while Robby slept. I held the sheep's face steady between my hands and I looked up close at the light in the sheep's eyes. The night went on and on. I kept counting and counting, sheep after sheep after sheep, until I saw a line of light coming through the crack between the curtains.

The next morning, after boilers on toast, Dad took us to Sunshine Hospital in the Holden. When we were in the car with him we didn't speak. I shared Robby and Dad's word-free language. All the windows were open and I watched as dust and crumbs and lost hairs and sand flew out the windows and into the sky where they joined the clouds and contaminants and refinery smoke. The car was clean.

We parked in Furlong Road, not far from the hospital.

When I got inside I looked for the sunshine but it was an absence, shut out by the roof and walls.

Dad walked up to a man behind a desk that said Information. 'I'm looking for my wife, Paula Flick.'

The man checked a folder and answered, 'F Ward.'

'F, F, F, F, F,' I chanted. 'F Ward, F Ward, F Ward, *good good good*.' My cells rotated in my fingertips. I was on end as we passed door after door after door on our way to F Ward. 'F F F feff feff. Mum! Mum! Mum!'

'Settle down, son,' said Dad. But I couldn't settle. 'Mum Mum Mum!'

She was there, under the sheet, in the long white bed of F Ward, like a mountain of snow. I ran to her and something fell and knocked behind me and someone said, *Easy does it.* In one jump I was on the bed against my mum, and she was holding me tight.

'Hello, little Jimmy,' she said. I breathed warm mint and vanilla and Impulse; she was still the same ingredients.

Dad stood at the bottom of her bed, tears gathering at the ends of his eye pipes. He wiped them and touched her feet where they were under the sheet. He said, 'Paula,' but only his lips made the shape of Paula; the sound was trapped by shame in his workings. Tears came to Mum's eyes, as if Dad's were contagious.

Robby stood quietly at her side and Mum took his hand and she said, 'Robby, I really am alright.' She squeezed his hand and he started to cry. She said, 'Really, what's all this?' and I held her tighter. 'Robby, my love, I'm alright, I promise,' she said, not letting go of his hand. If you linked up the lines between Mum, Dad, Robby and me we'd make a square that nothing could penetrate, like the backyard of Nineteen Emu.

'Are they looking after you alright, love?' Dad asked.

'They're looking after me fine.'

'Do you need me to bring you anything?'

'The food isn't five star, but I'll live.'

'Five star is what you deserve.'

'I don't need five star, love. Just you. You and the boys.'

'You've always got us.'

I didn't want to leave. Mum and Dad's talk to each other was a lullaby that could have rocked me to sleep.

The nurse came and read a chart in a blue folder on the end of Mum's bed. She said, *One more night I'm afraid* and Mum smiled weakly. 'Sorry, kids,' she said. 'I've tried to tell them I am fine.'

If we could, Robby and me and Dad would have taken a corner of the bed each and wheeled it out of Sunshine Hospital, down Furlong Road all the way to the Holden. We would have tied the bed to the roof with Mum on it and driven her home and she would have had all the air she needed, plus sunshine. I wanted to. Dad had the strength. But Mum needed the Ventolin. The hospital stored it in giant tanks under the highway outside. She had to be hooked up to the tanks to get her through the night.

I hid my face against her side.

'Come on, Jimmy. You can do it,' she said. 'I want you to be a good boy for your dad and do what he says and do what Robby says too, okay? Jimmy?' She put her nose against my hair. 'And make sure you have a bath. Robby, can you give him a bath?' she asked him.

The nurse asked if there was anyone Mum would like her to call to help with the kids.

'I can get another day off, love,' Dad said. 'Don't worry about that.'

Mum's face reached out to him – the mouth, the nose, the eyes, the forehead, the hair, the cheeks, all of it open and soft and reaching for him. She was as white as the sheet over her body. All her colour had been sucked out into the same hospital pipes that connected to the drips. She couldn't come home with us.

When we got back to Nineteen Emu, Dad spoke on the telephone to his boss at the refinery, Bill Philby. He nodded as he talked and said, 'Thanks, Bill, thanks, she'll be out tomorrow . . . She's fine. I appreciate it.' When he got off the telephone he said, 'Prick.'

After Robby had left for school Dad looked at his watch a few times as if it might tell him what to do with me. I put block on top of block and then I knocked them across the floor, then I piled them on top of each other then I knocked them down again, then I piled them up then I knocked them down. Dad stood at the sink wiping his mouth. He looked at the high cupboard then back at me, then at the high cupboard then at me. Then he said, 'Bugger this. Let's go, Jim.'

I stopped building. 'Where, Dad? Where?'

'The tip.'

'What for, Dad? What are we going to the tip for?'

'You never know, Jim,' said Dad, picking up the keys. 'It's the tip. Surprise city.'

'You never know, Dad. You never know.'

'Come on,' he said. 'Grab a hat.'

I took my hat from the low door hook and Dad took his from the high one and I followed him out to the Holden. There was no hesitation. He walked ahead of me, as if he was sure I would follow.

I climbed into the passenger seat and he got into the driver's and we drove out of Altona along Sunbury Road. It was never just my dad and me. The sun streamed across our knees in a single ray. Dad drove the Holden faster than Mum. He grabbed the gears as if he was showing them who was boss. He was the Bill Philby of the gearbox. He turned the corners more quickly. He leaned back as if he was sure the car knew what to do. Mum drove leaning forward, as if she doubted it.

We drove into a road that said *Bulla Tip and Quarry* and the smell was sweet and rotten in my olfactory. Dad sniffed the air, grinned and said, 'That's how we know we're in the right place, son.' He stopped the car and got out so I got out too and he never checked to see if I was following, he just knew I would.

I saw a crater but it wasn't moon, it was rubbish: plastic bags and pipes and baths and car seats and toilets and paint tins, all in piles under the sun where the pieces melted into each other. Everything was grey and white with bright pieces in between like shining plastic jewels – blue, yellow, orange and red. A man in a towel hat smiled and said, 'What would you blokes be after?' and Dad said, 'I'll know when I see it, mate,' and the man said, 'Right this way, fellers,' and I followed my dad to the salvageables.

There were stoves and lawnmowers and suitcases and dryers and buckets and tubing and wooden boxes and barbecues and bedframes and gutters and doors and fridges and taps and steering wheels and chairs and windows and radios, all left behind by previous owners. My juices rushed. Dad and the man in the towel hat let me run from part to part. Dad gathered wheels and pipes. I examined an engine. It was full of tiny pinpricks that let the water through. That's what caused the rust. I scraped at it with a rock, watching as the brown powder fell into the dust like a waterfall. I got down on my hands and knees and put my eye up close to a hole and I saw the light and the air on the other side. The air gave the engine extra power. Anything you attached to the engine would be unstoppable and a mystery to all mechanics, and only I could see that it was coming through the pinpricks in the rust.

'Son!' Dad called. 'Come on. We're done.'

Dad loaded his materials into the Holden and we exited the Bulla Tip and Quarry and Dad flicked on the radio and the song was *heartache tonight heartache tonight*. Dad sang along with it and when he looked across at me he smiled and the song kept coming out. It was like a light in the house that you never see switched on. I sang *heartache tonight heartache tonight* and our voices were the top and the bottom of the same tune and I did love the heartache, I did!

When we got home I helped Dad unload the Holden; the plastic seat of a chair without legs, a small cupboard, wheels and a pole. He never said, 'Come on, Jim, hurry up, come on, love, please.' He just got to work – a quick wordless man for me to copy.

Then we went into Dad's garage and he got out his welder and mask. He put the mask over my head, tightened the strap and said, 'Stay back, Jimmy.' From inside my mask I watched the bright and burning light of my dad at work. He joined the two pairs of wheels to the pole. 'It's the axle, son,' he said. Then he took the door from the small cupboard and attached it to the two sets of wheels, then on top of that he fixed the plastic seat of the chair.

'There she is, Jim,' he said.

'There what is, Dad, what?'

'Your go-cart, son.'

There was my go-cart. Time reverberated like lines around a drum. Breath filled my chest.

'Shall we paint it, Jim?'

'Shall we, Dad? Shall we!'

'All we got is green,' he said.

'Green it is, Dad, green it is!'

Dad gave me a brush and we painted together without talking and I didn't feel the need, not a single one. The brushes moved up and down, up and down as the wooden sides of my go-cart turned green.

'Okay, son. We'll go have something to eat and let her dry in the sun, hey?' said Dad.

My go-cart gleamed, four wheels and a door for a body with a seat and no steering wheel.

'Dad, it's got no steering wheel, Dad.'

'Steering wheel? Steering wheels are for sissies, Jim. Doesn't need a bloody steering wheel. That's the element of risk.'

'Okay, Dad, the element of risk. Okay, Dad, okay. Okay, Dad.'

We went into the kitchen and Dad made cheese sandwiches. The butter tore the bread and Dad said, *Nobody does it like your mum*. He leaned against the island, his eyes turning red and wet, with the memory of Paula. It was as if he could see her better when she wasn't here – he had the space. He poured us orange cordials and we took our sandwiches to eat on the step where we could watch the go-cart dry.

'Ready, Dad, is it ready?'

'How many times have you asked me that, Jim?'

'Five, dad. Is it ready, is the go-cart ready?'

He touched his fingers softly to the paint. 'Ready enough,' he said.

My core raced. I climbed onto the Jimmy-sized seat.

'Let's go,' said Dad. He pushed me on the go-cart out of the house and onto Emu Street, then up the hill of Cobham – up and up and up. I heard his breath behind me growing louder as we climbed, his outs shorter than his ins, as if the air was hard to let go – the very opposite of Mum.

Once we got to the top he said, 'I'll run beside you, okay, Jim? You okay? You ready?'

Dad looked excited, as if he was about to go down Cobham in a green go-cart instead of me.

'I'm ready, Dad, I'm ready.'

'Okay then.' He got behind me and began to push, faster and faster until his hands left the cart and I was speeding down Cobham, the wind in my face, the wheels rattling, the element of risk in full force. Dad ran just behind me, keeping up every step of the way.

'Wheeeeeee aaaaaaaaaeeeeeeeeee!' I was the same as the wind and the wheels and the speed of the go-cart. I was the same, the very same! 'Wheeeeeeeeeeeeaaaaaaaaeeeeeee!'

When we got to the bottom Dad, puffing and out of breath, said, 'How was that, Jim? Enjoy yourself?'

'Good, Dad, very good. Again?'

This time when we got to the top of the hill he said, 'What about going on your own this time, Jim, and I'll watch from the top?'

I looked at the long slope of Cobham.

'Come on, Jim. You can do it.'

My core jittered. 'Yes, Dad, yes, okay.'

He gave me one hard push then let me go and I was on my own but it was as if he was still there, running behind me. 'Wheeeeeeeeaaaaaaaaaa!' I shouted into the wind as the wheels and the axle vibrated me all the way to the bottom. I looked back and he was standing there, waving at me, and it was as if I had never seen him before. What drove crying? What was crying's engine?

Dad pushed me up the slope of Cobham eight more times, then he said, 'Jesus, son. I'm wrecked.'

We walked back to Emu Street, dragging the go-cart, and when we got home Robby was in the kitchen. He looked at our red and sweating faces as if he wasn't sure, and then I said, 'Dad and me made a go-cart. A go-cart, Robby!'

'That we did,' said Dad, taking a beer from the fridge. 'Go and show him, Jim. Take him for a ride.'

Robby looked at Dad like he didn't believe it, then he went outside and saw it for himself. 'Let's go,' he said.

Robby and me went further than Cobham, all the way up Maidstone, then we both got on the seat, him in front, me behind, and we went so fast that when we got to the bottom a wheel fell off.

'Oh no,' I said. 'Oh no.'

'Don't worry,' said Robby. 'It was my fault.'

'Oh no,' I said.

When we got home Dad was sitting on the back step reading the newspaper.

I held out the wheel. 'Sorry, Dad,' I said. 'Sorry.'

Robby looked at the grass, kicking at a stone.

Dad took the wheel and rolled it across the yard. 'Boys, if the wheels don't fall off your go-cart by the end of the day you haven't ridden her properly,' he said. Everything expanded, as if Dad's words had a power to release.

'And we rode her properly, Dad, we really did!'

Dad bought us a pizza for dinner and it arrived with a man in its own plastic case and it had pineapple. *Pineapple!* It was dessert and dinner mixed. The flavours filled up every hole in my system.

'That's one way to get him to shut up, hey, Rob? A Hawaiian from Pier Street,' said Dad.

'We need a fridge full,' said Robby, and they both laughed as if they knew a joke that I didn't and it was sweet music like a heartache.

After dinner we watched a movie in the sitting room called *The Thing* but when the thing went into the snow and came back the same shape as the man he was chasing I jumped and screamed, and Dad said, 'Jesus, we don't want the kid to have nightmares. Robby, you want to give your brother that bath your mother was talking about?'

And Robby said, 'Okay, Dad,' and took me to the bathroom. 'Get in the bath,' he said.

'I don't need a bath,' I told him.

'Yes you do. You stink.'

'Not tonight, Robby, not tonight.'

'You have to. Mum said.'

'Are you having one?' I asked him.

'I'll have a shower later,' Robby answered.

'Dad has showers,' I said.

'Not only Dad,' he said. 'Get in the bath, Jimmy.' I took off my shoes but that's all. 'You've got to take your clothes off, Jimmy.'

'No,' I said. I didn't like to take off my clothes. There was too much skin. There were parts of me I hardly ever saw and didn't want to see. I didn't know why they were shaped that way. If you pulled at those roots hard enough what would you see in the hole left behind? When Uncle Rodney shot the rabbit and cut its stomach open I saw a hole full of fibres like worms, black and purple and damp. My mouth filled with water and I vomited. Uncle Rodney laughed and said, 'Another weak stomach in the family, hey, Gav?'

'Come on, Jimmy, take off your clothes.' Robby stood with his hands on his hips beside the bath.

'No,' I said.

'Okay, then, you can keep your clothes on but you've got to have a bath.'

'Okay, then.' I sat in the bath with my trousers floating around me, my t-shirt rising up, my socks sticking to my feet. Everything filled with water.

Robby and me went to bed after the bath. Robby kept the light on and read Biggles. The cover of his book had a man standing beside a brown plane.

'Why is he Biggles, Robby? Why is he Biggles?'

Robby turned the page and didn't answer.

'Robby? Robby? Why Biggles?'

Dad opened the door. 'You boys alright in here?'

'Yes, Dad, yes,' I said.

He grinned suddenly. 'Good day?'

'Good day, Dad. Yes, good day.'

Robby looked over the top of his book and smiled at Dad. It had been a long time since Robby had given him one like that.

'Okay, well you can read a bit longer then it's lights out. I'll leave that up to you, hey, Rob?'

'Yep,' Robby answered, eyes back on his page.

'Night, boys,' said Dad, pulling the door to almost closed.

A little while later we heard Merle singing 'Going Where the Lonely Go' from the sitting room. Robby stopped reading. A shadow passed across his face. 'Whatever you do, don't go back in to see Dad tonight,' he said.

'Why?'

'It's Friday night.'

'So? So?'

'Just don't, okay?'

'Okay, Robby. No going in to Dad, okay.'

Robby put down Biggles and switched off the light.

Sometime in the middle of the night, I heard a smash. I jumped out of my bed and got in with Robby. 'Robby, did you hear that?' I asked him. Robby moaned. My cells sped up, like the go-cart at the top of the hill, gathering speed on its way down. 'Robby.' I pushed against him. 'Did you hear that?'

'What?' he mumbled.

'Listen.' We lay there, the warmth of his back against my front.

Something fell, as if it had been kicked. Robby got out of bed and closed the door. I wished Biggles was here with his brown plane.

'It's Dad,' said Robby.

'What will he do without Mum?' I asked him.

'Shhh . . .' said Robby. 'Don't say anything.'

There was another smash. Then the whole house began to fall – down down down, faster and faster. I gripped onto Robby as if he was strong enough to stop it.

In the morning Dad only looked at me for a second, when he picked up his coffee cup and took a sip. Then he went back to hammering the cupboard door that had been swinging loose on its hinges. There were vacuum-cleaner tracks over the carpet. I followed them, zigzagging between rooms. The carpet furs stood up as straight as soldiers. The dishes were done and put away. The kitchen floor didn't have cereal or hairs stuck to it. I could hear the washing machine rumbling from the laundry.

I could see there was a war going on inside Dad's head as he hammered. That's what made his neck sweat. Every day there were more men joining the battle. They shot arrows and bullets at each other and threw bombs full of glass and splinters. It hurt him to look at me or Robby because of the shrapnel caught in his eyes.

Why was it one thing one day and something different the next?

'I'm going to the hospital to pick up your mother,' Dad said, pulling his head out of the cupboard. 'Robby, you stay here with Jim, okay?'

Robby didn't answer.

Dad checked the new door screwed tightly to its hinge, then he left. I heard something smash outside, then the lid of the metal bin slamming down.

While Dad was gone Robby and me watched the television. Robby didn't want to do anything else. He didn't want to go into the wetlands to see if *Lady Free* had been flooded. He didn't want to look for snakes or show me his comics. He didn't answer a single question I asked him. What makes the television turn on? Where has the electricity come from? Where is the beginning of electricity? Robby sat staring at the screen without moving. I could feel vibrations coming off his skin. He only blinked four times from ad to ad. It made me speed up just being close to him.

When I heard the Holden in the driveway I ran to the door but Robby said, 'Let her get inside, Jimmy.'

'But I want to help her! I want to help her!'

'You will if you just wait till she's inside.'

I watched Dad through the window as he took Mum's hand when she got out of the car. As she smiled up at him her face became a heart. Dad led her slowly up the path. The closer she came to the house the faster I became. Any minute she would come through the door! Any minute! Any minute! And then the door opened.

'Mum! Mum!' I tried to climb her.

Robby said, 'Jimmy!'

Mum said, 'It's okay, love.' She came to Robby with me holding on to one side and she pulled him to her. 'Oh, my sweet boy, Robby, you did such a good job with your brother.' For a moment he was hidden by her wide, soft arms and I could only see the top of his head, his hair sticking to her dress with the static. Then he stepped back and his eyes were wet as if the pools inside them couldn't hold. Mum looked around the house. 'It's so tidy. Looks like you boys hardly need me here at all.'

'We need you, Mum, we need you.' I said. 'We really need you.'

'The boy's got that one right,' said Dad. He touched her arm, just at the elbow, quickly, as if he didn't know if the arm wanted it.

Later, when Dad and Mum were watching the news together in the sitting room, I went into the yard, lifted the lid of the garbage bin and looked inside. It was filled with the broken glass of a thousand shipwrecked Cutty Sarks.

For weeks after Mum came home from Sunshine Hospital Dad only drank beers. Every time it got to the end of Sunday I counted another weekend without Scotch whisky. I counted five in a row. For all that time Merle slept quietly between his paper sheets. There were no sounds in the night, and in the mornings when Mum stood at the kitchen island and stirred sugar into her tea, her face was as clear as the moon.

But when I stood in the yard of Nineteen Emu and looked into the sky, just before it turned to night, I could see a giant shadow full of tiny squares we were too big to swim through. Something was coming down over the house like a net.

Mum sucked on her puffer and went to work at Westlake and brought home slices for Robby and me that only she ate. Cherry and coconut and lemon, she sat on her blue kitchen couch, coconut rain falling over the covers of *Death on the Nile*. Her breathing tubes were clear. At the hospital the nurse took the throat vacuum and did to her channels what Dad did to the carpets. There was no dust on her tentacles and they waved freely; she was back at the start of the build-up.

On Saturday morning of the sixth weekend I was drying the dishes with Mum when the telephone rang. Mum picked it up.

'Hello, Rodney, nice to hear your voice,' she said. 'Oh no, nothing serious, I hope? . . . Of course . . . Yes, love, I'll just get him.' She put the telephone down on the bench, her forehead creased with lines, and called, 'Gav? Gav! Your brother's on the phone.'

Dad came in from behind the house where he'd been working on the hot-water box. The flame kept going out because the pilot was gone. 'Rodney?' he asked Mum, as if it was a surprise. Mum nodded, passing him the telephone. Dad put it to his ear. Uncle Rodney was the brother Dad spoke to the most. Dad was the oldest of the four and Uncle Rodney was just under.

'G'day, Rod . . .' Dad said, a smile in his voice. Then, as he listened, I saw the smile and the pink and the brown and the red and the black fall down from his face into the neck of his shirt. 'Jesus . . . Bloody Steve. Oh, Christ.' He shook his

head, back and forth as he listened. 'Was only a matter of time
. . . Yeah. Yeah. Thanks for calling, Rodney. Yes, they're fine
. . . Not right now, mate. I'll ring you tomorrow.' He put the
telephone back into the receiver.

'What is it, Gav?' Mum asked, looking worried.

'Steve had an accident,' Dad answered. Steve was the brother
he never saw. He did time for guns. Dad said he used to go
fishing with Steve and he never knew about the guns. Steve
stored them in the back of his ute in a silver box along with a
bucket of speed, and the police weren't even looking for them
when they found them – they were looking for stolen tools and
they found the guns and the bucket instead.

'What happened?' asked Mum.

'He hit a tree in his ute.'

'Oh no. When, love?'

'Early this morning.'

'Is he okay?'

I had never seen my dad's tears fall before, but he didn't have
time to close the gates and one escaped. It came out his eye and
stopped at his cheek. 'He's dead,' he said.

'Oh, Gav . . .' Mum touched his shoulder. Dad pulled away
as if she'd burned him.

'Steve was a prick,' said Dad, walking back outside. 'Him
and bloody Ray. Nothing fucken changes.' Soon Mum and me
heard hammering from the hot-water box.

Once I heard Mum talking to Pop Flick on the telephone about
Ray, another one of Dad's brothers.

'Oh no, Pop, I know, terrible . . .' she said. 'Are they saying
he raped her? Are they sure? . . . That's no good. Poor Ray.

I suppose I'm glad he's put away . . . I know . . . But still, I can't help but feel for him. No . . . shocking . . . I know, I know that.'

'What's raped?' I asked Mum after she got off the telephone.

'It's nothing, Jimmy. You shouldn't be listening when I'm on the phone.'

'What's raped? I should know, Mum. If it's a word then I should know the meaning. What's raped? I should know, Mum. I –'

'Alright, Jimmy, alright! Your father's brother Ray went to jail because he hurt a girl. He hurt two girls, alright?'

'Is raped hurting?'

'Yes, it is.'

'Then why didn't you say to Pop Flick that you are glad Uncle Ray is in jail for *hurting*? Why didn't you say that?'

'Because . . .' Mum took a breath. 'Because raping is hurting a person in a particular way.'

'What way?'

'A bad way. The worst way, Jimmy.'

'What way?'

'It's when a person forces themselves onto another person. That's what Uncle Ray did. He did it to two girls and now he's going to jail.'

'Did he know the two girls?'

She sighed. 'I don't know, Jim. I don't know anything about them.'

I watched as Mum took off her apron. She stood pulling at her lip. Raping. 'Alright, Mum. That's what Uncle Ray did.'

'Yes, that's what he did. Now forget about it. Let's eat lunch.'

I only met Uncle Ray once, at a Christmas at Pop Flick's. His nose was a lump like a mushroom and his eye had a tear down one side. A piece of his network was missing. Somebody took it from him. Maybe he was looking for it in the two girls. Maybe raping was a search.

'Why did that happen to Steve?' I asked Mum.

'Oh, Jimmy,' she sighed. 'Steve was a tough case.'

'But why?'

'Oh God, he drank too much. He had an accident in his car. He hit a tree, that's what your dad said.'

An accident is when something happens even though nobody did it on purpose. Gravity and other forces like tidal make it happen. Steve was in his car. It was still dark. Steve's headlights showed him the tree by the side of the road. The road went past the tree but Steve's hands on the wheel couldn't turn away. There was the tree, its wide branches full of sleeping birds, and nests and rustling leaves, growing up towards the stars, the sky still black, and Steve knew which way the road went, he could see it marked with broken lines, he could see the way, but there was the tree, live and growing up and up and up, a different pathway, and that's the way Steve took. That was the accident.

That afternoon, after Dad fixed the hot water, he got in his car and drove away. Mum watched through the window and chewed at her lip.

Robby came home from football practice. 'Steve died, Robby,' I told him. 'Dad took off in the car.'

'You don't waste any time, do you, Jimmy?' said Mum, rolling her eyes.

'What happened?' Robby asked.

'You don't want to know,' I told him.

'Yes I do,' Robby said.

'Steve had a car accident,' said Mum.

'He was drunk,' I said.

'Jimmy!'

'What?'

'You don't leave anything out, do you?'

'Where's Dad now?' Robby asked.

'He'll be home soon,' Mum answered.

Robby picked up the telephone and said, 'Hi, Mrs Davids, is Justin there?' and then, 'Can I come over?' After that he got on his bike and left.

Dad came home just before dark. In his hands was a bottle in a brown paper bag. He leaned against the island, his eyes red around the edges. 'I'll have my tea in the sitting room, Paula,' he said.

I ate fat noodles with cheese and bacon at the table while Mum stood at the kitchen island sprinkling salt over her bowl. She said, 'Your dad is feeling sad tonight, Jimmy. He's lost his brother. We need to be a bit quiet for him, okay?' She kept sprinkling.

'Steve was a prick,' I said.

'Don't use that word, Jim,' she said, putting down the shaker.

'What word?'

'You know what word. Steve was your father's brother. Imagine how you'd feel if something ever happened to Robby. We need to keep quiet around the house tonight. You can do that, can't you, love?'

I imagined something happening to Robby. I chose a volcano. The highest on planet Earth. Robby walked up its hot slope because he wanted to see inside; he didn't know about the lava.

It came spewing up over the sides and down towards him. Robby saw it coming — he started to run, but the lava was catching up. How would he get away? What would happen to him?

'Okay, Mum. Okay.'

That night we stayed out of the sitting room. The house was thick and heavy with the quiet we were keeping. I lay in bed and watched the shadows of sheep floating up and down the walls. They crossed from the window, moving up to the cornices, then down to the carpets — the shadows of sheep without the light. Soon I heard shouting. In my dream was a field but I couldn't tell if it was made of grass or water. It rocked, animals moved over the top of it, calling to each other with animal sounds. I couldn't tell if they were walking or flying. I heard my dad's voice, then Mum's, softer than Dad's, asking for something, *Please please.* But it mixed with the sounds of the animals calling over the water. Who was asking? Who wanted?

I got out of my bed and went to Robby's but it was empty. I'd forgotten Robby was at Justin's. I left the room and walked down the hall. I looked into the sitting room and saw an empty bottle on the floor and beside it the paper bag Dad had brought the bottle home in. A record spun round the player with no music. I smelled cigarette smoke. I kept walking. I heard voices rising and falling.

I passed the bathroom and the kitchen until I got to their bedroom. I stood in the doorway and I saw Dad hit Mum across the mouth with his hand open, *smack.*

'*Mum!*' I called.

Dad turned to me. 'For fuck's sake!' Steam rose from his pores.

Mum swung round, her cheek bright red, like a stop light under the skin. 'Oh no,' she said. 'Oh, no, Jimmy.'

Panic streamed through her and was transmitted to me. I ran from wall to wall, my cells spinning me around the rooms, one after the other. Hallway! Kitchen! Bedroom! Bathroom! Sitting room! Hallway! Nobody could stop me! The energy of the refinery that moved through Dad's arm onto Mum's face was now in my cells – *bounce bounce bounce* from wall to wall.

'Fuck this,' said Dad.

I was faster than the speed of light. I knew if it went on much longer I would disintegrate. The power of the refinery was blasting me apart *bounce bounce bounce*.

Mum ran at me; the bulk of her legs and back and bottom held me tight. It was only the mountain of her that was big and strong enough to contain me. She was shaking and damp. It was like being held by a storm. She carried me to my room and got into bed beside me. I heard the sounds of moaning, like something in trouble. Was it the animals in my dream? Was it me? Was it Mum? Was it Dad? Was it everyone in our family?

By the time Robby came home the next day, there was a bruise like a plum on Mum's cheek. The top half was turning black. I saw the vision of the blackening plum enter Robby's pupils, then his eye pools. He didn't speak. Mum looked at him and she didn't speak either, but her eyes asked for something from him. Robby knew what it was.

He took me through the fence and we crossed the trench, past the *Lady Free*, past the rusted car, further and further, until we came to Queen Street. We stood at the side, Robby holding my hand, and when there were no cars we crossed and walked towards the beach. Pelicans flew above our heads, their huge wings beating once, twice, three times against the grey of the clouds, then spreading wide and still as they rode the invisible currents, their heads resting back, as if they never got too fast, were never sent spinning by flames and heat. They circled above our heads, staying with us like guides as we walked.

The cool wind was in our faces, blowing back our hair and drying our eyes. Robby looked right into it. Out across the sea were ocean liners that seemed never to move, but were moving, moving, so that one day, even if it took a long, long time, they got there. We waded through water thick with seaweed, climbing across the sea urchins, and where they got too many, pricking my feet, I stepped in the places where Robby had stepped. When we came to the other side it was our own beach shared only with the black swans and pelicans and gulls. Far away on the other side, the flame burned a warning from its pole, never extinguished, fuelled by crude oil drawn from the centre, endless supplies that began with the earth's formation. The flame was the final result.

We ran through the shallows, kicking at the foam and watching it charge upwards. The birds spectated without movement, as if they were the audience and we were the show. We ran back and forth and any stone we saw we stopped and picked it up and threw it over the ripples into the sea, and any feathers we found we held for a while before letting the wind carry them back to the motionless birds. Robby found seaweed in wide rubbery strips and we looked up close at the lines and the circles, and felt its slippery surface before throwing it into the wind.

Robby pulled off all his clothes except for his underpants and I saw Dad in the thin of his arms and legs, and in the line of bumps under the skin down his back. He ran into the water, stepping high as if he could stop himself getting wet. He shouted and yelped and plunged, waving to me to come too, though he knew I wouldn't. I waved back and kicked my legs and threw sand at the water.

We stayed and stayed. We ate driftwood and shells and seaweed for our dinner cooked on a fire of stones. The invisible flames warmed our hands and turned our cheeks pink. We watched as the sun fell slowly down, leaving only the memory of its colours, orange and gold and red, and when the memory was gone we had to go back, we had to go back.

When we got home Mum's red suitcase stood in the doorway. Dad wasn't home. Mum was in the kitchen moving quickly from cupboard to fridge to sink to island, as if she wasn't sure what to wipe. The white of her black eye was mixed with blood.

'What's the suitcase doing there?' Robby asked. We knew the suitcase lived in the laundry behind the buckets. Mum used it to store winters.

'Why are you boys all wet?' Mum asked, cross. But she was the one who was wet; tears gathering under the pores, wanting to burst through. 'You're bringing sand in the house. Go and get changed.'

'What's the suitcase doing there?' Robby asked again, not moving.

'Nothing.' Mum's voice was thick with blocked water. 'It's got nothing to do with you.'

'But, Mum,' I said, 'it's a suitcase and it's in the doorway. It's in the doorway, Mum. Why?'

'No reason!' Mum shouted. 'No bloody reason! No bloody reason under the sun! Now go and get cleaned up like I told you!'

The suitcase bulged. I could see one of Mum's stockings caught in the zip. Robby and me walked to the bathroom. I kept checking the suitcase through the open door. Why was it there?

Dad came home late. I got out of bed and stood hidden behind the wall to see what he was going to do about the suitcase. Mum's tears finally burst through, drenching the ceiling like spouts from a fountain. He held her in his arms. 'I'm sorry, love. Please unpack it. Put it away,' he said.

Her sounds were muffled in his hold.

'This time it will be different, I promise. Please give me another chance.'

In the morning the red suitcase was gone. I got down on my hands and knees to look for evidence of where it had stood — there were four dents in the carpet, one for each corner.

I lay in my bed at nights and drew a line from week to week like a wave that rose with the number of beers. Three Sundays would pass, the wave growing higher, then on the fourth Sunday, sometimes the fifth, the wave would break and down the Cutty Sark would sail from the high cupboard, through the kitchen, along the hall and into the sitting room.

Mum tried to stay away, but she couldn't. She did Weight Watchers, but she gave up. She couldn't say no to slices and lemonade and extra gravy. She said, *Food is for enjoying, not counting.* Enjoying is when you don't want it to stop. My mum enjoyed vanilla slices. If she could, she would've crawled between the pastry sheets, pulled the custard in tight around her and slept in one. Her mouth would've been open all night so she never had to stop enjoying. Like gravy and chips, my Dad had magnetic powers. Mum had no defences for him. He got in underneath. He was like a slice: she couldn't give him up.

Part Two

For the next three years all the words Robby didn't say entered his bones and muscles, fibres and skin, and he grew taller and taller. The unspoken words were the nutrients taking him further from ground level. His eyes remained the same; they were no age, like water. He only ever answered my questions now when we were far from the house – only then would he help me with my obstacles. I had reached nine but I stayed small. Robby had reached fifteen and was taller than Dad. When Robby looked at him, his eyes were so big Dad had to turn from them. They were pools without bottoms. Under the water there were lands my dad didn't want to visit; he knew he would be a stranger, without language or a currency.

I had to go to school every day now.

'Do you understand, Jimmy? Is it clear?' my teacher, Mrs Stratham, asked.

I heard instructions but two of the sentences came to me at the same time, one on top of the other, like bunks. I didn't know which to choose; you can't have a top without a bottom.

I needed extra attention that Mrs Stratham had no time for. She wasn't paid enough to look after thirty ordinary kids and one retard. 'Have you considered a different program?' she said to my mother. 'Have you thought of Pine Centre?'

Pine Centre was two bus rides away. It was built on the outskirts so that nobody had to see. Once we went for an interview and the windows were high up and at first I saw nothing behind them but I kept looking and looking and soon I did see things behind them. But not whole things. Boys in half.

Dr Eric wrote a letter to the school that said I was their responsibility. If it wasn't for Dr Eric I'd have been with the half-boys at Pine Centre. Other teachers let me run but Mrs Stratham couldn't stand the pressure. I was cooking her from underneath. I might be the smallest part of the machine but I was the hottest.

When I thought of school my vitals grew heavy. I had to drag them. Every weekday morning was a fight with my mother.

'Come on, Jimmy, we have to go. I don't want to be late for work.'

'I can come to work with you, Mum. I can read my book for Mavis Tits.'

'It's *Tidd*, Mavis *Tidd*, Jimmy. No you can't. You're too old for all that now. You have to go to school just like everyone else.'

'But Mrs Stratham, Mum, Mrs Stratham.'

'What about Mrs Stratham?'

'Mrs Stratham is a crab.'

'Jimmy, don't say things like that! Esther does her best, poor thing. Not everyone knows how to handle you. You leave poor Mrs Stratham alone.'

'She doesn't leave *me* alone, Mum! She doesn't leave *me* alone!'

'Come on, Jimmy. Get your shoes on,' said Robby. He threw my school shoes at me across the floor. Robby was at Altona High. Sometimes he left the house early on his bike so he could play football with his friends on the oval. I'd seen his long pale legs sprinting across the grass towards the ball. Just beyond the ball was the goal. Robby knew where the ball needed to land. He sized it up, his legs propelling him forward towards his destination. Anything between him and the ball didn't enter his vision.

'Ham sandwich, Jimmy,' Mum said, holding it up for me to see. She packed it into my lunchbox. 'I want you to eat it this time, okay, love?'

A lot of times I didn't eat. If a bend in my pipe was too sudden the food got caught. It happened a lot at school because of the positions. Mrs Stratham said, 'Sit still while you eat, Jimmy. Everyone else can manage, why can't you?' Why couldn't I manage? Why couldn't I?

Mum put a banana in with the sandwich. 'Promise me you'll eat today.'

'Yes, Mum, yes, Mum. Ham sandwich for lunch, followed by banana. Orders from above.'

'Don't be cheeky,' she said. She took a plate from the fridge and held it out to Robby. Blocks of chocolate covered in little white ants sat in a pile; by the end of the day there wouldn't be any left. 'Robby, love, take a lamington to have with your lunch.' Even though I knew Robby didn't want the lamington, he took it and put it in his bag. He did it as a favour.

'See you, Mum,' said Robby. She reached up and kissed him on the cheek. He let her. There weren't many chances anymore.

I couldn't get the knots out of my laces; my fingers were as thick as slugs, and the knots were tricky. I picked and picked but the knots wouldn't loosen.

'For heaven's sake, Jimmy,' said Mum. 'You have to go to school.' She kneeled down beside me and grabbed at the laces. Everything was hard for her – hard to get down and hard to get up and hard to pull in the air. It hovered thickly around her mouth and Mum was barely strong enough to drag it in, and when she did it couldn't get past the dust to fill her tank.

I put my arms around her. 'I'm ready for school, Mum. I'll eat the ham sandwich.'

'Oh, Jimmy, my love.' She looked at me and hugged me and in flew the air.

Mum and me climbed into the Holden. Mum was wearing her apron that said *Westlake Nursing Home* and I was wearing my jumper that said *Altona Primary School*. I wished we could swap. Mum turned the key.

On the drive I stared out the window as everything rushed past. In the car I was the slow one. I wished the drive never had to end; I liked to feel the engine beneath us, rumbling and wobbling my mother and me, my mother's hand tight around the gearstick, jerking it one way then the other as she pulled the car from number to number, her fingers with the rings squeezing the skin, her nails painted pink. The streets and lights and houses and other cars outside the Holden never stopped moving. Sections might stop, but then all the other parts would work faster to keep the balance. The whole never stopped. I saw it from the inside of the car and even that was moving; my mother's hand, the windscreen wipers, the Doris tape singing 'Dream a Little Dream', my mum leaning forward to wipe the steam from the windscreen.

'Mum, does any part stop?' I asked her.

'What, love?'

'What part is always, *always* stopped?'

'What part of what?' She looked across at me. 'Do you have your raincoat in your bag, Jimmy? This doesn't look like drying up.'

'Mum – in the world. What part is always stopped?'

'What are you talking about?'

'You can see all the moving parts, but is there a part that is always stopped?'

Mum puffed her cheeks up with air and puffed them out. 'A part that is always stopped . . .'

'Yes, Mum. One part. One part that is always stopped.'

'Hmmm.' She frowned. 'If it's raining in the afternoon I'll be at the side street, okay? Don't come around here, it's too far to walk in the wet.'

'*Mum! What part is always stopped?!*'

'Don't shout, love. I don't know what part. Can I think about it today and then tell you tonight?'

'Yes, Mum, yes. Don't forget, Mum. A single part that is always stopped. *Always.*'

'Here we are, Jimmy.' She pulled up at the drop-off lane. 'Now quickly, hop out.' She checked her watch. 'I'm going to be late.'

'No answer no answer no answer,' I sang as I walked my heavy legs up the path towards the school gates.

Mrs Stratham was a crab just like the ones Robby and I used to find on the rocks at Seaholme before the concrete starts. When Mrs Stratham got home after a day at school, she pulled her human skin over her head and there was the crab, black shining eyes on orange sticks seeking out her prey. Beetles and rats and rabbits hid under her chairs, trembling. Mrs Stratham's bed was a rock and she didn't have blankets, only armour. She drank salt water from a teacup with her breakfast.

Mum said, *No more crab talk, Jimmy; it's disrespectful. Esther is trying.*

As Mrs Stratham stood at the front of the class I watched for the changes.

'Good morning, class, I hope you have all done the homework I set for you,' she said. She turned around to write on the board and I noticed that under her back piece was a cave. Her skirt wasn't long enough to hide it.

'Jimmy,' Mrs Stratham said, her crab lips snapping. 'You can do this one. What is three times thirty-three?'

The class went very quiet as they waited for me, the Detective of Threes, to solve the problem. I closed my eyes and saw more and more threes everywhere I looked. In every line of threes there was one other number — *six, four, one, nine, seven, seven, one* — but was the answer in the diagonal or the straight? Nobody in the class made a sound.

The threes kept coming. I couldn't see beyond them; it was an infinity of threes. I went from still to running, with no time in between. I got off my seat and ran around the chairs and around Mrs Stratham's desk and past the windows to the door and back again. '*Three three three three!*' I shouted, touching everything I could. '*Three three three!*' The answer lay on the surfaces and every surface was a clue. '*Three three three!*'

Crash! The lizard's aquarium shattered behind me. '*Three three three!*' I shouted.

Linda shrieked as the lizard ran across her feet. Suddenly everyone in the class was moving. I felt the air tear through me as the threes scattered, running for their lives. Girls were screaming, 'There! There it is, Mrs Stratham! There!' and the boys grabbed rulers and poked them into the shelves and under the desks.

'Children! Please settle down!' Mrs Stratham was on her hands and knees, looking for the lizard. Her skirt lifted at the back and I saw into the cave. It smelled of seaweed and fish. She waved her pincers wildly around her head and her crab parts dripped. 'You sit on that chair and don't move, Jimmy. Don't move.'

I saw the lizard beneath the map of the world, its grey tail close to South America. I stopped in my tracks, my eyes on the lizard. I was panting. The lizard didn't move a muscle and neither did I. I looked at the sharp spikes on the reptile neck, its green eyes, and long claws. I noticed how still the lizard was, completely stopped in all parts of itself. I took a deep breath and breathed out as slow as I could. I set myself to the clock of the lizard. Suddenly I knew the answer to the problem of the threes. 'Ninety-nine, Mrs Stratham. Three times thirty-three is ninety-nine.'

But Mrs Stratham never heard me. She was still looking for the lizard.

At the end of the day Robby and his friends, Justin and Scotty, were waiting for me outside the school gates. They stood with their legs apart over dragster bikes. Their hair was long and Scotty had an unlit cigarette behind his ear. Their bags hung loosely from their shoulders as if they hardly cared if the bag was there at all, it was up to the bag.

'Where's Mum?' I asked Robby.

'They wanted her to do the dinner shift,' he said. 'She left a message at the school for me to pick you up.'

'Feel like a ride?' said Justin.

I nodded.

'Get on,' said Robby. I climbed on the back of Robby's dragster and we got going through the streets, past all the other kids walking and past Mrs Stratham crawling into her Ford and past the slow mothers pushing prams. We went up and down, up and down and Scotty lifted his front wheel into the air and shouted, 'Fuck!'

I held onto Robby's shirt and felt the hard bones of his body as he pumped the pedals and we rode past the cracked driveway of Nineteen Emu, past its narrow door, and up Maidstone, then onto K Creek Road where the trucks carried the fuel in giant tanks at high speed into the city beneath the bridge. Robby pedalled faster and faster and Scotty overtook us, mouth open, hair blowing back, and shouted, *'Yah yah yah faaarrrkkk!'* But then Robby stood up on his pedals and pushed his legs up and down like pistons on a steamer, *push push push*, he went faster than all of them, even with me on the back, my bag swinging against his legs. *Thwack thwack thwack* Robby Robby Robby fastest of them all.

Just after Robby turned fifteen Mum said I had to move into her sewing room. If you cut our old room in half, the sewing room was smaller than one of the halves. 'Robby needs his space, love,' Mum explained. 'He's too old to share a room with you.'

'But why, Mum, *why*?'

'You'll understand when you get older, Jimmy.'

'What will he do with it?'

'With what?'

'The space.'

'I don't know. That's Robby's business. Help me carry your books into the other room.'

'The *sewing* room. Why don't you call it by its name?'

'It's not going to be the *sewing room*; it's going to be *your* room. Come on, Jimmy. Pick up your books and let's go. I want to get this done before Rob gets home.'

'Okay, Mum, *okay*.'

Mum's sewing room only had one small window and all you could see through it was a brick wall that held up the neighbour's house. In the corner of the room was the Singer on a table. There were racks of skirts and fabrics hanging from bars on wheels. Mum sweated while she worked. 'I was never a natural,' she said. She did it for a bit of her own to spend. 'For treats, hey, Jimmy?'

Mum's mother didn't teach her much because Mum was the last one of nine and by number eight she was done, so Mum was put on a ship from England leaving all the others behind. She couldn't remember their touch. It had evaporated.

When Mum tried to climb her family tree to find the ones she left behind, the branches broke beneath her feet. Even if you hacked at the tree with a stick, there was nothing growing. There weren't even insects, only dust. All Mum got was sewing.

'Bloody pain,' she said, trying to thread the needle one more time.

I missed the sound of Robby's breathing as he slept, steady and light. I always knew he would take another breath. There was a small beat between breathing out all the air, and taking more in. It was a suspension. When the next breath came I filled up with it. Now I was in the sewing room by myself, separated from Robby by a wall. I heard guitar music through the panelling.

I was dreaming that I was being built. I woke up just before I was completed. Concrete trucks were parked along the road, their loads turning to mix the water with the powder. I woke when the shovel went in, digging deep.

I came out of my room and saw Mum lying on the kitchen couch. She was on her back, one arm in the other as if she was making a sling for herself. Her nose was shining and red. I could hear the tentacles in her throat waving, but not fast enough to clear the dust. The *Home Sweet Home* pillow lay on the floor beside her. She looked like a big cake that wasn't cooked or ready for the world. *The Murder at the Vicarage* lay on the floor beside her. On the cover was a man leaning forward across a table, crying. Three other men stood around him looking worried.

'Mum?'

She didn't stir.

'Mum?'

My centre began to speed. Mum never slept in the day; there was too much to do. She had to prune and sweep and wipe and keep half an eye on me. Only at night did she sleep, when the darkness made a blanket and hid her uncooked bulk. My skin prickled.

'Mum?'

Robby came into the kitchen wearing his green and white football shorts. He had made it into the All Ones football team. Robby had muscles growing up his legs the same as the ones I saw in the rabbit that Uncle Rodney shot.

'Jimmy, what are you . . .?' He took another step inside and saw Mum. He gasped. 'Jimmy? Where's Dad?' he asked. His voice was light on top, but underneath it was dense.

Mum stirred, opening her eyes. When she looked up at Robby she forgot that her tubes were thick with dust and that her nose was swollen and that her arm was sore; she radiated. It was the same way she looked in the photograph when she first brought Robby home from the hospital and he was wrapped in the blue rug and was small like a present. *My firstborn*, she whispered softly as she traced her finger over the picture.

When she smiled at Robby I saw blood in the corner of her mouth. I went to her and held her and pressed my face against her swollen nose and she cried out, 'No, don't, Jimmy!'

Robby swallowed and the voice control box under the skin of his throat bobbed down then up again. His face had turned white. He walked out of the room.

'Robby, I'm alright . . .' she said. 'Jimmy, love, get me a glass of water, will you? From the fridge.' Mum pulled herself up to sitting. 'And my puffer from the bench.' Her voice sounded scratched. I didn't want to leave her; I wanted to leave the water instead. 'Please, Jimmy. A glass of water for Mum?'

I walked slowly to the fridge. When I opened it I heard something smash outside. Mum heard it too. Her head turned sharply to the window. She looked scared.

'Mum? Mum? Mum? Did you hear that?'

'My puffer, love?' she said. 'Quick.'

I left the water and got her puffer. I was starting to shake. Mum took a suck of her puffer, then she got up and went to the window.

There came a thump, like something against wood. I was speeding up, pressing against my own skin from the inside.

'Oh, Jesus,' said Mum. 'Oh God.'

I ran to the window, I ran to the door, I ran to the window, I ran to the door, I ran to Mum, I ran to the sink, I ran in a circle, then in another circle.

'Jimmy, stop. Jimmy!' She went to the back door and looked out and I followed her, and she said, 'No Jimmy, no!' and she pushed me back, so hard that I fell. 'Oh sorry love, sorry,' she said, taking me to the couch. Panic ran through her streams. Her eyes were stretched — she was going faster than me. She ran back to the window. 'Oh no, oh god Jimmy, stay there. Stay there on the couch and don't move,' she said, and her crying was shot through with fear. She grabbed her keys from the bench and she ran to the back door. I tried to follow her out but she pushed me back again, and locked me inside. 'Stay still Jimmy!!' she said. Through the glass I saw her go to the shed door, pull it open and go inside.

'No, Mum, no!' I shouted, but she couldn't hear me. For a moment there was nothing, then out came Robby and he was dragging my dad. Mum came out behind them. There was blood gushing from my dad's nose, and my dad was bending further and further down until he hit the ground.

Mum fell to her knees over him, holding up her arm, calling, 'No, Rob! No more! No more! Enough! Enough!'

I saw Robby go down onto the grass and I saw him put his hands around my dad's throat. I saw the words Robby didn't say, the things he wished for, coursing through the hollows of his bones, and wrap themselves around my dad's neck. 'That's the last fucking time!' Robby shouted. And Dad let him, he let him.

Mum screamed, 'No Robby!'

I began to bang on the glass *bang bang bang* and smash with my fists like wrecking balls *smash smash smash*. Robby and Mum looked up towards me. I smashed so hard the glass shook. I was going to smash the house of Nineteen Emu until there'd be nothing left but the stumps. I smashed and smashed and then Robby stood and went out of the yard through the back fence and Mum left Dad lying on the grass as she crossed the yard towards me. She opened the door and I screamed and smashed my fists against her.

She was crying as she crossed the kitchen with me against her, and pulled my coat from the hook. 'It's alright, Jimmy love, it's alright, it's your mum, settle down.' Her body was hot and shaking. She wrapped the coat around me, covering my head so the coat made a blindfold. She covered my ears and held me to her. Under the coat it was dark. The coat was over my face, bringing the world in close, muffling me, slowing me down. She held me against her, my ear to her heart, until I tuned myself to its beat. The sound filled up the space until there was nothing but the steady slowing pump of her heart.

Dad didn't come into the house at all that night; he stayed in his shed. Robby came home some time after dinner and went straight to his room – I heard guitar music playing through the wall. Mum asked Robby from the other side of his door if he wanted anything to eat but Robby said no. I looked out the kitchen window to see if there were any signs of Dad in the garage, but I couldn't tell. Later, Mum went out with a piece of sponge cake. I watched through the window as she tapped on his door. Her fist looked small and white under the shed light where the moths gathered and clung. Her body was wider than the whole doorframe, but her knock was soft and timid. Dad never answered the door.

Mum left the cake on the plate just outside it.

One night, a week after the last fucking time, I couldn't sleep. Dad wasn't home; he'd been taking a lot of extra shifts at the refinery. I lay in bed, closed my eyes and made a picture of him at work. His face was turned away from me, to hide the bruises Robby had left around his eyes, and the cut on his lip. I saw him scraping the refinery pipes with his steel brush, keeping the rust to a minimum. Even when Bill Philby called out, 'Time to go home, Gavin! Working day's over!' through his loudspeaker, my dad kept scraping. Even when the bristles on his brush wore down to nothing, just to stubs, and the last man had gone home to his family, there was my dad still scraping, locked in his battle with the rust.

I opened my eyes. There wasn't a sound in the house. I tried to listen for a single rustle or scratch or whisper – but there was only silence and darkness, as if it was the last page in the story. I stumbled out of my room, going slowly up the hall. I was shaking with cold, my heart was racing, my cells beginning to speed. Then I looked towards the front door and I saw one of

Dad's work vests on the coat hook, glowing and luminous. I went towards it like a beacon. I couldn't see any part of myself – only the glow of the vest in the shape of my dad. I got to the door and I reached for the vest. I took it off the hook and put it on and I was filled with the raw power of the refinery. I sat, my back against the door, feeling Dad's arms around me. I don't know how long I sat there, or if I was awake or asleep.

Mum found me. She bent down to me in her nightdress and I smelled warm Charlie. 'Oh, love, you funny boy.' She pulled the vest over my shoulders and hung it back on its hook. 'Come on, Jimmy, back to bed.'

On the weekends Dad mowed the lawn, tightened the taps, checked the pilot and watched *M*A*S*H*. Sometimes he took the Holden out to the TAB but he always came back at a reasonable hour. When she heard the front door open Mum's breathing grew deeper and she got out of my bed and went into theirs. *At least it's a reasonable hour*, she said to nobody on the way out.

After the last fucking time, Dad left the room whenever Robby came into it, even after his bruises cleared and his lip healed. He grew quiet around my brother; he could tell Robby was watching him with his eyes that missed nothing, storing information in the lands beneath the pools. Even though they seemed further apart, it was as if there was an invisible elastic connected to their ankles, keeping them joined. They always knew where each other was by the pull of the elastic. When it got too tight, which it did by Friday night, digging into the skin, sometimes pulling so hard it touched bone, Dad drank Cutty Sark Blended. It blocked his valves so his receptors didn't work. It was his only relief. But even after half a bottle, when the liquid had gone below the deck, he didn't hit Mum.

He started to spend more and more time in his shed. When I looked through the window I saw a bed resting against the roller door that didn't roll. 'When did the bed come?' I asked Mum.

Mum frowned. 'What bed?'

'The bed in the shed. Dad's new bed.'

'Don't ask silly questions,' she snapped. 'It's not his bed. Help me bring in the washing.'

I followed her out to the line. Dad's record player was in the shed too, set up on the workbench beside a small television. There was a coat hanger that had been untwisted and stuck in the top. During the week Dad lived in the house but then on Friday night he went into the shed, channelled shows through the hanger and listened to Merle sing, 'Someday When Things Are Good'.

Mum was lying. She knew it was Dad's shed bed. She knew he was sleeping in there. One night I saw her standing at the sliding door looking at his window. I saw her from the kitchen, lit up by the moon, hands and forehead pressed to the glass. Even with my developmentals I could see how much she wanted to be in the shed with Dad. She would have stretched out and been the bed for him if he'd let her. She was the same size. As Mum stood there she moved in time with Merle, *Memories of you, back through the years, the past my favourite dream* . . . The words penetrated the shed window, pushing their way through the atoms of glass in the sliding door to where she stood. She swayed to the song of her longing. *Memories of you, the past my favourite dream.* She never knew I was standing behind her in the moon room – watching.

Mum asked Robby to mind me while she did the late shift.

'Can we go into the swamp?' I asked him.

'Sure,' he answered. It would be the first visit in a long time. The light was fading as we left Emu Street. Soon it began to rain but we kept walking, the rain only enough to dampen the outside of our coats while the inside stayed warm with the heat transmitted from our solars. We came to the wetlands and Robby pushed open the gate. There were pelicans and swans and ducks on the stream. The grass was stiff and silvery green. Even though the wind blew there was stillness in the land underneath. Beyond the fields flames shot from the pipes of the refinery, gold and warning. Steam jetted into the grey sky, adding to the rain.

Water seeped through the grass under the pressure of our boots. I skipped to keep up with Robby as we moved deeper into the swamp. Mosquitoes hovered over our heads in busy clouds. Seaweed and froth, plastic bottles and tennis balls cut in half washed up at the sides of the stream. We stood at the edge as swans ran across the top of the water, their feet like Eskimo shoes, beating their wings, showing their hidden white feathers *flap flap flap* and up into the air.

Robby bent down and picked up a stick, stirring the water until clouds of mud swirled upwards. He looked across to the road, then back to the water. I could see his words and wishes circulating his tributaries. 'One day I'll leave this place,' he said. 'It's a hole.'

We walked around the rabbit warren and checked the burrows and Robby kicked at the sides so dirt tipped in.

On the way home I looked for the hole that was this place. I checked between clouds and blades of grass, and under rocks and down rabbit burrows and in clumps of reeds and behind patches of shrub, and in the water that ran beneath the bridge and in the plastic bottles that washed up against the banks of the stream and under the viewing bench and even in the far distance where the trains ran back and forth and the flame leapt from the pipe – but I couldn't see it.

'It's in you, Robby,' I said.

'What?' he asked.

'The hole.'

'Fuck off, Jimmy,' he said, walking ahead.

Part Three

For the next two years Robby grew even faster. Mist seemed to drift over the pools of his eyes so I couldn't check them for information. He hardly spoke, his long body feeding off his unsaid stores. How could Robby be so tall, his body stretched, his eyes obscured, and yet I still be here? I was eleven years old but at the same time I was not. How can opposite things be true?

In all that time, twenty-four months, Dad never hit Mum. The fight had gone underground, I could hear it bubbling in the pipes that fuelled the house.

I was in the sewing room not sleeping when I heard someone come home. It had to be Robby because Dad was on the night shift. I put one arm out from under the blanket and felt the icy air. After counting eleven seconds my epidermis began to freeze. Robby and Mum started talking in the kitchen. I pulled back the blankets and got out of bed. When I pushed open the kitchen door I saw Robby and Mum standing at the island. Mum stepped towards Robby and reached up to him – his body was so high and thin. His head bent towards her shoulder. She held him tight with the spread of her, and he let her, then she stepped back. She lifted the corner of her apron to her eye.

'Mum, I don't have to go,' said Robby.

'Yes, you do,' said Mum. 'Of course you do.' Mum's tears were rising up inside her, looking for the vents.

'I can wait another year.'

'What's the point of that? Your opportunity is now.' She swallowed hard.

'But you and Jimmy . . .' The lump in Robby's throat was swelling, making it more difficult for him to speak.

'You don't need to worry about me and Jimmy. That other business is in the past. You go and live your life. I'll break the news to your dad.'

If you turned on the taps at the sink tears would rush out. The apples in the wallpaper were damp with them. If you lit a match nothing would light.

I stepped through the door. 'Go where?'

'Jimmy.' Mum turned to me. There were pink dots in both her cheeks.

'Go where?' I asked Robby again. 'Where are you going?'

Mum came towards me. 'What are you doing up, Jimmy?'

'Where's Robby going?'

'Nowhere – nowhere at all. What were you doing listening at the door?'

'You said, *You go and live your life.* Go where?'

'Don't shout, Jimmy. You shouldn't eavesdrop.' Mum came towards me, frowning.

'You said, *Go and live your life.* Live it where, Robby? Where?'

'Jimmy, calm down,' said Robby. 'I . . . I'm thinking about going away for a while. On a boat.'

'Robby, we don't have to do this now,' said Mum, putting her hand on his arm.

'Don't we?' said Robby.

'What boat?' I felt my hairs turning in their pores, round and round, getting faster.

Mum sighed.

'What boat?' I shouted. 'What boat? Where?' Why weren't they answering me?

Mum smiled, but it was weak. It was only trying. 'He'll be with a team. He's going to catch more fish than the lot of them . . .'

Robby turned and looked at me and his eyes went down for miles, deep and brown. I ran to him and grabbed him around his waist and clung to him, feeling his heart beating through his shirt. He put his arms around my back and we held tight. Something was trapped in my particles, making them ache. It twisted in my throat and in my stomach and chest. I held on to Robby as if he had the power to release it, when I knew that he didn't. All he could do was release himself. *No, Robby.*

'Hey, Jimmy, it will be okay,' he said.

'No, Robby,' I said. 'No.' I gripped him tighter. 'No!'

'Hey, Jimmy . . .' He tried to separate us. 'I'll come back. I won't be gone forever.'

'No! No! No!' I shouted.

'Jimmy, settle down, come on. Your brother has to go.'

'No he doesn't. He doesn't *have* to go. He *wants* to go but he doesn't *have* to go.'

'Sometimes there's no difference, love.' She tried to peel me off him.

'No no no!' I shouted. 'No! Robby! No!'

Robby pushed my arms away hard, then he stepped back from me. I hit him with my mower blades as hard as I could. I kicked at his legs. I hit him over and over. I screamed, 'No! No! No!'

They tried to stop me, I don't know what they did, my vision was blurred. I hit him and hit him and hit him. I wanted to hit his face the hardest. I wanted to punch his eyes out. But they held me back.

'No, Robby!' I shouted. They tried to hold me down. 'No, Robby, no! Don't go!'

I kept kicking and screaming until there was nothing left. The pressure was gone. I was sore everywhere. I looked at Mum; her hair was sticking up, her cheeks were red and her face was sweating. I lay back in her arms and stared at the roof right through the ceiling. My eyes X-rayed the tiles and I could see beyond them into the empty world.

'Mum, is he alright?' Robby asked.

'He's fine, Rob. His tank's empty.' Rob and Mum pulled me up to sitting. 'Come on, Jimmy,' said Mum. 'You go and get some sleep, Rob, we'll be right.' Mum's breath sounded as though it was being strained through a sieve. The metal cross-wires were in the way of the flow.

'Are you sure?' Robby asked.

'I'm sure. You go. It's better that way. Come on, Jimmy, on your feet and let's get you to bed.'

I got to my feet. I was as loose as a rag.

When half of Robby was out the door he stopped and said, 'I love you, Mum.' Then he was gone.

Down she sat again, *boom*. Propped up by her elbows, she let her head fall into her hands. Even if I shouted she wouldn't have noticed me. She was with her firstborn, carrying him in his blue blanket, carefully, as if there was no more important thing in the world. I left her there, her tears catching in her fingers.

I went back to the sewing room on my own.

I didn't see Robby for two days; he was at Justin's or at practice. Then on the third day Mum said, 'Your brother is coming home early to see you, Jimmy. I want you to apologise to him, okay? You don't want him to leave without you apologising.'

When a picture of Robby entered my mental it hurt. Any picture. Just his knee or just his shoe or his mouth. If I saw the picture something in me went in the wrong direction. It was caught and couldn't find its way out. I couldn't stop anything. I had no powers. I had no vest and no refinery and no flame. I couldn't change things. I couldn't transform them. They were what they were going to be no matter what I did. Something was missing in my chemicals.

Mum put angel sponge cake on a plate and she made Robby a coffee and she said to me, 'Well, Jimmy?'

'It's okay, we'll be alright, Mum,' Robby said, smiling at her.

'Call me if he gets out of hand,' Mum said to Robby, then she left us.

Robby looked at me.

'I won't get out of hand,' I told him.

'That's okay,' said Robby. He sat on a chair so our eyes were level. He said, 'Jimmy, I really need you to be okay. For Mum. You have to be okay about this or I can't go. I won't go. Tell me the truth. Can you do this, Jimmy?'

I looked into his eyes – his guards were down, we were level, it was my rare opportunity, he wasn't on the way anywhere or doing anything else. I looked in and I saw the deep and powerful wishes, forces that hurt him to disobey. They were hurting him now. They would hurt him until he surrendered to them. 'Yes, Robby,' I said, looking down at his big hand holding mine. 'Yes,' I said.

He hugged me. 'You're a good brother, Jimmy,' he whispered. 'The best.'

Then Mum came back in. 'Let's all eat some cake,' she said, cutting down into the sponge.

In the nights after Robby said he was leaving I tried to count sheep but the sun was gone from the field. I could hear the sheep, but I couldn't see them. They called out over the top of each other without tune or sense, as if they were lost. *Bleat bleat bleat,* sheep after sheep after sheep.

I was at school battling the enemy the day Robby left. When I got home I knew he was gone as soon as Mum said, 'Chocolate crackle, Jimmy?'

'No thanks, Mum, no thanks.' I went straight to Robby's room. Mum had taken the sheets off his bed. I could see the mattress, stained with a dark yellow outline from all the times I'd got in beside him. I sat on the edge of the bed, tracing the outline until I met at the point where I started. There was a pressure in my chest, as if someone was pulling on my inners. I got up and looked in the cupboard. Robby's boots weren't there and neither was his blue check coat. I sat down inside the cupboard and made a wall around me with the remaining shoes. Most of the shoes Robby never wore; his feet were too long, but Mum kept them anyway.

Soon Mum came into the room. She bent down to me. 'Oh, sweetheart, Jimmy. We're going to miss our Robby, aren't we?' She held me to her and I smelled bread and vanilla. Over her shoulder I could see the coats and shirts and pants Robby had left behind, hanging like ghosts.

Dad didn't say anything about Robby leaving. After the last fucking time he couldn't get his words out because the apertures were blocked and to unblock them would need an operation that he might not survive, the way Pop Flick didn't survive. Pop Flick died on the table when his heart wouldn't start, it didn't matter how many volts they gave him. The things Dad couldn't say were so important, and so serious, that the smaller things, like *What a sunny day, hey?* and *How are you, Jimmy, my son?* and *I miss Robby* couldn't get past. I was the one in the house who said the most; maybe that's why I repeated.

The day after Robby left I was passing the sitting room when I saw Dad standing at the window. He held the framed photograph of him and Robby on the *Lady Free*. He didn't notice me at the door. Dad was on board the *Lady Free* with Robby and the fish. There was nobody else; just Dad and his firstborn. He stood and stood with the picture gripped in his hands.

A few days later Dad walked into the kitchen while I was eating baked beans on toast and he said to Mum, 'I want to take the boy to visit Rod for a few days.'

I stopped eating the toast — bean sauce dripped down the crust.

Mum turned around from the sink, rubbing her wet hands on her apron. There was a gap and then she said, 'You haven't seen Rod in ages, love.'

'About time, then,' Dad said.

Mum nodded as Dad's answer moved through her network, the new words illuminating her tubes. You could see them flashing under the surface of her skin, light then dark, light then dark. It was only Paula that managed me; she was the expert. 'When were you thinking you would go?' she asked him. Her hands were dry but she kept twisting them in her apron anyway.

'I've got holidays due. I'll call Rod. Maybe in a couple of weeks.'

Uncle Rodney lived on an island. It had a name that didn't work, as if it had been dropped, like a plate in pieces. What was it? Broken! Broken Island.

Mum stopped twisting her hands. In between her and my dad was air, floor, a lamp, a cookbook, a telephone, a bottle of orange juice, my toast, the empty bean can, my plate, Mum's book, me and the table. 'Alright, love. What a good idea.'

Dad nodded. 'Great,' he said, leaving the kitchen. Mum turned slowly back to the dishes, as if she had to be careful of something new in the house and she didn't know if it was great or dangerous.

We lay on my bed and I asked Mum questions. 'What will happen on the holiday with Dad? What will happen? What will we do?'

Mum said there was only one way to find out and that was by going. She said, 'You like your Uncle Rod and he could do with the company since Shirl's gone. I will miss you but you will have a good time and then you will come home and you can tell me all about it.'

'But, Mum, if nobody has done it before, and nobody knows what will happen, then how do I know that I will even come back home? Nobody knows how it ends because it has never happened anywhere before, so how do I know what the ending will be?'

'That's enough, Jimmy. You'll go and you'll come back and that's all you need to know.'

'But, Mum, why are we going? *Why?*'

'Because your father wants to take you on a holiday,' she said, turning off the light. She pulled up my top and drew letters on my back. *I LOVE YOU.* It was true, Dad wanted to take me on a holiday, but why? It hadn't been just me and Dad for a long time; not since Mum got sick and went into the hospital and Dad and me made the go-cart. Not since then. It was always Mum.

'Mum? When Dad and me go on the holiday will there —'

'Shhhh, love, shhhhh.'

It was late. I was lying on my bed looking for things to count when I heard Mum and Dad talking. I got up, crossed the hall and sat outside their door.

'But why now, Gav?' asked Mum.

'Why not now?'

'You've never wanted to before.'

Between each of their answers lay small spaces of thought. Dad didn't like the questions, but he knew Mum had to ask them. I heard a rope tugging on his plexus.

'Lost one son, don't want to lose another.'

'You haven't lost Robby, Gav. He's just finding his feet out there.'

'I'm not talking about the fishing.'

'You haven't lost him, Gav.'

'Don't pretend you don't know what I'm talking about.'

'Robby loves you.'

'Well he's not here.'

There was a small quiet gap, then Mum said, 'And Jimmy is.'

'Jimmy is.' The rope was pulling at its tightest in my dad. 'If I don't do something . . .'

'But . . .'

'Paula, I have to do this.' His voice was firm, but it took all his strength to keep it there.

I got up and I walked back across the hall to the sewing room – it was the first time my dad had fought Paula for me. I got into bed and I felt as though it was too small for me, the son who was still here.

Mum drove us to the airport. Dad wore his striped tie and his suit, and his shoes shone from when he'd polished them that morning.

'You look handsome, Gav,' Mum said, with a shy smile.

When we got to the airport I held on to her, not wanting to let go. I had to hide how much I was speeding by biting down. Mum faced me, holding my shoulders in her hands. Dad turned his head as if he didn't want to see. 'You'll be back before you know it, Jimmy,' she said. But it wasn't true; when I was back I would know it. There she'd be again.

I couldn't let go. I was clamped stiff to her warmth. 'Jimmy,' she said, looking into my eyes, 'do it for me, hey? For Mum?' I could see tears brewing in her pipes. Air hung in stubborn clouds around her face, refusing to go in.

'Goodbye, Mum,' I said, stepping back.

'I'll call you from Rod's, love,' Dad said, kissing Mum on the cheek.

'You boys take care,' Mum said, wiping at her eyes with the back of her hand.

I turned away. I couldn't look for her wave or her eyes as she left us. They would be in direct communication with my feet and my feet would run back to her, pulled by her need and by mine.

Aeroplanes lifted into the sky, the long row of windows too small to see a face behind. I closed my eyes, looking for sheep to slow myself down. I thought I saw them peering out from behind rocks, but I couldn't be sure. I tried to count them, hearing Mum's quiet numbers just before mine. I repeated the same number when I got too fast. *Seven seven seven* I blinked and the sheep became shadows without the light. I followed my dad's body-in-a-suit to the ticket counter.

Dad walked through a doorway with no walls, and no door. The doorway beeped and he had to go back and take off his boots. He walked through again just in his socks. His yellow nail poked through a small hole. Mum only cut mine, not his. When I walked through the doorway nothing beeped at all. After I got to the other side Dad smiled and said, 'Enjoying yourself, son?'

Was I enjoying myself? What were the signs?

We walked down a white tube that led to the door of the aeroplane. In we went, one by one. I followed Dad between the rows of seats. There were people ahead of me and people behind. I felt hot and itchy under my clothes. My centre trembled; I had never been inside an aeroplane before. I watched them flying over our house. They joined up to an underground computer the size of a factory and every plane that took off and landed made an electric green line across a glass map. Planes were the fastest living things.

When we got to seats 9A and 9B, Dad checked the tickets and said, 'This is us.' He put his bag in the cupboard above our heads and then he buckled me into the seat beside the window. 'You'll want the window, won't you, Jimmy?' he said.

I didn't know. A small seed of sickness, somewhere near the root, took hold in me. The air in the aeroplane was manufactured in the toilet, by machines just under the lid. The air came out of the bowl, down the aisle, entered my nostrils and nourished the seed, the same way blood and bone nourished Mum's roses. Ladies dressed up in orange hats and scarves like Sherry, the secretary at the dentist's, stood in the aisles and waved their arms in a pattern of up and down and side to side for directions. They said make sure you blow the whistle loud, and don't deflate until you're out of the water. Their lipsticks all matched their scarves. When their emergency dance finished they sat down and a picture of a seat belt came up in lights. Buckle up.

When the aeroplane started moving forward I gripped the seat.

'Be a while yet,' said Dad. 'Have to get down the runway first.'

My throat felt dry. The toilet air was cold and bleached. There was no space in it. The aeroplane got very fast and began to roar. I leaned back and Mum's scrambled eggs rose up to my throat as the plane left the ground. I gripped the armrests, closed my eyes and swallowed. I didn't move for a long time, as if my stillness was helping to drive the plane. Dad whispered in my ear. 'Open your eyes, son, and see how small the world is getting down there.' I opened my eyes and I saw the sea down below. My face went cold as the seed of sickness blossomed inside me. The toilet air couldn't reach my particles; there were sections going dry. I kept very still, suspended above the sea in the aeroplane without Mum.

A woman came wearing a hat and a badge that said *Tina*. 'Would you like to take the young one into the cockpit for a special treat?' she asked Dad, smiling.

'How about it, Jim?' Dad said to me.

I shook my head.

'Come on, Jimmy. It's a real treat to go into the cockpit. You can tell them about it at school.'

Cock. Cockpit. 'Okay, Dad.'

Dad unsnapped my belt and we got out of our seats. I followed Dad to the very front of the aeroplane. Tina opened a small white door. The captains steered the aeroplane by looking at a panel. Lights flashed orange, on off, on off. Rows of clocks told different times, arrows pointed the way. The sky was spread before us, never-ending space. If you pulled out the root did you see the same thing? Was the skin an optical illusion?

'Look down there,' said Dad, pointing.

I looked down and I saw the cracks between mountains, the walls looming black and steep. They were very dark and they went all the way into the earth's core.

'Bloody great, isn't it? Bloody beautiful,' said Dad.

Mum's scrambled eggs rose higher. I couldn't make my eyes operate; I saw only falling.

'Is this your first time?' asked one of the captains, pushing aside his mouthpiece. 'Pretty good, hey?' He leaned forward and pressed one of the buttons on the dashboard.

Tina put her hand on my shoulder. Her touch drew the seed like magnoplasm draws a splinter. My eggs rose unstoppably through the tunnel of my throat, out my mouth, splattering the back of the captain of the cockpit. He turned around to me as the eggs fell from my front. We both looked at them as they hit the floor.

Dad said, 'Christ, Jimmy.'

Then he said, *Sorry fellas* to the captains and Tina found a cloth and I heard, *Oh no, oh dear, sorry, oh no, oh no.* Dad led me back to the seat. He said, 'For Christ's sake.'

As we took our seats I saw the cracks again, like deep black mouths, the same as the cave under Mrs Stratham's armour. I saw my arms waving as I fell. My body spun round and round on the way down and I knew I would always be falling, the sickness no longer a seed but a network holding me in its grip like a triffid. 'My eyes!' I shouted. 'My eyes!'

'Quiet, son. Shhh.'

'Blindfold!' I shouted. Other passengers turned to look at us. 'Blindfold, blindfold!' I called again.

Dad held my knee and looked around us as if he wasn't sure.

'Blindfold, Dad!'

His fingers fumbled with the knot as he pulled off his tie — stripes ran sideways red black red black red black, all the way to the tip. He tied it round my head and everything darkened. I breathed in *two three four* out *two three four*, keeping each breath exactly the same distance. I brought the world in to darkness and breath and at last I began to slow down. In *two three four* out *two three four*. I pulled in deeper breaths than the ones I took at home because I needed the extra to have the same effect. Slower and slower, I was no longer falling but level. I leaned back and there was the chair ready to hold me.

From behind striped bars I saw Robby; he was the captain of the Indian Ocean. The ship was the *Cutty Sark*. Robby climbed the boat's sails and looked out for pirates and told the men to lower the nets, lower the nets. He was the one who could spot the fish – schools of bright orange carp swimming in circles around the boat. *Haul them up!* he called to the team. *Haul them up, boys!* And the team pulled up the nets and tipped them onto the deck and the fish poured out in a river of gold. When Captain Robby came down from the cockpit everybody cheered.

I heard Dad order a beer.

'Wake up, Jim.' Dad was shaking me. The aeroplane had stopped. He pulled the tie from my head. Light burned my eyes. 'We're here.' He got out of his seat and took his bag out of the cupboard above our heads. 'Come on,' he said.

I got out of my seat and followed Dad down the middle of the aeroplane. We came to a doorway where Tina was standing. She held out her arm to show me the metal stairs leading to the ground.

'Careful, son,' Dad said. He held out his hand.

I took it and we went out of the aeroplane and down the stairs into the glaring light, and then we stepped onto the grey tar of the airport. The sun was bright and hot, everything was shining under it. The lid of the sky holding it all was bright blue. I couldn't see one cloud.

'Sunshine,' said Dad. 'Makes a nice change.'

We walked with all the other passengers towards a building with two layers of windows. When we were close enough I saw Uncle Rodney waving through one on the top layer. I couldn't see his face, only his waving hand and his head. Uncle Rodney used to own a marine and tackle shop on the mainland; he sold bait and hooks and lines and anchors. He let me touch the hooks and the frozen prawns even though I was very small then and could have caused a breakage or tried to swallow a float. Then he moved to Broken Island and set up a new shop with less business but more time to fish. It was a lifestyle.

We got through the doors and Uncle Rodney came towards us. 'G'day, Gav. G'day, Jim. Let me take your bag.' Dad gave his bag to Uncle Rodney. Uncle Rodney put his hand on my back. 'You've grown, mate. You used to be a little feller. Jeez. Look at you now. Big man, you are!'

'No I'm not, Uncle Rodney,' I said. 'I'm the smallest in my class – and the oldest.'

'Alright, son, settle down,' said Dad.

'Well you look bloody big to me, mate,' said Uncle Rodney. 'Don't know if you'll fit in the bloody bed.'

Uncle Rodney took us over to his white car waiting in the car park. I climbed into the back seat and Dad and Uncle Rodney got in the front. The window went down without me turning the handle. 'Can you do that again, Uncle Rodney?' I asked him.

'What's that, Jimmy?'

'Can you press the window button again?'

He pressed it again and the window went down then up then down then up again. Uncle Rodney was pressing it then not pressing it then pressing it again.

'Aren't you a bit old for that, Jimmy?' Dad said.

'Never too old for the Statesman, Gav. You can get to know her better over the next few days.' Uncle Rodney pressed the button again.

'Never too old! Never too old!' I repeated.

'Easy does it, son,' said Dad.

The Statesman's internals were wrapped in wires, connecting up to the main control panel. They twisted round each other, just under the surface of the car, in all colours, each wire with a different signal and code. They put them in the metal, in the doors, the tyres, the boot, like the fibres in the rabbit, all connecting up to the control panel in front of Uncle Rodney. 'Uncle Rodney, how do you like your cock pit?' I shouted. 'Cock! Cock!'

'That's enough, Jimmy. Sit back and settle down.' Dad sounded scared.

'It's alright, Gav, the boy's no problem.' Uncle Rodney's voice was broader and wider than Dad's. 'Cock's a cock.'

'He gets a bit excited.' Dad lit up a fag and gave one to Uncle Rodney. They both smoked and talked about the weather and Uncle Rodney said how it had been a bit tough since Shirley left because there was no one to cook and how he always ate counter meals now and that was a lot of chicken parmies and chips and he patted his stomach where the belt stretched across and then the car went quiet. Outside the Statesman, palm trees with heads like giant pineapples swayed in a line along the sea.

When Uncle Rodney opened his front door a big grey dog with long legs and long hair came out and jumped on him. 'Ned is the missus's replacement,' said Uncle Rodney. Ned licked his face. 'Only a lot more affectionate. Say g'day, Jim. Ned loves kids.'

I touched Ned's head with my fingers and a small current entered my hand wires. We couldn't have a dog at home because its fur would clog Mum's air ducts. We couldn't have a cat either, or a guinea pig or a chicken or a mouse or a rabbit. Ned spun in circles, smelling Dad then me then Uncle Rodney.

'Settle down, Ned, and let Jim say hello.' Uncle Rodney smoothed his hand across Ned's head until the big dog was quiet and still. 'Say hello, Jimmy, he won't hurt you.'

Ned sat on his back legs and I went closer. Ned didn't blink as he took in the scent of me and made his decision. I looked into his eyes and I saw myself inside them; I was suspended in the same light as in the sheep. I felt my cells slowing down until they spun at the same speed as Ned's; there was no difference.

'Want to go down the beach, Jimmy? Have a swim?' Uncle Rodney asked.

'Can Ned come?'

'*Can Ned come?* Of course he can come! Can you imagine if I didn't bring Ned? He'd never forgive me!' Uncle Rodney sounded as though he was speaking through a loudspeaker. I saw grey fillings at the back of his teeth when he spoke. I saw more of Uncle Rodney's mouth than I'd ever seen of Dad's.

When Uncle Rodney picked up Ned's lead Ned ran around us in circles, his back end throwing the front end in a different direction. Uncle Rodney caught him by the collar. 'Easy does it, Neddy, settle down.' It was the same thing everyone said to me! The *same thing*!

'Go put your togs on, son,' Dad said.

'Okay, Dad, togs on,' I said.

Uncle Rodney took me and our suitcase to the room I would be sharing with Dad. I opened the case and took out the togs. I pulled off my shorts and put on the togs over my underpants. I put a t-shirt over the one I was wearing and went back out to Dad and Uncle Rodney.

'Ready?' Uncle Rodney asked me.

'Ready,' I said.

'You can take Ned, if you like,' said Uncle Rodney, handing me Ned's lead with Ned on the other end. We walked out the front door, Ned pulling me along the hot street. His power travelled through the red cord and into my arm — I could hardly hold him back. Ned was the leader from the animal kingdom. He only knew one language; there was only one world for him.

'Careful crossing the road, son.'

I waited for Uncle Rodney and Dad to catch up and then the three of us crossed in a line together. Ned pulled me down to the beach.

At home the beach on the other side of the wetlands was flat. Here the waves rose up as if an enormous hand was underneath, pushing the water back and forth. The waves transfixed me; I couldn't move. They rose up one behind the other, curling over themselves and breaking into white foam as they raced towards the shore. They were fuelled by the earth's refinery, steaming and boiling at the core, forcing wind and pushing up water through the cracks like a blowhole.

Uncle Rodney unclipped Ned from his lead and he ran down ahead of us. Uncle Rodney went after him. I wanted to follow, but I couldn't. I didn't have the powers.

'Go on, son,' said Dad. 'Jimmy, go down to your uncle. Come on, son, he'll think you've never been to the beach before.'

But I hadn't, not a beach like this.

Ned ran back to me, swinging round and knocking me over. He dropped a wet green ball beside me, his fur dripping water onto my legs. Uncle Rodney came up just behind him. I looked down to the water and saw a line that had been drawn across the sand where the last wave ended, like a boundary.

'You better throw that thing for him or he'll make me do it.' Uncle Rodney stood over me in his red and yellow togs with his chest covered in pictures as if he were the pages of a book.

I picked up Ned's ball and threw it as hard as I could. Ned raced after it as the waves kept coming and breaking and stopping and rolling back. They were always in the background of everything that happened and would happen. I ran up and down the hot sand throwing the ball to Ned and Uncle Rodney while Dad sat on a towel in his trousers and shirt. I ran faster and faster, big circles getting smaller. Then straight lines, then sideways lines, back and forth, back and forth, up and down, up and down, faster and faster sky sand waves dog sky sand waves dog sky sand waves dog faster and faster and faster.

'Easy does it, son.' Dad called out. 'Easy!'

'He's alright, Gav. This is the perfect place for a kid to go nuts. I don't know who's worse, him or the dog.'

One of my circles got so small and fast that I dropped onto the sand but I kept my legs turning me on my back, my legs kicking me around, spraying sand into the air. Ned barked. When I stopped I saw flashing rainbow lights. My heart pounded. If it exploded I'd die like Pop Flick. We went to his funeral. They put him through a tunnel and set him on fire. Dad kept some of the ashes in a silver eggcup with a lid and said, *One day I'll scatter them*, but Mum said, *That day will never come, Jimmy, just between you and me.*

I saw my Uncle Rodney laughing. Each puff had wings that carried it out over the ocean. Uncle Rodney brought over a bottle of water and splashed some of it over my face. 'I think Ned is going to like having you around, you're as crazy as he is.'

Dad stood up, pulling off his shirt and trousers. His boxers had stripes that went straight across – blue white blue white blue white blue white. I watched those stripes walk down to the water. Dad didn't stop to test the temperature with his toes, he just kept going and the waves parted, divided by his force, and went rushing past. I didn't take my eyes off him; the white skin of his inner body, the red of his outer, the green pictures on his muscles – maidens and anchors and birds with hearts in their beaks – the scar from the mower blade, the dark of his head.

'He's a good swimmer, your old man,' said Uncle Rodney.

I didn't know my old man could swim. I'd never seen it.

Dad held his hands in a high prayer above his head, then hooked his body over and went under.

I ran down to the boundary line. 'Dad! Dad!' I knew he couldn't hear me. The world under the sea had no sound. Whales spoke to each other by sucking the silence around them into the shape of what they wanted to say, then blowing it towards the other whales. My dad would never understand it, no matter how much he prayed.

I held my breath.

A dark circle tore through the froth. It was Dad's head. His body followed, and his stripes, lower now, as the water tried to take them from him. I could breathe again.

'Watch him catch a wave, Jimmy,' said Uncle Rodney. 'He was always good at it – better than any of us.'

I sat beside Ned and Uncle Rodney and watched a wave building behind Dad. He started swimming in front of it.

The wave grew bigger; Dad's arms were propellers churning through the water at top speed, carrying him forward just in front of the wave, as if he was trying to beat it. Then the giant wave rolled forward and tipped over onto Dad, but instead of sinking him, the wave carried him towards the shore, all the bubbles of silence bursting up around him with the message of the whales. I had never seen my father's mouth so wide. He beamed as if the sun was inside him.

'He's good, isn't he?' Uncle Rodney looked down at me. 'He always was.' Uncle Rodney was Dad's younger brother. Then came Ray the raper. Last came dead Steve.

'Yes, Uncle Rodney. Yes. Yes, he is good. He is good. Very good. My old man is *good*.'

'You want a swim?'

I looked out at the waves building and rolling and breaking. 'No thanks, Uncle Rodney, no thank you, no thank you.'

'Come on, kid. We'll show your dad how it's done,' said Uncle Rodney.

What could I show my dad?

'Come on, Jimmy. If Ned can, we can.' Uncle Rodney threw the ball out deep. Ned plunged out to where it floated, crashing through waves, his body covered by water. 'Come on, I'll be there to keep an eye on you.'

Uncle Rodney held out his hand to me. It was brown and beneath its surface I saw pale blue crisscrossing ropes. I put my hand in his and we walked into the water. 'Ooh, bloody cold that. We must be mad.' Uncle Rodney jumped up and down as if he could get away from it. I held his hand tight as the cold stiffened me. The ends of tiny pipes tried to poke their way through my skin. 'You okay, Jimmy? That's not too bad is it, kid? You okay?'

I shook my head. *No no no not okay no no not okay no no.*

'We don't need to go any further if you don't want to, mate. We can just stay here. We'll get used to it in a minute and then we can see if we want to go deeper, okay?'

Dad caught another wave, his eyes bright as he sailed past.

'You right to go under now, Jimmy?' Uncle Rodney asked me.

'No thanks, Uncle Rodney. No thanks. Not ready. Can I get out now, Uncle Rodney, can I? It was a great swim, thank you.' Even *that* made Uncle Rodney laugh.

'Sure you can, kid. Next time we'll go deeper. By the end of the week you'll be catching waves with your old man, you wait and see.' He led me back to shore and left me with Ned, then he joined Dad in the water.

I sat with Ned on the towels, salt drying on my skin, prickling under the sun, one hand on Ned's wet warm coat. Even though they didn't speak or shout across to each other as they flew along the water, there was a language between Dad and Uncle Rodney made of waves.

When they came out of the water, Uncle Rodney just behind Dad, I saw that they were both branches from the same tree. Uncle Rodney was taller but they both walked leaning back, legs happy to get there but the rest of them not so sure. Both had thick dark hair, and both had the same words written across their chests:

RIP MOTHER
BELOVED

After they dried themselves we walked back along the hot road to Uncle Rodney's house. Ned's head hung as he loped, his gums over the green ball between his teeth, the lead loose in my hand. The house we were walking to wasn't the one Uncle Rodney lived in with Shirley on the Gold Coast – she took that one after the split. The house Uncle Rodney had now was a smaller one that he bought after Shirley left him with hardly any dough. There weren't any of Shirley's flower paintings in this one; only photos in frames of Uncle Rodney on boats with giant fishes in his hands.

When we got back Uncle Rodney took sausages and bread and salad and sauce out of the fridge for a barbecue. Uncle Rodney and Dad cracked beers outside. We went onto the verandah. There were three long chairs covered in soft squares. The garden stretched green before us with a birdhouse on a tree in the middle. The garden surrounded the tree. All points from fence to tree were equal.

'Take a seat, Jim, stretch out,' said Uncle Rodney. I climbed on one of the long chairs and put the towel over my face to block out the rays. I hung my hand down so I could touch Ned's head as he lay on the deck next to me. The heat outside the towel was melting my outer coating. Uncle Rodney and Dad kept laughing at things while they fried the sausages and drank the beer. It was as if the waves and the sun had unblocked their valves. I liked the music it made – better than Merle Haggard.

I put tomato sauce on my sausages and bread. Uncle Rodney said, 'You want some sausages with your sauce, mate?' and laughed. Dad laughed too. Why? *Sausages with your sauce, sausages with your sauce.*

'Uncle Rodney,' I said into the heat, 'Robby left. He went away on a boat.'

There was a pause, then Uncle Rodney said, 'Is that right, Jim?'

'That's right, Uncle Rodney. That's right. That's what our Robby did. We're going to miss him, aren't we, Uncle Rodney?'

'Is it true, Gav?' Uncle Rodney asked. 'Has Robby pissed off?'

I pulled the towel from my face and saw Dad head for the esky. 'Yep.'

'You never said anything.'

'Didn't have to. Jimmy's done it for me.' Dad pressed his finger hard into his beer can. I heard a snap.

'Well I'm glad he *has* told me,' Uncle Rodney said. 'At least someone talks around here.'

'We can't ring him, we can't write him a letter and Mum doesn't know when he's coming home,' I told Uncle Rodney. 'You have to ask the fish, ha ha! Hey, fish! Fish! When is our Robby coming home? Any ideas, fish? Any ideas?'

'Good one, Jimmy. Ha! I like that. "Ask the fish!" Ha! At least you haven't pissed off. Not planning on leaving your old man, are you?'

I looked at my dad. For a moment he had left Uncle Rodney's yard and was searching for Robby through binoculars somewhere over the fence. Then suddenly he turned to me. 'You better not bloody leave me, kid.'

Sparks hit the sides of my bone cage. 'I better not, alright! I better not, Dad! I better bloody not! No way! No bloody way!' I jumped off my chair, then over it and back again.

Uncle Rodney and Dad laughed, their faces turned to me, as if I was the source of their delight. Me, *Jimmy Flick*!

After lunch we lay in a row of four, a long loose wire running between us, mingling our thoughts.

Me: yellow sun, grey fur, blue wave.

Dad: blue waves, yellow sun, Paula's brown eyes.

Uncle Rodney: yellow sun, grey fur, brown beer, Shirley's blue eyes.

Ned: green ball green ball green ball.

Soon all we saw as we lay there in the hot sun were colours, one on top of the other, mixing at the edges like one of the fridge paintings I did when I was small.

That night I lay on the guest bed while Dad and Uncle Rodney sat up and drank beer and talked. I heard Uncle Rodney say Steve's name.

'Oh mate, were you surprised?' Dad sounded as though there were tiny nails in his voice, little weapons to keep him safe, but from what?

'I guess not.'

'What I want to know is who the fuck came up with that much bail?'

'The last time I spoke to Steve he said none of the gear was his. It was the only time and he was doing it as a favour for somebody.'

'Bullshit. He was working for whoever paid his bail.'

'Oh shit. Poor bastard.'

'Poor nothing. A dozen fucken shot guns and a bucket full of speed. I could've been charged too. I already had Robby by then. Fucken idiot.'

'I know, I know.' Uncle Rodney sighed out.

'What the hell was he thinking?'

'He was never much big on thinking.'

'Too right.'

'Did you know I've still got his bloody ute up behind the shop.'

'The WB?'

'Yeah. He wanted me to mind it. He reckon'd he was going to come up and fix it and use it on the island to haul oyster baskets or some rubbish. I told him it was too hot for fucken oysters on the island, but he said he'd refrigerate the water or some bullshit.'

'Some bullshit is right,' said Dad.

Uncle Rodney waited. Dad was the oldest. Dad was the one who said what happened. But Uncle Rodney was going to try telling him something new. 'Steve copped it a lot worse from the old man than you or me, mate. Only Ray got it worse. I'm not saying that's an excuse, I'm just saying it happened. Did you know about the time Dad put him in hospital?'

'No.'

'You were long gone by then, and Mum didn't want you to know. Dad broke three of his ribs with his jemmy bar. The one he used for lifting traps. You remember that fucken thing?'

'Yeah. I remember it by the front door in case Brian Dixon ever came around.'

'Brian fucken Dixon. Bastard.'

'Dad said he was always ready for the enemy.'

'Yeah, but Steve wasn't the enemy, Gav. And Dad fucked him up well and truly. He was never the same. And neither was Mum. She got sick after that.'

There was a long silence between the brothers – two there, two missing.

'Do you remember Steve on that old horse of the Drakes', Rod? Do you remember how much he loved that horse?' Dad's voice was softer now. There were tears right at the back.

'I remember he slept in the Drakes' paddock. Mum couldn't get him inside. He had to be near that fucken horse.'

'He used to feed it all the breakfast cereal.'

'Is that where it went?'

'Jesus. Poor Steve.'

They were quiet again. I closed my eyes and saw the Drakes' horse flying over the roof with Steve hanging onto the tail.

I woke when Dad came into the room. I pulled in my resources, holding my breath until I didn't even take up one-third. Dad got in carefully, the mattress hardly dipped. He was very quiet, only taking in the breath that he needed and no extra. The air passed easily over his voice box, back and forth unimpeded. He stayed in his first position. I change positions a lot of times before the final. But Dad took his first and stayed with it. When his breathing deepened I knew he was asleep and then in my dream I was the guard and I wore a metal hat with a spear out the top and watched over my dad because that was my job and it always would be.

The next morning Uncle Rodney and Dad pulled the ping-pong table out of the garage. Uncle Rodney bashed cobwebs away with his bat.

I threw the tennis ball for Ned and he ran for it, picked it up with his teeth and brought it back. I ate my toast and threw it, I drank my juice and threw it, I brushed my teeth and threw it until Uncle Rodney said, 'At least finish brushing your teeth, Jim. I'm drawing the line there.' Ned was hot and shaking and wet and running running running but inside him was quiet and still.

I watched Dad and Uncle Rodney play ping-pong, puffs of laughter around their heads like the froth from the waves. Their arms were fast, their faces grinning, I saw my dad jump to the side. He jumped under, he jumped up, his arms out and his head back and then Uncle Rodney leapt and jumped and they sang out, 'Take that! Take that! You ole bastard! Ah! Still got it! Still got it, mate! Ha! Ah! Shot! Shot, you ole bastard! Come on, little brother! Take that, ha! Ha! Nice one, ha!'

In the afternoon we walked down to the beach again. Ned raced in circles and so did I and Dad didn't care. He was talking about boats and fish and produce from the shop. The sun shone hotly down on us as we walked along the road. Tiny rivers of sweat dripped down Mother Beloved on Dad's and Uncle Rodney's chests.

Oh, Gav, really, did you have to? Mum asked him the day he came home with his new tattoo.

That's how much I loved her, Paula.

Dad wore the stripes again. In his hand he carried cans of beer, his fingers between the plastic as if they were rings. Uncle Rodney packed oranges and bananas and cold cans of lemonade.

Soon Uncle Rodney asked, 'You been in touch with Ray?'

I sensed my Dad's cells go stiff, as if something was caught in the spokes. My dad didn't talk about Ray since Ray went to jail for raping. 'Not for about six months.'

'I spoke to him at Christmas.'

'How did he sound?'

'He's okay,' said Uncle Rodney. 'He lost the appeal.'

Dad huffed out air.

'He reckons Rockhampton is better than Brisbane.'

'Right.'

'He's still saying he didn't do it.'

'He did it,' said Dad.

After a while Uncle Rodney said, 'He asked about you and Paula and the boys.'

Dad wiped sweat from his forehead. He nodded.

We walked for a while longer, then Uncle Rodney said, 'Did you ever work out what Dad had against him?'

'What do you mean?' Dad asked.

'Why he had it in for him. Why he nearly killed him on New Year's Eve when we were at Portland. Why he hit him so much.'

'Maybe he knew something was wrong with him,' said Dad.

'Bullshit, Gav. There was nothing wrong with him. You know there was nothing wrong with him. Not back then.'

After a while Dad said, 'Bastard.'

When we got to the water Dad pulled off his t-shirt and went straight in. Uncle Rodney shook his head. 'Your old man, hey? My big brother . . .' He put his hand on my shoulder. 'It's good to see you both, Jimmy, bloody good. Coming in today?'

'No thanks, Uncle Rodney. Ned needs someone to throw the ball.'

'Suit yourself, son. Don't mind if I go in?'

'Don't mind, Uncle Rodney, don't mind if you do.'

'Make sure that dog doesn't wear you out,' said Uncle Rodney as he walked down to the water.

Ned knew the ball was coming; he waited, he watched, I threw and Ned ran. It was one thing over and over.

Late at night I was in the guest room not sleeping while Dad and Uncle Rodney were in Uncle Rodney's lounge room watching *Convoy* and drinking beers. Trucks sped down the highway as pictures of waves washed over me. I would fall back into soft water and then come sharply forward, my body jumping.

I got out of bed and went to the door. 'Ned,' I whispered into the hallway. 'Ned.'

Ned padded into the room.

'Ned.'

He climbed onto the bed. I put my hands on his head and listened for the messages. *Shhhhh . . . Jimmy . . . Listen . . .* Ned's warmth joined me to him and to myself, through him.

'I got to give up the booze, bro,' said Dad.

'Not our friend Fosters,' Uncle Rodney answered.

'Not the beers – the hard stuff.'

'Oh yeah? What's brought that on?' said Uncle Rodney.

'I'm getting older, mate. Robby's gone. Only one kid left. Can't take it like I used to.'

'Who can, mate? Who can?'

I heard the click of a beer ring, then laughter. Ned put his chin on my chest. The trucks of *Convoy* rumbled past the doorway.

'How's Paula doing?'

'She could be better. The asthma slows her down a bit. She works hard.'

'You guys okay?'

'We'd be better if I could stay off the hard stuff. I could come out of the doghouse once in a while.'

Rubby Ducky ten four ten four Silver Bear to Rubber Ducky. Trucks overtook, honking their horns.

'That fucken doghouse. Been there, mate,' said Uncle Rodney. 'Shirl ever let you out of it?'

'Not a lot, mate. Fed me from a bowl on the floor in the end. Put a collar round my neck and walked me round the block. Ha ha ha ha!'

It was as if they'd been laughing since they were boys, running up the Portland sand dunes with Stephen and Ray, sliding down on pieces of cardboard, beating each other to the waves, smiling across the water even as one tried to win against another. Four brothers joined by the sea and Mother Beloved and by Pop Flick. Pop Flick *the ole bastard* who hit them on Friday nights and Saturday nights and sometimes during the week until their feelings inverted, shot backwards and stole their language and drove them apart, drove them to jail, drove them into trees, drove them to Cutty Sark, split them, divided them and took from them Mother Beloved.

One night we went to the pub for a counter meal. Other men knew Dad and he introduced me to them. 'This is my son, Jim,' he'd say, his words crisp and proud.

I ordered a pink lemonade from Ginny.

'I'd like to see her Ginny,' said Uncle Rodney and Dad's eyes shot down to me and he tried not to laugh but he laughed anyway and then I did too. It was a bubble from the core. When I laughed they laughed more.

After I ordered my drink from Ginny I looked at the row of bottles lined up behind her, ready to pour – all at different levels, all different coloured glass and liquids. I traced the line of the levels with my finger and Ginny lifted up the pink cordial over my glass for more. At the end of the row hung the Cutty Sark. Its level was the lowest.

Dad said, 'Order whatever you want, kid.'

'Order the Oysters Kilpatrick, Jim. Let's make your old man pay.' Uncle Rodney winked at me.

'Who's Patrick?' I asked.

Dad and Uncle Rodney laughed again and so did I. More bubbles floated upwards, as if a man had been kicking underwater. The more you laugh the more you can. The pressure of the laughter behind Dad's skin puffed out the lines and the holes so they disappeared. Whatever came out with the laugh left a gap behind that light rushed in to fill. It shone out my dad's eyes. Uncle Rodney was a convector for it. He drew it from the sea and the island's earth and gave it to us.

'Chicken parmy, son?' Dad looked at the menu.

'Oysters Killed Patrick, Dad. Better call the cops.'

Ha ha ha ha ha ha ha!

After we finished dinner Uncle Rodney's friends came to our table.

'Hey, Jim, this is Amanda and Dave,' said Uncle Rodney. Amanda looked the same age as Mum but if you doubled her she still wouldn't be the same size. 'Pull up a pew,' said Uncle Rodney.

Amanda smiled and put a jug of beer and two glasses on the table. 'Hi, Gav — we haven't see you in ages.'

'Too bloody long,' said Uncle Rodney.

'He's right about that,' said Dad. 'Been working too hard.'

Amanda poured beers into everybody's glass. 'You southerners need to take more holidays.' She turned to me. 'Jim, are you having a good time on the island?'

'Are we having a good time? *Are we having a good time?* We are having the best time!' I spoke my words through a loudspeaker as if I was at the circus, like Uncle Rodney.

'How's the teaching?' Dad asked Amanda. 'You still at the island school?'

'Still there. It's good. I couldn't take working in a big school.'

'School sucks,' I said.

'Jim's not a fan,' said Dad.

'That's okay, Gav. It can suck if you've got the wrong teacher,' said Amanda. 'Remember Mr Bunt, Rod, when we were in high school?'

'I remember calling him something else,' said Uncle Rodney, grinning.

'Has Uncle Rodney got you fellas working in the shop yet?' Dave asked. Dave had even more drawings on his arms than Uncle Rodney. There was a picture of a man with a metal bucket on his head, underneath that was a fish.

'I'm waiting for that,' said Gav. 'Time and a half or nothing. Double for the kid.'

'Double for the kid!' I said.

'You reckon Jim'd like a day on the boat?' Amanda asked.

'Jim's not much of a sailor,' said Dad. 'The plane trip was bad enough. He went a bit nuts, didn't you, Jim? Not a fan of heights, hey?'

'There's no heights on a bloody boat, Gav. How long since you seen one?'

'Yeah, Dad. How long since you seen one?'

'Jeez, look at the cheek on the boy,' said Dad, ruffling his hand through my hair, his touch warming the follicles.

'Been bloody nice weather for a day past the heads,' said Dave. 'Amanda and me haven't been out for a couple of weeks – but *Ashley Lynne* is keen and ready.'

'I'm desperate for a break from marking tests. Give me an excuse.'

'We could make a day of it, what do you reckon, Gav? Before you guys go back,' said Dave, turning to Dad.

'Come on, Dad, let's make a day of it!'

Amanda said, 'Come on, Dad.'

It was as if my dad was standing at the top of a cliff and at the bottom was water and it sparkled but my dad didn't know how deep it was or what lay beneath. Everybody waited while he tried to guess. Then at last he jumped, his body a neat arc over the depths. When he reached the surface he waved up at us and said, 'Righto then, a day on *Ashley Lynne*! Let's do it!' He raised his glass, and everyone else did the same, knocking their glasses together so that beer tipped and frothed over the sides. I raised my glass too, the pink lemonade fizzing with beer as it spilled, the light behind it yellow and gold and pink.

'A day on *Ashley Lynne*!' I said, and it was a party.

Later that night, when we got back to Uncle Rodney's, the telephone rang and it was Mum. Uncle Rodney passed me the receiver.

'Hello, love, I miss you,' Mum said.

'Mum, there was waves and Ned was in the water, he swims, Mum, he catches the ball . . .'

'That sounds fun, Jimmy. Is it sunny? Is the weather okay?'

'Yes, Mum, sunny, sunny every day. I threw the ball very far but Ned always gets it, Mum, he *always* gets it; you can throw it anywhere. Anywhere! Anywhere, Mum!'

I saw a smile lift Dad's face from underneath as he watched me talk.

'Are you sleeping, okay?' Mum asked.

'No, Mum, not sleeping, not sleeping. Lining things up, Mum, lining things up. Ned is big. Really big. Bigger than a sheep, Mum. Mum, I can swim now. Uncle Rodney has a ping-pong table. Dad beat him, Mum, every time, but Uncle Rodney keeps trying, he keeps trying, Mum, even though Dad beats him. Uncle Rodney says *next time, mate, next time* and he tries again and again and Dad keeps beating him but, Mum, that doesn't stop him! He picks up his bat and tries again the next day. He tries all day, Mum. He doesn't stop. But Dad keeps beating him, Mum. He gets every ball, he doesn't miss, Mum! Just like Ned, Mum. It doesn't matter where the ball goes. It can go anywhere and he gets it. Dad is fast, Mum, but Uncle Rodney keeps trying, but, Mum, he'll never beat him, he never will. Not ever!'

'Jimmy, Jimmy,' Mum laughed. 'It sounds like you're having a good time. I love you, son. I love you very much and I am glad.' I heard tears in her vocals.

'Mum, Mum, what are you missing?' I asked her.

'What do you mean? I'm okay, love, you just go on having a good time and I'll see you in a couple of days, okay?'

'But, Mum, Mum, what are you missing? What are you missing?'

'Nothing, love, nothing. I'm not missing anything.'

'But you said, Mum, you said.'

'Yes, love, I am missing you, of course – I am missing you. But I know I'll see you very soon.'

I didn't cry. I didn't know where the engine of crying was, what it looked like. 'But Mum, what are you –'

'I love you, darling. Can you put your father on, love?'

I wished I had a manual for crying; I'd follow the instructions carefully from point to point, letter to letter, until I cried enough tears to fill the tray of a truck and then I would tip the truck in the hole in Mum and up it would fill, up and over the edge and nothing would be missing, nothing at all.

The next day it was windy and raining and Uncle Rodney said, 'Let's take the Statesman for a spin around the island, fellas.'

We got in and I pressed the window button and down came the window. I did it again. I did it one more time and then I didn't do it anymore. The button was there if I wanted to press it, in the same place just under the ledge – but I didn't need to press it anymore. Uncle Rodney turned the key, fuel charged through the passages and the Statesman hit the road.

Dad's arm rested against the open window and the wind blew back his hair. I stuck my arm out the window behind him and the wind bounced it back and forth. Ned put his head out the other side and the wind blew back his ears. The Statesman drove past the long lines of palm trees that ran beside the beach, tossing their pineapple hair in the breeze. Pelicans flew like white boats across the sky. The water kept changing; no one shape stayed the same – even when a single ripple found its shape, it was already on the way to another. There was no point of static.

I closed my eyes and I made a picture of Mum sitting at the kitchen table reading an Agatha. I chose *The ABC Murders*. She looked up from the page, her head turned to the window as if she was waiting for something. I listened to the slow drag of her breath. She needed the winds of Broken Island to blow back the dust in her tunnels.

'Can Mum come, Uncle Rodney? Can Mum come here?'

Uncle Rodney looked across to Dad. 'Of course she can, mate. Love to see Paula again. We'll organise it, hey, bro?'

'Great idea. I'll get on to it soon as we get home.'

I sat back as Mum floated around the body of the Statesman. Dad pulled his arm inside and pressed the button so his window went up as if he was scared of something.

When we got to the other side of the island the skies began to clear. Uncle Rodney picked up fish and chips and we took them to the lighthouse. We ate on the grassy slope looking up at the steeple, with its red circles at the top to warn the fishermen. Uncle Rodney poured sauce on the chips and every time I thought an obstacle would come it didn't. The seas of Broken Island had powers that thawed us. The invisible world had lost its language. Ned ate the chips we didn't want and the gulls came close for their share. I looked way out to sea and Dad said, 'Do you think Robby is on one of those boats, son?' It was the first time Dad had mentioned Robby in a long time. The first time he'd said his name.

'No, Dad, no. He's west. That's the Pacific. He's on the Indian. And those are liners carrying cargo, Dad. Cans and planks and car parts. Robby is fishing.'

'You're too smart for me, kid,' said Dad.

'I tell you what,' said Uncle Rodney, 'Robby will be working so hard he won't know which ocean he's in.'

'He knows how to work,' said Dad. 'He's a Flick, remember.'

'And one thing you can say about the Flick brothers,' I added. 'They know how to work.'

'Jeez you're sharp, kid,' said Uncle Rodney.

'Little bugger,' said Dad, messing my hair.

I lay in bed and listened to the hard coloured balls smacking against each other as Dad and Uncle Rodney played pool. The window was open and the light from the yellow moon shone through. Uncle Rodney had lit a coil to keep away the mosquitoes. If the mosquito breathed in the smoke from the coil, the smoke entered its body and did the same thing to its breathing apparatus as dust did to my mother's. But the mosquito is so much smaller than my mother that it couldn't manage the poison; its body burst. The coil glowed on the window ledge, going slowly round on its way to the middle where, with nothing left to burn, it would become the same ash that was left in Dad's egg cup after Pop Flick went through the incinerator.

I breathed in the smoke and lined up shadows: frame, curtain, coil, crack in wall, crack up wall, crack down wall, hook, suitcase, Dad's shoe, Dad's coat, Dad's belt, Dad's other shoe, pillow, my knee, my arm, my elbow, my hand.

Just as I was about to close my eyes I saw a faint line connecting the shadows, like string you take into a forest so you don't lose your way. Everything in the room was joined by the one line; the frame to the curtain, the coil to the crack, the belt to the shoe. I closed my eyes and in the vision behind the skin of my lids I saw the line stretch way out to sea, like cobweb blown by the wind, further and further; it crossed the Pacific until the Pacific became the Indian and it found Robby in his ship. It touched his shoulder and moved across the sleeve of his shirt and up to his eyes and across the top of his head and then the line went to all the other men on the ship, then all the way back to me. Everyone was joined.

'Don't know why we left it so long, mate. Madness.' I heard Uncle Rodney say.

'You get caught up in things . . . work. First holiday in – I dunno how long . . . too long, mate.' My dad sounded lighter, as if laughter had altered his weight.

'Too long is right. Pass me the short cue, will you?'

'Shirl wasn't too keen on visitors – don't you remember?'

Click went the balls.

'No Shirl now, mate.'

'No Shirl, true story. Bloody hell, mate. Nah, but you're better off.'

Smack went the balls.

'Shot! 'Nother beer?'

'Yeah, mate. Good to see the young fella again. Got to happen more often.'

'For sure, mate, going to make some changes when I get back. No more of the hard stuff, like I said.'

I closed my eyes and saw my Dad tearing through the surf towards me, getting to me as fast as he could. Mum wasn't there, only Dad. There was room for him. In Nineteen Emu Mum took up all the room. Her streams of love flooded the house; that's why Dad spent so much time in the shed. It was dry land in there.

As the brothers played and spoke and swallowed beer, and the balls clicked and smacked and sank, the sounds became a lullaby – not the one Mum sang to me when I was small; a different one, an accidental one made of men. Ned lay beside me, the power of the animal kingdom adding a harmony.

'Good idea. Save up for your retirement and come and live up here – the island life, mate, the island life,' said Uncle Rodney.

'Retirement, that's a good one. Bloody hell.'

Smack click.

'Two on the black.'

'Shit.'

Click.

'Two on the black.'

I drifted to sleep on the waves of the accidental lullaby.

One morning we left Ned at home with a bone and drove to Uncle Rodney's shop. Outside was a sign that said *Flick's Marine and Tackle* and Uncle Rodney showed me where he kept the bait and the hooks and the sinkers.

'Robby should be here,' said Uncle Rodney, his hands full of metal floaters. 'If he's taken up the love of fishing like his old uncle.'

'Yes, Uncle Rodney, *yes*. He should be. He *should* be.'

'Best fishing in the world on the island. Could get him a job on the mackerel boats. Better than the bloody crays, or whatever he's up to. He'd be better off here.'

Dad picked up one of the long rods standing in a row. 'Kid wants to get out on his own, I guess.' Dad didn't say anything about the last fucking time or what Robby did to his face.

'If he wanted work he could've got in touch. I could have sorted something out. Keep it in the family. Got long enough to be on his bloody own.'

'Kids do what they want. You did, remember?' said Dad. 'Remember bloody Sydney? Remember Sandra?'

'Bloody Sandra. Touché mate.' Uncle Rodney grinned. 'How could I forget bloody Sydney? Sydney and the stripper. Jesus.'

'What rods are you using lately?' Dad wanted Uncle Rodney to think about fishing rods and not Robby.

'The ultra-light is best for the flathead, but it cuts out the grunter bream. Dave sticks to his bloody heavy thing whether it means he'll catch anything or not. Stubborn bastard.'

Soon Amanda and Dave came into the shop. When Amanda saw me she gave me a cuddle. 'G'day, Jim. Excited?' I wished Amanda was my teacher.

We drove down to the pier and there was *Ashley Lynne* tied to the pole, her nose pulling at the rope. She was bobbing up and down and the sea was dark beneath her, sloshing and splashing up. 'Ahhh, Ashley, my love,' said Dave.

'Watch it.' Amanda pinched him. She pulled a basket out of the truck. 'Lunch,' she said.

'All aboard,' said Dave. 'Come on, people.'

There were boats tied up all along the pier and beyond them was the sea, no waves. It led to the line that said a person had died. I had seen it at Westlake Nursing when someone needed a monitor. It was the horizon and it was in all people but you only saw it when you were old. It circled the world but different countries got to see it depending on whether it was night or day. Inside me the needle spun around the dial, speeding up. The *Lady Free* was the only boat I had sailed and she was a fridge.

You had to step over one part where if you looked down you saw the sea. If you wanted to get on the boat that was what you had to do. Dave stepped over then Amanda did, then Uncle Rodney did. 'Right, Jim. You next,' said Dad tightly.

Uncle Rodney held out his arm to me from *Ashley Lynne*'s deck. 'Come on, Jim. The sea waits for no man.'

I didn't want to go. Four faces were waiting for me, smiling and trying to tell me it was a good idea. I looked down at the crack between the boat and the water. 'What about Ned?' I said. 'What about Ned? Ned is all alone today, Uncle Rodney, he won't like that, will he?'

'Ned will be okay,' said Uncle Rodney.

'Hey, Dave, put a plank across for Jim, will you? Might make it easier,' Amanda said.

'Sure,' said Dave. He pulled one of the bench seat lids out of *Ashley Lynne* and he turned it upside down and made a plank for me to walk across. I could not see the ocean and there was no crack. I took a breath and crossed and then I was in *Ashley Lynne*.

'Good on you, Jim,' said Uncle Rodney.

'Come on, Dad,' I said. Then Dad stepped on the plank and shook it and pretended to fall and Uncle Rodney said, 'Jesus, you haven't changed.'

Dave started *Ashley Lynne*'s engine the same way you start a car. He turned a key connected to her motor cord which drew up the petrol's energy and she rumbled for on. Dave turned *Ashley* away from the pier and then we were off across the sea, the wind blowing our hair as we cut through the water.

Ashley Lynne sped so fast she beat me. She took up all the movement; I had no choice but to be still. I saw the sides of the island thick with trees as we charged towards the horizon. *Ashley* roared in my ears. Soon Dad's face changed, as if the wind was blowing away the memories of everything that happened before so that he didn't know what had happened; he had no memory of worry. There was only *Ashley Lynne* and the island and the rings of forest and the sea.

Soon Dave stopped the boat and dropped the anchor so that *Ashley* bobbed in one place, held steady by the chain. Amanda pulled thermoses of tea and coffee from the basket and juice for me. The sun was midway up in the sky. It had no guard around it. There was no smoke transformed into cloud on either side. It was hotter.

The men got out the fishing rods and Dad gave me one and said, 'You need patience to fish, Jim. You got patience?'

I nodded. Did I?

'Amanda?' said Dave. 'You going to win catch of the day?'

'Oh, the fish love their Aunty Amanda. Bait me up, will you?' she said, putting down her coffee cup.

'Dave, mate, bait me up too while you're at it,' I said.

'Bloody clown,' said Dad, but not angry – proud.

Dave stuck prawns through our hooks and Amanda and me sat on *Ashley*'s edges with our rods dangling into the water. *Ashley* rocked me up and down and I held my rod and I was just one of everybody, not different, neither faster nor slower. We all had our own bodies but the bodies were an illusion. The invisible substance inside us was the same. I had patience. Soon I felt a pull. Uncle Rodney noticed my line going further out to sea and he said, 'Jesus, what's Jimmy got?'

I pulled back but I stayed slow.

'Give him a tug,' said Uncle Rodney. 'Come on, mate, a bit of a tug. Just let him know who's boss.'

I tugged.

'That's it, Jim. You're a natural. You still got him.'

Dad was looking at me and so was Dave. I watched my line pulling and my rod bend to give space to the fish. When Mum danced me round the carpet she took a step then I did. It was the same with the fish. I pulled back again.

'Okay, that's it, Jimmy, time to bring him in now. Wind your reel, that's it.' Uncle Rodney showed me how to wind.

'I can do it, I can do it,' I told him and I began to wind in my fish. I wound and wound and it got harder and harder and I used my strong hand and I kept pulling and the fish got heavier as if it was multiplying, and everyone on the boat was watching, including my dad.

'Go, Jimmy, go,' he said softly and then all things in *Ashley Lynne* were tuned to me as the silver fish rose from the water and into the sun, flicking and twisting on the end of my line. I was against it in a battle and the weight was heavy and about to break and everyone was shouting, 'Go, Jimmy, go! Jimmy, go!' and I pulled and the fish pulled and Uncle Rodney was right there, trying to help, but I told him, 'No! I can do it, I can do it!' And up and over went the fish, silver as mercury, onto the deck and he slapped and slid and I bent down to him and I tried to put my hand over him but he was too slippery and everyone was shouting and laughing, 'You got him, Jimmy! He's yours!'

'Look at the size of him!'

'Bloody hell!'

'A bloody great grunter!'

'Go, Jimmy!'

And then my hand landed on the back of the flipping fish and I felt him trying to move against me but my force stopped him. It was me over the fish. Then I grabbed at the hook trapped through his silver lip – my hands were shaking; I had never touched a fish before – and I unhooked it and I threw the fish high and everybody grew quiet as he flew through the sky, seeing his home the sea beneath him, knowing it was coming, only seconds away, able to hold on, only just, and *whoosh*, down he went.

It was so quiet, there was only the sloshing of water as *Ashley* bobbed on the surface above the fish now swimming deeper and deeper, away from the boat. It was a long quiet wait — which way would it go? Which way?

And then Dad cheered. 'Hooray! Hooray!' and clapped as if it was the show he'd waited so long to see and it was more than he'd expected. It was better, *better* even than he'd hoped for as he shouted and clapped and cheered on his feet for me, for me, and that was the sign for everybody else. 'Hooray! Hooray! Catch of the day!' they shouted. And I never needed to catch another fish. That was my fish.

The rest of the day I sat at the back of *Ashley* and watched the pathways of foam and froth that we left behind us melt into the sea and I ate Amanda's chicken sandwiches and tried something on top I never had before called avocado. 'I like it, Dad. I like it! Avocado!'

By the time we got back to the jetty all of the lines on Dad's face had disappeared and were hooked invisibly around me. Thank you, *Ashley Lynne*.

It was our last visit to the beach. In the afternoon we were catching the plane home.

'Oi, Jim,' Dad said, his eyes sparkling. 'Coming in?' He held out his dripping arm. The scar from the mower blade dragged down between the legs of his girls. The sun shone over us. He smiled. He was still and sure, his words with space between every one. Behind him, beneath the shining sun, the waves grew broad and blue, then curled over, smashing, sending white foam flying.

'Yes, Dad,' I answered. 'Coming in.'

I took his hand and he pulled me up from the sand. He led me in, pulling me through wave after wave of broken foaming water. It was as if he knew the water's direction, its intention. He wasn't scared of the change. I held back, and the line of our arms pulled tight.

'Come on, Jim,' he said.

'Can't do it, Dad, can't do it,' I turned to go. I could see Uncle Rodney standing on the shore, watching us.

Dad's arm stayed tight. 'You can do it, Jim.' He gave my arm a little jerk, catching me by surprise; I had to follow. He pulled me on through the water that rushed towards us, as if we weren't there, as if we were too small to make an impact on its shape. I couldn't stand. I gripped my dad's arm harder. My feet touched the sand and sometimes they didn't. We rose and fell together.

'Dog paddle,' said Dad. He was as firm as dry land – the Cutty Sark far away in the high cupboard to the south.

I kicked away at nothing, my breath quick, my dad a steady line as the world of water beyond him tipped and straightened. And then we were beyond the breakers and I could see where the wave began; a swell that sharpened as it gained a body and momentum. Beneath the ocean the engine of the earth roared, pushing the water forward, but here it was quiet, the waves smooth as glass. Up went my dad and me, over the top and down the other side. 'Bloody beautiful, isn't it?' Dad said.

'Bloody beautiful, Dad! Bloody beautiful!' I shouted across the sea.

I watched a wave coming towards us, growing higher and higher, thinner at the top as it curled over, preparing to crash over our heads.

'Take a breath, son.' Dad took hold of my hands and pulled me down under where it was quiet and the movement slow. I opened my eyes and he looked soft, made of water, like me.

We were one thing, connected by our hands leading to our arms leading to the rest of our bodies. I had begun with him and he ended with me. Waves couldn't break it, Cutty Sark couldn't, Merle couldn't, Mum couldn't; nothing could. I felt the wave passing over the top give us one quick pull, then we burst up into the sun. Dad let go of my hands, and the world above the water was shining and foaming with light and change.

The next wave that came was as solid and full as a mountain. 'Over this time,' said Dad, and over we floated. Far away down below I saw Uncle Rodney and Ned watching and then the rest of the island behind them and then I looked up and saw the whole endless blue sky.

When we came out of the water something that had been pressing on my chest, a weight that had been there for a long time, was gone. Miniature rainbows covered the wet sand. Uncle Rodney gave us a thumbs-up and I gave him one back. Ned barked and I ran towards him, water flying up around my feet.

Uncle Rodney and Ned stood with us at the airport. Dad held the suitcase. His shoes were on his feet, his coat was over his arm and his belt was looped through his trousers. We were going back.

'I'm going to miss you, Jim.' Uncle Rodney looked sad.

'Who will throw the ball for Ned, Uncle Rodney? Will you? Will you throw it?' I asked him.

'Not as often as you, kiddo.'

'What will he do? What will he do? Uncle Rodney, what will he do?'

Ned licked my hand with his soft tongue.

'Ned will miss you, and so will I. You've got to drag your old man up here again, Jim. Meanwhile, I'll be working on my ping-pong skills.'

'Ping-pong ping-pong ping-pong,' I said.

The aeroplanes roared overhead. One took off past the window, its wings like super knives to cut pathways through the air. Soon we would be on an aeroplane. My stomach moved to make room for the seed. 'Ping-pong ping-pong ping-pong ping-pong,' I said, louder. 'Goodbye, Ned, goodbye, Uncle Rodney, *ping-pong pong-pong ping-ping-ping*!'

'Settle down, son,' said Dad.

Another plane wheeled its way down the runway, propellers turning faster. Propellers inside me turned faster too. It was high up there, very high.

'Ping!' I shouted. 'Pong!' Where was crying? Were the switches somewhere inside me too? Why couldn't they be found? 'Ping! Ping! Ping! Pong!' I shouted. A little girl stared at me from behind the legs of her mother.

Dad put his hand on the top of my head. It was warm and strong and I felt all the ping and pong drawn from me as it travelled up my body and through Dad's hand. From there it entered his refinery and was purified to nothing. I turned to my dad and put my arms around him. I breathed in my old man and it slowed me down as if I had counted one hundred sheep.

Uncle Rodney said, 'My turn, mate,' and he hugged me, and if there was any fast left it was lost in Uncle Rodney's chest.

I went to Ned and put my arms around his neck. He stayed still as I held him, his centre holding us together.

'We've got to go, son. Don't want to miss our plane.'

'Yes, Dad, yes. Our plane.' I pulled away from Ned. Our time was over. Now there would be another time. What were the instructions for crying?

We put our bag into the tunnel and watched as it went behind the curtain, and waited for it to come out again.

'What happened to it in there, Dad?' I asked when the bag came out the other side.

'Not a lot, son. You didn't miss out on much.' He smiled.

I smiled too. 'I hope you're right, Dad, I hope you're right.'

Without waiting or stopping to check the temperature — the same quick way he entered the sea — Dad took my hand as we crossed the tar towards the steps that led up to the aeroplane.

As soon as we were in our seats we both leaned back and closed our eyes. The side of Dad's hard brown hand lay against mine, and we rested there, information travelling between us without obstruction: the changing shape of the sea, Uncle Rodney's voice, Ned, sun, sausages, green ball, pink lemonade, the Statesman's button, blue and white striped shorts. The messages, big and small, moved back and forth through the skins of our touching hands. We didn't wake until the lady said, 'Preparing for descent.' Dad blinked and swallowed and our hands pulled apart as we prepared for descent.

Mum was waiting for us just outside the airport, her dress blown back against her legs by the wind. She grabbed at it to hold it down. There was a scarf covered in berries around her neck that I had never seen before; strawberries and raspberries and blueberries and mulberries and all the other berries in the world there in Mum's scarf, her neck pink and sweet, and lipstick red on her mouth.

'Mum!' I shouted, running to her.

She put her arms around me and held me tight.

'Jimmy, my boy!' she said as if they were the words of her favourite song.

'Uncle Rodney's got a Statesman, Mum,' I said as we climbed into the Holden. 'The windows come down when you press a button.'

'Boy, did he enjoy pressing that button,' said Dad.

Mum and Dad's laughter was a harmony made of two tunes. One held up the other, lifted it, bounced it and caught it again. They took turns.

I rested against the back seat and a long breath of air that had come all the way from Broken Island was released into the body of the Holden.

That night I lay in the sewing room in my bed, eyes half closed, listening to the brothers' lullaby in my ears. *Smack click shit smack click shit two on the black two on the black shot mate shot.* I was drifting on the seas of Broken Island when Mum came into the room.

'It was good, wasn't it, Jimmy? Your holiday?' she said softly, sitting on the edge of my bed. I couldn't stop my weight tipping towards her. Beneath her words, I heard her wheezing breath, trying to push through its message.

'It went well, Mum, it went well.'

She smoothed her hand across my back. I rolled away. I wanted to trace the thread that joined shadow to shadow. Why hadn't I seen it in the house before, linking chair to cupboard to carpet to train? I wanted to watch it disappear, feel myself grow fractionally faster, my cells begin to spin, then just when I thought it was gone forever, see it appear again, making me as slow and sleepy as Ned lying on the hot sand.

'Goodnight, Mum,' I said.

There was a small gap of quiet. Mum sat in it, wondering, until she got to the other side.

'I love you, Jimmy,' she said. Then she left the room.

On Monday Dad put his green and glowing vest over his shirt and kissed Mum on the mouth. The pressing of their lips caused a chemical reaction that lifted the curtains. When Dad stepped back and looked at her I saw a thousand tiny lines that ran from his body to hers.

Even though my holiday with Dad was over it was still holidays from school, so I stayed home with Mum and drove her up the wall. We piled cheese on tomato on meat on milk on pasta sheets on meat on cheese, on and on and up and up and up went the layers.

'Your father loves lasagne,' Mum said as she greased the tray. She was pink and stained with the berries as she said it. *Your father loves lasagne.*

When Dad came home that night he didn't go to the sitting room and drink beers. He sat at the kitchen table while Mum got the lasagne ready and he spoke about a man called Marv who was too old to work but couldn't afford to stop. He talked about Marv's wife Julie and how she put him under pressure, though he could understand why, and how Marv didn't want to retire anyway. He said Marv used to be a fighter but he'd given up.

Mum nodded and said, 'Hmmm,' and, 'Oh,' and, 'Really?'

Dad kept talking. He liked Marv and he didn't like Marv, he was angry with Marv and Marv made him sad. He understood Julie and he didn't. He talked about pay and hours and break rates and output. At last Dad's valves were unblocked and the words flowed as easily as oil through the pipes.

As we ate the lasagne and drank our juice I looked at my Dad in the fading yellow of our kitchen and I saw how brown and bright he was. In the place of the red in his eyes were waves rolling over and foam bubbling up white and shining.

'It was good to see Rod again,' Dad said, putting lasagne on his fork.

'How is he without Shirl? Is he doing okay?' Mum asked.

'Better off. Shirl was always on his back about something or other. He's a free man now.' Dad took a long sip of his juice.

'A free man! Is that what you'd like to be?'

'Only love sets you truly free,' said my dad, putting his hand over my mother's.

'You know all the right things to say, don't you, love?'

'Old silver-tongue.' Dad turned to me. 'Did I ever tell you when I first met your mother?' he asked.

'Mum's told me,' I answered. 'Point Paradise.'

Mum smiled. 'You've got a good memory, Jim.'

'There she was,' said Dad, looking back at Mum. 'Sitting outside her little caravan reading a book. The wind was blowing her hair and lifting the pages. I couldn't take my eyes off her. The only time she moved was to turn the page.'

Mum looked at Dad. 'I was on a reading holiday. All I brought were books. Two weeks away from work with nothing to do but read.'

'And I was on a fishing holiday. All I brought was bait.'

'You smelled like fish.'

'You didn't mind.'

'I didn't mind a bit.'

'Point Paradise.' Dad shook his head. 'The most beautiful place on earth. When I die that's where I want to be buried.'

Mum looked at him and rolled her eyes. 'That's a long way off, love, if I've got any say in it.'

'A long way off!' I repeated. 'A long way off, Dad!'

Later, when Merle Haggard sang 'Holding Things Together', Dad took Mum in his arms and spun her around the kitchen. A chair fell as they twirled and Mum shrieked but Dad didn't stop to let her pick up the chair. Though he was small he could still get around her, as if his arms went on after they were finished. They wrapped her up tight as they danced so that every part of her was held, the parts I had never seen before and the parts I had. She was held so strong and so tight by my dad she could never come apart. I smacked my hands together and every finger had a partner to hit and the sound that came out was in time to Mum and Dad's feet as they danced over the lino squares — *black white black white black white* holding things together.

Three weeks after the holiday Dad came home and said some blokes were going to be laid off because of low productivity. He said, 'They could've given us bloody notice. I've been there for years.' When he spoke I heard all the days of rust caught in his vocals.

Mum crossed the kitchen towards him. 'But it won't be you, love. Maybe some of the men who are near retirement. Some of the older boys, but not you.'

'No one is safe. Not me, not any of us.' Dad moved away, opening the fridge door and pulling out a beer. He cracked the top and tipped it over his open mouth. If Dad was made of glass you would have seen the beer rushing through his network; beer through the tunnels of his legs, to his toes, along his arms, all the way to his fingertips, around his heart valves, into his breathing tubes and alveoli, up his neck and into his head until every part of him was flooded. What happened at the refinery that day would be drowned.

'Oh, love,' said Mum. She went to him, her face sorry, as if it was she who was going to lay him off, she who would tell him he wasn't wanted and had no place.

Dad walked out of the kitchen and into the sitting room. He turned on *M*A*S*H*. From against the door I heard Klinger say, 'You could let me try that nail polish,' but Dad didn't even laugh.

When Dad went to work the next morning he didn't kiss Mum and he didn't look at me and say, *Pass the juice, Bruce,* or, *Milk for your tea, squire?* He drank his coffee standing at the island. When Mum handed him his thermos he didn't say, *Thanks, love.* He just took it.

'It won't be you, love. You'll be fine,' Mum said as he opened the front door.

'I'm not worried about it,' Dad snapped back, as if there was one wrong thing to say in this world and Mum had just said it.

After Dad left it was as if everything in the kitchen had been thrown into the air and settled back down in the wrong places. It was unbalanced. There was only one person who could bring back the balance and that was Dad.

We went to the shops, we swept the floors, we went to Mum's work for the lunch shift, we sat in the sun and ate Lemon Softies and Mum drank tea but what we were really doing was waiting for Dad to come home, to see how he would be, what he would do.

I wished Robby was here. When I was on the holiday just with Dad I didn't miss Robby as much. He was there, but it didn't hurt. But now, without him, there weren't enough people to absorb the static; the rooms filled with it, buzzing and vibrating. I missed Robby so much my chest ached. When it was almost six o'clock Mum began to look at her watch. She looked at it many times. She checked her face in the mirror, she put on lipstick, she moved quickly across the kitchen in the same pathways over and over, then back to look at her face in the mirror, as if she wasn't sure about what she saw the first time.

I was sitting at the kitchen table setting up bridges to later smash when Dad came through the door. I could tell he was carrying the air from the refinery and it needed time to dispel. Mum went to him too quickly; 'Oh, love,' she said. 'How was it?' Her lipstick had a scent that reached his nostrils when she spoke and mixed with the vapours of the refinery still trapped in his head, and made him dizzy. I wanted to warn her, *Stand back, Mum. Don't speak.* But it was too late.

I followed the line around the kitchen, seeing it connect my dad's ears to his head that led to his hair which led to the fluorescent bar of light via the cord that hung down from the blind. Then into the quiet pocket of our waiting, I spoke. 'Are The Good Times Really Over?' Merle Haggard's song leapt from between my teeth without warning. Dad looked at me in the land between anger and laughter. A land like a horizon; if you put a foot too heavily on either side it tipped. There was a gap, then he laughed. Mum did too.

Dad took a beer from the fridge, smiling as he swigged. 'Are the good times really over?' he asked the bottle.

Dad didn't talk about Marv or Julie at dinner. Mum made shepherd's pie. When she cut through the potato roof, all the things the shepherd loved – carrots, potatoes, peas – rolled out onto the plate, steaming and soft, floating in brown sauce. When she brought the dinner to the table Dad didn't say, *Smells good, sweetheart,* or, *You know the way to a man's heart, Paula.* He sat without speaking, sticking forkfuls of the pie into his mouth and sipping from his beer. It was as if Mum and me weren't there.

That night I was lying in bed when I heard the muffled voices of Mum and Dad. I got out of bed, crossed the hall and stood just outside their door. 'They say half of us are going to go,' I heard Dad say.

'But you won't be in that half, love.'

'You don't know that.'

'You've got to have a bit of faith, Gav.'

'That's bullshit, Paula. I'm facing things.'

'Well, okay, if the worst does happen, we'll be right.'

'Living on what you bring in?'

There was a pause. The cells in my system began to spin. I felt tiny pins pricking the skin down my arms.

'When will you find out?'

'They'll start firing the end of next week.'

'It will be okay, Gav. We'll deal with it when we get there.' There was a small space and then she asked, 'Things have been good lately, haven't they?'

Dad didn't answer her. He didn't say anything. It was a gap that nobody reached the other side of. There was the rustle of clothes, the flick of the light switch, the pull of blankets. Then nothing. Mum and Dad lay suspended over the gap.

The tiny prickings in my skin reached my back and shoulders.

I went back to my room and got in bed. I took a breath and waited for a sheep. The house was different without even the *chance* of Robby. I closed my eyes and made a picture of him out at sea with his team. Where was his boat? I wanted to send a message to him along the line that travelled between waves. *Half*, I would say. *Half*, Robby, *half!* The message would rise and fall along the line with the waves beneath it until it reached his boat. One of the team would see its small red light flashing on the dark sea and the message would be pulled up on a rope and delivered to my brother in the cockpit, and he would hear it and come home.

Dad drank beer every night of that week. On Friday I crawled through the fence into the wetlands. I sat on the *Lady Free*, the grass now so high around her sides you could hardly see her. I closed my eyes and threw out my line and hoped that it might touch Robby's underwater. When I opened my eyes I looked across to the refinery. For the first time there was no flame from the pipe. It had gone out. Productivity was too low to supply it. With no flame would there still be refining and rust for my dad?

That night Dad said, 'I'll eat in here, Paula.' *In here* was the sitting room. Redness washed across Mum's face. It was blood transmitting the stored feelings. Mum brought him steak and onion and corn on the cob on a tray into the sitting room, then she came back into the kitchen and ate bread and jam standing at the sink. She curled the bread over and the piece was gone in two bites. Her eyes were blank without a single story to tell. After he finished dinner Dad came in, and, graceful as a dancer, reached up to the high cupboard, pushed past the vitamin C and the Panadol, and took down the bottle of Cutty Sark. The boat on the bottle sailed down into our kitchen, dropping anchor on the bench while Dad took the ice out of the freezer.

That night I was dreaming the room had a skin and I was the heart inside it, when I woke to the sound of glass smashing. In my dream I didn't know what kept me beating. The time between my beats was always different; the pattern was broken. I didn't know if I would make it to the next beat. I heard Mum say *'No, Gav!'* I heard something crash. There was a scream but I don't know which side of the skin it came from. The bed filled with warm water. It was the Indian Ocean making a visit, absorbed through the epidermis. On the other side of the skin the rest of the house began to sink. *Beatbeat beat . . . beat*. I kept my eyes tightly closed.

The next day Dad came home and told Mum that he'd been fired. 'No bloody loyalty,' he said. 'I'm a dollar sign and that's it.'

When he crossed the yard to go into his shed I saw that the water was gone from his body. Smoke drifted from his chest.

He was dried up like a desert. I wanted Mum to hose him the way she did the succulents.

I ran outside after him. Mum called me back. 'Stay away from your father, Jimmy. He's had bad news, okay? You stay away.'

'What happened, Mum?' I asked her. 'What happened? Why is Dad home?' It was only two o'clock. Dad didn't come home until six o'clock. 'Why did they fire him?'

'Shhh, Jimmy, take it easy. Just do something else.'

'What, Mum? What?'

'What about your manuals? Your blocks?'

'What about your manuals?' I copied her voice, rising in the middle, breathy.

'Jimmy!' she snapped. *'Don't!'* Tiny currents of electricity left behind from the firing zigzagged through the kitchen.

Mum made me sit in the sewing room with my manuals while she worked. I learned how the needle automatically threads and stitches. The levers at the base connect to the cotton and its all systems go. When Mum left to answer the telephone I went out into the yard. I turned an empty plant bucket upside down, and put it underneath Dad's high shed window. Then I stood on it.

Dad was staring into his open fridge. He was the centre and the light from the fridge came out in rays around him. All of the rest of the shed was in shadow. Soon he closed the fridge without taking anything out. He stood up and leaned against his workbench, his back to me. Everything in the shed radiated from him. The spanner, the saw, the rope, the car parts, the posters on the wall, even the dust particles, all joined to him by lines.

Dad slammed his fists down onto the workbench. 'Fuck!' he said.

I was ticking like a clock after too many windings. I gripped the ledge tightly, the bucket shaky beneath my feet. Dad sagged against the bench, putting his face into the bowl of his shadowy hands. Suddenly he lifted his head as if somebody had whispered to him that I was there. He swung around and saw me through the dusty glass. Though our vision was obstructed by dirt and cobweb and stain, his eyes held me suspended. Even if the bucket fell I would have hung there. I wanted to call out, but my throat was locked and wouldn't release the sounds.

When at last he turned away, shaking his head as if he could refuse me, I jumped off my bucket and ran inside.

Later I saw him coming up to the house. Just before dinner when I walked past the sitting room I saw the dark of my dad's head in his black recliner bobbing up and down to Merle, who sang 'The Fightin' Side of Me.' I saw his hand pour beer into his throat. The table in front of him was full of empty bottles. His ashtray was on the ground beside the recliner. It overflowed with butts. Two were on the carpet, like white slugs.

I went into the kitchen where Mum was making dinner. She put chops, carrots, green beans and potato on a plate with a white roll on the side and carried it in to Dad. She knew that after he ate he wasn't as drunk. Food particles battled the whisky and food, due to the heaviness, always won.

I heard Dad shouting from the sitting room, 'What the hell would you know about it?'

My heart beat faster. My hands kept getting in each other's

way, knocking against each other. The Saxa fell from the table, leaving a spill of salt across the floor.

'You and that bloody kid! He drives to me to it. You both do. Leave me alone!'

I got up from the table and walked to the sitting room. The dinner Mum had brought for Dad was on the floor. Beans made a path across the carpet that led to Mum and Dad where they stood facing each other.

Why was my mother in there? She knew not to stay when Dad was drinking.

'You leave him out of this. It's not his fault you lost your job.' Her face was red. There was chop gravy on her dress. Her hair flew round her face as if it was electric.

Dad stepped towards her. 'If he'd been normal we could've moved to Albany. I could've got the job on the rigs.'

'Oh, the bloody job on the rigs. Bloody Albany! You tried to get the job on the rigs and they said you weren't big enough or some rubbish. It had nothing to do with our son!' Her voice exploded from her.

I clung to the doorframe and watched sparks shoot from her mouth.

'Our son!' Dad shouted. 'He's not my bloody son! You must'a done some other poor bastard to get a son like that!'

Mum made the sound of an animal trying to escape. Then she came at him with the full strength of her body – with her arms that hung the washing and swept and vacuumed, with her legs that pushed the trolley of cans and packets all the way up the hill every Saturday, with her stomach where she put her dinners, and with the weight of her bottom that made a chair for her to sit on after another day done. Her hair now bright with currents that flicked into the air above, she pushed herself into him and he fell back against the coffee table.

'Stupid bloody woman.' Dad dragged a low growl up from under the carpet beneath his feet, pulling it past the fibres and giving it hard to my mother. He shoved her in the chest. I wished she was wearing a jacket made of knives and guns, all the knives tied together and the guns aimed and ready. I wished she was wearing it under her dress, but she wasn't. All she had was the bra and the cream petticoat I'd seen her put on that morning before she pulled her stripe and dot dress over her head.

Mum screamed and Dad hit her in the eyes. He was blinding her! He was blinding my mum! Who would see me if not her?

The sparks that shot from Mum's mouth ignited a trail that snaked across the carpet and set my feet alight. I ran with an unstoppable force into the room and hit Dad in the legs. He felt hard under my fists, as if there were metal fillings beneath his skin. I hit him in the stomach then he hit me back. Dad had never hit me before; it was only ever Mum. I felt the bones of my chest splinter from the weight of his hand. He grabbed my arm and pulled it and snapped it like a matchstick.

I swung at him with my other arm. 'No, Dad! No! No!' I shouted.

And then he shoved me hard against the wall. Merle Haggard sang 'That's the Way Love Goes' as I fell. I looked up and saw brown beer bottles filled with light as if a candle was burning inside each one. The carpet was wet with the ocean that flooded out of me.

Through the glass I saw Mum catch fire. Flames leapt from her body. She whipped at Dad with her burning branches, until he was crushed against the wall, hands over his face to protect himself from the heat. He dropped into his chair and let her burn him.

When she'd run out of fuel, Mum fell to her knees beside me, looking up at my dad. 'Our boy, Gavin, *our boy*,' she cried. 'Our son!' In her voice was the memory of a time when I belonged to both of them; neither his nor hers, their shared boy. Dad heard it too, but he couldn't look.

Mum kept crying as she half carried, half dragged me out of the sitting room and into the bathroom, where she wiped my face and took off my clothes. She fumbled with my clothes, trying to still her hands, trying to breathe in the air that might cool her and calm her.

She ran the sponge over my nose and arms and cheeks. My bones felt as if they'd been torn from my skeletal, like I'd seen Uncle Rodney do to the fish. My chest and arm ached. Blood dripped from my nose. Blood is always just under the skin; the skin is what holds it all in, like a membrane.

Mum gave me a pill from the medicine cupboard then she lay beside me on my bed in the dark of the sewing room, one arm under my neck. She gripped me. Her fingers hurt but I didn't stop her. My nose throbbed. What connected the nose to the face and the arm to the body? Was it veins? Was it wires? Was it nerves? Did the nose stay on the face for the same reason the arm stayed on the body?

When I next opened my eyes there was a strip of grey light between the curtains. I heard somebody walking around the house. I heard cupboards opening and closing, I heard Dad's cough, his vomit, his peeing, his flush, taps turning on and off. The last thing I heard was the Holden leaving the house.

I heard it go down the drive and then out onto the street and then away down the road and then I heard it go further. It kept turning and turning, stopping at lights, going left, going right, further and further till it came to the highway with six lanes of traffic rushing past and then it joined the highway and chose its lane, going further and further away until it drove into the centre of the setting sun. When I next opened my eyes it was morning.

When I moved in the bed my arm felt as if it caught on a hook inside, and hurt. I got up slowly, my body heavy and sore, and put my trousers over my pyjamas.

Mum was in the sitting room vacuuming the place in the carpet where I had lain the night before. When she saw me, she switched off the machine. Both her eyes were purple and swollen, as if she was wearing goggles. I heard the tentacles in her apparatus waving as they tried to move the dust. It made me want to put the vacuum cleaner to her mouth.

'Do you want your puffer, Mum?' I asked her.

'No, love, that's alright.' She came over to me, wiping sweat from her forehead. 'I thought you'd sleep in. I was going to come and check on you in a minute. Are you alright?' She touched my arm and I flinched. 'Oh, is that sore?'

I nodded.

'Oh no, Jimmy . . .' She lifted my top and gasped.

I looked down and saw a bruise spreading across my chest like a country on a map. 'Oh Jimmy . . .' She traced her fingers lightly across the bruise. Tears filled her eyes.

'Where's Dad?' I asked her.

'Not here,' she answered.

'Where is he?'

'He left.'

'Where did he go? Did he go to work?'

'No, no he didn't go to work.'

'Did he go to the TAB?'

'No . . .'

'Did he go to the bottle shop? Did he go the newsagent?'

'No, no Jimmy, he didn't go to any of those places.'

'Then where did he go?'

'I'm not sure.' She sat down on the couch, patting the space beside her.

I stayed where I was. 'When is he coming back?'

'Jimmy, your dad . . .' She searched for the words, pulling at her lips with her fingers as if there might be some hidden inside them.

'When is he coming back?'

'Your dad . . .'

'What?'

'He had to go.' Mum had no control over her pipes. As she spoke water came down over her face, as if her eye gutters were blocked: full with leaves and dirt and soil.

'Did he take the car?'

'Yes, yes he took the car. It's all he took.' She stood suddenly from the couch, pulling in air, straightening her skirt. 'Jimmy, we have to get ready for town.'

'Town? Why?'

'Because we do.'

'Will he come back?'

'No more questions – we have to go.'

'But, Mum, will he?'

'Let's get you dressed quick as we can, hey?'

'Where are we going?'

'Dr Eric's,' said Mum. 'Get a move on.'

Mum took me into town on the bus along Blythe Street. I sat beside her and counted the measurements of her breaths. Mine was in *one two*, hers was in *one* out *one*.

They didn't keep us in the waiting room long. The girl at the desk looked at Mum's eyes, frowned and sent us through.

'What happened?' Dr Eric asked Mum.

'Oh, it's nothing, really. It looks worse than it is.'

'I doubt that, Paula. What happened?'

'Oh nothing – it's not me I've come about. It's Jimmy.'

'You first,' said Dr Eric. 'What happened?'

'My fault – very silly. You know how you leave a broom leaning against a wall when you finish sweeping? You know how you do that? With the pile of dust ready to pick up? Well I went and stood on the broom and the handle of the thing came flying back at me and got me in the eyes. See how silly I was!'

Dr Eric didn't look like he saw how silly Mum was. She winced as he touched the skin around her eyes. 'If you had come in when it happened I would have insisted on stitches. But as it is, it looks like it will be alright.'

'Oh yes, good, I didn't think it was too bad.'

'It *is* bad, Paula.'

'Will you have a look at Jimmy?' She turned to me. 'He . . . oh dear . . . he got into a bit of a scuffle . . . his arm . . .'

Dr Eric looked at my arm. 'This will have to be X-rayed.'

'Will you look at his chest?'

Dr Eric lifted my top. He listened with his stethoscope. He felt my ribs. 'Paula, I need to know that it won't happen again or I will have to do something about it. Do you understand what I am saying?' Dr Eric's words were red lights flashing on off on off.

'Yes, Dr Eric, yes, yes I do. It's not going to happen again.'

'You've said that before.'

'It's different this time.'

'Different how?' Dr Eric raised his eyebrows.

'It just is.' Paula looked at the ground.

'I would like to know how it's different.'

'He's – he's gone.' She mumbled as if to say it loudly and clearly and properly would be too much news for her own ears.

'How long has he gone for?' Dr Eric asked.

'He's gone. He's not coming back.'

Still it seemed Dr Eric didn't believe her. 'This must never happen again – to you or the boy.'

'Please, Eric, is Jimmy okay?'

'He's okay, Paula. He'll need X-rays but I don't think anything's broken.'

'Oh good, oh God, oh thank God.' Mum started to cry again and Dr Eric passed her a tissue and a mint.

We had to catch another bus to Footscray Medical for the X-rays. Mum stared out the window and didn't speak a word. She only moved a muscle to check the map Dr Eric's secretary had drawn for her. The bus kept turning corners I'd never taken before. When I rocked against Mum my rib hurt and the hook inside my arm pulled at the socket. When we got to Footscray Medical a woman called Tracey stood me inside a telephone box and said,

'Stay very still, please. It's important.' Then she left and went into a sound booth where she sent the X-rays into me. I heard the radiation piercing my skeleton from inside the telephone box.

'We'll send the results to your doctor,' Tracey said to Mum when the X-rays were completed.

'How did they look?' Mum asked. 'Are they okay?'

'I don't read the X-rays, madam, I just take them.'

'So you can't tell? You didn't see any . . . any . . . damage?'

'Like I said, I don't know. You'll have the results back in a couple of days.'

Mum sighed, as if she didn't believe Tracey was telling the truth.

On the way back to Emu Street Mum took me to Lee Sam's on the corner and said, 'Choose a lolly, my love.'

I chose teeth. I stuck them in front of my own. Then I smiled up at Mum, pulling at her sleeve. 'Hello, Mum, how are you? Look at my teeth, Mum; Mum, look at my teeth. Hello, Mrs Flick, I would like to talk to you about your son, look at my teeth.' She laughed, then her eyes fill with tears again, then I ate the teeth.

When we got home Mum told me to have a rest in Dad's recliner. I lay against the valley of his legs and his back and his neck and Mum pulled the lever to bring up the footrest. 'You take it easy, Jimmy. I'll bring your manuals.'

I rocked the chair back and forth, back and forth. My chest and arm ached. Soon Mum came in with my manuals. She put them on my lap and then she turned on the heater full blast. 'I'll be back with cheese toasties, love. How would you like that?'

'Cheese toasties? Yes, Mum, yes, I would like that. With pickles, please. With pickles.'

'With pickles coming up, my man. Coming right up.' Mum left the sitting room and went into the kitchen. *Coming right up. Coming right up.* She was trying to pretend that Dad was here, that he still had his job at the refinery, and that he would be home for dinner at six.

I looked through my pile of manuals: vacuum cleaner, hot-water box, radio, hairdryer, toaster. I started with toaster. Electrical energy lived in the wall and entered the toaster through the socket. The more it tried the hotter the loops got. It's friction. Then the friction spread onto the bread turning it to toast.

Soon Mum came in with the cheese toasties. They were in fingers with pickles at the end in a small pile for dipping. I ate the cheese toasties and read my washing-machine manual. It was for Mum's new General Electric. Make sure the tap is tight before turning on the water. Weigh the pipe down in the sink to ensure there is no spillage. On page three there was a diagram of the engine. I couldn't see the back; they needed another picture for that. There were pipes in the engine that carried the water into the tub. The pipes were wrapped in rubber to stop electric shock. I traced over the pipes with my finger. I felt heavy and sore. I went back to page one for the instructions, then back to page three for the diagram. I linked them. The General Electric rumbled from the laundry.

All that day Mum cleaned. She dusted the china horses that reared up on the shelves, and the lady with the long skirt holding the umbrella and standing in flowers with the dog at her feet. She dusted the lamps and she wiped away the ring marks on the table from where Dad's beer bottles missed the coasters. She cleaned away gravy where it had splattered the table leg and she sprayed Zoom on the television and wiped that too. Then she got on her hands and knees and dipped her sponge in the bucket and rubbed at the lamb-chop stains on the carpet. Her bottom wobbled as she scrubbed. *Wobble wobble wobble scrub scrub scrub.* She ran the vacuum cleaner up and down the curtains until the dust even made me sneeze.

Mum was trying to clean away my dad. By nightfall only his shadow was left. She tried to clean that away too, spraying Charlie in the air where it hung. But Dad's shadow couldn't be cleaned away; it hovered over us as we watched the evening news — me in his black chair, Mum in her brown flower one. It hung, wanting us and not wanting us, unable to go, unable to stay, thin as air, passing through every membrane.

The next morning, and the next and the next and the next, I asked her, 'Where's Dad, Mum?'

'I don't know, son. You ask me that like I ate him for dinner,' she answered, her eyes on the screen.

I know she never ate him for dinner, even though he would have fit. It was as if my mum had no stomach, only empty space. If you ever visited you'd have to feel with your hands stretched out as you groped for something solid — it would all be space, the only thing to fill it the sound of her trying to breathe. There was a lot of room for my dad in there.

On the back of the milk carton was a picture of a M-I-S-S-I-N-G P-E-R-S-O-N. Her name was Samantha Billmore and she had metal wires on her teeth that channelled messages from her brain. 'Chew, Samantha, talk, Samantha, smile, Samantha.' Her face tipped when I poured milk on my cornflakes.

'What is a missing person?' I asked Mum as she put away the dries.

'What's that's, love?'

'What is a missing person?'

'Why are you asking me that, Jimmy?'

I pointed at the milk container. 'Is a missing person someone you miss?'

'Please don't talk with your mouth full, Jimmy.' She stopped stacking plates and put Samantha back in the fridge. 'A missing person is someone who has gone missing.'

'Does anybody know where they are?'

'I don't know. Somebody must. Poor girl.'

'So the missing person is not missing from everybody, only from some people?'

Mum put her hands on my shoulders. 'Jimmy, you have to go to school. We don't have time for talking.'

'But, Mum, there are people somewhere who know where the missing person is, aren't there?'

'I suppose there are,' she said, wiping drops of milk from the table around my bowl.

'Maybe if the person lived in a cave with only seals and polar bears and only talked to animals and didn't go onto the roads or into the towns and only drank from a coconut then they would be missing from all people, wouldn't they?'

'I suppose they would,' said Mum, pushing glasses into the cupboard.

'But they wouldn't be missing from the seals then, would they, or the polars?'

'Come on, Jimmy. We have to get ready.' Mum sighed and put the butter into the fridge beside Samantha.

'Is Dad a missing person, Mum?' I asked the back of her.

She stopped, her head still in the fridge. 'No, Jimmy, not in that way, he's not.'

'In what way is he, then?'

'What?'

'In what way is he missing?'

Mum huffed and pulled the hair back from her face. 'Oh, Jimmy . . .' I could see I was making her tired, but I had to know.

'In what way is Dad missing?'

'He's not missing – he's just . . . gone.'

'But, Mum, do you know where he is?'

'No. No, I don't. But if I wanted to I am sure I could find him.'

'You could find him?'

'I don't know . . . I haven't thought about it.'

'Because you don't want to?'

'Because I don't want to – you're right. I thought I explained this to you.'

'Can someone find Samantha Billmore?'

'No, but she is different to your father. She's only a little girl. Jimmy, get up. Come on, that's enough. You have to get ready for school.'

'So nobody in the world can find her?'

'Somebody can. Somebody will. That's why her face is on the milk, Jimmy. Now come on and get dressed.'

Just before we left the house the telephone rang. I picked up the receiver. 'Is your mother there, Jim? It's Dr Eric.'

'Yes, Dr Eric. Yes, she is. My mother is here.'

'Can you put her on?'

'Yes, Dr Eric, I can, I can.'

Mum held out her hand. 'Come on, Jim. Give it to me.'

I passed her the telephone.

'Hello, Dr Eric? Oh that's good news . . . that's a relief . . .' I saw tears entering her eyes. 'No, no, he hasn't come back. Yes . . . yes, I will. Thank you, Dr Eric.' Then she hung up. 'Seems like there's no broken bones, Jimmy.' She sniffed. 'Now let's get you to school.'

Mum walked me to school, leaning on a stick she'd bought at the chemist's. It curled over at one end with five dents for the fingers. She puffed as she walked.

'Enemy territory,' I said when we got to the gates.

'Oh, Jimmy, don't say that. You have to go,' she wheezed. 'Everybody has to go.'

'Enemy territory,' I repeated. I wished I could take her stick with me as a weapon.

'I have to work, Jimmy. I don't always like that very much, but I have to go. Sometimes we have to do things we don't want to. *Please*, Jimmy.'

I looked at Mum's face. It was white and damp with puffed half-moons beneath her eyes. I heard the tentacles waving in her apparatus, trying to clear the particles. She held her stick tight in her hand, knuckles white from the grip. Maybe she was scared that if she let go she would defy gravity and spin off into outer space. I saw my mother's white body in her dress with flowers on the hem, floating through the universe without cables connecting her to a spaceship. She would drift forever, turning round and round in the endless galaxy.

I gave her a quick cuddle. 'Okay, Mum, I don't want to, but I will.' I stepped away from her towards enemy territory.

'Thank you, Jimmy. You are a good boy. I'll make chips tonight and you can watch *Doctor Who*.' She kissed my cheek. 'My good brave boy.' There were tears in her vocals. But why, if I was going to school like she wanted? Why? Tears are from the sea of sadness and you draw them up through osmosis when things happen that you don't want. Your epidermis is born knowing how. It has the capacity, though you can't see it with the naked eye. Where was my capacity?

I walked up the path to school, the gravel crunching beneath my shoes. I didn't turn back to see Mum waving. I knew she was there, but I didn't want to. I took a deep breath and opened the doors to my classroom. There was everybody all as one thing, and then there was me, as another. School reminded me. Where was I from? Why was it this way? Who decided on the way it was?

Mr Napper, my teacher for the year, barely noticed me as I took my seat. He passed over me as if I was invisible. He never directed any question to me, if I needed to run or shout or turn in circles he just sent me out of the room. He never made anyone come and get me. He was letting the year go by. It was as if I walked into Mr Napper's class and was rubbed out like chalk on the board. In the early months I tried to get his attention, but Mr Napper's way of not caring took away my disruptive powers. It could have been his height; he was taller than Robby and could hardly see me. Mr Napper drove a fast white car with a red stripe and no roof. It dipped low at the front. The other kids hung onto the fence and looked at it in the car park and pointed at it and guessed how fast it could go. No one even threw a stone at it. You would have got the stone right into the seat because of the missing roof. Mr Napper would have sat on it when he got in after a long day of not noticing me.

At lunchtime I saw the trees on the other side of the playground and I ran to them. I saw the bikes parked in a row and I ran to them. I saw the gate, I ran to that, I saw the monkey bars and I ran to them. I covered all the straight lines first. When I got to the crossing points between lines I ran faster. The crossing points held powers times two that entered my feet and gave me double speed. After the lines I started circles; first big circles around the whole playground, then small circles, round and round, as small as I could go. Nobody could catch me! *Nobody!* Because I was faster than them all!

Mr Ashworth, the gym teacher whose gym I could never do, grabbed me by the elbows. If he hadn't held tight I would have fallen. The ground tipped and spun. I leaned against him.

'Jimmy, slow down, slow down. What's the hurry?'

I was too dizzy and out of breath to answer. I felt my heart inside me like a living creature. It knocked up against the walls of my bone cage, *bangbang bangbang bangbang*, pounding to escape and have a life of its own where it could eat what it wanted and watch television and read its manuals and not go to school and know where its dad went and how to get him back.

'Jimmy, you'll run out of steam. Have you eaten your lunch?' Mr Ashworth took me to the bench. Soon my breathing began to slow down. 'Okay, son?' Mr Ashworth asked.

I wasn't Mr Ashworth's son but he called me that. He called every boy that. 'I am not your son, Mr Ashworth.'

'I know that, Jim. Have you eaten your lunch? You know you need to eat lunch.'

'No, Mr Ashworth, no, I haven't. It's in my bag. It's in my bag, Mr Ashworth, keeping my pencil case company.'

'How about you go and get your lunch, Jimmy?'

'Yes, Mr Ashworth. Yes, yes, I will. It's ham, Mr Ashworth. It's ham and pickle.'

I sat under the shelter shed and ate my ham and pickle. Mrs Stratham crossed the grounds on yard duty. She looked at me with her black balls for eyes and she saw straight through my skin with her marine ability – all of my days and all the information in one look.

I couldn't swallow. I sat with a lump of ham and pickle obstructing my passage. When Mrs Stratham got to the other side, I spat out the lump, then I ran behind the bins. I stayed there after the bell rang and everyone went back to class; Mr Napper would never notice. They were one thing and I was another. 'Nobody is like you, Jimmy, you are my one and only, the most special boy in the world,' said Mum. I waited for Mrs Stratham to finish yard duty and go back inside. The hardest thing to do without Mum was wait. *Wait wait wait. Wait wait wait. Wait wait wait. Wait wait wait.* When I waited my cells vibrated so fast they reached boiling point. I had to move to cool them down.

I came out from behind the bins and I saw that the schoolyard was empty and that there was room to run. I got going from fence to fence. When I reached the posts I gave them a tap with my hand. Powered by the same force that was held in the crossing points between lines, I was about to go faster than the speed of light. There was visible light, heating houses and turning leaves green and helping the human being to see – and then there was me! Nobody could hold me back, not the fastest and most special boy in the world, Jimmy Flick! I ran so fast – fence to bench to fence to post to toilets to table to fence to bench – that I tore through the barriers of sound and light. My cells split from each other; I had no core, my limbs and fingers and head were blasted into space. I was everywhere, spread thin.

Mr Ashworth came running. He pulled the pieces together, jamming my hands back onto my arms and my feet back onto my ankles. My lungs were in his hands. He held them still so that the air could reach the ventricular. *Tell me what happened, talk to me, explain it, can you tell me, can you say it, how did it happen, Jimmy?*

When I tried to speak all the words wanted to get to the front at the same time, like runners in a race. But for Mr Ashworth, whose son I was not, I tried. 'Mr Ash, Mr Ash –'

'Ashworth,' he interrupted me.

'Ashworth, Ashworth – Mr Ashworth . . .'

'Slow down, Jimmy, take a deep breath and just tell me.'

I did what he said. I sucked oxygen through my mouth and down into my air passage until every cell got a portion. Oxygen was the glue, binding me together.

'That's it, Jimmy. Now what happened?'

'Mr Ash, Ashworth, I ran, I had to run, I had to run. I am very fast very fast, Mr Ashworth, very fast. Very special. I first did straight lines, then circles, very fast circles, Mr Ashworth. I was fast, I hid, I hid and waited. I waited I waited I waited . . .'

'Jimmy, slow down . . .'

Every one of my words had their eye on the finishing line and there was no stopping them now. 'I ran, I hid, I waited I ran, I – I – I – enemy territory, I told my – my mum, I told her, I always tell her. Mr Ash, do you know Samantha Billmore? She is missing. Missing, Mr Ashworth, missing. Can't be found, not by anyone.'

Mr Ashworth shook his head. 'Oh, Jim, what are we going to do with you?'

'How was it, love?' Mum asked me at the gate. 'Jimmy, was school okay?' She ran her hand through my hair.

'Enemy territory,' I told her.

'Oh dear,' she said.

'Oh dear,' I said.

We started to walk.

'Did anything happen?'

Pelicans flew in loops over our heads, and I mirrored them on land. 'Hot chips and *Doctor Whoooooooooooo*!' I shouted as I flew.

That night I woke up and heard Merle Haggard singing 'My Favorite Memory' from the sitting room. Dad was back! He was back! My heart raced. I didn't want to see him straightaway – I just wanted to lie there with my heart racing, knowing he was home. I closed my eyes and made a picture of him in his black recliner; he was wearing his work vest and nodding his head to the music. Bill Philby had given him his job back and the rust was waiting for him. It would never run out, productivity would never be low, the flame from the refinery pipe would never die.

When the song ended I lay in the gap and held my breath, before the next one came. When Merle started to sing 'Love Will Find You' I got out of bed. As I stepped into the hall I heard crying between Merle's words like an instrument he had never played before – one made from water and a pipe.

I went to the sitting room and peered around the doorway. The lamp was on and it wasn't the back of Dad's head in the recliner, it was Mum's, the skin of her wide arms pale against the black leather. Her head was in her hands and she was crying.

I stood in the doorway, squinting, my eyes unused to the light. Where was Dad? I looked around the room but I couldn't see him. I even looked in the places he'd never fit – above the blades of the ceiling fan, under the fringed shade of the lamp, beneath the couch – places I *knew* he'd never be. Mum was the only one in the room and she was crying, her shoulders rocking to Merle's tune.

I blinked and rubbed my eyes. Dad's recliner was using my mother as a transmitter, sending its tears through her and into the atmosphere.

'Mum?' I said.

She turned around to me, her eyes red, her face wet with the tears that had been pushed out of her eye-pipes. 'Jimmy, what are you doing out of bed?' She wiped her sleeve over her face.

'Is Dad coming back, Mum?'

'Oh, Jimmy, Jimmy . . .' She heaved herself out of the chair, sniffing and pulling her blue dressing gown around her tight. 'Come here, love,' she said, turning down Merle.

'Mum, is he?' I asked. 'Is he coming back?

'Oh, love. Your father . . . your father loves you. He couldn't . . . couldn't trust himself. Not after what he did to you.'

'But is he coming home?'

She shook her head. 'No, my love, no. No, he's not. Oh love . . . Your dad . . .' She was fighting the sounds of crying. 'Your dad is . . . he's . . . ashamed. I don't expect anyone to

understand. He loves you, Jimmy. Robby too. He loves you both.'
She took me in her arms and she hugged me so tight that soon
I wasn't on the outside of her blue gown, I was on the inside of
it. I could feel her tears, charged by the power of the recliner,
forcing their way through my pores, stinging as they entered.
The tears travelled my network, searching for a pathway but
were unable to find one. They were trapped in hidden pools
in my system, stagnant.

The next day when we got to the school gates Mum said, 'Okay,
Jimmy, ready to go?'

I looked up at the school. 'Enemy territory,' I said.

Mum frowned. 'Oh, Jimmy, is it really that bad?'

'It's really that bad,' I said. I turned to go but she grabbed
my hand.

'Bugger it,' she said. 'Come on, love.'

'Where are we going, Mum?'

'You can come to work with me,' she said, pulling me
along. 'If Mr Barker makes a fuss I'll tell him to make his own
spotted dick.'

I gave my mum a ten-point smile and we walked away from
enemy territory.

Mum wore her Westlake apron on the bus to save time. 'It's *go
go go* once I get cooking,' she said, tying the strings into a bow.

When we got to Westlake Mum took me out to the courtyard
where seniors sipped tea on chairs made of hard white lace.

'Hello, sweetheart, you're late,' said Gordon, tapping his
watch at Mum. 'I've been waiting with bated breath.' Gordon

was one of the seniors who'd been there the longest. Whenever he saw Mum it crushed his valves so the blood couldn't pump through. If he didn't take medication to keep them open, his brain would starve when she left the building. Gordon ate everything Mum cooked.

'Well you can unbate your breath, Gordon, because I'm here – and so is Jimmy. Keep an eye on him for me while I'm in the kitchen, will you?' she said.

Gordon raised his teacup to me as if it was a beer. I raised my fist back at him as if it was a teacup.

After Mum left I walked up and down the edges of the courtyard, my feet along the gutter. I touched my toes to my heels, keeping my feet in a straight line, up and down, up and down, and not once did I fall. It was better than school.

'Aren't you tired of that, son? You're sending me silly just watching,' Gordon said. 'How many times is that now?'

'Who's counting, Gordon? Who's counting?!' I sang back, putting a hop in my step.

Mum was standing over the big stoves in the dining room, stirring the giant pots, and ladling up the chicken soup when Gordon came up to her. 'Paula, if you weren't taken I swear I'd make you mine.'

Mum's face was pink and shining from the steam. 'Oh, Gordon, I'm too young for you – you'd never keep up.'

'We'll see about that,' said Gordon. 'Susan is driving us to the Point Cook bathhouse in the minibus today. Want to come?'

'I've got Jimmy,' Mum said.

'So? Be good for him too. An adventure.' Gordon winked at me where I sat at the bench finishing my banana custard.

Delia came and stood beside Gordon. 'Come on, Paula, come with us. Do you good.'

'What about the dinner?' said Mum.

'Bugger the dinner,' said Delia. 'There's plenty of time for dinner. Bring the lad. It will be fun.'

'Bugger the dinner, Mum! Bugger the dinner!'

'Now look what you've started,' said Mum. But she was smiling. We were going to the bathhouse.

'Do I have to take a bath?' I asked Gordon, who was sitting in front of us on the minibus.

Gordon turned around to me, his face between the seats. 'You don't have to do anything you don't want to, Jim. That's the only rule I follow.'

'I like that rule, Gordon, I like that rule *a lot*.' I rested back in my seat beside Mum. On one side was the cold of the window, rain dripping down, on the other side my mum leaning against me, warmth flowing through her streams.

Soon Susan stopped the bus outside a grey building with a dome. The seniors took a long time to deport; parts of them were broken. Each time the machine copied itself it made another mistake in the cells.

Mum lent Delia a helping hand as she came down the bus steps. I ran around the bus, touching the lights, touching the bumper, touching the mudguard. 'Look at him go,' said Delia. 'What a rocket.'

Inside the bathhouse people spoke a different language and held branches that they whipped against each other's backs, leaving pink leaf marks. 'Can I have a go, Mum?' I asked her.

'No one's hitting me with any branch,' she said. 'See if Gordon will let you give him a whack.'

'I took enough punishment in two wars for that nonsense,' he said, looking at the branch hitters as if they were enemy soldiers.

Mum and me and the seniors went into the steam room. Everyone else wore towels but Mum and me only took off our shoes. We sat in the steam and Mum leaned back as it rose up around us, hissing and wet. It carried our sweat up the walls and into the pipes and out to sea. The grapes and vines on Mum's dress clung to her legs, arms and chest. I held on to her hand in my shorts and singlet and the two of us joined a dream of heat and steam and water and it was just the rest Mum needed.

Afterwards we sat on long chairs and looked out the windows at the ocean, grey and chopping and deep, made up of all the drips that came down the walls of the steam room. Everything was joined.

Gordon sat on the very end of his chair and rubbed Mum's foot, his back bent, his legs thin with networks of tiny purple veins under the skin like rivers on a map. Mum's breathing, quiet as the air, dissipated by the steam, silently came and went. Mum said, 'Oh Gordon, that feels lovely,' and I got started on her other foot.

Gordon said, 'She deserves this, your mum. She works too hard.'

'You're right there, Gordon, I do work too hard. Maybe it's time I made a change,' said Mum.

'Make it with me, sweetheart.' Gordon's hands rubbed higher up Mum's leg. 'Make it with me.'

'Oh, Gordon! That's not what I meant.' Mum pushed his hand away.

'What did you mean, Mum? What change?' I asked.

'Oh nothing – nothing, for heaven's sake. Can't a woman say anything these days!'

Gordon winked at me and we kept rubbing.

On the way home Mum and me got off the bus at the shops. Mum bought cheese, lemon sponge, apple crumble, Monte Carlos, frankfurts, mayonnaise, ice cream, frozen potato puffs, peas, chops, caramel sauce, toffee squares and milk. When we got back to Nineteen Emu she said, 'Ooh, Jimmy, that steam wore me out,' and I helped her unpack the goods. She made a cup of tea for herself and poured me a glass of milk.

'Will Dr Eric get a letter from the school?' I asked her.

'Don't worry about that, Jimmy. You just enjoy yourself,' she answered, cutting two squares of crumble. 'I'll take care of any letters.' She picked up Agatha's *Winter Killing* and went into the sitting room and I followed with my manuals. Soon she was asleep.

I sat on the floor reading the vacuum instruction booklet. The vacuum was old and hardly sucked. Mum had to go over and over the same dust. The booklet was dirty at the edges with my fingerprints. It was important to clean the nozzle, not to forget about it, year after year. The dust hardened and blocked the exits. I got up and walked down to Dad's shed. The door was locked; only Mum had a key. I poked a stick into the lock but it broke, leaving half of the stick still stuck in the lock. I dug that half out with another stick then I went up to the house and got Mum's keys out of her handbag.

I tried all the keys until I got to the last one and I stuck it into the lock and it opened the door. I stepped inside the shed and Dad's remaining particles flooded my system. I closed my eyes and for a moment he was with me – his hands and his arms and his smile on Uncle Rodney's waves, the drawings across his back and chest, the scar on his arm – then I opened my eyes and let out my air and he was still missing.

I ran my hand over his things – his fridge with the stickers, his weekend bed and his tools – feeling the surfaces and the temperatures. They were all cold. I knocked my hand against the dusty glass of the window I had looked through so many times from the yard. Now I was on the inside. I picked up a paint can and shook it to listen for the paint, but the can was empty, or the paint had dried. I did the same with the jerry can, also empty. I opened the fridge – there was nothing in it, but I kept looking anyway, at the light and the silver bars. I traced my finger around the tools on the wall, following the line of my dad's drawings. I found a pen and I drew tools that nobody had invented before. I could have helped Dad fix the Holden with my screwner. He would have asked to use my hamm driver, I could have said, 'No, Dad, what you need is the spiver.'

In the corner of the shed was a clean empty space. Dad liked things tidy and put away. I looked at the tidy space and I saw the new bike that Dad had bought for me. It had a red flag on a stick that bended. When you rode very fast the flag vibrated. I wheeled my new invisible bike out of the shed and through the back gate. I was on the street. I climbed on the bike, wobbling at first, but because my bike had super powers I didn't need anyone holding the bike straight and I didn't tip.

I got going, pushing down on the pedals so hard my leg straps burned. I was pedalling, faster and faster, wind whistling in my ears, my flag vibrating. I was beating the cars. I leaned forward and opened my mouth and the wind dried my spit. I rode down the hill and around the block and past the house and around again. Soon I was transparent and there was no sound when the wind passed through me because I had no substance. I was no longer an obstacle. I was unbeatable. Thank you, Dad, thank you.

'What on earth?' Mum stood at the shed door. 'Jimmy, how did you get in here?' She was planted feet apart with her hands on her hips, and her face was flushed; there was no smile or softness. She was puffing. 'What the hell are you doing running round like an idiot in here?' She spoke as if she was taking over from Dad. 'Did you get my keys from my handbag?' She pulled the keys out of the lock. 'Bloody hell, Jimmy. You know you're not allowed in here! Get out!'

I raced past her and into the house and into Robby's room and I sat in his cupboard looking at his shoes, channelling messages through the laces. *Robby, have you caught enough fish yet? Can you come home? I don't know where Dad is, Robby.* It was the first time Mum let me stay there without coming and checking.

I stayed and stayed and stayed and Robby's cupboard grew darker and darker. In the end I came out myself. I didn't want to, I wanted her to come and get me but she never did. I went into the kitchen and found her boiling frankfurts. She hardly talked. When it was time for dinner she only ate her frankfurts, she didn't ask me any questions or tell me any news. And then after, her head was hung in her hands and her eyes were down and she didn't even look at me.

I woke up in the middle of the night caught in a black circle box. Everything had stopped. There was no next thing, but I was still alive inside the circle box. It held me tightly inside itself. Even if I exploded, my cells were trapped within the walls of the box. There was no escape. I couldn't move. *Mum! Mum! Mum!* I called but she couldn't hear me. Nobody could. I was nothing. I had living organs that beat and pumped and pushed but at the same time I was soundless and nothing. *Mum! Mum! Mum!*

Nobody came. I wasn't joined to the human race by sound or vision. 'Mum! Mum!' Time kept passing. I saw more and more of it in front of me, like a trap that didn't end. 'Mum! Mum!'

'Jimmy, Jimmy! It's Mum, it's Mum. Everything's going to be alright, Jimmy, Mum's here.' She took my bones, and the skin over my bones, and my trembling guts that the skin held inside, and she gathered it all up in the fat of her arms and pressed it close to her so I could I feel her heart beating its message to me from under her nightdress. *JimmyJimmy, JimmyJimmy, JimmyJimmy.* My mother penetrated the walls of the circle box that trapped me. In all of the world, she was the only person who could.

I had a wet face, wet sheets and wet legs.

'Oh, my boy,' she cried. 'Oh Jimmy, love, my little boy, I'm sorry, my special one, forgive Mum, please forgive me, I am sorry.'

Her tears added to my wetness. We made a pool.

'Jimmy, you need dry clothes, love. Come on.' She found clean pyjama pants in the cupboard, then she took me into the bathroom and tried to peel off my pyjama pants. I held the wet band in my fingers and pulled the pants back against me. 'No, Mum, no, no . . .'

'Come on, love. We'll be quick.'

'No, no . . .'

'It'll be over in one, two, three. Come on, love.'

I let her take off my pants. I didn't want to, but I did.

She took me to her bedroom, and into her bed. It enveloped me, as soft as clouds. I smelled Charlie on her pillowcase. My tubes and intestines and apparatus were pressed against her wide soft body. The blankets over us made a warm room with all extra space filled by my mum and by me.

I was in the place of my father. It was his side in the bed, but I only took up the room of one of his legs. Mum had the night lamp on beside her. I saw the spines of her Agathas lined up one on top of the other: *The ABC Murders*, *And Then There Were None*, *Death at Midnight* — all in a pile beside a box of white tissues, her Charlie bottle, her Intensive Care, her pink nail polish, a glass of water, her pearl necklace, her jubes.

I half closed my eyes until the water mixed with the polish and the Intensive Care made a puddle and tissues and crimes and blood and Charlie all mixed in together and shimmered. Mum switched off the lamp and pulled the blankets up to our chins. But I didn't want her to fall asleep without me. 'Mum, Mum, I can't sleep.'

'Yes you can, my love. Count sheep, Jimmy, count sheep,' she said into the back of my hair, her arm around my middle.

I closed my eyes and saw sheep crossing a small river. Some put their little tongues into the water, folding them up at the sides to make a funnel so they could drink. There were lambs and strong men sheep in a family. They stepped through the river, across stones. The water ran up over their knees. The men sheep helped the lambs and showed them where it wasn't too deep. They said, 'Cross over here, lambs, it's safer.' But the lambs didn't listen; they kept playing as the water rose higher. The mother lamb told them to hurry and cross because a wave was coming. 'Quick, quick, little lambs!' she said. She had seen the wave with the light in her eye and she knew how big and fast it was. 'Quick lambs! Quick, my little babies!' The lambs began to cross the stones but the water was flowing fast and the lambs weren't used to walking – they'd only been born a few days before – and the stones were unsteady and sharp. The lambs slipped and water flooded over the tops of their woollen coats. It didn't matter that the mother sheep and the men sheep stood on the banks calling, calling, the lambs were swept away by the wave.

'Mum! Mum! Help! Help!'

'Hush, Jimmy, hush. Big breath in and count with Mum. One . . . two . . . three . . . count with me, Jimmy . . . four . . . five . . . six, that's it – good boy . . .'

'Seven . . . eight . . . nine.'

'That's it – good boy.'

The next night Mum said, 'How about you sleep in my bed tonight, Jimmy.'

'Yes, Mum, yes!' I said. 'Your bed!' and went into her room. I got into her bed and the shape of me changed the shape of my dad in the mattress, as if I had always been sleeping there. My knee made a dip across where his back had been; my arm made a dent where his shoulder had lain. My head made a new valley in the pillow.

Before it was time for the light to go out Mum read her book and I read my manuals beside her. I examined diagrams of light bulbs and mower engines and sink pipes. When my eyes were tired I asked Mum to read for me. 'Please, Mum,' I begged.

'You can read to yourself, Jimmy. Let me read my own book.'

'But, Mum, you can read your own book out to me; that way you will still know what is happening and you will be reading to me at the same time, Mum. At the same time, Mum. Mum, your own book, Mum –'

'Settle down, Jimmy. Don't get yourself excited. Alright, I'll read to you.'

'But *your* book, Mum, *your* book.'

'Yes, my book, my book, alright. Shhhh. Settle down.

'And the car drove the roads at top speed. Whenever Jimmy changed gears the car got faster. He was a racer. A champion racer . . . Then he went home and baked himself a pie with apples and he took the cream from the fridge and he put some of the cream on the pie –'

'Not a made-up book, Mum, not a made-up book! Your book, *your* book. Your book, Mum!'

'Jimmy, shhh. You should be asleep. It's late.'

'I will settle down, Mum, I will settle down – but, Mum, only if – only if you read your book, *your* book!'

'Alright, alright. But don't blame me if you get nightmares.'

'Read, Mum!'

Mum began to read. '*. . . The earth was packed tight and dry and it was long work. After a couple of hours he decided the hole was big enough. He took the corpse from the back of the truck, unwrapped it from its now damp and bloody sacking, and placed it in the hole . . .*'

The tentacles waved slowly between her words as they blew away the dust and particles and hairs. I drifted. The ripples of her voice ran over me, bobbing me up and down, up and down.

When it was time to turn off the light Mum kissed me on the cheek. 'Good night, my little man,' she whispered. 'I love you.'

Charlie sent a message to me through my nasal – *Your father is never coming back.*

When I went into the kitchen the next morning I saw the back of Mum at the sink. Her apron with corns and tomatoes and onions in a row was tied around her middle. She was doing the dishes and she was crying. Tears dripped into the sink. When she dunked in her hands to scrub a dish, tears and dishwater spilled over the sides and dripped onto her slippers.

'Mum, what is it, what is it, Mum? Are you alright? Mum?'

She turned around, taking my shoulders in her hands, looking down into my eyes, her face white and scared. 'Oh, Jimmy, what will become of you if something happens to me?'

What did she mean? What is become? What will I become? What has to happen to my mother for me to become it?

She hugged me hard, pulling my questions into a tight bundle. 'Don't listen to me, love. Don't listen to me.'

I didn't know what I would become, but I knew I didn't want to become it without her.

She stood up, blinking away her tears. 'Jimmy, why don't we have a stay-at-home day, just you and me? We could watch a midday movie and if it gets sunny we could make a bed in the yard and have a rest out there. We could read our books. What do you say, my boy?'

'No school?' I asked her. 'No school again, Mum?'

'No school, Jimmy. That's right. How about it, hey?'

'Yes, Mum! Yes, Mum! Yes, Mum!' I ran around the kitchen, knocking over a chair. No school!

Mum sniffed and smiled as she picked up the chair. 'You're a funny one.' She took me in her arms as I ran past. Her hands, soaked with dishwater, wrapped around me. I smelled Sunlight Lemon Liquid. She pressed me against her bosom, squashing my ear back as she held me. With my unsquashed ear, I heard messages from her body's wires. *Your father is missing. It's just me now, little man. Please God don't let anything happen to me!*

I couldn't breathe. I was caught in her heat as it came up from under her dress and the pits of her arms and the fat of her chin. I was very small, all bones. The closer she hugged me the smaller I became until I was an insect like a flea or a termite that could hardly help her.

'Mum,' I said. It came out muffled. 'Mum!'

She set me back. 'My boy, what would I do without you?'

What would she do without me? What would she do? Where was Robby? How far out to sea? When would it be time for him to come home?

Day after day after day it was just the two of us – Mum lying across the blue kitchen couch, reading and sleeping, and sometimes making us chips and frankfurts.

'What about Westlake, Mum?' I asked her. 'What about Mr Barker and the seniors?'

'Don't you worry about Westlake, Jimmy. We're fine. I've got my savings. And your father left us with money. It's high time I had a break, so don't you worry about a thing.' She took another bite of her cheesecake and lay back against the couch.

The more she rested the less she walked. Her stick leaned against the wall by the front door unused; the five finger dents in the handle stayed empty. One morning she said, 'Love, do you think you can go and get your mother some milk from the shop? Do you think you can do that without getting into any trouble? I'm a bit tired for a walk today.'

'Yes, Mum, yes, I can do that! I can do that!' I ran around the room. 'Wheeeeeeeeeee!'

'Don't talk to anyone on the way, love,' she said, transmitting messages of urgency. 'We're alright on our own, you and me, aren't we?' Her face was a pale and shining flower, her breathing loud. 'Give me a kiss before you go, love, and remember, don't talk to anyone. You just go and come back, alright? No stopping or detours.'

'Yes, Mum! Yes! Yes! Yes! No detours and no stopping!' I did three laps around the kitchen, with a detour to the socks and a detour to the shoes. I was warming up for the journey.

'You can pick up some biscuits, too, okay?' Mum said, passing me my coat.

'What bikkies, Mum? What bikkies?'

'I don't know. Your choice, my boy.'

'Creamy centres, Mum? Jammy fingers? What about jammy fingers? Buttermilks? Cat heads? Cow chips? Lemon tuties? Mum, you like them, Mum, you like lemon tuties, or fruit pillows. Mum, fruit pillows so you can eat and sleep, ha ha!'

'You funny boy.' Mum smiled. 'Whichever bikkies you want, okay? Come here and give me a kiss and hurry back, my funny boy.' She leaned close and rubbed her hand over my head – I heard the rustle of wings. The moths that used to fly around the globe above Dad's shed door had found a new place to cluster since he'd left. I could hear their wings brushing the sides of Mum's tunnels, leaving dust around her valves.

'Pass me my purse, will you, Jimmy?' she said. She moved slowly, as if her own body was too big for her and the blood had too far to travel, the journey was too long and where would it find the strength?

I passed Mum her purse so she could stay sitting and she pulled out a fiver. 'Thanks, Jimmy.'

The telephone rang. 'Can I get that, Mum? Can I get that?' I raced for the telephone.

'Leave it, Jimmy, please. Just leave it.'

'But what if it's Dad? What if it's Robby? Robby or Dad? Robby or Dad, Mum!'

'Jimmy, it's the middle of the working day – it won't be Robby. And it isn't your father. It won't be anyone. Just a wrong number. You pop to the shops and pick up the goodies for your old mum, there's a good boy. Forget about the telephone.'

'Yes, Mum, alright, Mum,' I said. 'Goodies for my old mum. Forget about the telephone. Forget about Dad.'

'Off you go.' Mum nodded towards the door. 'The sooner you go the sooner you're back.'

I opened the front door and stepped onto Emu Street. I'd done the walk to the shops with Mum a million times but this was my first solo journey.

I kept my nose down and my eye on the line that joined cracks and bricks and fence posts. I followed it along the road as it wrapped its way around every stone and piece of gravel. If you followed that line you would get to the Indian where Robby was and if you kept following it further you could cross the sea and arrive on the edge of Broken Island where the waves carried the memory.

The street was very quiet. I didn't see anyone – nobody driving cars or running with dogs, no postmen or seniors pushing trolleys or mothers pushing prams or boys on bikes. I looked up into the sky and squinted. I saw a spaceship disguised as a cloud. There had been an explosion. The spaceship had dropped a toxic bomb. It fell slowly to its target, the earth, and when it hit it destroyed every living thing, including Mrs Stratham. Only Mum and me survived. There was no school anymore, no Dr Eric, no refinery, no Dad, no Broken Island. All gone. Just Mum and me and the corner shop.

I followed the line, chanting, *'Bikkies and milk, bikkies and milk, bikkies and milk!'* in time to my walking feet.

'Anything else?' Mr Lee Sam asked as I put the milk on the counter. Samantha Billmore's face smiled from the carton, the wire across her teeth like a fence in miniature. Mr Lee Sam narrowed his eyes. 'Well?'

'Biscuits,' I said.

Mr Lee Sam turned around to the shelf behind him. 'Which ones?' he asked me over his shoulder.

I looked up and down the shelf at Mum's favourites: angels, easy teas and cow chips. I stopped when I got to jam supremes. Mum never chose jam supremes. 'Supremes!' I said to Mr Lee Sam. 'Supreme surprise for my mum!'

'Okay,' he said, reaching for the packet. 'That's it?'

'That's it!' I copied. 'That's it.'

'Four dollars twenty, kid.'

'Four dollars twenty, kid,' I repeated, passing him the fiver.

He put the biscuits and the milk in a plastic bag and handed them over to me.

I walked out, the bag knocking against my legs. Back out on the street there still wasn't anyone around. My heart, the most vital of organs, pumped harder as I began to walk faster. The bomb that the spaceship had dropped leaked a poison into the atmosphere so I had to hold my breath. I couldn't follow the line to see if it joined on the way home as well as the way here.

Everything was still except me; I was the only fast and living thing. Everything else was the dead enemy — I had to make it home to my mother the mountain.

I don't know how but I took a wrong street, an alien street I had never seen before. Where had the street come from? Who put it there? I stopped still in the middle of it. I thought it was going to be Emu, I thought it was going to be our house at one end but it wasn't. I didn't recognise any of the houses or cars or plants or light posts. I was lost. I saw a curtain move behind a window; I was being watched. People with binoculars peered out at me, examining my moves. I spun in a circle, looking down both ends. My vision was shaky. I was going too fast. My hands bounced before me, I couldn't slow down. The air was all in my top half and filling up higher. The bottom half was vacated.

A boy rode past on a bicycle. 'Watch out, idiot! Get off the road!' he shouted.

Road? Was I on the road? When had I gone on the road?

I began to run, there was no time now for counting cracks or bricks or lines. I heard something drop. I turned and saw milk spilling across the road from Samantha Billmore's head. I ran faster. I couldn't see one thing that I had ever seen before. The bomb kept ticking. I turned and ran back. If I found the shop Mr Lee Sam would be there — he would know the way home.

But when I got to the end of the street there was no shop. The shop was missing, melted away with the toxic acid.

'Ah ah ah ah ah ah ah ah!' My blood moved around me too fast, too fast! 'Ah ah ah ah ah ah!' I was going to explode! 'Ah ah ah ah ah ah!' I was losing vision, my realities were blurring. 'Ah ah ah ah!' Then the bomb exploded, sending me spinning across the earth, my legs rotating faster and faster until there it was! There it was at last! The house with the brown roof, the slit instead of the box, the cracked driveway of Emu Street! Home!

I ran through the door. Where was crying to release me?

'Mum! Mum!' I called. 'Mum!' I ran panting and pounding down the hall into the kitchen – oven, sink, cupboard, fridge, table, bench, curtains, but no mother.

'Mum! Mum!' Where was she? Bedroom one, sewing room, bathroom, bedroom two and there she was, the white land of her spilling from her violet corner chair, eyes closed, her skirt pulled up and showing her legs, calves dotted with a thousand holes, the ends of tiny pipes in a pattern, all leading down to her network. *'Mum! Mum!'*

Her eyes opened. 'Jimmy,' she said, in a half-whisper.

I threw myself against her and felt her body, warm as a day on the beach.

'Careful, love. Your mum's a bit tired.' She moved me back and tried to sit up straight in her chair. The telephone rang from the kitchen. Mum shook her head. 'No, Jimmy, just leave it.' Her voice was full with wing dust, as if the moths were taking over and speaking through her. *Let us out.*

'Puffer, Mum?' I asked, going to her dressing table and picking up the puffer. 'It's a full one, Mum. Do you want it?'

'It's okay, love, got one here.' She tapped the drawer of her side table.

'Suck it, Mum,' I told her.

'Thank you, Dr Eric,' she said. 'But I know when to use the stupid thing.' She sat up and looked at me. 'What's wrong, Jimmy? Why are you out of breath? How were the shops?'

'Shops were good, Mum.'

'How long have you been back?' she asked, checking her watch.

'I've been back ages, Mum! Running around the yard warming up. Warming up and out of breath.'

'Did you talk to anyone on the way?'

'No one, Mum.'

'Oh good, now I can make myself a cup of tea.' She put her hand over her mouth and coughed – the moths were multiplying. 'I can't believe I fell asleep. I just popped in here for a quick sit-down. I was waiting for you to come back. I was worried . . .'

'Only one problem, Mum.'

'What's that, Jimmy?' she asked.

'No milk, Mum. No milk for your tea.'

'But you just went to the shops! What do you mean no milk?' Her face fell. 'What did you do with the money?'

'I did have milk, Mum. I did have. When I left the shop. Mr Lee Sam gave me milk and jam supremes, but Mum! Mum!'

'Yes, Jimmy, what? What? Where's the milk?'

I opened my mouth in case there was a stray word for me to say, but none came.

'Oh God, Jimmy,' she sighed. 'I'd kill for that cup of tea!' She shook her head. 'What happened to the money?'

Mum, Mum, I gulped like a fish.

'Well something must have happened to it, or you can give the money back to me.'

I reached into my pocket. 'Change, Mum! Change! See! I *had* the milk. I did have it, Mum!'

She huffed loud and breathy. 'Well that's great, love, I'm happy for you, but there's no milk now.'

I looked at the floor. My first solo journey and no milk.

She patted my head. 'Oh well, love, that's alright. I'm glad

you're home safe.' She came close. 'Just have to be powdered.'
She coughed again.

I took her hand and led her to the kitchen for tea with instant.

We were two when there used to be four. We were in half and
the house was changing. There were little red splats of food up
the walls, baked beans hid in the corners, porridge hardened
in the cracks, the cups grew rings inside. I counted them to see
how many days since Dad left but each time I finished counting
more rings came up from the bottom.

After the big clean Mum didn't clean again. She ran her
cloth over the top without rubbing. The dust left behind by the
moths in Mum's tubes piled up around the house. She coughed
it onto the statues and photo frames, the chairs and books
and lamps and shoes. It made a bed for mites and other living
things naked to the invisible eye. The vacuum cleaner leaned
against the wall, mouth closed, network empty. The crumbs of
lemon softies and fruit pillows and cow chips gathered in the
slits of chairs and couches. They cuddled Mum's stray hairs
and reproduced.

Mum let me wear the same thing every day. She said, 'We've
stayed indoors, love; no mud, no wash.' How many days in my
green stripes, my tractor socks, my red skivvy? She read and
read. She let me lie and trace. I kept my eye on the line between
objects. When the telephone rang Mum said, 'Oh leave it,' and
sometimes I heard her crying. Then the crying would stop, then
start again, then it would become the song of Doris. *Oh distant
man, Beyond the clouds, Rest your cheek by mine, Dance to me through the falling
rain, And be my love in time.* Then it would turn into crying again.

The supermarket delivered. Mum opened cans and tipped beans and spaghetti and peas into pots, then she flicked on the heat and said, 'Presto, there's dinner!' We ate with our feet up in front of the television; me on the recliner, Mum in the brown flower. News, police shows, murders, investigation and crimes. Every two days came another bottle of milk and there was Samantha Billmore, still missing.

Every day I was getting faster. Mum knew, didn't she?

'At last, no school. Isn't that what you've always wanted, Jimmy?' she asked. 'Can't you find a smile for your old mother today?'

I couldn't find one. Dirty towels and underpants and dresses and trousers and singlets spilled out of the laundry and piled up around the house – maybe my smile was under one of the piles.

One night I heard Mum talking to Robby on the telephone. 'No, Rob, love, we're fine. They changed the medication . . . Oh, it's getting better all the time . . . Yes, well, you'll be able to save a bit that way . . . Oh, he's the same, a bundle of trouble, keeping me busy . . . Oh, that's nice . . . Yes, he's well too . . .'

He's well too? Wasn't that Dad? She didn't mean me; I was the bundle of trouble. She meant Dad and she said he was fine, but how did she know he was fine when he wasn't here? Why was she telling Robby he was fine? Didn't she want Robby to know that Dad was gone?

'Yes, love . . . You just get on with the job . . .' She laughed. 'Yes, love. Oh no, never been better – Dr Eric is making sure of it. Goodbye, Robby.' She hung up the telephone. 'I love you,' she said, as if Robby was still there.

I walked into the kitchen. 'Why did you say Dad was fine, Mum?'

Mum swung around. 'What?'

'Why did you say Dad was fine when he isn't here and we don't know how he is? We don't know if he's fine or not. He could be fine, but where is the evidence? Why did you say that to Robby, that Dad was fine?'

'Oh God, Jim, I didn't say anything about Dad,' she said, sounding cross.

'You did. You said he was fine, but Dad's gone so how would you know if he was fine? How would you know, Mum? How, when he isn't here and you never answer the telephone?'

'He is gone, Jimmy. He is gone.'

'Then how would you know? How would you know?'

'He is gone! He is bloody gone!' she shouted.

'But Mum, how –?'

'Oh, for God's sake, your father is gone! He's gone!' She fell to her knees – the mass of her before me, crying. The air grew damp with her sobs. The crumbs and the dust and the mites and me couldn't escape her crying. It enveloped us. There was nothing I could do.

She stopped and looked up at me. 'Oh, little Jimmy, my little Jimmy,' she said. 'I'm sorry, my love.' The skin of her face was in patches of red and white. Wing dust sprayed from her nose and mouth in tiny dots.

'Help me, love,' she said, reaching for me. 'Oh, Jimmy,' she said, leaning on me as she pulled herself up. 'What would I do without my Jimmy?'

'I don't know, Mum, what would you do? What would you do without your Jimmy?'

We walked, slow and wheezing, to her room.

'Just a little rest,' she said. 'Then I'll be up to get your tea ready . . .'

Her hand in mine was cold. She got on her bed and I pulled the covers over her legs. 'Puffer, Mum?' I said.

'No love, no puffer. Just open the window a little. I won't be long . . . just a bit of a rest . . .' She closed her eyes.

I opened the window then I went back to her and stood by the bed. Every breath she took in she coughed when she got to the top. I put my ear to her chest and listened to the moths fluttering against her passages. Her eyes stayed closed. I kept watching, as if somebody had said, *Don't leave, Jimmy. Stay and keep watching.* Soon I saw a light around the room, like a halo. It circled the walls. Mum kept breathing, her chest rising and falling, the ins quicker than the outs. The light hovered over her, thickest at the head. Outside the sky was grey without sun.

Mum's eyes opened. For a moment she looked at me as if she didn't know me. Then the knowing came back, shining specks of it in her visions, and she said, 'Go into the kitchen, Jimmy. Leave Mum for a bit. Go and get yourself something to eat.'

I went into the sitting room and turned on the television and it gave the house some friends. I took a bag of chicken chips from the cupboard. I sat on the floor in front of the television and ate so many chips my mouth burned. Then I went back into Mum's room.

Her head was back, but the breath wasn't going in. She was covered in water.

'Mum! Mum!' I called.

Her eyes opened to narrow passes. I couldn't see the light. I pressed my fingers to the rims.

'Mum! Mum!' I called again. She pulled back from me, shaking her head, gulping at the air. Her mouth was wide open but the passage was blocked as the moths flocked to the entrance.

'Mum! Mum!' I shouted.

She grabbed at my clothes, trying to speak, making the sounds of a donkey calling and calling, her face white, eyes frightened, her body wanting the air, longing for it, needing it. Seconds were passing. There was nothing I could do but be her little man, watching as she tried and tried. Then she closed her eyes, and her body, so big and wide, arched like a bridge. Hard and stiff, her head went back and her eyes opened again but this time there was no light and no eye, only whites. Her eyes had rolled over to the other side, looking for a way to let in the air, searching for what was blocking the opening, then seeing the moths, thousands, swirling in clouds, wings beating as they struggled for space. Then her body dropped, slumped into the bed, soft and spent, her eyes closed, then it arched again, the eyes opened, and she made the sound of the donkey once more as it was squeezed and squeezed.

I called for her over and over. 'Mum! Mum!' but there was nothing I could do. Nothing I knew to do.

She arched her back one more time, her mouth opened wider than it ever had before, so wide I thought it would tear her face in two.

'Mum! Mum! No! No!'

Out rushed the moths, up in swirls. Clouds of moths flew over her, their wings beating them upwards from her mouth, each with a tiny eye in the centre of its wing, shining with light. I stood back as the room filled with light from the eyes in the moths' wings, then they flew towards the window, bunching at its open space, before flying out into the sky. They were gone. The room was empty.

'Mum, Mum!' I said, 'It's alright now, it's alright! They're gone!'

She didn't wake up.

'Mum, Mum! You can wake up now, they're gone, they're

gone!' I pushed her shoulder. 'Mum, Mum, you can wake up now,' I said. 'You can wake up!' She didn't move.

I climbed onto the bed and pressed myself to her, as I had pressed myself since I was a baby, to feel her, the land that was mine, but it was still. I held on as if by holding I could suck the life up from the earth's network and give it to her. I held on, myself growing damp as she was, mixing with the wetness of her, as if it could make us one person and not two – not two.

I held on as the light in the room faded to darkness, and then I closed my eyes and kept them closed as if I could become a dream and in the dream there she would be and there I would be. It wouldn't be earth, it would be another place, somewhere we'd never been before. It would be a story without pages or pictures and it wouldn't end, it wouldn't be over. I woke up, feeling her cold against me. I could feel crying in my cogs but it was caught, trapped. I couldn't let it go; the force would destroy me.

When I next opened my eyes I watched the room turn from grey to pink to yellow to grey again. Night came and went, mixing with day until there was no difference. I pulled Mum's blankets over me and lay close to her. I let myself slide back to where the sheep's light began, where it was always shining. I heard the telephone ring. 'Leave it, love, it won't be anyone. Wrong number.' I watched the light change again; pale orange, black, yellow. I was slowing down, setting myself to the clock of Mum. When I breathed I only took in the tiniest puffs, just enough for the smallest rise and the smallest fall. With each breath I took in less. The telephone rang and rang. 'Oh, just leave it, Jimmy, we've got each other, we're alright on our own, aren't we, love?'

I rubbed my hand up and down her arm as if I could transmit life through my cells into hers, over the elbow, up to the shoulder and down again, her skin hard and cold beneath my fingers. 'Pop down the shops, love, be a good boy.'

'Yes, Mum, yes. For jam supremes, Mum. Supreme surprise.'

'Funny boy. Don't be long, love. I'll miss you.'

'No, Mum, I won't be long.'

'We're alright, you and me, just the two of us, hey?'

'Yes, Mum, just the two of us. Milk for your tea? Milk for your tea?'

'My good boy, my little man, I'll miss you, little man.'

'I won't be long, Mum. I won't be long!'

'I know you won't be long, my love. I know.'

'You know, don't you, Mum?'

'I do, Jimmy.'

'Good, Mum. Good.'

'I love you, Jimmy.'

'I love you, Mum.'

I never went to the toilet; I don't know what came out of me or where it went. I never left her side at all.

I heard knocking on the door: *knock knock knock. Knock knock knock.* I tried to push in underneath her while I waited for the knocking to stop but she was stiff and heavy. At last the knocking ended and it was just the two of us again.

Sometimes I got out of the bed and went to her bathroom where I drank from the tap, putting my face close to the spout, holding out my tongue like the lambs, feeling the cool and living water entering my parched tubes. Then I went back to the bed and climbed in under the blanket. I held on as the land of her turned to winter.

Part Four

'Wake up, Jim, wake up!'

Men lifted me into the air. I looked for my mother in the bed but she was gone. I saw the shape where she had been; the full round valley, the low dips and gentle rises. I opened my mouth to call for her but I couldn't make any sound. I turned in time to see men carrying a narrow bed through the door with a body beneath a sheet. I tried to follow but it was too late.

'Haven't you been able to contact anybody? What about the father?'

'We're trying. Apparently he left a couple of months ago.'

'Keep looking. And didn't the neighbour say there was a brother?'

'Yes, and she also said he was off the coast of Kalbarri somewhere on a fishing boat.'

'That's just great. There's an uncle too. Up north. Has anyone tried him?'

'We're trying.'

When I opened my eyes I saw that I was in a bed with a policeman standing on either side. Their words floated over my feet.

I closed my eyes and rolled them back so I could look inside. I saw the skin sac that enclosed my network, but the network itself was gone. There was only empty space; I couldn't see the boundaries.

A man stood beside the bed. He said, 'Jim, are you awake? Can you hear me?' The man's voice was warm, like a small fire of twigs and coal. 'Jim? Can you hear me?' I opened my eyes. I was in a bright white room with a row of beds. Above every bed was a window. I tried to swallow but my throat felt dry. The man passed me a glass of water and I took a small sip.

'Do you think he might be ready for something to eat?' A woman in a white dress put a tray with egg and baked beans and a glass of milk and peaches in syrup beside the bed.

'We'll see how we go,' said the man. He looked down at a notepad in his hands. 'Your name's Jim, right? Jim Flick?'

I nodded.

'I'm Andrew,' he said. 'I'm here to help you.'

I listened to him, but it was as if he was talking about somebody else. Here to help who?

'Jim, do you know what happened to you?'

What happened to me? What did he mean? I opened my mouth to ask but I was prevented; something was blocked.

'Jim, you've been through a tough time. The good news is your uncle is coming down to get you. Rodney – you remember him, don't you? Rodney?'

I nodded. Rodney was from another time.

Andrew put his hand on my arm. 'I am sorry about your mother, Jim.'

Sorry? What did he do?

Andrew stood up. 'You don't know where your father is, do you, Jim? We don't know where to look.'

The smell here was like Blitz floor cleaner. I looked at the tray of food and I didn't want any of it. I lay back, the pillow cool beneath my head. I was on my own; Andrew must have left.

'We need the bed, Andrew. There's no reason for him to stay. When's the uncle due?'

'Any minute.'

'You better be right. He needs to be out of here by the end of the day.'

'He still hasn't spoken.'

'There's nothing wrong with him.'

'He's in shock.'

'We can't let him have a bed. There has to be someone or he goes into state care – but not this part of state care.'

'Just until the end of the day.'

'I'll be back at five. Then that's it.'

'Okay.'

'What's his name – have you figured that much out?'

'Jim. Jim Flick.'

I rolled back my eyes and watched as the empty space where my network should have been began to fill with rusted engines and wheels and belts and fans and glass and gearshifts and exhaust pipes and radiators and Coke cans and old tyres. I was being stretched.

'Well, Andrew?'

'Please, just one more night. The uncle called, he'll be here at nine am. He couldn't get a flight any earlier.'

'The boy can't stay. There are children who need the beds. If there's something wrong he needs to be in a psychiatric ward.'

'No, he doesn't need that. He's just lost his mother. He was in the room with her for four days.'

'These beds are for sick children.'

'Okay, okay. I'll take care of it.

'Now, please.'

'Okay.'

Andrew helped me out of the bed, his hands against my back. I could feel the warmth between us but it was only happening to my outer casing. I was external to myself, watching from a new land. The police had taken my words at the entrance, locking them in a box and storing them in alphabetical order alongside the other mutes'.

'Come on, mate, we need to get you out of here.'

My legs shook as Andrew took my hand and led me out of the hospital.

'How long since you saw your uncle?' Andrew asked as we drove.

I looked for the line between shops and gutters and lampposts and buses and bins but it had disappeared.

'Can you remember when?'

The road was crowded with cars and trucks and a motorbike, all pushing to get to the front. Vehicles took the empty places then vacated them, seeking others. There was empty space changing shape, but no connecting line.

'What about your father? When did you last see him?'

I could hear Andrew's voice, as warm as the first time, but it was like the television being on without watching it.

'We know your brother is away on a boat. That's pretty exciting, hey?'

His voice came and went, mixing with the rumble of the car's engine. But I had nothing for him. I was wordless.

Andrew stopped the car at a building of pale bricks with a broken window and bars across. Outside the building was barbed wire and some writing in pink, purple and green painted across the side. The writing had its own code, indecipherable to the naked eye.

'It's just for the night,' said Andrew. 'Until your uncle comes.'

We walked towards the building. I read the sign out the front.

LATITUDE
South Western Juvenile Shelter

Andrew led me through double doors, his hand on my back. A woman came towards us. She had hair as short as a man's and she was a man, and she was a woman at the same time. She gave us a small difficult smile, as if it was the last coin in her wallet.

'G'day, Julie – this is Jim,' said Andrew.

Julie looked at me with lines deepening across the top of her face. 'You never told me he was so young, Andy. You sure you're in the right place?'

'There's nowhere else. It's not for long. He just needs a place to sleep.'

'Sounds like he's looking for a hotel. Do you know how short we are at the moment?'

'Come on, Julie. The kid has been through enough. He hasn't spoken since they found him.' He put his hand on my shoulder.

'Okay, Mr Bleeding Heart.' Julie looked at me and wrote something down. 'Welcome to Latitude, Jim,' she said.

'His uncle will be here to pick him up tomorrow morning. He doesn't have anything with him except a pair of pyjamas someone at the hospital gave him.' Then Andrew's voice dipped low, as if he had a secret to share with Julie. They spoke and looked across at me and spoke again. Julie shook her head. They had to move closer to me to make room for a girl walking past. She was as dark as chocolate and wore fur boots and chewed gum, and she said, 'S'cuse me, boss.' Now Andrew and Julie were close enough for me to hear what they were saying.

'She had no living relatives. It's the father's brother who's coming for him – he doesn't know where the old man is either. Disappeared off the planet – could be dead for all we know.'

'Okay. But if the uncle doesn't show up in the morning I'll be calling you. They'll eat him alive in this place.'

'No worries, Julie. Thanks.' Andrew turned to me. 'Your uncle will be here in the morning.' I could see his bleeding heart through his shirt. It was on its knees, hands pressed together. Then he walked out and I was left with Julie.

'Come with me,' she said.

I followed her down a long corridor that ended at a small room with a bed and a sink and a poster on the wall of hands

gripping each other. Above the poster it said *Wash your hands*.
There were bubbles rising up around the hands but there was
no body, the hands ended at the wrists.

'You'll have to stay in here, Jim. It's our sick room. It's all
we've got left. I'll come and get you soon for dinner.' She opened
a door in the corner. 'There's a toilet in there. I'll bring soap
and a toothbrush, okay?' She waited for something that didn't
come. 'Okay then,' she said, and left the room.

I sat on the bed, my back against the wall, and turned off
my remaining switches. Even then I kept breathing. It was as
if I was hooked to a small plastic pump hanging in the air
somewhere over my head, pulsing *in out in out*, but not because
of anything that I did or wanted. It was made to, by gravity
and tides, forces greater than one human being. But there was
nothing to breathe for.

I don't know how much time passed before Julie opened the door.

'Come on,' she said. 'Dinner.'

She led me to a room with tables and chairs. People came out
of doors and sat at the tables. They were young the way Robby
used to be, but older than me. Their hands were all hidden in
their sleeves, as if they were scared somebody would try and
cut them off. Maybe the poster in the bathroom was a warning.

'You don't have to talk but you should eat. You'll sleep better
tonight,' said Julie.

She took me to a place at one of the tables. I kept one half
of my bottom on the chair and the other almost off. I tipped
the chair back and forth. My leg wasn't strong enough to hold
me; I could feel it shaking.

Julie put a plate with chips and peas and steak in a puddle

of sauce on the table in front of me. When she walked away I pushed the plate to the middle.

A girl with sores on her face sitting opposite me said, 'You got to eat — you're skinny enough. You want to grow, don't you?' Each sore was a mountain with snow on top.

A boy with muscle slung across his shoulders sat down beside her. 'Eat him yourself, Jennifer. You know you want to.'

'You know *you* want to,' Jennifer said back to him. 'Paedophile.'

'You have to be over sixteen to be a paedophile, Jennifer. Like your old man.'

'Like *your* old man,' Jennifer said. She laughed and I saw milk inside her mouth.

'Where are you from?' a boy with a backwards cap asked.

'He doesn't talk,' said another girl. Her teeth were broken and they'd cut her gums the ends were so sharp. There was blood on her lips in the shape of her broken teeth.

'I tried that for a while,' said Jennifer. 'At the end of two days my brother said, "Hey, Jen, you stink like shit," and I forgot I didn't talk and I said, "Fuck you!" Dad was listening and he said, "You've been faking it, you silly bitch!" But it was good for two days. They thought I was in toxic shock from seeing someone's leg severed, or their head come off and the brains come out. My brother knew I was faking it.' Jennifer sucked on a chop, oil around her lips, then turned to me. 'Are you faking it? Can you talk or what?'

I was falling like dust, slowly, as the old world outside of me went on, not knowing that I'd left. I was in Latitude, where everything fell.

'I asked you a question,' Jennifer said, putting her chop bone back on her plate. She took a long drink of her milk. 'Just because you can't talk doesn't mean you can't hear.' She moved close to my ear and shouted, *'Can you hear me?'* The notes of her shouting tumbled over each other down my canal until they reached little drums beaten by automatic sticks.

I began to shake, as fast as the sticks, arms and legs and head, shake shake shaking, I was a firecracker, spinning across the room.

'Ha! Look at him go!'

'You pressed his button, Jennifer!'

'Go, kid, go!'

'Ha ha!'

'Go go go!' I spun to their shouting. 'Go! Go! Go!' I was zipping off the walls, sound ripping through me, the flames of the refinery pipes jetting from my heels.

Then suddenly there were arms were around me. 'Can't you lot be trusted for one second?' Julie shouted as she held me. 'Jennifer, get back to your room! Taylor, that's enough. Jim, it's okay. Nothing's happened. Calm down . . .'

Julie took me back to the sick room. 'I'll have to lock you in, Jim. Someone will come to check on you soon.' The man and the woman in Julie battled each other for territory. 'It's the best I can do.'

Then she was gone. I rolled onto my side on the bed as darkness moved over me.

There were no stars or suns or planets or moons or seas – nothing to count or wait for, no light from the eye of the sheep.

Only the dust from the wings of moths remained. It thickened the air; slowed my falling.

When the door opened again I was still on my side; I hadn't moved. Uncle Rodney walked into the sick room with Julie behind him.

'Good morning, Jim. Your uncle's here for you.' She was smiling like Uncle Rodney had come for her instead.

Uncle Rodney's face was grey, as if somebody had shaded him in with a lead pencil. There were grey loops under his eyes and grey lines across his forehead, where the pencil had been pressed harder.

'Jim!' he said, coming towards me. I heard crying resonating in his engine. He shook his head and kneeled in front of me, putting his arms around me. 'Are you alright, Jim? Are you okay?' He looked up at Julie, his voice quick and scared. 'Is he okay?'

'Like I said,' she answered, 'we've only had him for the night. They needed the beds at the hospital. I suppose they wouldn't have let him out if he wasn't okay. He hasn't spoken since they found him. I don't know what's normal for him. He hasn't eaten much either.'

Uncle Rodney looked back at me. 'We'd better do something about that, huh, Jim? A man's got to eat, huh? You'll be okay, Jimmy. It's going to be okay.' He stood up. 'Thanks for looking after him,' he said to Julie, taking my hand in his. 'Come on, Jim. Let's get you out of here.'

As we passed through an open door I saw Jennifer and Taylor and Danny sitting against the fence. There was music playing from a silver box and Danny was moving his hands up and down as if they were gutters with water flowing through. Taylor was chewing as she watched Danny. Her white piece of gum was tossed around inside her mouth like a fish in a sea storm, the teeth coming down on it, the tongue throwing it from side to side.

Jennifer waved to me. 'See ya, Speechless. Don't let 'em trick you into it!'

I turned away as Uncle Rodney led me through the gates and down the steps to a waiting car.

Uncle Rodney opened the door and I climbed in. I rested back on the seat, closing my eyes. Uncle Rodney started the car.

'Jimmy, we're going to catch a plane back to the island tomorrow, okay? You can stay with me for a while – until . . . I've set up the spare room for you, okay? We need to go to your place first, though. Just to pick up some of your gear. Sort out a couple of things, okay?'

When I looked across at Uncle Rodney it was as if I was seeing him through an unwashed window.

'When are you going to talk to me, hey, Jimmy?' He glanced at me, then back at the road. 'Are you hungry? You look thin, Jim. You need to eat, you know.' He turned off the radio in his car. 'I'm sorry about Paula, Jimmy.' I could see how much each word hurt his mouth when he spoke it. *I'm sorry about Paula.* 'We're going to track down your old man and everything is going to be alright. Ned will be happy to see you, Jimmy. He's missed you.' His small laugh was tired, its little engine weak. He looked ahead and the talking stopped.

When he saw a petrol station he turned into its driveway. 'You need to go to the toilet, Jimmy?' he asked. Outside, customers filled their tanks with sauce from the core, sucking it up through pipes then pressing the handle. Uncle Rodney shook his head and sighed. 'Okay, you stay there. I'll get us something for breakfast.'

I watched him walk into the petrol station. I saw him go to the fridge and choose. Soon he came back to the car with sandwiches and chocolate milk. He passed me a sandwich with chicken squeezing out the side. I picked up the chocolate milk.

'Good on you, Jim.' Uncle Rodney started the engine.

I sat with the chocolate milk in my lap as Uncle Rodney drove back out onto the highway.

'Go on, drink it, Jimmy. Stop stuffing round.' He stuck the straw into the automatic drinking hole and passed it back to me. 'Drink it,' he said.

I took the milk, put the straw to my mouth and sucked. Cold chocolate milk flooded the system.

Uncle Rodney breathed out. More road passed. Uncle Rodney twitched, his hands rubbed up and down his leg. He looked at me then at the road then at me then at the leg. 'I didn't know your dad wasn't around,' he said after a while. 'Nobody told me. I saw you . . . not even five months ago – Jesus it feels like yesterday. Things were alright then, weren't they? Back in January? I didn't know he'd left. I didn't know you and Paula were there alone.' Uncle Rodney shook his head.

'The neighbour – what was her name? – Mrs . . . what was it? She said to the cops that he'd been knocking your Mum around . . .' Uncle Rodney shook his head. 'Is it true, Jimmy? It's not true, is it?'

Puffs of white cloud hung in the sky. They were very still, not one part of any cloud moved. No new things formed.

'Fuck, Gavin . . .' Uncle Rodney kept shaking his head, then he took in a deep breath and sighed one out. 'Bloody hell.' He undid the window and did it up again. 'Poor Paula.'

The inside of me slid out of my ears like steam, spectating from above. Uncle Rodney put his hand on my shoulder. There was bone underneath the skin that connected the arm to the body. There were tubes wrapped around it transporting chocolate milk to my organs.

Uncle Rodney kept talking. 'I can't get hold of your brother. He's out at bloody sea somewhere. You'll have to stay with me until we get something sorted. But I have to work. I've got Dave minding the shop while I'm here, but he can't keep that up.'

Uncle Rodney drove the car into Emu Street. It was like looking at a diagram from one of my manuals but the connecting lines were missing; there was nothing joining me to the house or the house to the road or the road to the world.

'I'm sorry, Jimmy, you'll have to come in with me. I have to see if I can find something that might tell us where your dad is. Or Robby. And we need your things.' He reached across me and opened my door. There were tiny black dots of hair over the bottom half of his face. If my eyes were small enough I could have looked straight down the hole at the end of every hair and seen into the memory bank behind Uncle Rodney's skin. 'Come on, Jimmy,' he said.

I followed him up the path; I saw my old footprints in the concrete, I saw Mum's spade, her bucket, her kneeling pad, her glove. Doris began to sing, *Won't you tell me that you love me? Won't you tell me that you do?*

'I'm sorry you have to deal with this, Jim. Jesus.'

He opened the door and we went into Nineteen Emu. I looked around the kitchen at the curtain with roses and sparrows, the Sunlight Lemon, the wallpaper apples, the teacup, the upside-down dish rack, the apron with rows of roosters and suns hanging over the stove, and I felt the pull of sleep coming up from underground. I saw the window with chips in the frame, the vase without flowers, the magnets holding lists and recipes . . . The force from underground pulled on the bones in my arms and legs . . . The puppy salt and pepper shakers, the kitten poster *We are in this together* with one kitten hanging from a branch about to drop, the other with his eyes wide, reaching out a paw . . . Sleep pulling on my chest cavity, my neck, through my face to my eyes. I couldn't resist the force. I lay back on the kitchen couch where my mum read her Agathas and I closed my eyes.

'You just stay there, Jimmy. That's a good idea, have a rest.' Uncle Rodney talked as he looked at papers by the telephone. He began to speak to someone. His voice came in and out, like a radio station not tuned, almost catching voices, then missing again.

'No bloody idea . . . I don't know . . . It's a mess . . . Asthma . . . No, she was pretty sick. Nobody knew . . . Oh shit . . . Gavin was knocking her around . . . I know, I know, it wasn't even five months ago he was on the island with Jim. Shit! Things seemed okay, really okay . . . No, the kid won't speak, not a bloody word . . . Oh shit, mate, she had nobody here . . . I don't know . . . oh Jesus . . . I don't know. Give the dog a drink will you? . . . Yeah, he tips his water out. Bloody idiot dog . . . Yeah, mate, tomorrow afternoon . . . No, he's asleep . . . Yeah mate, thanks.'

It was dark. Moths beat their wings, multiplying as they flew around my face, their dust in my nose and eyes. I flapped at them with my hands, but they came in closer. The more I coughed the more they multiplied. I couldn't see through them.

'Jimmy! Jimmy! Are you okay, kid? Are you okay?' Uncle Rodney shook me awake. 'You were dreaming. Were you dreaming? Are you alright?'

I sat up and saw that Uncle Rodney had Mum's red suitcase beside him.

'Are you okay?' he asked me. I nodded my head. 'I packed some things for you, Jim. I don't know if I got what you wear, but we can pick up anything else you need on the island.' Uncle Rodney held up Mum's numbers and lists book. 'This is Paula's diary, right? No numbers in it for your old man. You don't know where he went, Jim? Did your Mum say anything? You've got no idea?' He looked at me, waiting. 'Jim, it would help if you could talk to me.'

I knew what he wanted but I didn't have access; there was nothing I could do for my Uncle Rodney.

'Oh shit.' He went to the sink and poured himself a drink of water. Then he opened the cupboards and closed them again. 'You want a drink, Jim?' He brought me a glass of water.

I tipped it into my mouth and felt it drip down.

Uncle Rodney put his hand out for the empty glass. 'We may as well get going. I got us a hotel near the airport, okay? Is there anything you want to take from the house? I don't know when you'll be back again.'

My manuals lay strewn across the kitchen table — oven, washing machine, vacuum cleaner. The black and white drawings blurred before me. The diagrams didn't belong to the instructions. Letters and numbers crossed paths, on was off and off was on. They were mistaken. There was nothing I wanted to take from the house.

I looked down and saw tracks across the floor that ran deep into the tiles. I stared at them, narrowing my eyes for increased vision. The cracks led to the ground under the house and they kept going until they got to the earth's core and then they penetrated the core and ended up in space, but lower space. The space underneath goes down and down and spreads. In it you see only the shadows of things. There wasn't one thing existing without the under-space — it was there all the time, but nobody looked. You had to be empty to see it.

Uncle Rodney sighed and picked up Mum's red suitcase. 'Okay then, let's go. We have to drop the car back on the way, then we'll get something to eat. Come on, Jimmy.'

I followed him out of the house, my eyes on the case.

Uncle Rodney didn't speak on the drive to the airport. He watched the road and pulled sharply at the gearstick and ran his hand through his hair and turned the radio on then off. He sighed and shook his head. He looked across at me, then out the window, then back at me, then at the road, then out the window, then at the road again. He rubbed his hand over his face, as if he was trying to clear something away.

We left the car at a parking lot, then Uncle Rodney waved at a taxi and that took us to the airport hotel. When we got to the hotel I drank chocolate milk straight from the carton in the lobby restaurant. Uncle Rodney put chips in front of me, he put steak in front of me, he put ice cream and Coke in front of me, but I only drank the chocolate milk.

'You can't keep this up, Jim. You have to eat,' he said.

I sat on the chair in room seven while Uncle Rodney lay on the bed, and we watched the television. I don't know what was on. When I next opened my eyes I heard cars racing around the room, getting louder as they came closer, then fading.

Uncle Rodney was lifting me to the bed. I heard men on the television cheering for the cars. Uncle Rodney lifted me as though he didn't want to wake me but he didn't know — only Mum knew — that I was always awake, like a clock that doesn't stop ticking.

The next day we went to the airport in another taxi and Uncle Rodney put the red case into the square frame, then he led me down the path that moves whether you are walking or not. Up in the sky aeroplanes cut through the air, leaving tears in the atmosphere, revealing the under-space. I couldn't take my eyes from it. What is the past? If it happened, does it still live anywhere? Is it gone after it happens? Does anything keep it? Was memory stored in the under-space?

Our plane flew high over the land then out over the sea. I hardly looked. Uncle Rodney gave me a magazine and a man in a white suit with medals saluted me from the cover.

When we came out at the airport on Broken Island, Amanda was there to meet us.

'Amanda!' Uncle Rodney called.

Amanda didn't look at Uncle Rodney; she looked at me and I saw that her eyes were full of tears that didn't belong to her. They belonged to the Flick brothers but only she could produce them.

'Hi, Rod,' she said, giving him a small quick hug. She turned back to me. 'I think you've grown taller by this much.' She held up her fingers and made a pinch. I looked between the fingers, through the glass doors of the airport and saw the sea.

'It's a bit cold for a swim, mate, but we could take Ned down for a walk if you like,' said Uncle Rodney. 'We could throw the ball for him.' He looked at me, tiny flickers of changing light in his eyes. Above his head the airport fans spun around and around. You couldn't see the air they were moving. Some things, like air and electricity, are invisible.

We walked towards the black rubber path going around and around beneath the fans. Uncle Rodney picked up Mum's red suitcase and the doors knew to open as we came closer; invisible sensors gave them knowledge of our approach. Their slide was smooth as they closed behind me.

We walked towards the Statesman in the car park.

'Thanks for coming, Amanda,' said Uncle Rodney.

'No problem. I hope everything's okay . . . Whatever I can do.'

'It'll be okay . . . one way or another.'

They looked at each other, as if I couldn't decipher their codes.

'I just wish I knew where Gav was. Gone bloody walkabout,' said Uncle Rodney.

'What about Jim's brother?'

Uncle Rodney shook his head quickly at Amanda, as if he didn't want her to ask about Robby. 'Think we'll stay in tonight. We'll order pizza from Stella's. You like pizza, Jim?' He touched my head.

I pulled away; the touch didn't belong to me. Uncle Rodney looked at Amanda and sighed.

'Anything we can do, Rod, please, just let us know. Dave has made you a tuna casserole. If you're anything like my Brett, Jim, you'll hate it.' She smiled and climbed in the front seat beside Uncle Rodney. I got in the back and it was the same row of buttons that undid the same windows, the same road, the same island, sea and sky, but the line between them was gone and I didn't need to press the button and never would again.

When we came to Uncle Rodney's house Ned came to the gate. He jumped up and put his paws on the front fence.

'You can open the gate for him if you like,' said Uncle Rodney. 'But be ready.'

I opened the gate and Ned jumped up on me, almost knocking me over. He wasn't careful with me, as if I was about to break, or had already broken. He was fast and wild and living.

'Easy does it, boy,' said Uncle Rodney.

I put my hands on Ned's shoulders, and messages carried by his blood came to me from the animal kingdom. The animal kingdom is in our world but it's another world too. It has no people or extinction. It only has plants with leaves that are damp with dew and if you tip the leaf it makes a spout for you to drink from. That way you never run out of water. All the secrets for survival are in the animal kingdom. Ned was from it even though he was in this world too. I looked in his eyes and I saw the light from the eye of the sheep, like lamps to show the way.

I didn't do anything but sit in front of him and look. Ned didn't turn from me. With my back sensors I could feel Uncle Rodney behind me, watching. I touched Ned's head, the bone that covered his brain, the storage box of the pictures he carried inside, and he sent me messages through my fingers: light, sun, running and stillness. I pressed my face to Ned and smelled him and he leaned into me and allowed me.

'It's good to see Ned again, hey, Jim?' Uncle Rodney said. 'Come on, we'll take him out the back and you can play with him.' Uncle Rodney's voice was lighter.

I followed Ned, who followed Uncle Rodney, who carried the red suitcase, through the house.

Uncle Rodney stayed inside while Ned took me into the yard and showed me where he slept and his toys and his shed and his lead and his bone.

Uncle Rodney brought out a drink of water and I drank it, keeping one hand on Ned's back.

I sat with Ned in the yard the whole day until it turned to night. Uncle Rodney spoke on the telephone, his voice travelling through the yard, the wind blowing it over the grass in small pieces.

'Any idea? Where the hell? He was there when it happened. A bloody mess alright. No way. No, I can't take him. There's nothing here for him. Christ, who'd run the bloody shop?'

Uncle Rodney came out with a beer and some spray in a can. 'For the mozzies,' he said, spraying me, then drinking from the beer can.

He put steaks on the barbecue. They sizzled pink and Ned sniffed around the gas cylinder.

'I wish you'd speak to me, Jim. So we can sort this out. Are you going to speak to me?' Uncle Rodney formed words with his lips and his tongue and the words travelled along invisible waves to the trees and the grass and the clouds. I watched the world receiving them as Uncle Rodney waited. After a while he said, 'Bloody hell.'

After looking at me not eating steak and potato and tomato Uncle Rodney said, 'You can watch some telly if you want,

Jim.' He turned on *Doctor Who* then went into the kitchen to do the dishes. He left a packet of chips out for me. I put one chip at a time into my mouth. I kept my mouth on each chip long enough for the olfactory to wet it, and then I swallowed and down it went via my bowser. I sat with Ned close enough to smell his fur and we watched the doctor save the universe with electrodes and a bug.

I lay on the double bed in the guest room at Uncle Rodney's and looked at shadows in the last of the light: windowsill, cupboard, tennis racquet, open door, photo frame, curtain; each shadow as separate as the island itself.

In the morning Uncle Rodney came into my room and said, 'Jeez, you like a sleep-in, don't you, kid? It's nine o'clock.'

But I wasn't sleeping. There were lights inside me and all night they stayed on red. Ned was across my legs, his heat and weight transmitting solar and lunar into me.

Uncle Rodney ran his hand through his hair that was sticking up all over his head. Then he rubbed his eyes. 'Jim, come and have breakfast and we'll have a talk about what happens next.'

All my clothes were still on – even my shoes. They had left skids of dirt across the bottom of Uncle Rodney's sheet but he didn't notice. I followed him to the kitchen and he poured me water and then he poured me milk. I drank the water. It cleaned out my radiator. Uncle Rodney put food in a metal bowl for Ned. Ned ate it, his jaws throwing it back. 'You don't see *him* saying no,' said Uncle Rodney, sounding tired. 'You need to eat, Jimmy. What's the problem with eating? I'm going to fry you some eggs, okay?'

I watched him crack eggs into a frying pan. If you crack open an egg before it's cooked you will find a baby bird inside. It won't have feathers yet, only skin. Its eyes will be black seeds in its head. It will be wet and its skin as thin as tissue and it won't know anything. No pictures or words or messages yet in its mind. The shell stopped any coming through but as soon as you crack the egg then there is no protection and everything enters the bird through the skin and the black seeds, in a rush of information. If the bird isn't strong enough to hold the information it tips forward from the broken shell, its head hanging from its neck like a grape too heavy for the vine.

'What have we here?' said Uncle Rodney, pulling a small box from the cupboard. 'Cocoa . . . I don't know how old this is, but if we mix it with milk it will make it chocolate. How about that, Jim? Will you have chocolate milk?' He poured some cocoa and two spoonsful of sugar into the glass of milk and he stirred it round and round, the white of the milk turning brown.

He put it down in front of me and I touched the glass and it was cold against my fingers. I lifted it with Uncle Rodney watching and I drank it and it went down my pump and charged through my pipes.

'At least there's something you like,' said Uncle Rodney, smiling and turning his eggs over. He poured himself a cup of tea and buttered two pieces of toast, then he scraped the eggs onto the toast.

The telephone rang and Uncle Rodney picked up the receiver. 'What time, mate? *Now?*' He glanced at me. 'Shit . . . Alright, I'll be there . . . Yeah, no worries. A bit more notice wouldn't go astray, though . . . Yeah I'll see you in a bit.'

After Uncle Rodney got off the telephone, he passed his hand across his mouth and across his face and walked around the kitchen and washed a dish then left it in the sink then washed it again then wiped down the bench, missing the spilt milk. Steam rose from the eggs on the plate. He looked at me, then out the window, then at me. He checked his watch then he checked the clock hanging above the stove. He picked up the telephone. 'Come on, Dave, come on . . .' Dave wasn't answering.

Uncle Rodney turned to me. 'Listen, Jimmy, I've got to go to the shop for a while. There's an order coming, I have to be there. You'll be alright by yourself, won't you? I'll leave Ned in charge.' He pulled a bag of chips from the cupboard and put it on the table. 'Don't leave the house, Jim, okay? Just stay there and eat the breakfast I made you and watch the telly. I'll be home in forty minutes. See the clock?' He pointed to the clock on the wall. 'When that says ten o'clock I'll be home again, okay? Then we can go and do something. Just stay here and watch the box with Ned. Don't even go out the back, okay? It looks like rain.'

He took his coat and he was gone. I sat with Ned and watched the television. The superhero walked up a building with only his feet for suction, as if he could defeat gravity. But nothing can defeat gravity. Even a spaceship only defeats gravity from within the craft. Outside there is still gravity, pulling the contents of the earth towards itself. Gravity is a greater force than water and if the two are put together then that equals THE END.

I watched as the dark green superhero flashed the silver enemy with a red laser. The enemy caught fire then the flames cleared and there was only smoke left and a small hole in the ground where the enemy had once stood. The superhero said, *That should stop him!* A girl whose dress was pulled in so tight she had two stomachs fell against him and he put his strong arms around her. He kept his goggles over his eyes. Ads came on.

I looked out the window and saw low grey clouds in the sky. I picked up Ned's red lead from where it hung across the back of the chair. Then I clipped Ned to the lead and opened the front door.

We walked down the road, light rain falling on our heads. Ned kept the lead pulled tight and straight. I felt his desire travelling up the fibres into my fingers.

Soon we were at the beach. A woman with grey hair stood in her garden, watering her gnomes. She waved at me when I walked past. There was nobody on the sand and nobody in the water except for two men with black skins out on surfboards. The sky was grey with the light behind it, moving down to another deeper grey that was darker and wet. The second grey belonged to the sea but these were only names and words. The clouds and the sea were the same thing with different amounts of water penetrating.

I unclipped Ned and watched as he raced down to the shore, barking at the waves. I followed him to the edge, letting the water wash over my ankles. I watched it drag at the hems of my tracksuit pants. I watched the waves pull out, leaving the sand shining and damp, reflecting light.

I looked out to the horizon. It was the last place; you couldn't go further. It was a circle around the planet Earth that tried to keep the people in and only some went beyond it. It wasn't advisable; beyond it there were no warranties. My bare feet moved towards the horizon as if the horizon was calling them, calling and calling with a voice my feet had no power to refuse. The swirling water tugged at my clothes, turning them dark. The water was over my knees now as wave after wave came tumbling towards me. Out the back they rose like mountains, then as they gained speed they rolled over, crashing and breaking into white spray and froth, too fast for their own weight and the pressure and the speed behind them.

I heard howling. I turned around and saw Ned sitting on the shore, tilting back his head, jaw open as he called to me. The water was now up to my chest. The music of wind and wave and dog howl was as hollow as a tunnel. I kept going deeper, the water now up to my neck. The sea was heavy and smooth and parted as I moved my arms but there was always more behind it, rushing towards me. I couldn't stand, and then I could, and then I couldn't and then I could and then I couldn't. Waves washed over the top of me. I went under where it was still and slow and muffled and then I came up again and heard my dad calling me. 'Jim! Jim! Son! Jimmy!' But his calling turned into the howling dog, which soon rose higher and became the howl of the wind. A wall of water too high to climb came thundering towards me. I looked up to its shining pinnacle and tried to read its message in the last seconds, but then it broke over the top of me, and it was too late. I went under, my throat on fire, water in my nose and my mouth. I was pulled in all directions and thrown sideways and back, then everything went quiet. I saw particles of dust slowly falling. I reached for a face I couldn't see. 'Mum?'

I lay on the sand, my throat and nose burning as Uncle Rodney kneeled beside me, the still clouds behind him, hiding the sun. I saw its bright rays around the edges.

Uncle Rodney was pressing on my chest. 'Oh God, Jimmy, oh God . . . Jimmy! Jimmy!' he said and in his voice was the voice of all Flick brothers – Rodney, Gavin, Steve and Ray – four brothers calling for me – willing me, willing me.

I coughed and out came hot salty vomit, the same as I'd seen in the rabbit. I opened my mouth and the air rushed in.

Uncle Rodney gripped me against him, saying my name, *Jim Jim*, as Ned watched over his shoulder, waiting without movement, the light in his eyes at the back the same light.

I lay in the double bed on cool sheets and Uncle Rodney sat beside me.

'Jimmy, I shouldn't have left you by yourself,' he said when I opened my eyes. 'What was I thinking? I should never have . . .'

Another man who was with Uncle Rodney took my temperature with his glass tube of mercury, waiting for my reading to enter the liquid. He felt under my arms and under my throat, his fingertips dry and cold.

Uncle Rodney said, 'What do you think, Brian?'

The man nodded. 'A bit out of your depth here, aren't you, Rod?' he said.

'The boy's alright, isn't he?'

'The boy is fine, but you can't afford to have something like this happen again. I don't know how you made it in time.'

'Nance in twenty-two was in her garden when she saw bloody Ned howling on the shore. She called me and I got straight in the car. Thank god for Ned, hey?' Uncle Rodney shook his head. There was blood and shadow all through his eyes and the skin of his face. He patted Ned's head but his sensors were trained on me.

'What are you going to do about it?'

'I don't know.'

'I'm not sure that you are going to be able to provide him with what he needs . . .'

'He's got nowhere else.' Uncle Rodney ran his hand through his hair.

Brian packed up his case. 'Let me talk to a couple of people and see if I can help.' Before he left the room he turned to me. 'You're lucky your uncle found you in time,' he said, as if it was a warning.

Later Uncle Rodney brought me hot chocolate and chicken chips. He sat beside the bed with electricity shooting from his pores, draining his battery.

'Jim, I know you don't want to talk . . . I was a lot older than you when my mother died, but . . .'

Water dripped from Uncle Rodney's eye pipes. I looked into the round water of his tears and saw Mother Beloved wearing a scarf around her head. In her hands was a basket of sultana cakes. *Sorry. Sorry, boys*, she said.

'I didn't feel much like talking either,' said Uncle Rodney. 'It will get better, Jim.'

I watched as he rubbed more tears away from his nose and cheek and chin.

Three days later I sat with Ned in the backyard while Uncle Rodney spoke on the telephone. For most of the three days he had been trying to find a place for me to live. I put my arms around Ned's chest and listened to his heart beating blood to his vitals. I rested against him, my only living source. Like me, he couldn't cry.

Amanda came to the house. She didn't knock — she just opened the door and called, 'Rod?'

'In the yard!' Uncle Rodney called back. She came outside where Uncle Rodney drank coffee and watched me throw the ball for Ned. I only threw it a step. Ned caught it in his jaws and dropped it between my feet. I threw it again and again.

'How are you doing?' Amanda asked Uncle Rodney.

'I don't know.' Uncle Rodney shook his head. 'I just don't know.'

Amanda smiled at me. 'Good to see you up and about, Jim.'

I threw the ball again and Ned caught it.

'I have to get back to the shop, Amanda. I've had to close for three days. Missed a load of tourists from Tokyo. Ian bloody Webb couldn't resist telling me. I can't afford it.'

I saw Amanda nod her head. She looked at me and her face was sad. 'But he's family.'

'I know he's family! But he nearly fucking drowned! I nearly fucking lost him! I don't know what I'm doing.'

'Take it easy, Rod. Dave will take a couple of days off to watch over the shop while you sort this out.'

'Sorry, Amanda.'

'You've got nothing to say sorry for. *I'm* sorry. I brought you potatoes with bacon.' She came to me and she took me hard and quick against her and kissed the top of my head. 'Hang in there, Jim,' she said.

That night I was lying on the bed when Uncle Rodney came in. 'You alright, Jim? You need a glass of water or anything?'

I shook my head.

He sat on the chair beside the bed. 'Jim, you know I care . . . oh God . . .' Rodney sighed loudly, and blew out a column of air. 'You can't stay here, Jim. You need better care. It's not on the island. You're going to be placed with a family for a while who take care of special kids. Special kids like you, hey?' He bent forward and he held me so tight the meat between my bones was crushed. 'Oh Christ, what a mess. Jesus. I'm sorry, little fella,' he said, and Ned climbed on the bed and laid his head on my knee.

Uncle Rodney took me on another plane ride back to the mainland. I closed my eyes and floated with the dust in the world where outer and inner space joined. The seat dug into the bones of my arms.

At the airport Uncle Rodney and me stood in a queue and soon a taxi came. Uncle Rodney put out his hand and the taxi drove close to the kerb and stopped. The boot popped open and the driver got out and put Mum's red suitcase into it. We climbed into the back seat and Uncle Rodney said, 'Thirty-five Cook Road,' and the driver of the taxi knew where to go. Soon the car stopped outside a house with 35 on the letterbox. Uncle Rodney paid the driver and we climbed out.

A woman who'd been waiting in a white car crossed the road towards us. She was tucked into her black suit, the bottom matching the top, and she carried a leather briefcase. 'I hope I'm not late,' said Uncle Rodney, putting out his hand.

'Not at all. I'm early,' the woman said, shaking Uncle Rodney's hand. 'Jan Watts.'

'Rodney Flick,' said Uncle Rodney.

Jan Watts looked at me and smiled. 'This must be Jim.'

'This is Jim,' said Uncle Rodney. Tears rose up in him; he could hardly breathe.

'Hi, Jim. Today we're going to get you settled into a new home. The Reeds live right in there. Pretty big house, isn't it? What do you think?'

'He hasn't spoken since . . . much . . . since they found him,' said Uncle Rodney.

'Right . . . that's right. That's okay. Anne will have him talking again in no time. She's had plenty of experience.'

Uncle Rodney took my hand in one of his and the red suitcase in the other, and we followed Jan Watts up the front path of 35. We knocked on the door and a boy opened it and he was big with freckles that came close to touching. He looked at me then up at Uncle Rodney and he said, 'What the hell do you want?'

'Liam! That's no way to greet someone!' a woman said, coming up behind him. 'What do you say when someone comes to the door? What do you say?'

'Fuck off?' said Liam, looking at me.

The woman sighed. 'Go to your room please, Liam. You can stay there until I come and get you.' She turned the boy around and pushed him gently on the back. 'Go on, off you go.'

Liam scuffed his shoe into the floor as he left.

'Sorry about that,' said the woman. She put out her hand for Uncle Rodney to shake. 'I'm Anne White.'

Anne White's eyes were pink and melting at the rims, as if she'd looked into too many fires. Inside the rims the balls were pale blue.

'Hello, Jim,' she said, leaning down to me. 'I'm so glad you are coming to stay with us. I hope you'll be happy here.' She called over her shoulder, 'Deirdre!'

A girl smaller than me came to the door. Her hair was in a long plait that hung over her shoulder, like rope.

'Come and meet Jim.'

Deirdre took Anne White's hand and looked at me. 'I'm not nine yet,' she said.

'Jim, this is Deirdre,' said Anne White. 'She lives here too.'

'And so does Liam,' said Deirdre, rolling her eyes.

'Yes, Liam lives here too,' said Anne White. 'Jim has already met him.'

'Liam's dad can't walk,' said Deirdre. 'But his arms are double strength.'

'Thank you, Deirdre.' Anne White smiled at Uncle Rodney. 'Let's all go into the living room and have a talk. Deirdre, will you show Jim the play things in the big chest?'

'Yes,' she said. 'But he can't touch my doll, Melanie. She won't sing if he touches her.'

'No, he won't touch your doll. Show him the trains. And the car with the remote control.'

'The remote control doesn't work,' said Deirdre.

'Show it to him anyway, please. The two of you might be able to fix it.'

'Okay,' said Deirdre. She took my hand and led me to the toy chest in the corner of the room. She pulled me down to it, putting a black plastic car on the floor in front of me. Then she looked in the box again and found the control panel. Wires came out the top. She put it into my hands. I held onto it as I listened to Uncle Rodney, Jan Watts and Anne White discuss my cases.

'Over the years I've worked with plenty of antisocial behaviour,' said Anne White.

'It's not that he's antisocial,' said Uncle Rodney. 'He's a social kid. He's just . . .'

'Traumatised?' said Jan Watts. 'Since the loss?'

'Yeah — yeah, he's traumatised. I'd keep him, but I don't think it's the right thing,' said Uncle Rodney. 'I don't know what I'm doing. I don't want him to get into trouble. He still isn't eating properly, and he hasn't said a word. I can't find his dad, or his brother. He's always been a bit . . . different.'

'I've been fostering children ever since I had kids of my own over twenty-five years ago,' said Anne White, 'and Jan's report on Jim doesn't scare me too much. When he's more settled he can go to school here. We are part of an active community. I think the company of other kids who are in a similar position can be very helpful. And the island is only a plane ride away. You can visit whenever you want, Rodney. And when you track down the rest of his family we can talk again about what will happen to Jim.'

'It's been great to meet you, Anne. It's a relief to know he'll be living here.'

I heard a shout from upstairs.

'Excuse me, Rodney,' she said. She went to the bottom of the stairs. 'Liam!' she called. 'I'm coming up there in a minute to see what you're doing!' She turned back to Uncle Rodney. 'Do you know, my husband Jake and I have decided that Jim will be our last foster child. It's been wonderful, but we just don't have the energy we used to. I think that makes Jim a bit special, don't you?'

Deirdre sang, *When you dance, sweet Melanie, When you do a dance for me I can see your knickers, Melanie,* and I couldn't hear Uncle Rodney's answer.

Uncle Rodney kneeled opposite me, looking into my eyes. I looked into his but there was glass between me and their light, as if he was a mirage.

'You're going to be okay here, Jim.' He put his arms around me. A tear came out his pipe. I had never seen a single tear of Uncle Rodney's before and now I was seeing too many to count. 'Ned is going to miss you, mate.' He wiped away the tear. 'I'm sorry about all this. But you're going to be alright here, aren't you?' He set me back. 'You are, aren't you, kid?'

I knew Uncle Rodney wanted words, but I didn't have any for him.

Jan Watts and Uncle Rodney walked through the front door leaving me with Anne White. She took the red suitcase Uncle Rodney had left behind. 'Let's get you settled in, Jim.'

'Liam wrote *fuck* on the wall,' said Deirdre.

'Deirdre!' said Anne White. 'Please don't use that word. Liam has been spoken to about what he did. You are not to repeat that story anymore, do you understand?'

'Yes,' answered Deirdre as we walked upstairs.

'And you are never to use that word.'

'What word?' asked Deirdre.

'You know the word I am talking about. Don't use it again or you'll lose a star from the rewards board.'

'Yes, Anne,' said Deirdre. She turned around to me and said *fuck* without the sound.

Anne White opened the door to a small room where Liam sat at a desk in the corner tipping back and forth on his chair.

'You'll be on the bottom,' said Anne White, pointing to a set of iron bunks. 'Don't do that please, Liam.'

Liam stopped tipping. He had his eyes on me.

'I want you to make Jim feel welcome, Liam. You remember what it was like when you first came, don't you? How you felt a bit lost without your Aunt Leanne?' Anne White began making up the bottom bunk with the blankets and sheets. 'I'm pretty sure that's how Jim feels. So, Liam, maybe you could show him some of your games and show him the yard and where you've been helping Jake clear the ground for the vegetable patch. Okay?' Anne White sounded tired, as though every word was one too many. She smoothed her hand down the blankets on the bed. 'This is your bed, Jim.' She pulled my red suitcase to the cupboard. 'Do you mind if I unpack your things, or would you prefer to do it yourself?'

I looked at the red suitcase, then the window where I could see the single branch of a tree. Birds swooped up to the sky so I couldn't see them, then down again so I could. I heard singing. *Won't you tell me that you love me? Won't you tell me that you do?* The sky was bright and grey. I didn't know why I was in Cook Road. I closed my eyes and saw the world underwater. It was slower and cooler; there weren't beds or fosters – everything drifted. Each shape could have been something else.

'It's almost six. You kids go outside and show Jim the yard,' said Anne White, unpacking the clothes from my case and putting them into the cupboard. 'I'll call you for tea when it's ready.'

I followed Liam and Deirdre down to the bottom of the yard to look at a patch of dirt inside a wooden square. 'That's for the vegetables, when Anne gets time,' said Deirdre.

'Why don't you talk?' Liam asked me.

'Because he doesn't want to,' said Deirdre. She pointed at the square. 'We can plant strawberries – wild ones that I can feed to my doll because they'll be the right size and they come with a daisy.' Deirdre stuck her finger into the dirt and twirled it. 'The daisy grows off the side.'

'Strawberries don't grow here, dickhead,' said Liam. 'They need farms.'

'Don't call me a dickhead.' Deirdre pulled out her finger and threw dirt onto Liam's shoe.

'Then don't be one.'

'I'm not being one.' Deirdre picked a stone up from the ground. 'Wherever this lands is where I'll plant the first strawberry.' She threw the stone and it landed in a corner of the square.

'You'll be gone before you see a strawberry in that dirt, Deirdre,' said Liam. 'Anne doesn't want to keep you. You wet the bed.'

Deirdre screwed up her face. 'You shut up, Liam. Your dad can't even walk. You're the one who needs a nurse to teach him how to read.'

'You're the one who needs a nurse to show her how to piss in the toilet,' said Liam. His smile only lifted half, as if the other half was damaged.

Deirdre stuck out her bottom lip and she shook her head. She turned and walked back up to the house. 'See you at tea, Jim,' she said over her shoulder. 'I'm helping Anne serve.'

Liam sat down on the wooden frame around the square of dirt. He picked up a stick and dug a hole, flicking fresh dirt onto the grass. 'A Chinese man blew both my dad's legs off in the war so I had to live with my Aunt Leanne and her boyfriend Gary when I was just a baby. Gary's whole wall was made of beer cans; every time he finished a beer he'd keep the can and add it to the wall. But then my cousin Tyler took a rifle out of Gary's gun cupboard. Aunt Leanne reckons the gun cupboard was locked and she told the courts that, but the time Tyler took me to see the guns it wasn't locked. The courts didn't believe her, anyway. Tyler left jam on the door. He'd been eating a jam sandwich. Then Tyler shot the neighbour, Mrs Connelly, in the neck and even though her son did mouth-to-mouth on her she ended up in intensive and never came out. I wasn't allowed to live with Aunt Leanne after that. Tyler went to Stateside. He doesn't speak to me anymore.' Liam broke his stick in half.

'Aunt Leanne said my dad should get more than just sickness benefits; he should have got a medal because he probably blew off a few men's legs before he lost his own. My mum ran away with a man called Dave who had both his legs. Aunt Leanne said my mum had two faces; one for my dad and one for the devil.'

Liam got to his feet. 'Come with me,' he said. I followed him behind a shed. He pointed to a row of three iron drums that stood against the fence. 'They hold a hundred gallons each,' said Liam. 'One is for burning, one is for weed poison and one is for water.' He knocked against the side of the drum for water with his fist. 'One day the cat fell in,' he said.

'Jim! Liam! Tea's ready!' Anne White called from the house.

'Coming, Anne!' Liam shouted back. He picked up another stick and trailed it across the end of my shoes, bumping it up to my ankles, then down again and across the ground. He drew an X into the dirt then turned and walked up to the house. I stayed for a moment longer, looking at the row of drums – one for burning, one for weeds and one for water – then I followed him.

When I went inside Anne White said, 'This is Jake.'

'G'day,' said Jake. Jake was as big as a double fridge. His stomach pushed out the top of his trousers. There was only hair round the sides of his head, not on the top.

'You can sit there.' Anne White pulled out a chair for me. 'Beside Deirdre. Deirdre, you are helping me with tea tonight, aren't you?'

'Yes, Anne,' answered Deirdre. 'Then I get a tick on the chores and rewards board. Only seven more to a star.' She stood in front of a poster filled with empty boxes going down.

'You won't get a tick if the food is cold,' said Anne White. 'Come on.'

Deirdre brought meat and pumpkin and chips and peas to the table and a jug for the gravy.

'I hope you like roast lamb, Jim,' said Anne White, smiling at me.

Deirdre put a glass of water near my plate. 'I hope you like water,' she said.

Anne White frowned at her. 'Sometimes after kids stay with us for a while they call Jake Dad,' she said. 'You just take your time, Jim, and when you're ready you can call him Dad too.'

'Dad,' said Liam putting a chip in his mouth.

Jake stopped eating his lamb. 'You watch yourself,' he said.

'Oh, he's alright, aren't you, Liam?' Anne White put her hand on Liam's arm. 'Did you show Jim the backyard?'

Liam nodded, his eyes on his plate.

'I showed Jim where the strawberries will go,' said Deirdre. She turned to me. 'Anne White's is the best foster home. I went to another one and you had to do jobs all the time like cleaning out the garage and that's where the father went. He kept all the things he liked the most in there. He liked it in there more than the house even though there was no heater or fan. I didn't stay there long, did I, Anne?'

'No you didn't, Deirdre. Would you like some more peas?'

'No thanks, Anne. I'm leaving room for dessert.'

'Good girl.' Anne White turned to me. 'Jim? Not hungry? At least try a chip.' She turned my plate around so the chips were the closest. 'Go on.'

I picked up a chip.

'Good boy,' said Anne. 'Wasn't so hard, was it?'

I turned the chip in half-circles. I kept both directions even, turn turn turn.

Jake looked over Anne White's shoulder at the television playing in the other room as he ate. Liam didn't say anything.

When the telephone rang Anne White got up from the table and answered it.

'Hi, Rodney.' She looked across at me and smiled. 'He's settling in fine. No problems at all.' She held the telephone away from her. 'It's your Uncle Rodney,' she said to me, then she spoke back into the receiver. 'Oh, he'll be really pleased when I tell him. In three weeks? How lovely. Well we've got him eating chips, so that's a start. Yes . . . oh yes . . . I'll tell him. Thanks, Rodney. Bye.' Anne White hung up the telephone. 'That was your uncle,' she said to me. 'He's already planning a visit. Isn't that lovely?'

Later I lay awake in the bottom bunk, under Liam. In the darkness I held my hand up to my face, then away from it, then close to it. I could only see the shadows of my fingers; my fingers were hardly there. Everybody else was asleep. The streetlamp outside communicated the only light. There wasn't much, as if the source that supplied it was running low.

I got out of the bed and went to the cupboard. Liam rolled over in his bunk. As quietly as I could I pulled open the doors. On the top shelf I saw the dark outline of the red suitcase. I pulled the case to the ground and sat beside it. I felt the sides of the case with my fingers. Then I unzipped it and pulled back the lid. I got inside, making myself small. I reached outside the case, pulled the lid closed over me, and zipped up what I could. The zip squeezed against my skin. I touched all sides of the case. My head pressed against the end. The suitcase held me; I was contained within it. At last sleep infected me.

In the morning Liam unzipped me and the light came in. 'Good morning, Matchbox Boy,' he said. 'Sleep well?'

Rain fell from the sky the whole day. Anne got out the games from the cupboards. 'For you boys,' she said, taking Deirdre's hand. 'You can bake biscuits in the kitchen with me, Deirdre.'

Liam watched the television and didn't play any of the games. I stood at the window and looked up to where the rain came from. I traced the pathway of a single drop. It was falling fast; I had to train my eyes. It didn't touch any of the other drops on the way down. The water knew its direction; the instructions were inbuilt.

'Jim?' Anne White stood in front of me. 'Jim? Earth to Jim?' She shook the towel she held in her hands. 'Don't you think it's time you had a bath? Come on, before dinner.' She leaned down and held out her hand to me. 'Come on. I don't want to have to carry you – my back would break.'

I stood up. She took my hand and led me to the bathroom. She turned on the tap. 'Here's your towel, there's the soap and there's a face washer. I'll leave you to it, okay?'

I nodded.

When she left the room I watched water running from the tap. The pipes led to a pool under the house. Moss and algae grew up the sides. It didn't matter that Jake poured in bleach, the moss kept growing, turning the walls of the pool soft and dark. Green tentacles reached out, waving.

The bath was slowly filling, steam rising. I got in. There was nothing contained inside my skin. I had vision but I wasn't made of solid material. I closed my eyes and rocked to the sound of the water falling into the bath. I felt her strong arms lifting me. My hand rested against her chest. She was there when I called. Sometimes I called just to see if she would come. She always did. When Robby was at school and Dad was at the refinery she put on Doris and danced with me across the carpet, space between our faces as she smiled and sang. *I see your eyes in the starlight, I hear your laugh everywhere, I feel your touch in the sunlight, I know your voice in the air.*

The water kept filling the bath. My shoes and jumper and trousers grew heavy. I lay back and let the water close over my face, hot enough to burn. I held my breath. I could hear knocking from under the surface. I began to spin, water rushed into the spaces, as if I was a ship full of holes out at sea. The water came higher and higher – it was going to sink me. I held my breath. I was on a pathway deep under the ocean, heading towards the light in the sheep's eyes. 'Mum! Mum!' I called.

'Jim? Jim? What on earth?' It was Anne White pulling me

from the water. Liam was behind her, sticking up his thumb at me, and Deirdre was staring from the corner of the bathroom, Melanie gripped to her chest.

'Let's get you out of these for heaven's sake.' Anne White started to take off my clothes. She didn't know that it was my clothes holding me together, that beneath them was cold skin and the root and the hole under the root and beneath that, nothing at all. I twisted and struggled against Anne White.

'Calm down, Jim. Calm down. You can't take a bath with your clothes on.'

I opened my mouth to speak but there were no words, only *water water water* in a long hard stream into her face, blasting her to liquid mercury, hot with my temperature. *'Aaaaaaaaaaaahhhhhhhhhhhhh!'*

I kicked her as hard as I could in her chin, then in her blue doll's eye, then in her leg. I bucked and went as hard as a board and I bit at whatever was close to my mouth.

'Jake! Jake!' Anne called. 'Help me! Jake! Deirdre, get Jake! Quickly!'

Jake came and held my arms beside me, and Anne White pulled off my clothes until I was only the skin. There was nothing binding me. I was in pieces, stripped. I vomited bathwater onto the floor at Anne White's feet.

'Help me get him into bed,' she said.

Jake carried me. I let him. I didn't belong to myself.

'I'm sorry, Jim. There's been a lot of change.' She smoothed the sheet across my chest. 'But you need to learn that no matter how hard things get, you have to treat others with care.' She touched her chin where I had kicked. 'It's never acceptable to hurt someone.' She got up and switched off the light.

I got out of the bottom bunk, pulled the suitcase from the cupboard and climbed inside. I zipped up what I could. The sides of the case held me in like a membrane. I could hear my own breathing *in out in out* as if I were the lungs.

In the morning Liam unzipped me. 'Morning, Matchbox Boy.'

Anne White sent Deirdre, me and Liam into the yard to pick lemons. School was starting soon; these were our last days of leisure. Anne White told me that I would be in the same class as Liam.

'Lucky you,' said Liam, pulling off a green lemon.

'They kept you back two years, didn't they, Liam?' said Deirdre.

'Yep. Because I told the teacher to go fuck herself.' He picked another green lemon and threw it on the grass.

'What did she do?' asked Deirdre.

'She said "Where did you learn language like that?" and I said "From the fuck-off dictionary that my dad kept as a coaster for his beer glass."' Liam pulled off another green lemon and threw it at the fence. 'The other kids laughed but the teacher said I couldn't stay.' He kicked at the bricks that were going to be the edge of the vegetable patch. 'Nobody wants the older kids.'

'It's true,' said Deirdre. 'When I turn nine nobody will want me, but by then my nan will be back from her holiday and she'll take me to live at her B & B.'

'Bullshit and bullshit,' said Liam. He picked up a loose brick from the top of the garden wall. 'Put your finger under here, Flick.'

I didn't move.

'Don't do it, Jimmy,' said Deirdre.

'Go on, put it under here,' Liam said. He pointed.

'Don't do it, Jimmy – he'll hurt you,' Deirdre said.

'Go on, Flick. Just because you can't talk doesn't mean you're a chicken. This is what the kung-fu men do. It doesn't hurt. You just think it won't hurt and it won't. Go on.'

I listened to the wind blowing the trees. It had come all the way from outerspace, generated by the tides when the moon turned its face.

Liam grabbed my fingers and he put them on the brick and he put the other brick down on my fingers and he pressed.

'Stop, Liam, you'll hurt him,' said Deirdre.

Liam kept pressing down on the brick.

'Don't, Liam, don't,' Deirdre whined.

'*Don't, Liam, don't,*' Liam sang back. 'It doesn't hurt you, does it, Flick? You're a kung-fu man, right? You can't feel anything, can you, Flick?'

The wind from outer space first blew past the stars, gathering their dust and sending it in clumps to planet Earth. The end of my fingers tingled.

'Stop, Liam!' Deirdre shouted.

Liam's smile tore open his face and I saw a red crack. Inside it was the gun that shot Mrs Connelly and the son doing mouth-to-mouth.

Liam pressed the brick down harder. Deirdre screamed and pulled my hand out from under it. My fingers were bleeding and scraped and squashed. The nail of one was pushed into the skin. Deirdre was crying.

'Shut up, Dee Dee, crybaby,' said Liam.

Deirdre cried louder. Then she picked up a handful of dirt and threw it at Liam's face.

Liam rubbed the dirt from his eyes and mouth. 'It'll be you next,' he said to her. 'And it'll be your head, not your fingers.'

Deirdre turned and ran up to the house.

Liam picked up my hand and inspected my fingers. Flames jumped from under the nails. 'Kung-fu, man, aren't you, Flick?' he said, then he dropped my hand, pulled down his trousers and weed against the fence.

Anne White took me to the hospital with Deirdre while Jake took Liam to the football field to train him into consequences.

Emergency was underneath the other parts of the hospital. Children came and went, some with bruises under their eyes, some with trails of snot from their noses, some screaming. Deirdre played with Melanie, near the toy box. She sang to friends only she could see, her voice as soft as a butterfly. I sat and took in breaths. I could see the air; it had a vapour and travelled in currents around the room. Anne White read magazines and watched a television up in the corner too high to change the channels.

After a long time of waiting a doctor called John looked at my crushed fingers. He put them in a machine to take pictures of the bones. The bones are hollow. You could play music through them.

'He doesn't seem to be in too much pain,' said the doctor.

'But he should be in pain,' Anne White said. 'Shouldn't he? Something's not right if he can't feel this.'

John cleaned my fingers and said, 'We'll put them in plaster; only one is broken and it's a small break. You're lucky, Jim.'

While a nurse wrapped my fingers in wet white sheet I looked down through the floor of Emergency and saw the cemetery where all the children that didn't get fixed in the hospital lived. They were talking to each other. *Everything is on its own*, they said.

On the way home Anne White turned to me from the front seat.

'Are you okay, Jim?' she said. 'I'm sorry about Liam. He is a good boy, really, and I have to give him a chance. But I can see I'd better keep a closer eye on him — especially around you.'

'What about around me?' Deirdre asked, leaning forward from the back.

'You do a good enough job of taking care of yourself,' said Anne White, looking at Deirdre in the rear view mirror.

Deirdre slumped back against the seat, crinkling her nose.

'Jim, please let me know if you are alright,' Anne White said.

I was only Anne White's foster, like Deirdre and Liam. We were all pretending. What was alright? My organs were pumping. I wasn't in the cemetery. Was that what Anne White and John and Jan Watts and Uncle Rodney were all making sure didn't happen? Was that what Emergency was for? To stop it? Why?

Liam slept in another room that night. 'Just to give Jim a breather,' Anne White said.

'I'll miss you, Matchbox Boy,' Liam said, pulling his pyjamas from the shelf. 'Who will unzip you in the morning?'

It was the first time I would be alone in the room for the night.

'Sleep well, Jim,' Anne White said from the doorway. 'I hope your fingers don't feel too bad.' She was a painting wet at the edges, her pale colours dripping out of the frame.

When she left I closed the door and sat down on the bed. Liam's bunk hung over me. I closed my eyes, holding myself very still. In the floating world the dust was the same colour as the yellow stripe of the bee. The rest was black. If I held my breath, refusing any oxygen or hydrogen, I could see the dust shining.

'No, Liam, don't! Don't touch her!'

I opened my eyes when I heard Deirdre scream. The room was so light it made me blink. I looked at a poster stuck to the wall beside Liam's bunk. A man on a motorbike with one big leg on the dirt, the other on the pedal, looked down at me. The man held his helmet under his arm ready to put on his head as soon as he started his engine. The poster had white creases across it, and the edges were curled, as if it had been stuck to a lot of walls. Underneath the poster was a small photograph of Liam standing beside a man in a wheelchair with his arm around him. Liam's head was the same height as his dad's head. The dad had been brought down by the wheelchair.

I went to the cupboard and pulled out the red suitcase. I opened the lid, touching the silky material inside. The suitcase's stomach was empty and hungry after all the years of waiting in the cupboard for a change. I slid my fingers into the thin pockets under the lid, touching the cool edges. There was a smaller pocket, inside the big pocket, that I hadn't found before. I slid my hand in, feeling slowly from one end to the other. I touched something hard and stiff, like cardboard. I pulled out a photograph.

There was my mother and father when they were young, before my mother had her miracles. She was wearing a long dress with frills around the sleeves. Her feet were bare and one of them was lifted. My father was holding her from the side. There were trees on the edges and grass underneath. The wind blew my mother's hair up around her face. She was smiling as she tried to hold her hair back from her mouth and her eyes with her hand. Behind Mum and Dad was the cliff, and beyond that, the ocean. Mum used to read with her chair beside the cliff while Dad climbed down it and fished. He never forgot she was there, it didn't matter how much the fish pulled and jumped. You could see Mum's hand coming shyly round my dad's other side. The photograph was faded from the darkness of time in the hidden pocket of the suitcase.

After a long time of looking at the picture I saw a line that ran from my mother's fingers, curled up to my father's hair, and twisted and knotted through the locks. Then it seemed to end. My skin prickled as I searched; I felt myself grow hot. Then at last I saw the line coming down from my dad's hair, over his shoulder and joining up to my mum's waist. My heart pounded. I wanted to be slipping and sliding up and down that line as if it was a ride at Luna Park and I was miniature and could fit, sliding from one to the other, mother to father, father to mother, forever.

Downstairs a door slammed, and I heard Deirdre and Liam shouting.

I turned the photograph over.

Point Paradise Caravan Park, Point Paradise
Gavin and Paula

It was my mother's writing; I knew the round ups and the leaning downs, the i's with hardly a dot, and the thin u's. It was as if

I was looking at a code from another country so far away you couldn't find it on the atlas.

That night I didn't zip myself into the suitcase. There wouldn't be room for all the feelings coming from my pores. I needed space; I had *glad*, I had *want*, I had *maybe*, I had *Mum and Dad*.

I turned off the light and climbed into the bottom bunk holding the picture by the edges. I didn't want my fingers to contaminate it. I tried to hold exactly one millimetre, balancing it between my bandaged hand and my unbandaged one. But what if I fell asleep and the photograph was squashed beneath my bulk? What if it slipped through a crack and no matter how much I searched, or Anne White searched, or Jake searched, or the police, or the army, the picture would be lost forever, never to be found, always missing without an answer? I got out of bed and turned on the light. I balanced the picture on the table beneath the photograph of Liam's dad.

I kept my eyes glued. I was the night guard of the photograph. My fingers throbbed a forward pulse beneath the stiff bandage.

In the morning Liam stood beside the bed looking down at me. He was wearing his pyjamas; row after row of brown anchors leading down to his ankles and a sea of carpet. 'You look small in that bed, Flick,' he said. 'But in the suitcase you look big.' He picked up the top of my blankets, and waved them up and down. 'I'm emptying your fart bag,' he grinned. 'Did you like having the room to yourself?'

I shivered, my eyes on the photograph behind him.

He turned around. 'Who's that?' He leaned in close to the

picture. 'The man looks like you.' He picked up the photograph. 'Is that your dad?' He swung around to me. 'Is it?'

I got out of the bed and held out my hand.

Liam looked back at the photograph. 'Is that your mother? Come on, Flick. Talk, will you? Is that your mother?' Liam sat down on the chair still holding the picture. 'If it's not your mum, your old man's a root rat. My old man's a root rat even though he's in the chair. The ladies still like it. They climb up on the bars and hang off them with a drink and a smoke and they lift up their skirts so my dad can see the edge of their underpants. The skirts get stuck on the hooks he nails into the armrests before the ladies get there. They come around from the hospital. The hooks are to protect him from his enemies but they're good for hooking the ladies' skirts too. Ha ha!' he laughed. 'Is your old man a root rat?'

My arm ached from holding it out as I waited for Liam to give my photograph back. I tried to grab it but Liam held it high.

'She's nice, your mum. Lucky my dad never met her, or he would have rooted her. Then we'd be brothers. Liam and Jimmy, partners in crime.' He turned the photograph over and looked at the words. 'We'd be in the headlines. *Gun Crimes Across the Nation.* We'd be famous.' He touched my mum's writing. 'What does it say?' he asked me. 'Do you know?'

I stepped towards him.

'Is he still alive, your dad? I know your mum's dead — Anne told us. But what about him?' He smoothed his fingers over my dad then at last he gave me back the photograph.

I looked at it again and the picture led me straight to the cliff where I could watch them together, Mum and Dad.

'Let's see if Fanny Bite will give you chips for breakfast, Flick,' he said to me, leaving the room.

I put the photograph back against the wall under Liam's dad and followed him out the door.

As I walked downstairs I could feel the floor beneath my feet and the railing in my hand and the air entering my tubes, as if I had never felt them before. I breathed in deep and the oxygen charged my engine, turning the lights green for go.

Jake, Liam, Deirdre and Anne White were already sitting at the table. I went to my chair and joined them. I ate toast. It was dry at first but I added more butter, then I took a sip of milk to wash it down.

Anne White nudged Jake. He smiled at Anne White. 'You're a miracle worker, Anne.'

'Can I write on your bandage?' Deirdre asked. She picked up my arm and lay it on the table, then she got a texta from her pocket and wrote, *Deirdre your sister was here.*

'Do you think you're his sister, Deirdre?' said Liam.

Jake looked up from his bacon.

'Of course I'm his sister,' said Deirdre. 'And you're his brother, Liam. Didn't you know that?'

'Okay, Deirdre, just leave it there,' said Jake.

'Okay, Dad,' Liam said, putting egg onto his fork. Jake frowned.

After breakfast Liam said, 'Deirdre, come up to our room.'

'What for?' she asked.

'Because I said so.'

'That's not a reason.'

Liam looked at me. 'Because Flick wants you to.'

'Do you, Jimmy?' Deirdre asked me.

Something was forming in the core. My sensors were

awakening; the wind in the photograph had set my cells in motion. I nodded my head.

'You do!' she said. She put her small arms around my neck and held tight. She smelled of sugar. When she let go she took my hand and pulled me along the row of bedrooms until we came to mine and Liam's. She led us in and she looked at Liam and said, 'Well, what?'

Liam took the photograph from the desk and showed Deirdre. 'They're his mum and dad. His mum's dead . . .'

'Liam.' She shook her head and frowned at him.

'What?'

'You shouldn't say that.'

'Why not?'

'You'll make Jimmy sad.'

'But his dad's not dead. Just his mum.'

'Dads don't count.'

'Yes they do. They count more. Just because you don't have one.'

'I do have one and he's not in a wheelchair.'

'Bullshit, Deirdre. You don't have a dad.'

She snorted air out of her nostrils, then turned to me. 'What did you want me to come up here for, Jimmy?'

'Have a look at this.' Liam turned the picture around and gave it to Deirdre. 'Read what it says.'

'Point Paradise Caravan Park, Point Paradise,' Deirdre read out. 'Gavin and Paula.' She turned the photograph back around. 'Is that your mum?' she asked me.

'Yep,' said Liam. 'And the man is his dad. You can tell. Flick looks almost exactly the same as him.'

'Your mum was pretty, Jimmy.'

'Yeah, but she's dead,' said Liam. 'It's his dad that's alive.'

'But his dad doesn't want him or he wouldn't be here. So his dad may as well be dead,' said Deirdre.

'But it's his *dad*.' Liam turned to me. 'I've left every foster home to get back to my dad. I hitch or catch a train or a bus. But I don't get my hopes up. Jan Watts says not to. *You're old enough now to lower your expectations, Liam.* I lower them lower and lower but I never lower my expectations enough because when I get there Dad says, *Bugger off, you little bastard.* When I'm eighteen I'll go and live with him. I can cook for both of us. I'll keep his fridge full of tinnies and we'll get a dog and I'll train it to pull Dad's chair round the house so Dad can use his hands for smoking and changing the channel.'

'I like dogs,' said Deirdre. 'Maybe I'll come and visit.'

'Maybe I won't invite you.'

'Maybe you'll still be in jail.' Deirdre stuck her tongue out at Liam and gave the photograph back to me.

'Do you want to find your dad?' Liam asked me.

'Do you, Jimmy?' said Deirdre.

My dad was missing. It was one thing I knew. I didn't know the other things I should have known; I never did know them. But I knew my dad was missing.

'Do you, Flick? Just nod, that's all you have to do.' Liam came close to my face and spoke very slowly. 'Juuusssstttt noood, thaaattt's all youuu haaaavveee tooo do. Do you want to find your dad?'

'He can understand you, Liam. He just doesn't want to talk.'

'Flick,' said Liam suddenly, 'if you can understand me, then answer me. It's not a hard question. You have a dad. Here he is in the photo. If you want to see him, then nod for a yes.'

'Liam, don't pressure him.'

'Deirdre, he's *got* a *dad*.'

'But even if he has a dad, so what? You got a dad and you're still here.'

'Fuck you.'

'Fuck you.'

Liam grabbed Deirdre's arm near the elbow and squeezed. Deirdre squealed.

I looked at the woman who was my mum. I saw the way the line wrapped around all of her fingers and travelled up along her arms and curled itself around her ears and then ran across to her dress and then spread out from her to the trees and then kept on going out of the frame of the picture. Then I saw that the line entered the picture again and ran back to my dad. The line began with him; he was the starting point. It came out of his hand, the hand closest to the frame, and then it crossed to my mother, and back to him. It went full circle. My dad was at the beginning and the end.

'Yes,' I said. 'Yes.'

They both turned to me.

'He can talk!' said Liam.

'Jimmy! You talked!' Deirdre grabbed my hand.

'He can bloody talk.'

'I always knew he could talk,' said Deirdre.

'No you didn't. You're just saying that now, Deirdre.'

'I *did* know.'

'Bullshit.' Liam turned to me. 'Say something else, Flick.'

'He doesn't have to talk just because you say so.' Deirdre put her hands on her hips. 'Just talk when you want to, Jimmy, not because Liam tells you to. He's not the boss.'

'I am the boss. I'm fourteen at my next birthday.'

'Yeah, but nobody knows when that is, so you'll always be thirteen.'

'Fuck off, Deirdre.' Liam pushed her in the chest.

I held the photograph up to Liam and Deirdre. 'Mum and Dad,' I said.

Liam looked at me in surprise. 'You really can talk.'

'Yes, he really can,' said Deirdre.

'Why didn't he before?'

'He didn't have a reason before.'

'He does now, don't you, Flick? You got to go find your old man.'

'Don't pressure him, Liam.'

'He's got an old man. He has to go and find him.'

'Why?'

'Because it's his dad. Jake's not his dad. The man in the picture is, Dee Dee. He's got one.'

'But you've got one . . .'

'Shut up about that, Deirdre. I'm warning you. Shut up.'

'Okay. But I'm just saying . . .'

'Jimmy has to go and see his dad. You know he does.'

Deirdre pulled at Liam's sleeve. 'What if he can't find him? What if he can't find him and he hasn't lowered his expectations?'

'Of course he'll find him. We'll help him.'

'How can we help him?'

'We'll organise it. We'll make a plan for him. Now that he can talk.'

'Jimmy –' Deirdre took my hand – 'do you want us to make a plan?'

It was happening so fast. Like the hand beneath the sea that made the waves, something was pushing us.

I nodded.

'And we won't tell Anne. We won't tell anyone, will we, Deirdre?'

'Not if you don't want us to, Jimmy, we won't.'

Liam put his hand on my shoulder. 'No way will we tell, Flick.'

'Even if they torture us,' said Deirdre, her face serious.

'Even if we were going to die.'

Deirdre looked at Liam as if she didn't understand his mechanics. 'You never did anything nice before, Liam. How come you are now?'

'If his dad's not dead he needs to see him.'

'Nothing was different after you saw your old man.'

'At least I got an old man.' Liam grabbed Deirdre by the end of the nose and twisted. 'Yours fucked your mum and ran, she was so ugly.' He twisted harder.

Deirdre screamed and Anne White came in. Deirdre pressed against her, crying.

'This is the last time I'm doing this! You kids have worn me out!' Anne White said.

Anne White and Jake took us on a picnic with other fosters beside a brown river. When we got out of the car I walked across the grass to the edge. Life drifted across the top of the water; birds, boats, plastic, feathers that had fallen from the wing, but under the surface nothing lived. The river was a moat to the floating world. You just had to cross it. I waded in to my ankles and watched as water rose up against the sides of my shoes.

'Come back from there, Jim!' Anne White called to me.

I stepped back and squatted on the muddy bank to examine the wet lines left across my sneakers. I put my hand to my chest. My organs pumped against my palm.

There were rugs spread across the grass and there was a picnic table and it was covered in containers of food and some was on plates – lamingtons and oranges, cut up, sandwiches with Vegemite and biscuits and cakes and frankfurts with sauce. The fosters ran across the grass chasing the ball. Jake was the coach. He kept running and blowing his whistle and shouting, 'That's it, Liam, faster, stay down the sides, boy, that's it, don't let them get ahead!'

I sat beside Deirdre on the grass not far from the river. She was combing Melanie's hair. *'Dress me up and play with me, touch me softly, be my love, all I want is you, don't go, don't go, don't go,'* she sang. Her words were like water over pebbles. *'Oh how I love you, touch me, touch me, don't leave don't leave me, don't leave me.'* She put her doll in my lap. *'Touch me softly, touch me . . .'*

Adults fed the fosters, passing plates of donuts and sausages and cakes. A foster mother brought a plate of sausages and chips to Deirdre and me. The fosters were all different sizes; there were other big ones, like Liam, and other smaller ones, like Deirdre. We were loose from each other and from the adults. We had come from somewhere but that place was gone – our lines had no ending.

I was going to look for my dad. The line began inside him, put there by the refinery, then it moved out from him into my mother, entering her stream and setting her to life. Was I joined by the same line?

I watched the river, my eyes resting on its surface. At first I thought the water was static but as I watched I saw that it *was* moving. The surprise movement was slow but it was there, forward.

'Do you want me to come with you?' Deirdre asked.

I shook my head, keeping my eyes on the momentum of brown water.

'Do you know how far it is from here?'

I shook my head again.

'Anne has a map book. That's how she knows where to find her fosters.' Deirdre stuck a sausage into sauce and took a bite. She picked up her doll, leaving a smear of red across its cheek. She lifted the doll to my ear. Her fingers smelled of sausage. 'I will wait for you,' she sang. '*Kiss kiss*. I love you, Jimmy, *kiss kiss*. *Touch me, touch me softly* . . .' She passed me the sausage and I ate it.

That night Liam and me and Deirdre sat on Deirdre's bed with the lights off. We were looking at a book of maps with a torch Liam took from Jake's storage shelf.

'Don't ask Liam anything because he can't read,' said Deirdre, flicking through the pages. The torch lit the bottom half of Liam's and Deirdre's faces.

'I can't read but I can smoke,' said Liam, sticking the torch in his mouth and shining it on the ceiling. 'What's more fun?'

'Don't do that, Liam,' whispered Deirdre. 'We can't see.'

Liam aimed the torch onto the maps, lighting up the black crisscrossing lines over the page. 'Point Cale, Point Eddington, Point Elsworth, Point Dixon . . .' Deirdre read out.

'Point Dick,' Liam interrupted.

'Point Crap,' Deirdre giggled.

'Point Crack.'

'Point Arse.'

'Point Paradise,' I said.

They both looked at me, their faces shadowy, smiles gone. 'Point Paradise,' they said, as if they'd just remembered.

Downstairs Jake and Anne White cleared the table and picked up the toys. *They better be asleep, Jake, I can't do this again — what were we thinking, taking on Jim? I don't know how much hope there is for him . . . I always said the day I started thinking like that about any of them would be the day I needed to stop. I don't know if there's anyone inside there at all, Jake. How can I think that about a child? It's not right.*

Deirdre ran her finger down a long line of names, her lips moving as she read them out under her breath. She turned page after page. I heard the flutter of paper and Liam's breath as we waited.

'When you find him,' Liam whispered, 'tell him you can't come back here or I'll drown you. Show him your broken finger and tell him I did it. Tell him I'd never give you mouth-to-mouth like Mrs Connelly's son. I could if I wanted — I know how — but I wouldn't. I'd let you drown before I did that.'

'Found it.' said Deirdre.

Liquid rushed through my tributaries, like the fluid used to make the flames jump high.

'Bingo,' said Liam.

'What's bingo?' asked Deirdre.

'You're dumb,' said Liam.

'You're dumb. No wonder your dad said fuck off.'

'No wonder yours topped himself.'

'He did not.'

'He did so. Anne told Jake. That's why you're here. He overdosed because he couldn't get a job.'

'He did not.'

'Did so.'

'He topped himself but it wasn't because he couldn't get a job.'

'Then why?'

'Because if he didn't top himself the dog men would get him — he owed them money. They'd take the silver cages off the dogs' mouths and let them at him. That's why I'm here; the dogs would've hurt too much. You're here because you aren't old enough for jail.'

'Point Paradise,' I reminded them.

'Yes,' said Deirdre. 'Map two hundred and one.' She flicked through the pages. Point Paradise was on a map. There was a number. I was coming tightly together, beginning to spin, pain behind every rotation. Point Paradise! The wind and the cliffs and the waves coming in one after another behind my mum and dad where they stood, the camera resting on the branch of a tree, set to automatic, my dad running back to her, not wanting to be away for longer than a second, rushing back so he could put his arm around her and feel the warmth of what they would become if they stayed together. He had to be quick before the light and the flash saying it was too late *too late* the picture is already taken.

'Map two hundred and one. Found it.' Deirdre held up the book.

Suddenly the door swung open and Jake switched on the light.

'What the hell?' I saw the words coming out of Jake's mouth in a sonar wave. His face was red and as round as a balloon. 'Leave each other alone and get into bed!'

We scattered like marbles. I went back to my room with Liam. He climbed up onto his top bunk and I climbed into the bottom. I knew the photograph was there on the wall beneath Liam's; I was linked to it by Map Two Hundred and One.

'You're going to need money,' whispered Liam. 'You have to catch a train or a bus or a plane.'

'Where will we get the money?' I asked.

'We got to steal it from Jake. I don't care if I get busted. I'm not staying here anyway.'

'Where are you going?'

'Morecroft. Juvenile home. Until I'm eighteen. Then I'll go and live with Dad. He can't walk, so what can he do about it? He can't get out of his chair and chase me out with a stick, can he? If he calls the cops I'll tell them it was him who never locked the gun cupboard, not Gary. Dad said he did lock it and the jury believed him because of the wheelchair, but he never did. I know because when I went there it wasn't locked. I just went halfway down the stairs and pulled it open. It was easy.' His bunk creaked beneath his weight. 'Goodnight, Jimmy.'

'Goodnight, Liam. Goodnight.'

In the photograph stuck to the wall above mine, a younger Liam stood with his arm around his dad, their heads level. It was the wall of fathers.

Liam and me were at the back of Anne White's yard behind the shed. Liam dragged his hand along the three big drums, *clink clunk clonk* up and down. He threw a handful of mud into the drum of water then he dragged over an empty wooden milk crate and turned it upside down. 'Climb up,' he said to me.

I climbed up and the crate wobbled.

'There was a man in the city who cut up bodies and put them in a tank like this.' Liam knocked the side of the drum with his fist. 'But it wasn't water in there – it was acid and the acid fried the bodies, only leaving the bones and the teeth, and that's what gave the man away to the cops. There were five people in one tank plus a dog. The man could fit them all in because they had no bodies. The acid melted the flesh away in sixty seconds.' He leaned against the drum. 'Have a look over the edge, Flick.'

I leaned over, my hands on the rim.

'See yourself?' Liam asked. 'That tank is taller than you.' He threw in another handful of dirt. It disturbed the surface, leaving holes. 'The man didn't do it alone. He had accomplices. He was the ringleader of his family. He did the killing and his brothers and his uncle and his cousins helped him cut up the bodies. They were the ones who bought the acid, poured it into the tank, put in the pieces and stirred. Can you swim, Flick? If you got into that tank the water would go over your head, but if you could swim you'd be alright.'

I looked into the water until it was as if I was under the surface. Everything was slow and soft, at first floating, but then falling. I was going down . . . I stepped back, the breath entering me sharply. The crate almost tipped.

'Careful, Flick,' said Liam.

Deirdre came down from the house carrying something in her hand. 'Map Two Hundred and One,' she said, passing it to me. 'I tore it out.'

'Open it, Flick, let's have a look.'

Deirdre was on one side and Liam was on the other, the three drums behind us as we leaned towards the map. Deirdre pointed. I followed the line of her chipped yellow nail polish to the end of her finger where it joined the map. Point Paradise.

'We are here,' she said, then she drew her finger across slowly. 'And Point Paradise is . . . here. It's not that far, Jimmy. If you had money, you could catch a bus.'

'Then that's what he'll do,' said Liam.

Deirdre dropped her hands from the map. She looked at Liam. 'What will he do if his dad's not there?'

'He has to try,' said Liam.

'But what if . . .'

'It's his dad. He has to try.'

'But . . .'

'If he doesn't try then he may as well be dead – like his mum.'

'Liam!'

'I have to try,' I told her.

Deirdre turned to me. 'Are you sure, Jimmy?'

'Of course he's sure.'

'I have to try,' I repeated. 'I have to try, Deirdre.'

'You do,' said Liam. 'We're going to get him some money. The bus could be more than twenty dollars.'

'How are you going to do that?'

'We're going to steal it from Jake. I told you.'

'Be careful,' said Deirdre.

'Be careful,' copied Liam.

I lay on my bunk with the lights off and looked at the inside of dust. It was as if I had lenses attached to my eyes and they could magnify the particles. I saw little bright circles joined together by glowing bars. I watched them lifting up and sinking. At first when I looked I couldn't see any pattern, but I kept watching. I watched all night and just before the morning I saw one. The circles expanded, pulling the bars of light taut, about to burst apart, and just when I thought they would separate they began to move in towards each other again. The circles never stopped moving and the bars holding them together didn't break, even though they were only made of light, not rope or chain or rubber.

When I opened my eyes I saw Liam's red face hanging over the side of his bunk, looking in at me. 'Your eyeballs were moving so fast I was waiting for them to explode,' he said. His head disappeared back over the top and down came the anchors.

It was Sunday morning and we had just finished breakfast. Anne White was tidying with Deirdre.

'Come with me,' said Liam. 'You're the decoy.'

'What's a decoy?' I asked him.

'Something for Jake to talk to while I do the deed.'

'What deed?'

'Stealing the money, Flick, remember? Jake's got plenty. The government pays him for looking after us. It's compensation, like when you crash your car.' He grabbed my arm. 'Come on.' He took me outside where we could see Jake's truck parked at the side of the house. You had to walk up steps to get inside. 'Jake is working under the truck. You go hang around him and act like you're interested in what he's doing.'

'Okay,' I said. 'Jimmy the decoy.'

'That's right, but, Jim, you can't talk. You're not going to talk to him, are you? He can't know that you talk.'

'Okay, Liam, okay. Jimmy the decoy who doesn't talk.'

Liam grinned. 'Funnyman Flick,' he said. Then he headed for Jake's truck. It said *Towing 24 hours*. Jake hooked up broken cars to his bumper and towed them to the tip. It took all his strength to face the road at three o'clock in the morning. And all that time in the car wasn't good for his diet. Anne White made him pack Tupperware salads but he liked pies and sauce and hamburgers from the takeaway more.

I went to where Jake's legs stuck out. I didn't know what to do. Soon he came out on a tray with four wheels, as if he was the dinner. 'Jim,' he said, 'I didn't know you were there. Anne's inside.'

I shook my head. Then I pointed to the wheels of the truck.

'Big bloody things, aren't they?' said Jake. He went close to the tyre and felt it with his fingers. 'Have a look at the treads on these, Jim.'

I came closer to Jake than I had ever been before, and bent close to his tyres.

Jake touched the grooves in the rubber with his finger. 'See how worn the treads are? That's how many bloody cars I've towed.' He looked at me and smiled. 'Like trucks, do you, mate?' He put his hand on the body.

I heard a small bump coming from the front end.

Jake looked up.

I grabbed his hand and led him to the back of the truck. He let me take him, as if he was proud of the development. I pointed to the towing hook, raising my eyebrows.

'Yes, Jim, that's the most important thing on the truck. That hook is what puts your dinner on the table.' He tugged on the chain that joined the hook to the crane. 'Unbreakable,' he said. Could pull a bloody trailer full of elephants if I needed to.'

I smiled up at Jake, and touched the chain. There was another bump from the front. Jake frowned.

I ran back to the tray with wheels, beside the truck and lay down on it. I pushed myself under the way Jake did. My ceiling was dark steel, thick with the rust of towing.

Jake grabbed my feet and pulled me back out. 'Jim! Don't

do that. Don't ever do that. The truck's not a toy. Don't even touch it unless I'm here.'

I nodded and smiled.

Jake sighed. 'It's good to see you making an effort to get involved, Jim. Just leave the truck alone when I'm not around.' He'd forgotten about the noise in the cabin. He was used to a lot of noises from all the kids he'd looked after, some his own and some he pretended.

I smiled, nodded some more and then I left him there. When I passed the cabin Liam was gone.

After dinner, up in our room, Liam fanned green money out in his hand. 'Eighty bucks, Flick. Now you need somewhere to hide it.' He looked through his cupboard. He threw t-shirts and shorts and singlets across the floor. He pulled out a black pouch. 'For sunglasses,' he said. 'I took it from the chemist. I never got the sunglasses; only the pouch.' He pushed the money into the pouch then he gave it to me. 'Hide it under your mattress.'

Anne White took us to crafts. I watched the way the paper squares fell to see if the angles and colours matched. 'Don't you want to use the paper, Jim?' Anne White asked. When I didn't answer I saw her roll her eyes at another foster mother.

Deirdre made a doll from orange pipe cleaners with a cork for a head. She drew little black crosses on the cork for eyes and wrapped a piece of material around its middle for a skirt. Deirdre called her pipe doll Silver. *Take me to heaven, Silver, oh, take me to heaven,* she sang, turning Silver through the air. *'Lift me on your back and fly me to the stars . . .'*

Liam told Anne White he was too old for crafts but she said, 'You can be creative at any age.'

Liam created a gun from clay. When Anne White turned her back to pour cordial he aimed his clay gun at her head and fired.

When Anne White went to help with the sandwich plates, Liam spoke to Deirdre. 'He's got to go before school starts,' he said, his face tight with a purpose. 'Before everyone knows who he is and that he lives here.' Liam looked as old as his father, each freckle the mark of another year, merging into each other across his cheeks.

'Speak to Silver and she can tell me,' said Deirdre, stretching out Silver's arms.

'Don't be an idiot.' Liam grabbed Silver and bent her, leaving clay on her pipe-cleaner arms.

Deirdre grabbed her back. 'Tell Silver or I won't help.'

'Alright, alright. Give her to me,' said Liam.

'Don't hurt her.' Deirdre passed Silver back to Liam.

'Silver, tell Deirdre that Flick has to leave before school starts. Tell her she has to ring up the buses and ask when one goes through Point Paradise from here. She has to get the number. She has to do it when Anne can't see. Tell her or I'll use you to wipe my arse.' Liam passed Silver back to Deirdre.

'Liam!' Deirdre patted Silver's cork then held her to her ear to listen to Liam's message. She listened for a while, nodding her head and saying, 'Hmmm . . . hmmmmm.' Then when Silver was finished she said, 'Don't worry, Silver – Liam is just sad because his mum has two faces and his dad likes his smokes more than him. Silver, tell him I will call the buses when Anne is doing the ironing in front of *The Bold and the Beautiful* because she never turns it off even for one second and sometimes she cries and even on the ads she stays and puts her iron down to sip her coffee. That's when I'll call. Tell him that, Silver. And tell him if he uses you to wipe his arse you'll put a pipe cleaner through his dick and his wee will come out in his shorts. I love you, Silver, *kiss kiss*.' She kissed the cork and passed Silver back to Liam.

'*Silver, I love you, kiss kiss*.' Liam rubbed Silver against the crotch of his trousers and threw her in the air. She landed at Deirdre's feet.

Anne White came back in and saw. 'Liam, you are really pushing your luck.'

'Liam, you are really pushing your *fuck you*,' Liam whispered.

In the afternoon, while Liam was at his reading lesson, Deirdre and me waited for *The Bold and the Beautiful*. Just before it came on, Anne White dragged out the ironing board. Deirdre took my hand and we went into the kitchen and Deirdre looked up buses in the telephone book. She called them and we waited and waited and she made me check on Anne White and Anne White was sniffing and sipping and ironing and at last Deirdre spoke to the right person who said the South Eastern Bus leaves from High Street Depot at midday on Saturday. Deirdre wrote *midday* down on a piece of paper, *Saturday*.

She folded up the piece of paper and I followed her to my room.

'Where's the money?' she asked me.

I pulled the pouch out from under the mattress. Deirdre folded the piece of paper three times, kissed it then put it in the pouch with the money and the map.

'You have to get a taxi to High Street,' said Deirdre. 'You'll get lost. I've been to High Street – it's big with tunnels and trains and there's a place just for the buses but you have to speak to them and tell them. I'll write down what you have to say. You have to pay for your ticket. You have to give them the money, okay? Jimmy, if your dad tells you to get fucked, you can take your suitcase and I'll take Silver and Barbie and you can come to my nan's B & B with me, okay?'

'Okay, Deirdre, okay,' I said.

Anne White gave us Cokes because it was Friday afternoon and in only one more week school was starting so enjoy your freedom. We sat in a row along the fence beside the empty vegetable patch. The red can felt cold and heavy as a bomb in my hands.

'How are we going to get him out of here without Anne and Jake noticing?' Deirdre asked, sticking her finger into the hole at the top of her can.

Liam took a long drink, then he turned to me. 'Flick, you have to say you're sick and you have to go to bed. Then you can sneak out to the taxi that we call for you when Anne and Jake take me to training. Taxis are used to coming for the fosters. You got to talk, Flick, you got to tell the taxi driver to take you to the bus stop. He'll know where to drop you.' Liam burped, sending Coke vapours over Deirdre and me. 'When Anne sees you're gone I'll tell them that I made you walk to the mall by yourself to buy me cigarettes. I'll tell them that I said to you if you didn't do it I'd stick your head in the toilet and flush and then when they punish me I'll put holes in Anne's couch with a cigarette, don't worry about that. I'll push my cigarette into the plastic cover until it melts right through and burns the flowers. Fuck her. I've got cigarettes saved. I could smoke them but I don't want to. I only will when they find out you're gone and that's when I'll say it was my fault and they'll take me in the cop car to find you because I was your last contact, and every time they see a kid that almost looks like you I'll say, *That's him, that's him!* We'll go and search the kid but it won't be you because you'll be on the bus on the way to Point Paradise.' Liam finished his drink, threw the empty can into the air and kicked it with his foot. 'I'll smoke the cigarette when the cops are interviewing me too. I'll say, "Get me a lawyer."' He turned to me. 'Even if your dad says he doesn't want to see you, don't listen, Flick. Just sit in his house –'

'Caravan,' Deirdre interrupted.

'Just sit in his caravan and say, *If you send me back to the foster home, Liam David Lescock will kill me.*' Liam jumped off the fence, put his hands around my throat and squeezed. 'And I will, you little bastard, I will.'

I let him squeeze until I could feel the sides of my throat pipe touch.

Deirdre kicked Liam just below the knee. 'Leave him alone or I'll get Jake.'

Liam let go of my neck and I fell forward off the fence.

'Get Jake, I don't give a fuck,' he said, standing on the empty can.

I lay on my bed holding the sunglasses pouch and the photograph. The photograph was crushed; particles of my parents had entered the skin of my hands the way, if you leave it, water goes into a potato. The picture of the cliff, my mum in her dress, the grass beneath her feet, and the sea beyond the cliff were inside me, like osmosis.

For the whole of the next week Liam and Deirdre made plans around my head. It was all they talked about: the map, the taxi, the bus, the caravan park, what I would say, what my dad would say, what I would do if he wasn't there, what I would do if he was. When they weren't planning they were fighting.

Deirdre wrote a list of the words I needed to use: *How much? Where is it? What time? Hello, Dad.* 'After that you have to think of the words for yourself, Jimmy.'

'He'll know what to say — he just has to get there,' said Liam.

'Did you know what to say?' asked Deirdre.

'It doesn't make any difference what I say,' said Liam, pushing her in the chest.

Anne White took me to Cook Road Medical to have my cast removed. 'This shouldn't hurt,' said the doctor. I held out my hand. The doctor cut with the pruners, until my cast was in half. I read *Deirdre your sister* but the rest fell to the floor. 'Perfect recovery,' said the doctor, inspecting my fingers. They had changed colour, turning pale without the sun. There was dried blood around the nail. 'Can you move your fingers for me, Jim?'

I kept them motionless.

'He's still coming to grips with things,' said Anne White, as if she was saying sorry.

In Anne White's car on the way home I wriggled my new fingers in my sleeve. They were ready.

Early on Saturday morning Deirdre told Anne White I was sick. 'He vomited and it missed the toilet, Anne. I cleaned it up with the hand soap,' she said, smiling at Anne White. 'Are you glad I cleaned it up?'

'Yes, Deirdre, thank you.' Anne White pressed her palm to my forehead. 'But it's not good news you are sick, Jim.' No messages entered, as if her hand wasn't connected to the rest of her. 'Maybe you do feel hot.'

'He just needs to go and have a rest, doesn't he, Anne?' said Deirdre, sweet as a lolly.

'Yes, I suppose he does, Deirdre,' said Anne White. 'But it's Liam's game this morning. Maybe he can rest in the car while I watch the game and meet with his teacher.'

'But he could vomit again and it smelled like the compost when Jake digs it into the ground. You need to wear a mask. Plus he could be catching,' Deirdre said.

Anne White shook her head. 'That's true . . . It's good of you to give it so much thought, Deirdre, but I have to see Liam's game. The other foster parents will be there and so will Liam's teachers for next year. Jim has to come. I can't have him home alone.'

'I could stay home with him, Anne. I could read to him if he can't sleep. I don't mind.' Deirdre smiled up at Anne White.

'Oh dear . . . oh no, I don't think . . . Let me talk to Jake. Thank you for being so helpful, Deirdre. Maybe you can take Jim to his room now and I'll go and speak with Jake.'

Deirdre took my hand and led me to the bedroom.

'Get into bed and look tired,' she whispered.

I got into my bed with all my clothes on, even my shoes.

Liam came in wearing his football shorts. His cheeks looked flushed and full with the plan. 'What happened?' he asked Deirdre. 'Did she say yes? Can he stay home?'

'I don't know,' she answered. 'She's asking Jake.'

'He has to stay home.'

'Anne has to talk to Jake. If he says yes . . .'

'But if he doesn't stay home he can't get on the bus.'

'Anne is –'

'And then he can't get to Point Paradise and see his dad. He's got to see him, Deirdre!'

Deirdre pulled a book from the shelf and opened it on her lap. 'We don't even know if his dad is at Point Paradise. He could be anywhere. How do we know?'

'We do know. That's where he is. Where else would he be? It said it on the photograph.' Liam frowned.

'That photograph is a hundred years old, Liam.' She looked up at him. 'Get out! When Anne comes up to check on us she has to see me reading and being good and if you're here she won't. Get out. Quick!'

'Okay, okay,' said Liam, leaving the room.

Deirdre started to read but the words weren't from the book; they were made up and the longer they went on the more they became a song instead of a story. 'And then the man stood up and he looked tall, his shoulders were so strong he could lift a horse or a car and he said, Hello, hello, my little boy, I love you, I will never smack you, I will never take you into the garage, I will never say, Count everything on the shelves, that's all you have to do, count everything on the shelves. Keep counting, keep counting, how many how many how many, that's it, little boy, that's it, lean forward a bit more, that's it. I will buy you snacks and you can choose whichever snack, I will never say too expensive put it back, choose something else. I will just say eat up, eat up, because I love you . . .'

I felt my eyes closing, as if there was no plan anymore, it was just me and the song of Deirdre. I was with her in the garage. I took her hand and I said, Come away, come away, and she said, I can't, he's too big, and I said, You can, and she said, I can't, he's too strong, and I said, Yes you can. Look! Look! I took matches from my pocket and I lit one, then with the other hand I shook the open jerry can so the petrol sprayed up, and I threw the match into the shimmering air *boom!* and we ran and ran and we changed what happened so that it didn't happen. We made it different.

Anne White and Jake were standing at the door. Anne White was smiling at Deirdre.

'You're a good girl, Deirdre. I wish all my children were as good as you. It's lovely to see you reading to Jim.'

Deirdre smiled back and her eyelashes were like two fluttering wings over her visions. 'I like reading, Anne.'

Jake took Anne White's hand. 'I think they'll be fine. The important thing is that Liam will be out of the house with us,' he said, as if we couldn't hear.

Anne White nodded. 'I think you're right. I'll drop back at half-time to check on them.' She put her hand on my forehead again. 'You don't have a temperature, Jim. Could be gastro, but if you don't feel better by this afternoon we'll take you to see the doctor, okay?'

I nodded then closed my eyes, as if I was very tired.

'Best idea is to sleep these things off,' said Jake. 'Come on, Anne, we don't want to be late.'

'Thank you, Deirdre, it's very kind of you to stay home with Jim when you could be coming out with us. I'll put a tick on the board and it will add up to a star.' Anne White patted Deirdre on the head. 'I'll see you at half-time.'

'Okay, Anne. And don't worry — I'll take care of Jim.'

'Thank you, Dee Dee,' said Anne White, then she and Jake went downstairs.

Liam put his head in the room. 'Flick,' he whispered. 'Flick, you're going. This is it – you got the all-clear.'

'Get out, Liam!' Deirdre hissed. 'They'll be waiting for you!'

'I'm going, I'm going. And remember, Flick, if you come back I'm going to kill you.' Liam's eyes flashed green. I smiled at him. He smiled back and light came from his eyes in a ray. 'Good luck, Flick,' he said, and then he was gone.

As soon as we heard the front door close Deirdre pulled back my blankets. 'Quick. Quick, Jimmy.' She looked scared and happy. 'You need to bring something to wear at your dad's. You have to have pyjamas. You've got pyjamas, right?' She didn't give me time to answer. 'We have to ring up the taxi now. We have to do it fast. Come on!'

I got out of the bed and followed her to the telephone.

'Have you got everything? Have you got the money?' she asked, pressing the numbers.

I nodded, gripping the pouch in my hand.

Deirdre tapped the table with her finger. 'Yes please, yes please, thirty-five Cook Road. Yes, to High Street, where the buses go . . .' she said. 'Yes, alright, we'll wait at the door. Thank you. He's only small, so you have to take special care. He's a high-needs kid . . . Yes a *foster* . . . Please hurry, he doesn't want to miss the bus.'

She hung up the telephone, scribbled something down on a piece of paper and passed it to me. 'This is Anne's number, put it in your pocket. Ring it if you get lost or if your dad's not there or he doesn't want you. The taxi is going to be here *very* soon, Jim. The driver's going to beep the horn, okay?' Deirdre grabbed my hand and I could feel her network pulsing hotly through her skin.

We sat against the door, everything suddenly still and calm. I heard a single bird sing to its missing friend. *Won't you tell me that you love me? Won't you tell me that you do?*

'What will you say to him, Jim, when you see him?'

I didn't know.

'If he's not in the caravan you can come back, okay? I'm staying until my nan's B & B is ready so it will be a long time, if I don't drive Anne crazy. I will still be here, okay?' She put her arms around me and held me. 'I love you, Jimmy. I love you.'

Then the horn sounded from the taxi outside and she pulled open the door. 'Quick Jimmy. Tell the taxi – quick!'

I went to the taxi waiting at the kerb and I pulled open the heavy door. A man was in the front and he said, 'Hop in, kid.'

I climbed into the taxi.

'Pull the door shut tight, okay?' said the man. 'High Street, right?'

I held the money pouch and nodded. My heart pounded in the centre *hurryhurry hurryhurry hurryhurry*.

As the taxi moved away from the kerb I looked through the window at Deirdre, who stood at Anne White's door, waving to me, smiling, and it was as if I was her little boy going on his first solo adventure. Goodbye, Deirdre, goodbye.

I looked out the window as the taxi drove along the streets. There were other cars, bicycles, houses, cats, clouds, painted stripes along the road, bins, lights, windows, fences, birds, wires from house to house but I didn't belong to them. I was between worlds, like the horizon. The hum of the engine vibrated through my skin, quickening my cells.

'So where are you going?' the driver asked.

'Point Paradise,' I answered.

'Never heard of it,' the man said. 'But it sounds alright.' His elbow hung out the window. 'Mind if I smoke?'

I didn't mind.

He lit a cigarette and the smoke drifted around the car. I was an arrow in the middle, heading for the target.

I unfolded the photograph in my hand; white lines ran across my mum's neck and my dad's chest. The edges were torn. Deirdre had left a green cordial stain in the corner and Liam had left a tear.

'Not far now,' the man said. 'See up ahead?' He pointed and I saw signs and traffic and the cells of all the people through their skin. I saw their tubal systems making their legs move quickly across the streets as they ran to their trains and buses. The taxi driver dragged back his last mouthful of smoke, then blew it straight up into the air. I watched a slow grey snake wind its way around the body of the taxi.

'Nice day for a trip,' the man said. 'Wish it was me going.'

The man drove the taxi to the gutter. The red numbers on the taxi meter said sixteen dollars. I gave the man two ten-dollar notes and he pulled out his box and gave me back four. 'Good luck,' he said. I stuffed the four into the pouch.

'Thank you, thank you,' I said. 'Thank you, driver.'

The world outside the taxi was cold and brightly lit, as if the sun wanted nothing in shadow. Cells I had forgotten were speeding up inside me, organs I couldn't remember having began to beat. I walked towards the sign that said BUSES with a picture of a bus underneath. I read the noticeboard, flashing with green lights matching the buses to the stops. I read down the list looking for Point Paradise. What did Deirdre say?

Which bus? Was it all buses, or just one? I squeezed the pouch in my pocket.

People were rushing past carrying bags and suitcases, holding hands with their children, saying goodbye and hello, knowing which bus took them to Paradise Point.

'You okay, lad? You look lost.' A man in a green suit looked down at me. His cap leaned forward over his face, making shade for his eyes and nose.

'Point Paradise,' I said.

'Point Paradise . . . hmmmm.' He led me to the ticket counter.

'Can you see him?' The man asked the woman sitting behind the glass. 'He's a bit on the short side.'

The woman leaned forward and stared at me. 'Where to, dear?'

'Point Paradise,' I said. 'Midday.'

'What?' she asked, her voice muffled by the thick glass. 'Point where?'

'Point Paradise,' me and the man in the leaning hat repeated. 'Midday!'

The woman looked at a screen and pressed buttons. 'Dock three, dear. You better hurry. The bus leaves in ten minutes.'

'How much?' I asked.

'Nineteen dollars,' she answered.

I pulled two more ten dollar notes out of my pouch. Two ones came out with it, falling to the ground.

The man picked up the ones and gave them back to me. 'You right, lad? You got it?'

'Got it,' I told him. 'Got it.'

He passed the money through to the woman behind the glass. She took it and gave me back a dollar.

'Come on,' the man said. 'Dock three.'

I went with the man in his green suit as if he was the sergeant of the station, knowing every bus and every train and every sign and every shop for snacks and where was the toilet and which train passed through the tunnel at what time, making sure they never collided, sending passengers flying through the air, forcing them from the windows of the train as they shattered, flinging them against the hard stone walls, crushing them against the steel wheels and rails, sparks flying as both drivers hit the brakes, seeing the lights of each others wagon's streaming through the darkness *stop stop stop!*

'It's okay, we'll get there, calm down. You don't have to race, lad,' the man said as we trotted through the crowds. 'I can hardly keep up.'

We came to dock three, the third bus in a long line, and the man stopped at the open door. 'G'day, Eric,' he said to the driver. 'The boy wants to go to Point Paradise.'

'Then he's got a long day ahead of him.' Eric grinned.

'He's all set. Go on, lad. Up you go.'

I climbed up the bus steps, giving Eric my ticket as I passed.

'Just in time,' Eric said, pulling a lever that sent the bus door sliding closed. 'We'll stop at the Point around seven this evening.'

The man in the leaning hat waved at me through the glass. Then he was gone from my vision, but in some other part he would never be gone and that's a memory.

I walked down the almost-empty bus looking for my place. Just behind the driver there was a mother holding a baby wrapped in a blanket. She stared out the window over the top of the baby's head. There was a small brown bear, a coloured ring with bells, a packet of cigarettes and a bottle of milk on the seat beside her. The mother, eyes as empty as caves, jiggled the baby.

I kept walking and I passed a woman halfway down whose hair shone silver-blue. She held onto her purse and nodded at me. The lenses of her glasses were so dark I could only just see the shadows of her eyes. Behind the old woman was a sleeping man with yellow and green skin. He leaned against the window, his yellow face pushed up against the glass. There were beer cans beside him sliding out of their paper disguise. Mosquitoes had bitten his fingers and left them red and itchy. Some of the bites were scratched open.

Further back were two teenagers touching in every part they could. Arms touching legs touching cheeks touching bottoms. They looked at each other as if there were hardly the words to be found for what they felt – only touch could tell it.

At the very end of the bus I found my seat.

Eric drove out of dock three and into the traffic. The bus was a solid box with edges that held me up over the cars and the people and the roads, like a building that had tipped over and been given wheels and mechanics. The engine hummed and vibrated as it moved through the city. I could see the side of the mother's face at the front of the bus close to the window, still jiggling the baby, her nose almost touching the glass, as if she wished herself through it, closer to what she was leaving behind.

I leaned back and felt the warmth of the engine through the walls as it charged the lights and the automatic door and the windscreen wipers. Nobody looked at me. I didn't belong to the mother or to Eric or to the sleeping man or to Deirdre or the taxi driver or Anne White or Liam or Jake or the bus guard. I was separate, with no memory of being joined. My recollection reached a fence and was stopped, as if what was on the other side was dangerous.

Soon we were out of the city and driving down a wide highway with six lanes of traffic. Sometimes two cars would be driving in opposite directions and if you looked far into the distance it seemed as though they were being drawn to each other, each vehicle generating its own horizontal gravity. Each vehicle was a magnet for the other and the force was beyond human power – it didn't matter if the drivers pressed the brakes, they couldn't stop the collision or prevent the fatalities. I held my breath as the car sped towards the bus faster and faster and then when I was sure it would hit, the car would miss and there was air between the vehicles and one more time we would live until the next car.

I sat motionless. There were my organs, my eyes, my hands, my sensory receptors, but it was as if they were accidental, not belonging to me, like an experiment made to happen, but not my choosing.

I don't know how much time passed. I never did. Sometimes one minute was longer than one year. Sometimes a morning was longer than a night. Time was increasive, like elastic. The bus drove on and on and on, though time itself could have been stopped, or moving so fast it couldn't be counted. The white lines on the road repeated, one after the other after the other. I was in suspension, riding the spaces between the lines, waiting to end or begin. It was the same with my eyes open or closed. It could have been a dream at night or it could have been real living. The bus rocked to the sound of its own deep rumbling. Nothing hurt. Not a single part. I was hurtless, weightless. I rested against the side of the bus and it rocked me like a cradle. Outside the light changed, moving from midday to afternoon.

Some time before dark Eric stopped the bus at a petrol station and the mother with the baby and the man with the bitten fingers and the old woman, tired from sitting, climbed slowly down. I watched through the glass as they walked into the light of the petrol station, the light glowing but at the same time sad, as if it couldn't reach far enough or bright enough to show what was there. I watched as everyone lined up for snacks then I got up and went into the bus toilet and, keeping my eyes closed, I used it. After, I flushed bright green and it smelled sweet and sick. I washed my hands in the small sink.

Back in my seat I watched Eric through the window. He was sitting at a table inside the petrol station. Eric looked down at his dinner then up at a television high on a wall, then down at his plate then up at the television then down at his plate. He shook salt and pepper over his dinner. My mouth felt dry. Soon the people walked back to the bus and Eric wiped his mouth and paid, eyes still on the television. When he came back onto the bus he said to me, 'I'll be dropping you off in an hour, okay? Make sure you're awake.'

I nodded.

We kept driving, the bus warm and darkening, and then the shining sea appeared before us, the night falling quietly over the top. I expanded as the sea entered my vision. I met the body of water with my inners; my linings stretched. 'It's always here,' I said to nobody.

I kept my eyes on the ocean as the bus followed the narrow road down the mountain. The mother was asleep, her blanket around her shoulders, her jacket beneath her head. The old woman had taken off her dark glasses and her eyes were closed. The man only opened his eyes to take sips from his beer can. Eric and me were wide awake.

The road kept going down. The sea shone as the moon rose. I could only see the things in front of me. There was no history. The round moon over the sea and the cold glass, and Eric, and the warm rumble of the engine was all there was.

Soon I saw lights and a sign too small to read, and Eric drove the bus off the road. He kept the motor running and called to me, 'Hey, kid! Your stop. Point Paradise.'

I got to my feet and walked down the bus between the seats. 'Where is the caravan park, Eric? Do you know? Do you know, Eric?' My voice sounded like it belonged to somebody small without powers or a map or lines to join him.

'It's the only thing in Point Paradise, mate.' Eric spoke as if his answer was a joke. 'See the sign?'

I did see the sign but there wasn't enough light to read it.

'Anyone coming to meet you?' Eric asked me.

I shook my head. 'No, Eric, no. No.'

Eric frowned. 'Just follow the path into the park.' He pointed at a narrow road leading into the darkness on the side of the highway.

'Yes, okay, Eric. Okay, Eric.' I looked down at the other passengers and I saw the mother wake up. She opened her eyes and blinked at me. There were no messages to decode. There was nothing left in her, it was all in the baby. The old woman woke too, and nodded and smiled as if to say, *Go on, go on. Go on, Jimmy Flick.*

Eric opened the bus doors and cool air rushed at me as I stepped out of the bus. Thousands of road particles that didn't know my foot was coming were forced into a different position. Eric closed the doors and the bus drove out onto the road. I stood and watched as it disappeared down the mountain.

After the bus had gone it was very quiet. There was only the sound of the night, a hushing, like a blanket coming softly down. I went close to the sign. *Point Paradise Caravan Park*, I read in letters bleached by the sun. Underneath the words was an arrow pointing the way. I looked up at the sky and saw the first stars.

I followed the arrow down the dirt road that ran off the highway. The cool wind that blew over me was the same wind that blew in over the water and across the cliff and over my mum and my dad in the picture. Time didn't change it; the currents moved around planet Earth, cleaned by the rainbows after the rain, passing over the same places, new and ancient. I heard the music of the sea as water rose and fell, changing the shapes of rocks, pounding at the cliffs, wearing away the sea floor. I kept walking forward.

Soon I saw rows of caravans with yards and chairs, satellite dishes and flowers in pots, and through every window I saw the blue glow of the television. Every caravan leaned towards the sea, as if they were straining to hear its music. They all had names — *Traveller*, *No Looking Back* and *Freedom* — but the caravans couldn't move. Their wheels were dug deep into the ground so you could only see the very tops of the tyres. Electrical cords were tied around their bases and the cords went right into the ground, and though I couldn't see it, I could hear the central network at the core, supplying electricity to the televisions, powering the voices inside, giving them news and things to sell on the ads. I didn't see anybody outside. The salty coolness of the sea entered my sensories as I walked past the rows of trapped caravans.

I came to a brick house with a light at the front, and a small black square beside the door that said *Office*. I walked inside and on the desk there was a bell to ring so I rang it and I rang it and I rang it until I heard someone say, 'Alright, alright! Calm down!'

A woman came through a door behind the desk with her hair in a high ball. Pieces hung down at the sides like Deirdre's princess doll and she wore bright pink lipstick. Her eyebrows were pencil lines and over her eyes there were blue clouds. Everything was pulled down, as if there were hairs attached to every pore and somebody was tugging on them.

'You're not on your own, are you?' the woman asked.

I nodded yes.

She frowned. 'What do you want here?'

'My dad,' I said.

'Your dad?'

I nodded again.

'Your father is here?'

I nodded.

'You sure about that?'

I nodded again. There was no other choice.

'Who is he?'

'Gavin Flick. Flick, Gavin. My dad.'

The woman shook her head slowly and the blue clouds over her eyes came down low. A smile played on her mouth, not sure whether it was safe to stay. 'Is that right? Gavin Flick is your father?'

I nodded.

'You'd better follow me.' She came out from behind the desk. 'Derek!' she called over her shoulder. 'Start without me – I'll be back in a minute.'

We walked out of the office and onto the path that ran between the rows of caravans. As the woman walked I could see every part of her flesh through her pants from behind. There were little stories hidden in the dips.

Soon she left the main path and took a track that was narrow and bumpy away from the lights. The park had almost run out of caravans. I could only see two, both small and white; one was close and the other one was further. I followed the woman past the one that was close until we came to the last one. *Happy Times* was written across the side. It had a small window and its wheels were dug the deepest. Beyond *Happy Times* I could see the same cliff that stood behind my mum and dad in the picture. Beyond the edge of the cliff the moon rose over the sea, full and shining white, indentations in its surface, giving it shadow. I saw steps on it leading underground. Every moon has a core with a network in the centre.

The woman pointed to *Happy Times*. 'This is Gavin's,' she said. 'Ha!'

There was a small light in the caravan's window – somebody was home.

I took a deep breath.

'Come on,' said the woman. She walked just ahead of me along the three squares of cement up the steps to the door of the caravan, her vapours blown back into my face as she guided me: perfume, cooking meat and cigarettes. She knocked on the door of *Happy Times*.

Nothing happened.

I looked up and I saw that the sky was the sea upside down. They reflected each other; but which one was the mirror?

The woman knocked again. 'Gavin,' she said, her mouth close to the door. 'Someone here to see you.'

There was a muffled answer from inside.

'Gavin!' she sounded cross. 'Open the door, will you? There's someone here to see you.'

I stood at the bottom of the three steps. He was here; I heard him moving. All points came together in me, forming one single beat. Dad Dad Dad Dad.

'What is it, Denise?' Dad opened the door.

'Look who's here,' said Denise, as though she knew a funny trick was about to be played on my dad. She held out her arm to me. I was the trick.

Dad looked at me and his mouth fell open.

'I'll leave you to it, shall I?' said Denise.

Dad stood swaying in the doorway.

'I don't want any dramas, Gavin,' Denise said. 'Sort this out in a hurry, will you?' She turned and walked back down the path.

'Where's his mother?' Dad called to her.

She didn't stop.

He called again. 'Denise? Where's his mother?'

'No mother, Gavin. He's here on his own,' she called back. 'Sort it out.' And then she was gone and it was just Dad and me.

Dad shook his head as if something was too big to believe. There was my dad's mouth, his eyes, his arms, his legs, chest and shoulders, but there was no life in them, as if they were powered by yesterday's resources. Like the lawnmower blades still swinging after the engine has been turned off – it's only a matter of time. I smelled Cutty Sark mixed with the same medicine they used in Emergency.

'Jimmy,' Dad said, still shaking his head. His mouth hung open. His face was made of rags. His eyes floated in Blended Scotch; the Cutty Sark had dimmed the light. He held out his arm.

I took another deep breath, climbed the steps and went through the door.

Happy Times was a land of bottles, some brown for beer, some see-through and others green. They stood in the corners and they filled the sink and they stacked up against the walls. There were bottles on the television and there was a chair with a bottle on it next to an ashtray, and there was a bed not made and there was a towel and soap, and everything, including my dad, was shrunken to make room for the bottles. Merle sang 'I'd Trade All of My Tomorrows' as the Cutty Sark sailed the currents.

'Wh . . . wh . . . where's your mother?' he asked me. 'Where's Paula?'

'She couldn't . . . she couldn't . . .' I told him.

He frowned. 'What?'

'She couldn't, she couldn't . . .' My words were jamming at the toll gates. 'She couldn't, she couldn't . . .'

'Jimmy, what? She couldn't what?'

'She couldn't she couldn't she couldn't . . .'

'For Christ's sake, Jimmy! What? What?'

'She couldn't she couldn't she couldn't she couldn't breathe! She couldn't breathe! She couldn't breathe!' The words pushed past the gates, their message on repeat.

Dad stood looking at me, too soaked to absorb me, or the words I was saying.

'She couldn't get it in,' I said again. 'She couldn't, Dad! She couldn't! She couldn't!'

His mouth kept opening and closing. He was older than when he left. All the waves of Broken Island were gone from him. The crude oil was clogged, unrefined in his network. The only thing to flow was whisky. It rushed thinly through him, faster than blood, more effective. He shook his head as if he was trying to clear something from it, to make space for what I told him.

'She couldn't get it in,' I said.

'What are you talking about?' Dad slurred.

'The air, Dad. The air! The air! She couldn't breathe.'

'What the hell are you saying?'

I took a deep breath. 'Dad, Dad. Mum was in the bed and she couldn't get the air in and the puffers were empty, Dad. All of them in the house empty and there was no Robby and no you. There was only me, and I left her when she sent me to the shops. I went to the shops, Dad, and I got lost. The streets all changed their order and the houses changed their places and when I got home she couldn't breathe. I was with her and she went back, Dad, ahahahaaaaaa!' I made the sound of my mother pleading with the air, begging for it to save her. 'Aaaaaaahhhhhhaaaa aaaahhhhhhaaaa!'

Dad fell down into his chair. Whisky came out of his pipes and dripped down his face.

'She couldn't get the air in,' I said from a quiet and faraway place.

Merle sang 'If I Had Left it Up to You' as Dad got up, staggering towards the sink. The glass tinkled. I looked around *Happy Times* and nothing was connected to anything else or to me. What was the reason for it all? I looked at the bottles and in some there were cigarettes sitting in the dregs. There was a newspaper, there were thongs and socks and a cap and a fishing rod and little lead weights still in their plastic, but I couldn't see the reason.

This man standing at the sink, his back to me, was the man in the photograph. Those were his hands gripping the metal edge — the same hands that had first held me, connected to the same arms — but there was no line from those hands to me.

Dad turned to face me. 'How did you get here?' His lips struggled to loop themselves around each word. They didn't meet at the ends, so that the sounds fell out the sides.

'Bus,' I answered. 'With Eric.'

I looked at the walls and saw there was a hole beside the bed where the wall was crushed in, as though someone had hit it with a fist.

I wanted to put my hand in it to see how it fit.

'Where are you staying? Who are you . . . who are you with? Robby? Where's Robby?' It was as if each of my dad's questions was a journey he wasn't equipped to make.

'No Robby,' I said.

'Just you?'

'Just me,' I said. 'Just me, Dad.'

'What are you here for?'

'For you, Dad,' I said. 'For you.'

'Jesus,' said Dad, as if I had spoken the worst words of all. He picked a bottle up from the floor and turned it in his hands, looking deep into the glass, then he smashed the bottle against the sink. He picked up another and smashed it against the cupboard. He picked up bottle after bottle, smashing them against every surface. Merle kept singing 'If I Had Left it Up to You' as the glass rained down on us, shining and glittering. Pieces of glass fell into my hair, into my pockets and socks, and into the cuffs of my trousers. Down it fell, *down down down*, burying me.

At last, like a storm that was finished, Dad stood panting, against the wall. He said, 'You better go back where you came from.'

I climbed out from under the glass, shards still trapped in my ears and my armpits and under the lids of my eyes, and I said, 'Okay, Dad, okay,' and I walked out of *Happy Times*.

I pushed through bushes and trees until the moon showed me a small path that I followed until I reached the cliff. I stood close to the edge, looking out at the endless sea, silver and rippling in the light of the moon. I felt myself drawn as if the sea had a magnetic force and wanted to absorb me. I heard the waves crashing against the rocks down below, disintegrating into white foam and spray.

I saw the pathway across the surface of the sea that led to the moon. It had a silent voice that communicated to me through airs. *Hello Jimmy, this way, this way.* I wanted to cross it, more than I'd wanted to find the hole eleven years ago to push myself through, her second miracle.

'Jimmy, come back into the caravan.' It was Dad. I hadn't heard him coming up behind me.

'Come on, Jimmy,' he said. 'Come back from there.'

I stayed where I was, the moon's pathway stretching out before me, waiting.

'Jimmy.' Dad put a hand on my shoulder. 'Come on, come with me.'

I didn't move.

'Jimmy.'

He pulled me back. 'Come on.'

I let him lead me along the track back to his caravan, as if I had no powers of refusal, no remaining will. Merle was quiet when we went inside. The glass was swept away. Dad's eyes were red and he moved slowly. He said, 'You can stay here for the night then in the morning you have to go.' He showed me the bed. 'There, you sleep there.' He sat in the chair and turned off the light.

I climbed on the bed and turned to the wall and I fit my hand in the hole and I kept it that way until morning.

When I next opened my eyes I saw Dad standing over me and it was as if his blood had stopped. He swallowed but there was no liquid. He was shaking: his head, his nose, his legs, his neck, his hands, all trembling. It was the last of his motor. 'Get up, Jim,' he said.

We walked to the office. When Dad opened the door Denise came out. She wore shorts that were more like underpants, and thongs, and each toenail was orange. She smiled and she said, 'Surprise, surprise.'

'Good morning, Denise.' Dad looked down at me. 'Where you staying, Jimmy?'

'Anne White's,' I answered.

'Do you have a number?'

'Yes,' I said. 'Yes.' I pulled the piece of paper that Deirdre had given me from my pocket.

'Who's Anne White?' Dad asked.

'My foster mother.'

'Christ,' he said, looking at the ground.

'Is there a problem?' Denise put her hands on her hips.

'Can I use the telephone?'

'Long distance?' Denise asked, raising the pencil lines on her forehead.

'Yeah, long distance.'

'I'll be timing you.' Denise tapped her watch, her lips tight around her cigarette.

'Haven't you got better things to do?' said Dad, picking up the telephone. His hands were shaking so much he kept hitting the wrong numbers. 'Oh fuck,' he mumbled.

'You want me to dial it?' Denise said.

'I got it, Denise,' said Dad. Then slowly and one at a time, using all his mind powers, my dad pressed the numbers. He passed the telephone to me. 'Tell them to come and get you,' he said to me while it rang. 'Tell them you'll be at the Point Paradise service station on the highway. Don't say anything about me.'

Denise frowned at him and he shook his head at her.

Anne White answered the telephone. 'Hello? Anne speaking.'

'Anne White,' I said. 'Anne White.'

'Yes, this is Anne speaking. Who is this?'

'Anne White, it's Jim. Jim Flick. Jim Flick.'

'Jim! Is that you?'

'Yes, Anne White. Yes, Anne White, it's me.'

'Oh, Jim! Jim! Where are you? Are you alright?' Anne White started crying.

'Point Paradise service station on the freeway.'

'Point Paradise! Jake! Jake!' she called.

Jake got on the phone. 'Point Paradise, Jim? On the Eastern Freeway?'

'Yes, Jake, yes.'

'On the Eastern Freeway? Just near the border?'

'Yes, Jake, yes.'

'We'll be there in . . . five hours, Jim. Don't move. Don't speak with anyone. Sit tight and we'll be there soon.'

'Are you okay, Jim? You're not hurt?' It was Anne White again.

'I'm okay,' I said. 'I'm okay, Anne White.' I heard her sniff, then I hung up the telephone.

I looked across at my dad. He was standing in the office doorway, like a dead silhouette. Streams of light came off his black shadow.

'Come on,' he said.

'You heading out already, Gavin? They won't be here for hours. Aren't they coming from the city?'

'Mind your business, Denise,' said Gavin. 'Get back inside and feed Derek.'

'Doesn't the kid need some breakfast before he goes?'

'Don't you worry about my kid.'

'Suit yourself. See you, Jimmy,' said Denise, her mouth a tight purse, all the creases headed for the clip.

I walked along the highway behind my dad. Trucks roared past, not slowing, almost crushing us. We followed the yellow stripes of paint along the road until we came to the service station, its electric lights glowing with the energy of petroleum and oil. We went in and Dad bought a coffee, an orange juice and a pie with sauce. We walked back outside and Dad took me to the low wall that ran along the side near the parked cars. He said, 'Sit down and drink the juice.'

I sat on the wall and tipped the juice bottle up over my mouth and down went the juice.

Dad watched me. 'You came here all by yourself?' he asked.

I nodded.

Tears came out of his eyes with no other signs of crying. The tears travelled in messy zigzags down the skin of his face, getting spread in the hairs and the corners of his mouth. What was generating them?

'Bloody hell, Jimmy. Bloody hell.' He kept shaking his head, as if it was the only move he was sure he could make. He sat down on the wall beside me. He looked at his watch, then he crossed his arms. Cars drove in and out of the station. He said, 'You got to leave me out of the picture, Jim.'

I smelled Cutty Sark vapours when he talked; the whisky was using my dad as a channel.

'Yes, Dad,' I said. 'Yes, Dad. Out of the picture.'

He took a sip of his coffee, his hand shaking around the cup. He shook his head and threw the rest of the coffee onto the grass, then he got to his feet. He sighed out. He walked across the concrete towards the road, then he came back. He sat down again next to me and we kept waiting as the sun rose higher and grew stronger over our shoulders. There were no words between us. Cars came and filled up on fuel. I saw their owners go inside the petrol station jangling keys, buying cigarettes and Mars Bars and newspapers. The wall felt hard and cold beneath me.

Dad checked his watch again. We kept waiting. My legs grew stiff. Neither of us moved. Time kept passing. Dad began to rock forward and back, forward and back. A rocking that could barely be seen by the naked eye, only felt. He looked at his watch one last time, then he said, 'It won't be long now, Jim. Just stay here and wait, okay? Don't move until they get here. You won't go anywhere will you, Jim? Until they get here?'

'No, Dad. I won't move, I won't go anywhere.'

'It won't be more than an hour,' he said. He looked at me, then he took my arm and held it tight, just above the elbow. 'Jimmy . . .' he said. I felt Dad's clamp, like pliers, its hardness, but there were no messages coming through. 'Jimmy . . .' And then he let go, got up off the wall and walked across the black of the service station ground, his thongs slapping against his heels. I watched as he walked back onto the highway and I saw my only chance leave with him, sitting on his shoulder like a parrot on a chain.

I stayed on the wall and looked at tiny lights sparkling in the concrete at my feet, but there was no pattern; I didn't need to search. When I had to go to the toilet I went inside and I didn't look down.

You have to aim, Jimmy! You have to look. It's getting on the seat.

No, Mum! I don't want to look! I don't want to see! No, Mum, no!

Come on, Jimmy. For Mum. Please look.

No! No! Mum! No! No!

Alright, alright, love, don't shout. You don't have to look.

You look, Mum, you look!

Alright, love. I'll look for you. Mum will look for you.

There was a knock on the door so I put my hands under the tap then I opened the door and walked back to the wall. I don't know how long I waited. I wasn't counting. I closed my eyes and made a picture of the silver pathway made by the moon. I didn't change positions. I stayed sitting, my legs hanging down from the wall. Car after car, hour after hour. Nobody saw me, as if my outline had been lost. Every time I blinked I saw the pathway. If I left my eyes half-closed it shone, beckoning me. I looked up to its leader, the glowing moon, then back down at the path.

Anne White and Jake drove into the station. When the car stopped near the wall where I was sitting, Anne White opened the door and came to me. She looked more tired than ever. 'Thank God, Jim.' She squeezed my hand. 'Get in the car.'

I climbed into the back seat and Anne White shut my door and climbed into the front. 'I am glad you are okay. What were you thinking, Jim? Why did you run away? Why did you come here?' Anne White turned around to look at me as she waited for the answer; there was none. She faced the front again. 'This is it for us,' she said to Jake. 'No more.'

Jake drove the car out of Point Paradise.

When we got back to the house Anne White sent me straight to my room. 'You'll need a rest,' she said. 'You can eat in here tonight. I'll bring your dinner.' I heard the door click when she left. Anne White had locked me in.

I didn't look at anything: not the wall of fathers or the poster or the cupboard where the red suitcase lived. I was the body without the network. There was nothing left in the world for me to do. I didn't move.

Anne White opened the door and came back into the room. She carried a tray with a bowl of soup and an apple and a piece of cake on it. Steam rose from the bowl of soup. I tried to see when the steam disbanded to become air but my eyes missed; it was impossible. Anne White placed the tray on Liam's desk, then she turned on the desk lamp.

'Come and sit down,' she said, patting Liam's chair. I sat down. She touched the tray. 'I just think it's easier for tonight if you stay by yourself, Jim. Give you a bit of time to think about things. Liam can bunk in with Deirdre.'

She touched the apple on the tray. 'I'm afraid you'll be leaving us soon, Jim,' she said. 'Please don't think it's because you're not a very special boy, because I can see that you are.' She was trying to talk but there was a wave washing up through her throat. 'I'm just . . .' She looked towards the window. 'You're a good little boy, Jim. I'm sorry.' She walked to the door and opened it. 'Jake and I were very worried,' she said. 'Something bad could've happened. Something very bad.'

She left the room.

I didn't touch the soup or the apple or the piece of cake. What bad thing was it that hadn't happened?

I turned off the light on the desk and I lay on the bunk and watched day turn to night. After a long time I heard somebody trying the lock. *Click* one way *click* the other. The door opened. It was Deirdre.

'Jimmy,' she said, coming to the bed. 'Jimmy.' She took my hand and kissed it.

I rolled onto my side. 'How did you get in?' I asked her.

'I took Anne White's key,' she said. 'I'd do anything for you, Jimmy.'

Did crying start at the upper most or the lower most? I didn't know.

Deirdre kneeled beside the bed in the dark. 'What did he say?' she asked.

'Leave me out of the picture.'

She crawled in beside me and put her leg over mine, then she tucked Melanie against me. 'Hey, Jimmy, Liam and I never told Anne you were going to find your dad. Even when Anne said, *You should have kept a closer eye on him, Deirdre*, I never told her. They were going to call the police – they didn't want to, they were scared of the negligence – and then you called.'

'Thank you, Deirdre, thank you,' I said.

'They're sending you away, aren't they?' she whispered. 'Into Stateside?'

'I don't know. I don't know.'

'I'll come with you,' she said. 'You can hide me in your suitcase and when we get there you can cut my hair and they'll never know I'm a girl.' She put her arm across my chest. It was warm. I could feel her blood going round full of messages, but I couldn't feel my own.

Soon Deirdre got out of the bed and left the room. Melanie was still on my pillow.

In the morning Anne White unlocked the door and said, 'Time to get up, Jim.' I ate breakfast at the table with everybody else. Deirdre kept her foot against mine. Jake didn't look at me, as if I wasn't there. There were sparks coming from the ends of Liam's hair, like he'd been electrocuted while I was away. Anne White said to keep to our routine. My chore was sweeping the path and Liam's chore was raking the leaves. Anne White hung up washing and kept an eye on us.

She went inside when the telephone rang and as soon as she was gone Liam stopped raking and said, 'What happened? Did you see him?' His eyes were wide and scared, as if his life depended on my answer.

I didn't say anything.

'Come on, Flick, don't act like a retard. What did he say? Did he tell you to fuck off?'

I nodded.

He picked up a roof tile that was lying against the fence and he threw it on the path and it shattered. He picked up another one and did it again.

Anne White came back out and she said, 'Do you want to go to Stateside with Jim, do you, Liam? Is that what you want?'

'Fuck off, Anne,' he said, picking up another tile.

'Don't speak to me like that, Liam,' said Anne White. 'You know not to speak to me like that.'

'Get fucked, Anne! You're not my mother! You're not anybody. Fuck you!'

'Liam!' Anne White came charging towards him and he said, 'Fuck you!' and raised his hand. He was quick, his hand so fast you could barely see it, up towards her face, as if he'd slashed a thousand faces.

Anne White cried out, 'Jake!', her hand to her eye, blood coming from under her fingers. Jake came running. Liam and me stood, neither of us moving. Anne White pointed and said, 'Liam!'

Jake saw the tile in Liam's hand and he grabbed it and twisted Liam's arm behind him and pushed him inside.

It was our last week; Liam, Deirdre and me were all leaving. Anne White told Jan Watts over the telephone that she couldn't manage.

'Not even me?' Deirdre asked her when she got off the telephone.

'I'm sorry, Dee Dee.' Anne White pulled away. Seven stitches ran under her eye like a trench to catch the colours. Her eyes had no blue left; you could see through them. Jake couldn't go to work because he had to make sure nothing else happened with the fosters.

It had been raining for days; everything was drenched. We watched television while we waited for the end. Anne White spent a lot of time with her church group or upstairs in her room. She let us do more things and eat more chips. Jake had to give the orders. After Anne White cooked the dinner she took hers upstairs on a tray – only Jake ate with us and he kept the television on.

I only moved if an adult applied force. I tried to see how little I could breathe and Liam sulked and trained and did his chores if Jake's hand was around his neck. Deirdre pulled off all her dolls' clothes and painted green arrows between their legs. The rain fell and fell.

My blood ran slowly around my network; I knew the quiet floating world was coming closer.

Uncle Rodney called the house. I heard Jake telling him I was going to be transferred and that Jan Watts would explain.

'We can't keep him anymore, Rodney, so if you aren't here by then he'll be going into Stateside and you can contact them . . . it's not going to be our concern anymore.'

Jake came into the living room and said, 'Your uncle is coming for you today, Jim.' Next he said, 'Don't do anything stupid before then.'

The only time Jake wasn't there, guarding us, was after he dropped Liam back from training.

'I'll be an hour, Anne,' he said. 'I have to give one of the boys a hand at work; I've got no choice.'

'No longer than an hour, Jake, please,' said Anne White.

After Jake had left, Liam said, 'Can we go outside, Anne? It's not raining.' He had mud up his legs and across his cheeks and on his top.

Anne White looked through the window. 'Yes, yes, you can all go outside,' she said, then she left the room to go upstairs.

Deirdre got up and followed Liam out the back door. I stayed sitting.

Anne White came back downstairs and saw me in the lounge room not doing anything or getting any fresh air or letting off any steam.

'Go on, Jim, you too. Outside with the others.' She lifted her arm to show me where the door was, and I got up and walked outside. I stood beside the lemon tree heavy with lemons almost ready, not much longer now, and closed my eyes so that only the sounds could enter. I narrowed it down to birds and leaves and a car.

Liam found me; he said, 'Come with me, Jimmy.'

I followed him to the bottom of the yard. Deirdre was there throwing stones into the three drums, which were all over-flowing with water. I listened to the stones land with a *plink*. 'Hello, Jimmy,' Deirdre said, smiling.

'You stand next to the drums, Jimmy,' said Liam, 'and tell us whose stone lands first.'

I went close to the drums and waited.

Liam stood behind the line made out of a stick and threw. A stone hit my cheek.

'What did you do that for?' Deirdre asked Liam.

'I didn't mean to.'

'Yes you did.'

'No I didn't, I was aiming for the drum.'

My cheek stung where the stone had hit, but as if it was hurting someone else and not me. Who was that person? Why was he here?

'Come on, Deirdre,' said Liam. 'Go again.'

They stood behind the stick that was the line and threw again and a stone hit me in the forehead.

Deirdre squealed. 'Liam!'

'Shut up, Deirdre,' Liam said, walking to the drums. He looked in over the top of the end one. 'It's the deepest it's ever been,' he said to me, pulling a crate over to the drum. 'Have a look, Flick.' He touched the crate.

I stepped onto it and looked into the water in the drum and saw myself moving on the surface.

Liam stirred the water with a stick and the different parts of me rippled and separated, like waves in miniature. I couldn't stop looking into the water, as if the water was the magnet and I was the metal. It drew me to itself.

Deirdre pulled me off the crate by the back of my shirt. 'Remember the cat,' she said to Liam.

He turned on her. 'I never put the cat in,' he said, his mouth twisting.

'I know,' she said. 'It fell from the branch.' She looked up at the tree leaning over the drums. 'Jake cut the branches back after that, didn't he, Liam? After he found the cat.'

'I didn't do it.' Liam's face flushed.

'I didn't say you did.' Deirdre stood, feet apart in the mud. 'Did I?'

'Yeah, you did. Why don't you fuck off?'

'Why don't you?' Deirdre's feet squelched and mud curled up around the ends of her gumboots.

'Why don't you?' Liam poked her in the chest with his stick. She stepped back. He poked her in the cheek. Then he put the stick under her chin and lifted it.

'Stop it!' she said.

'You stop it.'

'Why are you doing this?' she asked, pulling the stick away with her hand.

'Doing what?'

'Why are you being so mean?'

He threw the stick at her feet. 'Fuck off.'

Deirdre shouted, arms stiff by her side, 'He caught the bus and he went all the way there and he saw his dad like you said, he tried but the dad didn't want him! His dad said, "Leave me out of the picture." He didn't want him!' She started to cry. 'He didn't want him! His dad didn't want him, Liam!'

'I said fuck off!' They were both shouting now.

'There was no more he could have done, Liam. He tried! The dad didn't want him. So what?'

Liam pushed her hard and she landed on her backside and her hands gripped the mud beside her. 'So nothing!' he said. 'Leave us alone!'

I watched as Deirdre got to her feet. 'Come back inside, Jimmy. Don't stay out here.'

I didn't move.

'He doesn't want to go inside, do you, Jimmy?' said Liam.

'Jimmy, come on.' Deirdre took my hand and pulled. 'Don't stay out here.'

'He's not a little girl. Deirdre. He wants to stay out here with me, don't you, Flick?'

'Don't you?'

I nodded.

Deirdre hit me in the chest with her fist. 'I hate you, Jimmy!' she said. Then she turned and walked up to the house – her skirt, her boots, her muddy hands, the back of her head, her dark plait, its blue ribbon frayed at the edges, all had given up.

'Come and check this out,' said Liam, looking into the drum. 'Here's where the cat was.' He banged on the drum with his fist, *bang*. 'It was raining then too. It was a white cat with bent whiskers and it was always at the back door. It didn't belong here or anywhere but Anne felt sorry for it so she gave it milk and then it came back and she said to me, "I always end up with the ones nobody wants."' Liam banged the drum again. 'I picked up the cat from the back step where it waited for Anne and it scratched my cheek.' He pointed to a place near his ear. 'Right here,' he said. 'But I didn't let him go. I walked down to the drums. I held the cat tight; there was no way I was letting him go. I decided. If you decide then that's it – the cat could have scratched out my eyes and I wouldn't have let go.

'I got to the drum and I threw in the cat and when it tried to come up for air I pushed its head under. It kept coming up and I kept pushing it under. It bit my fingers and it tried to swim but I kept pushing it down. I could see the whole of the inside of its mouth. It was bright pink and it had row after row of teeth like a shark's. Its whole mouth was open, trying to breathe, and then when it went under its eyes never closed – even when it was dead its eyes stayed open.'

He looked at me. 'Climb in,' he said. 'Come on, let's see if you can stand.'

I knew I couldn't stand because when I was on the outside of the drum it was much taller than me. I stepped onto the crate and I pulled myself up. Liam helped me. The water was cold on my legs when I swung them over.

'Lower, come on,' said Liam. 'Go lower – hold on to the sides.' He watched as I went lower.

When I was all the way in I held on to the sides with my fingers. I looked up into the sky and I saw that it was made of water, as if the sky had turned to sea, and it was falling in my eyes.

Liam banged at my fingers with the stick where they gripped the edge of the drum. 'Let go, Aqua Boy! Let go!' he said.

I moved my hand away and gripped on with the other but then he hit that too.

Whack! 'Let go, Aqua Boy!' *Whack!*

I kept changing hands and kicking with my legs and the rain was beneath me at the same time as it was over me.

I felt Liam's hand on the top of my head push me under as if I was the cat and it was me who kept coming back, me drinking Anne White's milk, me nobody wanted. I went under then I struggled and his hand came off for a second and I grabbed at the air but I couldn't get it in. My passages filled with water; I coughed and gulped and more water came in. I could hear something roar, like a shout, but it wasn't from outside of me, it was from somewhere deep in my own network.

When I came up again I saw Liam's face and all the features were sharp and serious, every cell and fibre working hard towards the one thing as if there was no other thing more important than this. He had decided.

I came up for air only to give him something to push against. Then I was under and I couldn't feel the sides of the drum anymore; there was nothing to hold. Every part of me hurt; my chest, my eyes, my throat, my back, my ribs, my face and stomach, legs and arms were all bursting with the pressure of the water filling every space.

I saw my mother, her body a bridge in the bed as she arched. I saw her mouth open, fighting for air, as if she'd always been at war, the battle keeping her starving no matter how much she ate. Now we were in the same fight. Tighter and tighter and hotter and hotter, my mother before me, her eyes rolled back as she fought, and then suddenly nothing hurt at all. The fight was finished. Everywhere was quiet and soft, and in the darkness of the barrel I saw particles of the light that burned in the eye of the sheep.

The tiny lights drifted like dust, bouncing from my fingertips when I reached out to touch them. The sides of the drum disappeared as the water spread; there were no sides, everywhere was soft and soundless. The water was a cool safe home around me. I surrendered to the floating world: all of my parts underneath, my root and the hole left behind, my cells, all drifted in the light from the eye of the sheep.

Part Five

And then I heard shouting and calling, and I was in the mud on the hard ground, no longer drifting or weightless, and there was a face over mine, covering my mouth, blowing air deep into my passages. I struggled against it but there were no limits to its force. The air knew what it wanted and where it wanted to be and it kept coming and coming, insistent, sure, as if in the final seconds it had made up its mind. It was Liam breathing life back inside me.

I coughed and coughed and when I opened my eyes Liam was shaking my shoulders, and his face was white. 'Jimmy! Jimmy!' he cried loudly. It was full of sound and breath, like choking.

But it was too late. My epidermis was here but all my living inners were in the light. I closed my eyes and found myself drifting again. Somewhere there was shouting and calling. Was it Jake? I heard a siren; the same one that called for my mother was coming for me. I was joining her. My skin was shaken, there was a mask over my face. I let it. I let it all. There was no one and nothing to fight; the fight was finished. I breathed and it both hurt and it didn't. I was observational only.

My body was put in the bed. Liam was still crying. It was a music trying to enter, but I was impenetrating. The instruments of it went on and on. Jake shouted, 'What the hell happened?' but there was no answer, only the music of Liam's crying, then Deirdre's. It linked with his and took over. She stood at a door then the door was closed and I was alone, then I closed my eyes and I was in the light again. It was there for me. The waves of my brain had discovered it in the barrel. There was no time anymore.

Then Uncle Rodney was at the house. His face floated into vision; he said, *Hang in there, hang in there, Jimmy.* His touch was made of glass. Didn't he know – all change was only change on the way to the same place? The only place for me was in the water, in the light, with my mum where I had begun and where I ended.

Jan Watts was there and I went with her and Uncle Rodney to the hospital and a man said, *Don't move, don't move,* as I slid into the tunnel and I didn't move, I was never going to. Another man took my blood and I watched it shoot into the bottle and the way it rushed was a surprise, as if there was still life. A man came close with a torch and his words were *no evidence of injury just in time I'd say.* Injury was when something took a bruise and the blood turned hard so it couldn't pass on the nutrients. It stuck under the skin and turned a person into an immovable.

I didn't see Anne White anymore. Just before Jake pushed Liam into the car, Liam said to me, 'I wasn't going to let you drown,' then he started to cry. Deirdre was saying, *Jimmy, Jimmy.* I couldn't speak. She threw herself against me. 'I love you, Jimmy,' she said, then she stuck Melanie into the pocket of the red suitcase. Uncle Rodney drove us to the airport and he led me into the body of the plane and put me in a seat and a lady said *do you want a drink* before she found out I was inanimate.

There was the sound of lifting, the roar of the engine, the turn of the blades through the sky. I drifted. I never left the light for a single second. I could be in it eyes open or closed.

The plane headed down and there was no difference between take-off and landing. They were the same. Uncle Rodney said, 'Jimmy, we've got to get you home,' and he got me home and Ned came to me. He whimpered and put his heavy paws on my shoulders but my eyes couldn't look. They lifted above.

Uncle Rodney said, 'Your father is coming, Jim. He called me after you went to see him. He's coming, Jim. I didn't want to tell you until I was sure. But he called again. He is coming.'

Uncle Rodney kept checking the clock and his watch and getting up and looking out his window and then sitting down, then getting up again. There was a knock at the door.

Uncle Rodney jumped up and pulled open the door and it was my dad. He crossed the room towards me; he didn't know I had left the living beings. The television was on. There were men chasing each other through the streets, their ties flapping back over their shoulders. My dad was in the room. I wasn't joined. My eyes stayed on the screen as the men kept running. When they got to a building or a wall they jumped right over the top.

My dad said, 'Oh God, Jimmy.' And he put his arms around me. I couldn't feel their pressure. He began to rock me back and forth, his arms tight around me. I was like a silkworm in a cocoon. I couldn't be reached. He kept rocking. Again he said, 'Oh God, Jimmy,' and his warm breath in the shape of my name entered my ear. Again, 'Jimmy,' he said. And he kept rocking and I felt his heat. He kept rocking and I could feel him pushing past the barrier of my skin. I didn't want it. I screamed. My dad didn't let go. He kept going, kept rocking back and forth, back and forth on Uncle Rodney's couch until I began to flood back into myself too fast for my streams, too fast, and too much.

'No!' I screamed. 'No!' I wanted only the light from the eye of the sheep, but my dad didn't let go. 'Mum! Mum!' I called. The same hands that had hit and pushed and punched my mum now held me as the force rushed hard through my skin. It was going to split me, and tear me, and I would come out, all of me pouring onto Uncle Rodney's floor, but for my dad's arms holding me together. He was over me, greater than me, and he said, 'Jim, son . . . Jim, son . . .' over and over, and his hands were around my body so that the old imprint from the first time he ever held me was awakened. I was awakened.

Part Six

It was almost night. Dad and me were sitting on the long chairs on Uncle Rodney's verandah. There was a glass of milk in my hands, and in the sky a single star. The clouds behind the star were grey and silver and purple. Dad kept very still as he sat; he was in the narrow land that ran between lost and found and he didn't yet know his way. But there was no Cutty Sark left in him; only the spaces left behind, like the roads after a storm when the puddles have been washed away. Potholes, wet streets, houses that had been damaged, furniture floating, ending up in the wrong places — that was my dad, saved from the flood. He looked at me and said, 'It was your coming all that way on your own that did it, Jim. If you could, then I could.'

I had shown my dad; I, Jimmy Flick, had shown him. 'It was a long way, Dad. A long way.'

He nodded. 'It was.' Then he said, 'I'm not sure I know how to do this, Jim. But I want to try.'

I drank down my milk in one long swallow, then I wiped my mouth on my sleeve. 'I'll give you a chance, Dad,' I told him.

Lines like arms spiralled around us. They reached up into the sky and joined us to the clouds and the single star. They connected me and my dad to each other, and to the world.

Uncle Rodney came through the back door. 'I'll pick up some beers,' he said.

Dad said, 'I'm not drinking.'

'Staying off the hard stuff, hey?' said Uncle Rodney.

'Off the soft stuff too, Rod. It's over.' His voice was sharp and tough, like he was ready for the fight.

There was quiet for a while, only the sound of crickets calling in the night on their leg bows. Uncle Rodney said, 'You can stay on the island, Gav — at least for a while. Keep close.'

'You sure about that?'

Uncle Rodney leaned against the railing of the verandah and looked at the sky; more stars had joined the single. 'There are alcoholics on the island, Gav. Some of the worst.' He grinned, before becoming serious. 'I know what I'm dealing with.'

Dad shook his head slowly. 'Right.'

'I can get you work on the boats. You'd be home early so you could be there for the kid. I could help out a bit. Amanda knows someone too. And you know she works at the school. She wants to help.'

'Right.'

'Be good to have you fellas close for a while. Family.'

'Yeah.' My dad was stiff, as if he wasn't used to the word and it stuck.

I took his hand. 'Yeah, Dad.'

Uncle Rodney's phone rang. He went back inside. Dad and I sat and looked at the light; it kept changing, like the sea. It went from pale at the bottom to dark blue to almost black. Soon Uncle Rodney came back outside. He was smiling. 'That was your brother, Jimmy. He's back on dry land.'

For the first time that night I slept, as if my father had a power that ran through his inner liquids and was potent with sleep. The steam came through like osmosis and travelled through the lids of my eyes, heavying and drooping them so that I fell into a place both empty and full, where up was balanced by down, and down by up. I slept with my father close, the warm broad panel of his living back against mine. In the morning I saw that the lines were there between all things but the line that led to my mother was gone.

The tears moved down my streams, catching the pain and carrying it through my pipes and down my legs and into the earth. I looked up through water as the world shook and wobbled. Dad was awake and he said, 'Jim, I am sorry.'

Epilogue

Dad, Uncle Rodney, me and Ned sat on the island pier, watching the sun go down. It was crossing to the other side to give them a turn, giving space to the moon that would soon be above us. White birds dipped and rose over the waves looking for the shining tails of fish just below the surface, then swooping for them, beaks as sharp as arrows. My dad sat beside me. We weren't touching but his flesh went out beyond where it was visible, giving me a cloak which I could sit inside. Uncle Rodney sat next to my dad, joined to him by the waves they had surfed, the wives they had lost, by the drawings on their arms, by Mother Beloved and by me.

Ned was with us, his messages running easily through him, with space between each one, coming through him like water. He was the go-between, going between the animal kingdom and this one. I watched the waves as they rolled and crashed towards us, one after another, never stopping, always changing. I knew what was making them come, I had been there and I would always know.

Someone shouted. 'Jim! Jimmy!'

I turned and saw Robby coming up the pier, his thin legs sweeping him towards me.

'They told me at the shop you might be here.' Robby was speaking to my dad but he was looking at me, only me, Jimmy Flick, the one brother who had lived the same years and seen the same things and was there when she died. He came close, bent down, put his arms around me and he cried and so did I, so did I, and I knew where crying was made; it was made in me.

Acknowledgements

Special thanks to Jane Palfreyman, Ailsa Piper, Richard Walsh, Sue Walsh, Christa Munns, Luke Elliot, David Francis, Madeleine Meyer, Gail Jones, Dmetri Kakmi, Peta Murray, Ali Lavau and to Marc, for taking Sonny into the wetlands.